Betrayals
Gina Caimi

POPULAR LIBRARY

An Imprint of Warner Books, Inc.

A Warner Communications Company

POPULAR LIBRARY EDITION

Popular Library® and the fanciful P design are registered trademarks
of Warner Books, Inc.

Cover photo by Palma Kolansky

Popular Library books are published by
Warner Books, Inc.
666 Fifth Avenue
New York, N.Y. 10103

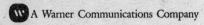 A Warner Communications Company

Printed in the United States of America

First Printing: March, 1989

10 9 8 7 6 5 4 3 2 1

For Fred Hanzlik

The dream was destroyed
but love endured.

PROLOGUE

She flinched as the harsh glare of the fluorescent lights hit her, full force. *Why did I come in here*? she wondered, shielding her eyes against the bathroom's relentless brightness. The walls, the ceiling, the sink, and the huge sunken tub were all made of gleaming white marble, as were the artfully concealed toilet and bidet. All of the custom-made fixtures were eighteen-carat gold.

She'd always felt that the decor was a bit much—the Hollywood version of a bath in an ancient Roman bordello. But at the moment, she was more preoccupied with trying to figure out what she was doing there. She wasn't even sure who she was anymore. The last thing she could remember was someone jabbing a hypodermic needle into her arm. Whatever she'd been given must have been strong enough to knock out a bull elephant. She didn't know just how long she had been asleep.

She was dying of thirst.

That's why she'd come in here, she finally realized. She

wanted a glass of water. Still feeling groggy, she stumbled over to the seashell-shaped marble washbasin, her bare toes sinking into the long, curly fleece of the wall-to-wall flokati carpet.

She was about to slide a glass out of the clutches of its mermaid holder when she noticed the gold razor blade lying on the shelf above the sink. It was her monogrammed coke blade—the one she'd used to cut the lines she'd snorted earlier. Like the half-remembered fragments of a dream, disconnected images began to take shape in her mind. Wanting to end them, she looked up from the razor blade, only to be confronted by her reflection in the mirror.

There she was again, in all her dubious glory: her long, platinum-blond mane, carefully disheveled to give the impression she'd just fallen out of bed after a night of debauchery; big blue eyes with a double fringe of false lashes; sensuous, glossy mouth, always wet and invitingly parted. The one and only Lara Layton—Hollywood's hottest sex symbol, and resident dirty joke.

Will I never be rid of her? she wondered.

She didn't understand why she was still in her work clothes. The ivory lace negligee clearly revealed every voluptuous curve of "the body that launched a thousand fantasies."

Suddenly, everything that had happened before she'd been knocked out came back to her in a rush. She grabbed on to the scalloped edge of the sink with both hands. The marble was as cold as the rage beginning to build inside her. She knew it wasn't over. He would only force her to do it again tomorrow, and there was no way she could stop him.

Or was there?

She pushed herself away from the sink. For a long moment she stared thoughtfully at the reflection of what she'd become. Then slowly, almost languidly, as though she were performing a task she'd been looking forward to for a long time, she peeled off one row of her false eyelashes, and then the other. She did the same to her other eye, and dropped the thick, spiky lashes into the sink. They lay there like exotic-looking centipedes. She turned on the dolphin-shaped water faucet as high as it would go, and smiled as she watched the lashes swirl down the drain.

Reaching for the soap, she scrubbed off the layers of theatrical makeup, rinsing her face over and over until she felt clean again, even though the water was almost scalding. Not bothering to dry it, she popped out the contacts that changed her eyes from pale gray to Technicolor blue. Stepping quickly around the gold filigree partition, she dumped the tinted lenses into the toilet and flushed them down.

"That looks better already," she had to admit when she'd finished studying herself in the mirror. Vestiges of Loris Castaldi were beginning to emerge. She was almost able to recognize herself. Now she needed to destroy Lara Layton for good.

With a feeling of reckless joy she hadn't known in years, Loris pulled out the hairpins that secured the luxurious, platinum-blond fall to her own shoulder-length hair. When it was hanging from one hand, like a spill of obscene cotton candy, she reached over and picked up the gold razor blade. Lock by spun-sugar lock, she sliced away at the fall, until there was nothing left except the bald netting.

Would that be enough to stop him?

Impulsively, she grabbed a chunk of her own hair. A slight flick of the wrist was all it took—a single, fluid motion of the blade—and an entire bleached strand of her hair floated down to the carpet. The more she chopped off, the better she felt. In a few moments, all of her hair was lying in clumps at her feet. Tentatively, she ran a hand over her scalp. It felt like the soft fuzz on a newborn infant. No one could mistake her for Lara Layton now! She couldn't remember the last time she'd felt so free. She laughed. She could hardly wait to see his face when he saw what she'd done to his creation.

It suddenly occurred to Loris that he could always put more makeup on her, and she had several pair of backup contacts, plus a whole closet full of falls and wigs.

What else could she do?

A glimmer of light shimmering off the edge of the razor blade caught her eye. It answered her question. She watched as she glided the blade downward toward her raised left wrist. The soft, translucent skin had never seemed more vulnerable; the solid gold blade gleamed hard and sure against it. She ran the sharply honed tip over the network of delicate blue veins a couple of times—quick, light strokes, just to test it—and was surprised to find that her movement merely caused a stinging sensation.

With a mildly curious detachment, she wondered how deep the cut would have to be in order to be damaging. She pushed the tip of the blade into her skin, just to the left of the first vein, and watched it sink all the way in, as far as it could go. She took a deep breath, held it in, and pulled the razor blade clear across her wrist.

It didn't hurt at all. She was amazed that it was that easy. Then, the thin red line running the width of her wrist began to open, as slowly as the petals of a flower in a time-lapse sequence. Blood gushed out, pouring all over the scalloped sink. She never thought there'd be so much blood. Dropping the razor blade into the washbasin, she turned on the faucet, but there was so much blood the water couldn't dilute it quickly enough. Suddenly, she was afraid. For the first time, she realized what she'd actually done. She never thought there'd be so much blood!

Grabbing one of the towels off the rack on the filigree partition, she quickly wrapped it around her wrist; it was soaked through in seconds. Her lace negligee was sticking to her bare skin in warm, wet patches, and the clumps of bleached hair strewn at her feet were now dyed crimson. She unwound the blood-soaked towel in order to wrap another, larger towel around it, and was stunned by the sight of the gaping hole in her wrist.

Unchecked, blood quickly filled the wide gash and began to overflow in thick spurts. Now she was really scared. She was tempted to call for help; the telephone was only a few feet away. But she was even more terrified of what he'd do to her. Surely he would lock her up in the nut house and throw away the key; the insurance would cover all his losses.

Blood dripping from the tips of her shaking fingers, Loris retrieved the gold blade from the sink. How the hell had it come to this, she wondered angrily as she plunged the razor blade into her other wrist.

PART I

CHAPTER
One

"Loris, please sit still, baby. How can I fix your hair for Daddy if you keep turning your head away?"

"But, Mommy, it's fixed already." Tired of her mother's endless fussing, the child slid down as far as she could in the back of the limousine, pulled her feet up, and plopped them down on the plush edge of the seat.

Her mother gasped, and with a single sweep of the hairbrush, knocked her daughter's feet off the seat cover. She let out a sigh of relief when she saw that the chauffeur's attention hadn't strayed from the winding country road. The glass partition between them was closed, yet she lowered her voice almost fearfully. "Don't put your dirty shoes on the seat, Loris." Quickly, she brushed the edge of it, though even the child could see it hadn't been soiled.

"Don't worry, Mommy. My shoes are real clean." Loris stuck both feet straight out; the unusually wide space between the front and back seats allowed her to do so easily. "See?" This was the first time she had worn her new Mary

9

Janes. The soles were practically spotless, the black, patent-
leather tops so shiny she could see her reflection in them.

"I know, baby, but this is genuine suede," the young
woman said, her tone hushed in awe. "It stains if you so
much as look at it. See how soft it is?" Slowly, with a kind
of longing, she ran her hand over the door panel. "Did you
ever see anything so lovely?"

Tilting her head back, Loris examined their surroundings.
The interior of the Rolls-Royce was upholstered entirely in
suede, and a plush carpet in the same shade of pearl gray
covered the floor. Beside each window a gleaming silver
tube held a single yellow rose. "Is this Daddy's car?"

"Yes, baby."

"It's very swanky, isn't it?"

Angela Castaldi couldn't help smiling at her daughter's
typically solemn judgment. She was such a serious little
thing. Not quite six, she spoke and acted with a maturity
that was disconcerting at times. Tall for her age, and
unusually graceful, she was the most beautiful child Angela
had ever seen outside of the movies. Her face was a perfect
oval. She had her father's wide, pale-gray eyes and fine
bone structure, but her skin was even whiter than Carter's—
almost translucent. Mercifully, she'd managed to inherit her
mother's best features: heavy, blue-black hair; a long, thick
fringe of lashes; and lips with the soft, sensuous curve of a
daVinci angel.

Angela adored her. She had been seventeen when Loris
was born and people often mistook them for sisters. Since
Carter had been posted to Saigon two years ago, and since
her family would have nothing to do with her anymore,
Loris was all Angela had to live for. Sometimes she was
afraid she loved her too much—that so much love was too
great a burden for a little girl to carry. She knew she didn't
deserve such an exceptional daughter, and that also frightened her. She had often heard that the sins of the father
were visited on the child—but what about the sins of the
mother?

More and more frequently during the past two years,

Angela would wake up in a cold sweat and, shaking with a nameless terror, would rush over to her sleeping child to make sure she was still breathing. She ended up letting Loris sleep in the double bed with her so that she could check on her whenever she awoke.

On especially bad nights, when the shadows that filled the bedroom came alive, creating shifting, changing visions of evil even as they concealed them, Angela remained vigilant until the light of dawn filtered through the windows. Only then would she let herself drift off into a fitful sleep, Loris's vulnerable little body still clutched in her protective embrace. But no matter how careful she was, she still feared that retribution would ultimately find her.

"Mommy," Loris cried, tugging with both hands at the sleeve of her mother's new dress. "Please, Mommy!"

It took Angela a moment to break free of her terrifying thoughts. She forced a smile. "What is it, baby?"

"You went away again."

The look of hurt and bewilderment on her daughter's face reinforced Angela's feelings of inadequacy as a mother. "Oh, no, I . . . I was just thinking."

Snuggling close, Loris buried her face in the warm softness of her mother's breasts, as if only the most primal of contacts could reassure her. "What about?"

"Why, about seeing Daddy again, of course." Angela laughed, a bit too gaily. "And how wonderful everything's going to be now."

Loris turned her head and stared out the window. "Why is Daddy's house so far away?"

"It's not that far. Newport is only about a hundred miles or so from Manhattan."

"Is that as many miles as Vietnam?"

Angela smiled indulgently. "No, baby, Vietnam's thousands of miles away. I showed it to you on the atlas, remember?"

Loris stuck her chin up, the way she always did when she felt she was being treated like a baby. "I know. That's why Daddy doesn't come to see us anymore."

"But Daddy's home now." Sliding her arm around her daughter's delicate shoulders, Angela gave her a reassuring squeeze. "He's home for good."

Loris stuck both feet straight out and carefully aligned them so that the buckled straps on her Mary Janes matched perfectly. "How long is Daddy going to stay with us before he has to go away again?"

"That's what I've been trying to tell you, Loris. He never has to go away again."

"Never?"

"No, never."

Loris dropped her feet as abruptly as she'd raised them. "Yes, he will."

"Loris, you make it sound as if Daddy wanted to leave us. He had to go," Angela insisted. "His assignment in Washington was over, and they needed him in Saigon to . . ." She was unable to recall the reason Carter had given her for his unexpected transfer. "To help end the war," she finished lamely. She gave Loris a bright smile. "But I know how much he missed you. He's just dying to see you."

Shrugging off her mother's arm, Loris sat up again. "Then, why didn't he write to us for so long?" she asked reproachfully. "He even forgot my birthday."

"I told you, Loris. Your Daddy's a very important man. Important people don't always have the time to write," she explained. "That doesn't mean he doesn't love you. Daddy loves us both very much."

Loris made a face. She knew the excuses her mother always made for her father practically by heart, but she still had trouble believing them. Sometimes, she thought her mother didn't really believe them either. "So, how come he waited three whole days to see us if he missed us so much?" she persisted. "And if he really and truly loves us, then why didn't *he* come to get us, instead of—"

"Oh, look, baby." Angela cut her off with a high, shrill laugh. "Look at the beautiful horse."

Loris gasped with wonder when she looked out the window and saw the black stallion galloping across the meadow toward them, with long powerful strides. His delicate legs were a blur, and his hoofs seemed never to touch the ground. "Come here, horse!" Fearlessly, she threw her arms out the window of the moving car, eager to embrace the new experience and make it hers. In her excitement, she was barely aware of her mother's fearful cry, or the arm she'd wrapped around her waist. "Over here, horse!"

The Thoroughbred halted a few yards from the fence that separated the wide, grassy field from the two-lane highway. He stood there, sleek muscles quivering under his glistening hide, as though he were considering the child's request. Then, with a proud toss of his mane, he turned his head and glanced over his shoulder, ignoring the Rolls as it passed.

"Oh, make him come back, Mommy," Loris pleaded.

"There are more, Loris. Over there." Angela pointed out the window with the hairbrush she was still holding in one hand. "See? There's a mommy horse and a baby horse."

Loris let out a squeal of delight when she caught sight of them. The mare, who was moving with a leisurely gait so her colt could keep up with her, had a coat the color of amber. The colt was black, with an amber mane and tail that gleamed like burnished gold in the sunlight. Pawing the ground impatiently, the stallion waited as the pair approached him.

It was a sign, Angela told herself. *They* had finally sent her the sign she'd been begging for. She drew in a long breath of air that smelled of freshly mown grass. It was the first free breath she'd drawn in almost two years.

"Why are all the houses so short?" Loris asked, referring to the two-story brick farmhouse they'd just passed. "And where are all the people?"

"This is the country, baby. It's always peaceful and quiet here. How would you like to live here all the time, Loris, instead of that dirty, noisy city?"

Loris gave up her search for more horses and turned to look at her mother. "Can I take Annie with me?"

"You can take all your dolls. But I'm sure Daddy'll buy you a whole bunch of new ones."

"I want Annie."

"From now on, you can have anything you want, baby." Angela pulled Loris away from the window and turned her around so they were facing one another again. "But first, you've got to let me fix your hair."

"No." Wriggling out of her mother's reach, Loris put both hands in front of her face to ward off the hairbrush. "No more."

"Don't you want to look beautiful for Daddy?"

Loris squirmed uncomfortably in the stiff organdy party dress her mother had stayed up most of last night to finish. It was white with red polka dots, and had bright red trim at the neck, short, puffed sleeves, and a full skirt. The satin ribbon around her waist matched the red bow in her hair. "I don't care how I look."

"Don't ever say that!" Angela couldn't have sounded more shocked if her child had just uttered a four-letter word. "You don't realize how lucky you are. Most little girls would give anything to be as beautiful as you."

"Why?"

"Because when you're beautiful, everybody wants and admires you." A wistful smile softened Angela's strong-boned features. She had missed being a beauty by a nose: a Roman nose that proclaimed her heritage and caused her much regret. "If a girl is a beauty, and knows how to make the most of it, she can have anything she wants in this world—even if she was born with certain . . . disadvantages."

"But, why?"

"That's just how it is." She might have been explaining an immutable law of nature, like the sun rising in the east and setting in the west. "So, don't ever say you don't care about how you look." She raised the tortoiseshell brush again. "Now, be a good girl and let me fix your hair."

Loris wasn't sure she wanted to be a beauty; it was too much fuss and bother. She shook her head stubbornly.

Her mother's eyes took on that sad, hurt look that always made Loris feel so bad. "Don't you want to make Mommy proud of you?"

With a resigned sigh, Loris let her hands drop in her lap, and was rewarded with an almost desperately grateful smile.

"When Daddy sees what a beautiful little girl you've become," Angela said, excitement building in her voice as she smoothed out Loris's curls, "he's going to be so proud to be your father he'll never leave us again. Then, we're all going to live together . . . like a real family!"

Loris's large eyes widened until they seemed to fill her face. "Daddy's going to live with us?"

"Yes, baby."

"For keeps . . . just like Betty's daddy?"

"Yes!"

"Is that what he said on the phone the other day?"

"Well, not in so many words," Angela admitted, "but—"

"I knew it." Loris pulled her head back, evading her mother's reach. "I just knew it wasn't true!"

"But it is true," Angela cried. "Daddy always said we'd live together once he got a permanent assignment in Washington. Why else do you think he's invited us to his home? He's never done that before, has he? He always visits us at our place."

Loris slanted her mother a wary look. "So how come he did, then?"

"So we can finally meet his mother and father, maybe even his older sister," Angela insisted. "Because we're going to be part of his family, too, now. That's why."

Loris lowered her eyes again. "I wouldn't be so sure," she said, staring at one of her patent-leather shoes.

Reaching out, Angela put a finger under Loris's chin and lifted her face back to hers. "Has Mommy ever broken a promise to you?"

"No."

"Didn't I tell you Daddy would be coming home for good one day? Well, he has, hasn't he? And now, everything's going to be just like I always promised."

Loris looked anything but convinced.

"Do you think God would listen to your prayers night

after night, for so many years, and not answer them,
baby?'' Angela asked softly. ''Do you?''

''I don't know.''

''No, of course he wouldn't.'' God might not deign to
answer her own prayers, Angela knew, because she'd been
living in mortal sin for so long, but how could he deny her
daughter, who was innocent of sin? No one could deny such
a beautiful child—not even Carter.

'':Besides, I've had a sign!'' Angela laughed, much louder
than she'd intended, unable to contain the rush of joy that
filled her with a certainty she thought she'd lost forever.
''Everything's going to be just like I promised you, baby.
You'll see.''

She carefully wrapped one of Loris's curls around her
index finger with the brush. As she did so, she began to tell
her about all the wonderful things that were in store for her.
Not wanting to spoil her mother's happy mood, Loris sat
there silently, her hands folded in her lap. Slowly, inexorably,
she felt herself being drawn into the familiar spell that was
being woven around her.

''We're all going to live together in a great big house in
the country,'' her mother was saying, her voice as soft and
caressing as her fingers. ''And you're going to have lots and
lots of friends. Everyone will want to play with you, from
now on.''

Lulled by the low, mesmerizing voice and the steady
movement of the car, Loris had trouble keeping her eyes
open. These were the same words her mother repeated when
she tucked her into bed every night, evoking images that
glimmered with hope before they merged with her dreams.

''You'll go to the very best schools. You'll have piano
lessons, and you'll learn to speak French. Then, when
you're all grown up, you'll take your rightful place in
society with the rest of your father's family.''

Loris's eyes flew open. She knew the sequence of events
by heart, the way most children know the story of Cinderella
or Little Red Riding Hood, so she realized that her mother
had gotten ahead of herself. ''And now that we're going to

live in the country, I'm going to have a dog, just like Lassie," she prompted, eager to get back to her favorite part of their fairy tale.

"That's right. And you'll have lots and lots of toys, and pretty new clothes."

"You forgot the pony," Loris reminded her. "Tell me about the pony!"

"I was just getting to that." The smile her mother gave her implied that she'd deliberately kept the best part for last. "Daddy's going to buy you your very own pony—a snow-white Arabian with a long, flowing mane and tail." With the tip of the brush, she slid the last curl off her finger. "It's going to be the most beautiful pony in the whole world."

"And the fastest!"

"And the fastest," Angela agreed. "You'll learn to ride, and jump the hurdles, and—"

The sudden, loud honking of the horn cut Angela off, making her jump. The limousine had come to a halt at the end of a wooded country road. She'd been so involved with Loris that she hadn't even noticed when the car had turned off the main highway. Swiveling in her seat, she glanced out the side window, and drew in a sharp breath.

The Rolls-Royce was idling in front of a huge, wrought-iron gate. A tower stood on either side of the gateway, constructed of the same granite stones as the high, spike-topped wall that stretched as far as she could see. An iron-bound portal opened at the base of one of the towers, and a giant of a man stepped out. In spite of the brass-buttoned charcoal uniform and gold-braided cap he wore, he gave the impression of being a bouncer in a disreputable bar.

With a discreet nod in her direction, he walked over to the gate, a large key dangling from his gloved fist. Because of his height, he was forced to bend over to insert the key in the lock. Through the vent in his jacket, Angela caught a glimpse of the revolver strapped around the small of his back. Straightening up again, he swung one side of the gate out of the way with a single, effortless motion, then walked the other side of the gate open.

The breath Angela had been holding came out in a rush as the Rolls glided through the arched entrance. "Oh, my God, we're here." Quickly, she ran the brush through her straight, waist-length hair, then stuffed it in her purse.

Loris sat up on the edge of her seat, straining to get a closer look through the front windshield. Giant oak trees lined both sides of the seemingly endless driveway; all of them were exactly the same size and height. "Mommy, how do they get the trees to grow all the same?"

"What, baby?" Angela murmured distractedly. All she could think of was that in a few more minutes she would see Carter again. She had the sensation that her heart was swelling, pushing against her ribs, ready to burst.

Loris turned to face her mother again. "How do they get—"

"Now, listen to me, Loris." Her hands trembling, Angela fiddled with the red bow in Loris's hair. "In just a few minutes we're going to see Daddy again, and we're finally going to meet his family. Promise me you'll be on your best behavior."

"You don't have to worry about me, Mommy," Loris assured her. "I'll be good."

"Oh, you're always good, baby. I didn't mean it that way." Her hands fluttered down to Loris's polka-dot dress and proceeded to fluff up her puffy sleeves. "But, you know how shy and quiet you get whenever you meet people for the first time? Try not to do that now. I want them all to see what a bright little girl you are and . . . and how well you get on in society, and . . ." In spite of her effort to speak slowly so the child could understand her, she mumbled her words out of nervousness. "But, if you hang back or . . . or hold onto my hand like you always do, they'll think you're still a baby."

"I am not a baby," Loris protested, sticking her chin up. "Anybody can see that."

"Then, you know what I mean?"

Loris hesitated, not quite sure what was expected of her. Her mother was waiting for her answer, her face glowing with hope and excitement. "Yes, Mommy."

"I knew you would, baby." Bending over, she inspected the shine on Loris's shoes and tugged at her white anklets, even though they were already as far up as they could go. "I just know you're going to make a big impression!"

Loris wasn't sure what a big impression was exactly, but she decided not to ask, for fear of being thought a baby. "I'll try my very best."

Sitting up again, Angela gave her a brilliant smile, which contrasted sharply with the almost desperate look in her eyes, and confused Loris even more. "Please try, baby," she pleaded. "It's really important that Daddy's family approves of you."

"Why?"

"Because if they don't, Daddy won't be able to live with us for good. Do you see why it's so important now?"

Loris still didn't understand what she was supposed to do, but she knew she had to do it properly. She nodded anyway.

The limousine had come to the end of the long, oak-lined road and surrounding wooded area; not so much as a shrub or a wild flower remained. The great expanse of manicured lawn that now sprawled before them seemed to have been flung across the gently sloping hill like a lush green carpet. A forty-room Victorian mansion crowned the level hilltop, gleaming in the crisp September sunlight, blinding in its whiteness. A Victorian garden edged the marble-columned veranda, its neat, triangular beds reflecting the formality of the nineteenth-century mansion.

To one side of the house—approximately a city block away—was what Angela guessed to be a clay tennis court adjoining an orchard. Farther away there were cutting and vegetable gardens. At an equal distance on the other side of the mansion stood a marble terrace enclosing a swimming pool. Lounge chairs and café tables sporting colorful striped umbrellas dotted the lower level around the Olympic-size pool; a matching awning sheltered the bar and swivel stools on the upper level, next to the bathhouse, which was a miniature version of the main house.

The brilliant blue water of the pool rivaled that of the ocean sparkling at the foot of the other side of the hill. Perched on a bluff that jutted out over the strip of private beach below was a turn-of-the-century gazebo. The last roses of summer climbed its latticed sides and clung tenaciously to its fanciful gingerbread roof.

"Gosh, Mommy," Loris breathed, too awed to speak above a whisper. "It's just like in the movies."

All Angela could do was nod in agreement as the limousine negotiated the last curve of the circular driveway, gravel crunching under its wheels. She'd known that Carter came from a wealthy, socially prominent family, but she'd never expected anything like this.

The joy and excitement she'd felt about seeing him again began to drain out of her slowly. She knew then that his family would never allow him to marry her. How could she blame them, when it was obvious even to her that she didn't belong here? The slow, dull throbbing behind her eyes that signaled the onset of one of her spells started.

"Mommy, which apartment does Daddy live in?" she heard Loris ask, her voice an echo, bouncing off the long, dark walls of the tunnel. "What, baby?" As Loris repeated the question, Angela was able to focus on her words and leave her dark thoughts behind. "This isn't an apartment house, Loris. This is Daddy's home . . . all of it."

"All of it?" The child stared thoughtfully up at the mansion, clearly comparing it with their railroad flat on the Lower East Side as the Rolls glided to a stop in front of the entrance. "It's something else, isn't it?"

Angela laughed in spite of herself at Loris's favorite new expression. "Yes, baby, and so are you." Impulsively, she threw her arms around Loris and hugged her close, drawing hope from her warm, beautiful little body. And, suddenly, anything seemed possible once more. After all, Carter had invited them here. He wouldn't have done that unless he believed that she and Loris belonged with him.

Joy and excitement spread through her again, and she couldn't wait to see him. Releasing Loris, she grabbed her pocketbook off the seat, pushed the car door open before the chauffeur could get to it, and jumped out.

The look the chauffeur gave her as he stopped beside the door, his outstretched arm falling impotently to his side, made Angela realize she'd blundered. He held her gaze while he waited for Loris to climb out of the car.

Angela saw nothing but contempt in his eyes. He had to be comparing her with the women in Carter's social circle—women, she knew, who were as accustomed to riding in chauffeured limousines as she was to taking the subway. The dull throbbing started up behind her eyes again. If she couldn't even get the chauffeur's approval, how would she ever be able to win over Carter's family?

Before she could reach for the brass knocker—a huge ring held in the maws of a lion—the front door began to open slowly, soundlessly.

CHAPTER
Two

The liveried butler peered through the narrow opening in the doorway. When he was finished looking down his long nose at Angela, she half expected him to slam the door in her face. He regarded Loris as though she were a pet who had not been properly housebroken. Finally, he let them in.

As mother and daughter started across the entrance hall, he held up a white-gloved hand, bringing them both to a sudden halt. "Would Madam please wait here while I announce her arrival?"

Angela nodded self-consciously.

With measured steps, the butler walked over to the small but superb Vanrisamburgh table in one corner. Its veneer was of flamed mahogany with contrasting scrolls of satin-wood, edged in gleaming, intricately wrought ormolu; its top was Sèvres porcelain. Though originally designed for serving coffee or hot chocolate, the table currently held a telephone.

While the butler used the phone, Angela took in the rest

of the opulent decor. An immense cut-glass chandelier, sparkling like clusters of diamonds, vied for domination of the entrance hall with the wide, burnished-mahogany stairway. A full-length Gainsborough portrait, framed in lushly carved gilt, hung on one wall. Against the opposite wall, as if swollen by its own importance, stood a bombé marquetry commode by John Cobb, flanked by matching torchère stands. Instead of candles, the unique bombé pedestals held tall crystal vases overflowing with freshly cut flowers that were so exotic they could only have been grown in a greenhouse.

Though Angela was incapable of naming the styles of the exquisitely wrought furnishings or the masters who'd created them, she had no trouble recognizing the genuine article when she saw it. Each carefully collected piece was a painful reminder of the difference between Carter's background and her own. Every black and white square of the highly polished marble floor diminished her.

Someone just like her father had painstakingly created the perfect symmetry of that marble floor. But her father would never have been allowed to walk on it once it was finished. Even though her father had taken great pride in his work and considered himself an artist, he was just a common laborer to people like Carter's family. Surely they would always think of her as equally inferior.

"Mommy," Loris called in a loud whisper. "Mommy, the man is talking to you." Those were the first words Loris had dared to utter since they'd entered her father's house. Unknown people and places always intimidated her, and she sensed the tall, thin man's disapproval of them both. She moved closer to her mother but, remembering her earlier instructions, resisted the urge to grab her hand.

Angela hadn't realized that the butler had hung up the phone and was now addressing her. When she became lost in her thoughts, only her daughter's voice could find her. Blindly, she reached for Loris's hand and clung to her, the one steady point in the constantly shifting landscape of her

life. The child looked up at her mother with a combination
of surprise and relief.

"Would madam please follow me?" the butler repeated
for Angela's benefit. "Mr. Kingsley will be receiving you
in the library."

"Yes, thank you." In an attempt to explain her odd
behavior, she added, "I'm fascinated by this house. It's the
most beautiful one I've ever seen."

The insufferably superior look on his lean face let her
know that he didn't need her to tell him. "Of course, there
are other, even more famous summer cottages in Newport,"
he allowed as he led them down a lushly carpeted hallway.
"The Breakers and Belcourt Castle, for example, or Marble
House."

Angela was amazed that what she thought of as a palace
was considered a mere summer cottage in Newport.

"But the best people find such flaunting of wealth and
opulence somewhat recherché." A self-satisfied little smile
curved his lips as they passed an open doorway that afforded
a tantalizing glimpse of the wonders within. "King's Haven
is renowned for its restrained elegance."

"Oh, yes, it is elegant," Angela eagerly agreed. Having
failed with the chauffeur, she desperately needed to win the
butler's approval. "I've never seen anything so charming.
No wonder you're proud to be part of it."

He stiffened as though he found her attempt to treat him
as an equal unseemly, perhaps even offensive. Angela realized she'd committed another social blunder. Looking away,
she caught sight of the largest living room she'd ever seen,
and slowed her steps to get a better view.

The main drawing room, as it was actually called, could
easily have contained the living room of her modest apartment five or six times over and, in fact, had been decorated
to give the impression of being a number of rooms without
walls between them. Oversized, overstuffed sofas and chairs,
upholstered in a variety of watercolor silks, were arranged
in groupings around rare tables and occasional pieces like
shimmering pastel islands in a wall-to-wall, powder-blue

sea. They were in the process of being shrouded by a team
of uniformed maids, who were systematically working their
way from one end of the room to the other.

Angela hurried to catch up with the butler, dragging Loris
along with her. "Why are they putting sheets on all the
furniture?"

"Dust covers, madam," he corrected archly. "We're in
the process of closing up the summer cottage."

"Closing it up? But why?"

"Because the season is quite over." His tone implied that
such an explanation would have been unnecessary with
anyone but her. "Mr. and Mrs. Kingsley and their daughter
returned to their Fifth Avenue apartment yesterday."

Angela halted abruptly, making Loris stumble. "You
mean, Carter's family isn't here?"

"Certainly not, madam." He sounded shocked that she
could even consider such a thing, confusing Angela even
more. She had no way of knowing that to remain in
Newport even one day past the designated seven-week
season was deemed déclasse.

"Mr. Kingsley, Junior, will be staying an additional day,"
he added. "I'm told an important matter needed attending
to." The withering look he cast over his shoulder as he
continued on his way made it clear that he held them both
responsible for this serious breach of social etiquette.

Disturbing questions began to surface in Angela's mind
but, as she'd been doing for the past three days, she
managed to ignore them. Without another word, she followed the butler until he came to a pair of huge, carved-oak
doors.

"The library, madam," he announced, sliding the double
doors apart.

Unlike the other rooms Angela had caught glimpses of,
the library had a solid, darkly masculine look to it. The
patterned parquet floor was bare, except for two large
Oriental rugs. The antique Bijar created an island of comfort
in front of the baronial fireplace; its primarily maroon tone
blended with the oxblood Chesterfield couches resting on it,

facing each other across a lacquered sea captain's chest that served as a coffee table. At the far end of the library, in front of the silk-damask-draped window, an antique Tabriz, all golden tones, gleamed under a Louis XIV bureau plat and fauteuil chairs.

Row upon row of leather-bound first editions lined one entire wall; gilt-framed, early-eighteenth-century English landscapes and hunting scenes were displayed on the others. An impressive collection of silver trophies, won over the years by the Kingsleys' prize Thoroughbreds, shone proudly atop the marble mantelpiece.

"Would madam please wait here? Mr. Kingsley will be with you presently." He hesitated in the doorway, as though concerned about leaving them alone with so many precious objects. Then, clearly obeying orders, he reluctantly slid the doors closed.

"Mommy, I don't like that man," Loris admitted now that she was safely alone with her mother. Craning her neck, she looked at the carved walnut ceiling looming twenty feet above her, then stared into the fireplace, which was large enough to swallow her up whole. "I don't like this place so much, either."

"Why do you say that, Loris?"

She gave a rueful little sigh. "This house doesn't kiss me."

Her words caught Angela by surprise, wounding her. She hadn't realized her daughter also knew that they didn't belong here. "Oh, but it will, baby," she insisted. "This house will be full of love for you once everybody gets to know you."

"I wouldn't be so sure," she murmured in her serious little voice.

"Loris, aren't you happy to see Daddy again?"

Loris shifted uncomfortably from one foot to the other. She'd learned from experience that if she let herself get too happy to see her father, she'd be that much more unhappy when he left her again. "Yes, Mommy," she said. She knew that's what her mother wanted to hear.

"Then you must smile, especially when you see Daddy, so he knows how happy you are to see him. You remember what Mommy told you before?"

Loris stuck her chin up proudly. "I remember."

Angela rewarded her with a loving smile. "I'm so proud of you, baby. You look just beautiful."

"So do you, Mommy," Loris returned unhesitatingly. She hadn't gotten used to her mother's strange new outfit yet, but to her, she was still the most beautiful mother in the whole wide world—and always would be.

"Do you think Daddy will like the new me?" Angela tugged self-consciously at her mini-dress. The white, black, and red Op-art-patterned shift she wore was a copy of a St. Laurent, inspired by the paintings of Modrian, and was the latest rage. In an attempt to impress Carter's parents that she was up on the latest fashions and, therefore, worthy of him, Angela had accessorized it with white plastic go-go boots and a shoulder bag with a Mary Quant daisy motif in black and white.

Just as she was wondering what could be keeping Carter so long, a hidden door in the wood paneling at the far end of the wall opened and he stepped into the room.

The world went silent around Angela. She was totally incapable of speech or movement. It was as though her mind had shut down in self-defense, unable to handle such a sudden, overwhelming jolt of emotion without short-circuiting.

Carter was silent also, and just as motionless, though he seemed more uncomfortable than overwhelmed with emotion.

The navy-blue cashmere blazer and crisp white linen trousers he wore emphasized the lithe, elegant lines of his body, making him appear taller than just under six feet. The double row of brass buttons gleaming down the front of his jacket bore the insignia of an exclusive yacht club; the same insignia was embroidered in red and gold on his breast pocket. A monogrammed handkerchief was crushed softly inside the pocket, and a silk paisley ascot added a touch of casual elegance to the open collar of his white shirt.

He'd grown a moustache since she'd seen him last. It lent

a needed touch of virility to his boyish features, but he still appeared years younger than thirty-two. His ash-blond hair and sideburns were longer, in keeping with the new fashion. His hair was wind-blown, Angela suddenly realized, as though he'd just been sailing, and his perfectly tanned skin made his pale-gray eyes seem even more startling in contrast. Vaguely, she wondered how he could have acquired such a deep tan in only three days. -

He flashed her one of his boyish, utterly irresistible grins. "Hi, Angela."

In an instant, Angela went from total paralysis to unrestrainable joy. "Carter!" Launching herself across the room, she threw herself in his arms and kissed him full on the mouth.

Carter staggered back several steps, as much from the unexpected impact of her body against his as from arousal. *She can still do that to me*, he thought resentfully, trying to extricate himself. He managed to pull his head back, but she tightened her arms around his neck, seeking to bring his mouth down to hers again. "Angela, we're not alone," he muttered, nodding toward a spot just past her shoulder.

Accustomed to showing emotion freely, Angela had always been openly affectionate with Carter in front of her own daughter, so she knew he wasn't referring to her. Turning her head in the direction he'd indicated, she saw a tall, thin woman standing just inside the doorway.

She seemed to be in her mid-thirties, or perhaps her manner made her appear older than she really was. She was wearing a pants suit, which was quickly becoming a popular alternative to mini-skirts, in a charcoal flannel pinstripe. Her light-brown hair was pulled back severely, twisted into a merciless little bun that was stabbed clear through with a bright yellow No. 2 pencil. It was impossible to tell what color her eyes were; the large, thick glasses she covered them with seemed designed to allow her to see other people clearly, while making it difficult for anyone to see her. As she stood there watching them, a steno pad clutched in one hand, disapproval thinned her lips into a single, hard line.

Angela's arms slid from around Carter's neck and she stepped back.

"This is my secretary, Miss Prescott," he said stiffly. Unlike Angela, Carter wasn't accustomed to public displays of emotion.

Removing the handkerchief from his breast pocket, he wiped his lips clean of Angela's lipstick, but not of the taste of her. He'd been right to invite her to the cottage, he realized with satisfaction. If he'd gone to see her at her place, he'd probably have ended up in bed with her, as he had the night before he'd left for Saigon. And, once again, he'd have been incapable of doing what needed to be done.

Something in the way Carter had cleaned his mouth—as if he'd meant to wipe away every trace of her—made the reckless joy Angela had felt at seeing him again shrivel up inside her. The vague presentiment that had been nagging at her for days pressed behind her eyes, trying to force its way into her consciousness. With a toss of her long hair, Angela turned and eagerly motioned to Loris to join them.

Loris was busy tracing a pattern in the maroon carpet with the tip of her shoe. Her heart was pounding.

"Is that little Loris?" Carter asked, having finally noticed her. He might have been speaking to an acquaintance whose child he'd met once. "Why, I hardly recognize her, she's grown so."

"Yes, she's quite a little lady now," Angela said proudly. "Come on over here and say hello, Loris."

A frown disturbed Carter's perfect features as Loris walked over to them. "Angela, I thought I'd made it perfectly clear on the phone the other day that it wouldn't be a good idea to bring the child. We have important matters to discuss."

"I don't remember you saying that, Carter." There had been a lot she'd been unable to grasp when they had spoken. At the time, she'd put it down to a bad connection.

"I made a point of it."

"Did you? I can't imagine how I missed it." She laughed lightly, and was surprised at the harsh sound of it. "But, even if you did, I wouldn't have had the heart to leave Loris home. She's been dying to see you again. She hasn't talked about anything else for three whole days except seeing her da—'' She stopped herself just in time, biting down on her bottom lip to keep any more indiscreet words from tumbling out. She glanced guiltily at the secretary.

"You may speak freely in front of Prescott," Carter assured her. "She's well acquainted with our . . . situation."

Was that what they'd become, Angela wondered, a *situation*?

"I'm sure you'll agree it's best not to subject the child to a serious discussion." His left eyebrow went up a fraction of an inch.

As if that were part of a secret code between them, Prescott, who hadn't moved so much as a muscle since she'd entered the room, immediately took control. Without breaking stride, she walked over to the writing table, pushed one of the buttons on a special console, tucked her steno pad under one arm, and went over to Loris. "Loris? That is your name, isn't it?"

Loris nodded and moved closer to her mother.

Prescott gave her a thin-lipped smile. "Such a pretty name. And such a pretty little girl." Bending over until her face was level with Loris's, she held out her hand. "How would you like to go to the kitchen? Cook will give you something delicious to eat."

Loris shook her head adamantly and moved even closer to Angela.

"Wouldn't you love a great big glass of chocolate milk," she persisted, "and a big fat slice of layer cake?"

Loris grabbed her mother's skirt. "No!"

Prescott's hand dropped to her side. Unaccustomed to dealing with children, she'd quickly run out of ploys. She straightened up and looked over at her boss, as though expecting further instructions.

"Angela?" Carter said archly, shifting the problem to her.

"Loris, what's the matter with you?" Angela chided. "You haven't even said hello to Daddy. Now, go and give him a big kiss and tell him how happy you are to see him, just like you told me before."

Loris shrank against her mother's side, her fingers tightening around the clump of fabric she was clutching. From under her long lashes she looked up at the beautiful stranger who was her father. She was caught between fear and longing.

"She's not usually like this," Angela was quick to assure him with a desperately cheerful smile. "She's really very outgoing and extremely bright for her age. I guess she's just so overwhelmed at seeing you again, Carter." One by one, she pried Loris's fingers loose. "That's all she talked about in the car on the way up here—how much she missed her daddy, and how happy she is that we're all going to be together now."

"Angela, please," Carter said tightly. "Don't make this any more difficult than it already is."

"Why, she's even learned a song, just for you," Angela rattled on, "to celebrate your homecoming! Go on, baby." With a tiny push, she propelled Loris directly in front of her father. "Show Daddy how beautifully you sing." She didn't notice the exasperated look that passed between Carter and Miss Prescott because she was too busy prompting Loris in her husky contralto, "We all live in a yellow submarine . . ."

"A yellow submarine," Loris chorused obediently, "a yellow sub—"

"For God's sake!" her father cut her off angrily. "This is neither the time nor the place for such an exhibition!"

Loris's mouth remained open, though she was too ashamed to utter another sound. Angela's eyes had widened in shock and she seemed frozen to the spot. Even the usually impassive Prescott looked uncomfortable.

The butler broke the strained silence by inquiring from the main entrance to the library, "You rang, sir?"

Prescott was the first to recover. "Yes, Finley," she said. "Would you kindly accompany the child to the kitchen and see that she's given a glass of milk and some cookies or cake?"

The butler pulled himself up haughtily and regarded Loris as though she were a mongrel he'd just been ordered to take for a walk. "Very well, madam."

"Go on, Loris," Prescott said with a stiff smile.

Seeking protection, Loris turned to her mother, but to her horror, she was nodding in agreement. "Please, Mommy," she pleaded under her breath, "don't make me go with that man. I'll do just like you said from now on—I promise."

"Do as the nice lady says, Loris. Mommy and Daddy have to talk now." Her mother's voice was subdued once again, faintly hollow, and her eyes held that deep sadness that always made Loris feel so bad. Not wanting to upset her any more than she already had by not singing the song right, she reluctantly obeyed.

"Well, shall we get on with it?" Carter stepped behind the Louis Quatorze bureau plat he used as a desk, and, with a sweep of his manicured hand, indicated where Angela should sit.

CHAPTER
Three

Angela sank into one of the fauteuil chairs in front of the writing desk; Miss Prescott took the other.

"I've been meaning to talk to you about this for some time, Angela," Carter said without looking up at her. He paused to clear his throat.

"There are a lot of things I've been wanting to talk to you about, too, Carter, but can't we talk in private?"

"Miss Prescott's presence here is vital. We need her as a witness."

"A witness?"

"Yes. You see, I've had my lawyers draw up a letter of agreement." He cleared his throat again and lifted several legal-size papers out of a hand-tooled Fabergé document box. "I believe this is a more than equitable settlement—very generous, in fact." He gave her a smile that managed to be both humble and smug at the same time. "My lawyers certainly think so." He set the original down, then handed them each a copy.

"I'm confident you'll think so, too, Angela, once you've read it," he hurried on. "All you have to do is sign it. Prescott will witness it."

Angela looked from one to the other. She felt totally disoriented. Nothing was as she thought it would be. "What's going on here?"

"You have only to read the document to understand," Carter said, making an effort to be patient with her. He felt he owed her that much.

Halfway through the second paragraph, Angela gave up trying to decipher the legal jargon, which was incomprehensible to her. "I don't understand any of this."

With a sigh of utter frustration, Carter ran his hand through his sun-streaked hair. He was accustomed to having other people take care of his problems. Because of its private nature, he'd been forced to deal with this situation himself. He was beginning to feel the strain. He turned to his secretary. "Will you please explain it to her, Prescott? I don't seem to be doing a very good job of it."

"I'll do what I can, Mr. Kingsley." She leaned toward Angela with a certain eagerness. Her defense against the normal chaos of life was a relentless efficiency. No problem was too big for her to tackle, no detail too small to warrant her attention in her tireless pursuit of order.

"Miss Castaldi, what we have here is a letter of agreement between Mr. Kingsley and yourself," she explained. "It clearly states that your . . . association with Mr. Kingsley has been terminated." She heard Angela's gasp of disbelief, but continued as though she hadn't. "In appreciation for your years of service to him, Mr. Kingsley believes a settlement of fifty thousand dollars is appropriate. And you will continue to receive a monthly check for five hundred dollars toward the support of your daughter, if—"

"*My* daughter?" Angela interjected. For the first time, she seemed to understand the significance of what was being said to her. "She's *his* daughter, too!"

Prescott pushed her glasses firmly against the bridge of

her nose. "That has never been legally established, Miss Castaldi."

Angela turned to Carter for vindication. "Carter, you know better than anybody that Loris is yours. You know the first time we . . . that I was a . . . I'd never been with a man before you!" Carter squirmed uncomfortably in his seat but said nothing. Angela turned back to Miss Prescott. "In all these years, there's never been any other man but him!"

Prescott was thrown for a moment by the emotional intensity of Angela's outburst, the very real despair darkening her eyes. She'd been led to believe that the young woman was just another cheap little gold digger. She fixed her attention on the document; there was something immensely reassuring about the blocks of precise black letters, the even spaces between the lines, and the perfectly executed margins.

"If you would please turn to page three, paragraph two, Miss Castaldi," she resumed, "you'll see that all Mr. Kingsley requests in exchange for this generous settlement is that you 'cease any and all claims on him forthwith, and all contact or attempts to contact him shall likewise desist as of this date. The aforementioned Loris Castaldi shall continue to bear said name, and she will not now or at any future date lay claim to any monies or titles relating to Mr. Kingsley or his estate, nor at any time or in any manner presume upon a blood tie that does not exist either in fact or before the law.' "

Prescott glanced at Angela to see whether or not the young woman had fully understood what had just been read to her.

The blood had drained from Angela's face. "I don't believe this." Sitting up abruptly, she grabbed on to the edge of the bureau plat with both hands. "Your father's forcing you to do this, isn't he, Carter? You could never do such a thing to Loris or me. I'd stake my life on it!"

"Angela, I—"

"You were willing to marry me when we first found out I was pregnant, but your father made you promise to wait until—"

"This has nothing to do with my father!"

"And he pulled strings to have you transferred to Saigon, hoping to break us up for good. I see that now."

"I asked him to have me transferred," Carter admitted irritably. He hadn't expected her to give him any trouble; she never had before. "I thought you were smart enough to have figured that out by now."

"After the last night we spent together, how on earth could I have thought that?" For two years, Angela had lived on the memories of that night. She leaned toward him, her eyes wide with pain and bewilderment, but all he noticed was the way her full breasts strained against the patterned fabric of her dress. "Don't you remember that night?"

Carter dropped his eyes. It was because of such nights that he'd allowed what he'd always known was an unsuitable relationship to go on for so long. "You may as well know the truth, Angela. I'd intended to tell you that night that the main reason I was going away was because it was over between us. I tried to tell you, but . . ." He wasn't used to defending his actions, and resented her even more for making him feel guilty. "For God's sake, how was I to know you'd wait for me for two years!"

Her hands slid off the edge of the writing table into her lap. "But, I told you I'd wait for you."

He shrugged off her remark. "Everybody says things like that when they're in the throes of passion."

"No, not everybody," she said ruefully. "My mother waited faithfully for almost six years in the old country until my father had made enough money to bring her and my brothers over here. That's how the women in my family—"

"Angela, listen to me." Carter cut her off, looking deeply distressed. "I'm sorry if I misled you. I was merely trying to let you down easy. I want nothing more than to make it up to you." To prove his sincerity, he reached over, took a signed check for fifty thousand dollars out of the Fabergé document box, and tore it to shreds, except for the right-hand corner. "Prescott," he announced magnanimously, handing her the corner, which bore a printed number, "please void this check and issue another in the amount of seventy-five thousand dollars."

Miss Prescott didn't seem the least surprised by his gesture. "Certainly, Mr. Kingsley."

"No," Angela protested before the secretary could get to her feet. "I don't want seventy-five thousand dollars, Carter."

A cynical smile distorted the perfect line of his lips. He'd obviously expected her to hold out for more money. "How much do you want?"

"I don't want any money. When have I ever wanted money from you, except to help me raise our daughter?"

"You must want something," he said matter-of-factly, as if that were the customary procedure in such matters.

"I want you to do what you've been promising me for years . . . to marry me and give Loris your name!"

He laughed as if she had told a mildly amusing joke. "That's out of the question. I couldn't marry you now, even if I wanted to."

That slow, dull throbbing started up again behind Angela's eyes. Part of her wanted to let it take over, wipe out all thought and feeling, yet she fought to hold it off. She couldn't give in to one of her spells now—she had to think of Loris.

"But, what about all your promises?" she demanded. "And all the promises I made to Loris in your name? For years we've been living on nothing but promises! How can I tell her that none of them will come true now? I can't . . . I won't let you do that to her!"

A look passed between Carter and his secretary before he asked, "What do you intend to do about it?"

"I . . . I don't know," Angela admitted. "But I'll do anything I have to make sure Loris is recognized as your daughter and gets a chance for a better life."

Carter and his secretary exchanged a meaningful little smile; they'd clearly considered this eventuality as well. "You have one of two options, Angela. You can either sue me for breach of promise, or bring a paternity suit against me. Am I right, Prescott?"

"Yes, Mr. Kingsley."

"I hope you're aware of the consequences of such an action. It's true that the scandal you'd cause could be somewhat damaging to my good name, but your name would also be smeared all over the tabloids, and Loris would be branded as a bastard before the entire world." He leaned across the table, as though prompted by concern for her. "Now, how do you suppose your father would react to that?"

The throbbing pressure behind Angela's eyes intensified at the mere mention of the father whose honor she'd betrayed. She hadn't seen him since the night he had found out she was pregnant. He had thrown her out of the house. A deeply religious man, he'd made her mother and brothers take a sacred vow to the Virgin Mary never to see or speak to her again. A few weeks after Loris was born, she'd taken the baby to his house, hoping for a reconciliation, only to find that he'd moved away from the neighborhood he'd lived in from the first day he'd set foot in America. Because of the shame she'd brought her family, he could no longer hold his head up in front of his friends and neighbors.

Angela forced herself to take several deep breaths. That always helped to stop the throbbing and dissipate the distancing haze it produced in her mind.

"And what purpose would taking me to court serve?" Carter was saying. "When it's all over, you wouldn't be any better off than you would be if you signed the letter of agreement."

"Mr. Kingsley is right, Miss Castaldi," Prescott was quick to confirm. "Even if you were to win such a case—which is highly unlikely, considering his position in society—the court would merely award you a monetary settlement."

"However, the court might not be as generous with my money as I am," Carter chimed in.

"As for a paternity suit, you do realize it would be encumbent on *you* to prove that he is the father of your child?"

"But he *is* the father of my child!"

"Let's assume you were somehow able to prove that," she allowed. "Once again, the court would merely order Mr. Kingsley to pay you child support, which he's already willing to do on his own."

"So you see, Angela," Carter added, without missing a beat, "you have nothing to gain by suing me. No court in the land can force me to marry you."

"But, we have a child!" When she got no response from Carter, she turned to his secretary. "Doesn't that mean anything?"

Prescott carefully adjusted her glasses. "I'm afraid Mr. Kingsley is right again, Miss Castaldi. Under the law, no one can be forced to marry against his will."

"Then, what's going to happen to Loris?" Angela cried. "Everybody keeps forgetting about her. Doesn't she have any rights?"

With a weary sigh, Carter sank back in his chair. "You win, Angela. I'll make the settlement an even one hundred thousand dollars, on condition that you sign the document right here and now."

She stared at him as if she were seeing him for the first time, and noticed the tiny beads of sweat on his forehead. "What are you afraid of, Carter?"

"I'm not afraid of anything," he returned defensively. "I merely want to put my past mistakes behind me and make sure they don't spoil my plans for the future."

She shook her head. "It doesn't work that way. Sooner or later we all have to pay for our sins."

"I *am* paying for mine," he snapped contemptuously. "One hundred thousand dollars' worth!"

Angela flinched as if he'd struck her; her voice shook when she was finally able to speak. "I wouldn't take a million dollars. No amount of money can make it up to Loris for not having a father, or for being despised for the rest of her life because she's illegitimate."

"You should have thought about that before!" he threw back in her face. "My father found us the best doctor on Park Avenue to take care of it. You refused. So don't blame

me for what happens to your little bastard! You brought this
on her yourself!'' Righteous anger brought him to his feet in
one swift motion. ''And you might as well know this, too,
so you'll stop deluding yourself once and for all about my
marrying you. I'm engaged to marry someone else. The
announcement's going to be in next Sunday's *Times*.''

Angela felt something wrench inside her. She knew she
was trembling uncontrollably—she could feel it—but it
wasn't her, it was someone else.

''Good God,'' Carter gasped.

Miss Prescott jumped to her feet. ''Miss Castaldi, what's
the matter?''

Angela's face had become masklike, her eyes were veiled,
and though she was shaking severely, every muscle in her
body was rigid.

Carter and Miss Prescott exchanged a baffled look. This
was one eventuality neither of them had anticipated.

Bending over, Prescott grabbed Angela by the shoulders
and shook her, hard. ''Miss Castaldi, can you hear me?''
There was no response.

''What do you think it is?'' Carter asked. ''An attack of
some kind?''

Angela was able to see and hear them both, but from a
great distance. Everything was far away. It was as if a wall
of glass had descended between her and the rest of the
world—an opaque, impenetrable wall.

''She seems to be in shock.''

''Well, how the hell do we bring her out of it?'' Carter
didn't bother to hide his concern. A scandal could wreck his
impending marriage, as well as the brilliant political career
his father had planned for him.

Stepping resolutely over to the bureau plat, Prescott
picked up the receiver of the house phone and dialed the
butler. ''Finley, you may bring the child back now,'' she
said when he answered. ''Quickly, please.''

''Do you think that's a good idea,'' Carter protested
feebly, ''under the circumstances?''

''She seems to be inordinately fond of the child. Let's

hope *she* can bring her out of this. Otherwise . . ." Leaving the worst unsaid, she hung up.

"Otherwise, we'll have to involve someone from the outside," Carter finished grimly.

A feeling of shame managed to penetrate the nothingness enveloping Angela. She couldn't let Carter see her like this. She fought to get air into her paralyzed lungs and break free of the forces threatening to drag her under completely. Gripping the arms of the chair, she pulled herself, somewhat shakily, to her feet.

"Miss Castaldi, are you all right now?"

"Yes, I . . . I'm fine." She felt so ashamed, she was unable to look at either of them. "I don't know what happened. Is there a . . . a bathroom I can use? I just want to splash some cold water on my face."

"Yes, of course." Prescott pointed to the side door she and Carter had used earlier. "My office is through there. The powder room is the first door on the right as you enter. Would you like me to help you?"

"No!" Angela put a hand up, as if to ward off a blow. "I can manage. Thank you." Her face hadn't quite returned to its normal color, and her eyes were still a bit glazed. Only by concentrating on putting one foot in front of the other was she able to make her way out the door.

"Thank God!" Carter exclaimed with the most genuine religious fervor he'd ever been capable of.

"You're going to be late for your appointment," Prescott reminded him. "Cocktails with the Reynoldses at the club, remember?"

"Damn!" He checked his wristwatch automatically. "I can't leave. I've got to settle this today."

A smile of perverse satisfaction further thinned Prescott's lips. "I think you've done enough damage for one day, don't you? You'd better let me take care of it from here on in. Besides, you put off doing anything about this problem for six months." Her tone implied that if he'd taken her advice, none of this would be happening now. "What's one day, more or less, at this point?"

"I suppose you're right," Carter agreed reluctantly. Actually, he was relieved that he had a legitimate excuse to leave. Thank God for good old, reliable Prescott. He gave her a suitably grateful smile. "I know I can trust you to take care of everything."

"Don't I always?" From behind her thick lenses she fixed him with a level stare. "But you might have told me she's in love with you."

Carter checked his watch again. "Call me tonight. I don't care how late. I want to know what happened."

"Of course."

"Will you be driving back to New York this evening, as you'd planned?"

"Certainly. And I think it would be best," Prescott added quickly, eager to wrap things up before Angela returned, "if I were to drive her back in my car. The state she's in, we don't know what she might say to the chauffeur."

"But first, you've got to get her to sign that damn document." If his father found out that he'd failed to get Angela permanently out of his life, he'd never hear the end of it.

"Let me handle this, Carter. We're not dealing with one of your little sluts this time." Her tone had been harsher than she'd meant it to be, but she was upset that he had not taken her completely into his confidence. "I'll take care of everything, just as I always do."

Carter resented being reminded of the times she'd covered up for him, the many difficult situations she'd gotten him out of. She treated him like an ineffectual child, as if she had taken lessons from his father! Still, he had to admit, she always behaved in a properly deferential manner when others were present.

She was the only female he had ever known whom he couldn't charm the pants off. She was also the only woman, including his exquisite but featherbrained mother, for whom he'd ever felt a twinge of respect. If anyone could get him out of this mess, Prescott could, but it would be one more thing she had on him. He flashed her what he hoped was his most disarming smile. "Take care of this for me, Pres, and there'll be a nice bonus in it for you."

She gave him a strange look, then turned away before he could decipher it.

"I'll be waiting for your call," he reminded her, going over to the side door just as Angela returned. Once again, he forced a smile of tender concern. "Are you feeling better, Angela?"

She nodded. The cold water had sobered her. She felt like a mortally wounded animal that wanted only to get back to its den, to die with some last shred of dignity. "I just want to go home now."

"But first, Angela—"

"Don't worry, Carter." Her tone was flat, defeated. "I won't sue you." She looked up at him then, trying not to see how beautiful he still was to her, in spite of everything. "And I don't want your money. Nothing could ever get me to sign that letter. *You* may be capable of denying Loris her father, but I never will."

Prescott's eyes narrowed as she studied Angela. The young woman was obviously a fool when it came to men—but then, most women were. Still, she couldn't help admiring her. There weren't too many people in this world who couldn't be bought; in fact, Prescott didn't know any, personally. But everyone, she knew, was vulnerable; everyone had one precious thing he valued above everything else. She was an expert at finding and manipulating it. She'd just discovered Angela's.

"Now, Angela, be reasonable," Carter was insisting impatiently. "You know you—"

Before he could cause any more damage, Prescott cut in. "Mr. Kingsley, you'll be late for—" she began, only to be cut off herself.

"Mommy!" Loris cried, squeezing through the narrow opening between the double doors. In her eagerness to rejoin her mother, she hadn't given the butler a chance to open the doors the rest of the way.

Nor did Prescott. "That will be all, Finley."

Her abrupt words, and the sharpness of her tone, brought Loris to a stop as well. Immediately, she sensed that something was wrong. She could hear it in that strange silence that prevailed when a child entered a room unexpectedly; she could see it in the way they immediately changed their expressions. Her mother turned away, as if she couldn't bear to look at her. When her father stormed out of the room, Loris knew that the worst had happened.

And it was all her fault.

"I'm sorry, Mommy," Loris said, fighting to hold back the tears. "I really did try. Honest, I did."

Slowly, as if reluctantly, her mother turned her face away from the window and looked at Loris, for the first time since they'd gotten into Miss Prescott's car. "It's not your fault, baby," she said with a soft smile that made Loris feel even guiltier for having failed her. "Try to get some sleep now. You missed your nap today." She turned to stare out the window again, although she seemed uninterested in their surroundings.

Twilight was wrapping an indigo blanket over the sleeping countryside, and the trees whizzing past the car from the side of the road were visible only in silhouette. The dark branches swaying in the wind looked scary to Loris, like long, skeletal arms that could reach out and grab her. She slid over to the far corner of the back seat and sank down as far as she could go.

She couldn't remember ever feeling so bad.

Slowly, she turned the strange word over in her mind, as she had while she was having milk and cookies in the butler's pantry earlier. She still didn't know what an *exhibition* was, only that she'd done it, making her father so mad now that he'd never love her. She was sure that's why her mother wouldn't look at her. A single tear slid down her face, and she had to bite down on her bottom lip to keep from giving in to more of them. Was what she'd done so bad that her mother would stop loving her, too?

With each silent smile Loris's fear and guilt deepened, making it impossible for her to sleep, though she pretended to do so for her mother's sake. She couldn't wait to get home, where her mother would be herself again. She sat up expectantly when Miss Prescott finally pulled up in front of their building on the Lower East Side.

If one were going to be a kept woman, Prescott couldn't help thinking as she eyed the run-down brownstone, one could manage it with more style than this. Despite his faults—and Prescott knew he had many—Carter could never be accused of being stingy. Living in such a modest place had to have been Angela's idea. Perhaps it was her way of refusing to be treated as a kept woman. And, as the peeling vacancy sign indicated, she'd chosen to live in furnished rooms. The poor girl had obviously believed Carter's promises of marriage.

Directly across the street from the building where Angela lived stood a storefront mission, dedicated, as its neon sign blazingly proclaimed, to Christ the Savior. A five-foot-high, four-inch-thick cross, connected to the front of the building by a horizontal, V-shaped iron bar, hung suspended over the sidewalk. The huge cross, not unlike a theater marquee, flashed its message of salvation at regular intervals.

Miss Prescott cut the motor. "Here we are."

Angela stared up at the windows of her apartment, like a prisoner being returned to her cell. Her face was still unnaturally pale but her eyes were clear, and she appeared composed.

Almost too much so, thought Prescott uneasily. "Are you feeling better, Miss Castaldi?"

Angela nodded, but made no move to get out of the car.

Prescott shifted her position so that they were facing one another over the top of the seat. "I know how painful all this has been for you, but after a good night's sleep, I'm sure you'll realize things aren't as bad as they seem to you now."

Angela smiled. "Have you ever been in love, Miss Prescott?"

For once, Prescott was too thrown to respond.

"I didn't think so." Angela shook her head as though she actually felt sorry for her.

Prescott stiffened defensively. "Love is the last thing you should be thinking about. It's love that's brought you to this sorry state of affairs."

Angela didn't need to be reminded. "All right, baby, we're going," she told Loris, who was fidgeting in her eagerness to be home. "First, thank Miss Prescott for driving us back."

"I realize I have an abrupt manner," Prescott said, before Loris could speak, "but I'm only trying to help. This is neither the time nor the place, but we must talk. May I call you tomorrow? We could have lunch."

"No, thanks." Angela was polite but cool; she'd seen the secretary slip the letter of agreement into her large shoulder bag.

"Nobody admires your pride more than I do," said Prescott sincerely. "But pride is the one thing you can't afford right now. You've got to think about your future."

Angela laughed. Something in it set off a warning bell in Prescott's head. She leaned over the back of the seat. "Are you sure you're all right?"

She answered with a shrug. Even if she wanted to, Angela knew she could never get Miss Prescott to understand how she felt. For years she'd been living in dread, waiting for God to mete out the inevitable punishment for her sin, and now that He had, all she felt was a strange sense of relief. It was over. She didn't have to hold her breath anymore.

"Wait!" Prescott called out as Angela grabbed the door handle. She quickly removed a card and a pen from the breast pocket of her jacket. "Here's my business card. You can reach me at the office from eight to six. And," she added, scribbling, "this is my home number." She offered her the card. "Please let me help you."

Angela laughed again. Throwing open the door, she got out of the car.

"I'll keep it for Mommy if you want," said Loris.

"Yes, why don't you?" Prescott handed her the card, then watched as the child tucked it carefully into the side pocket of her dress.

"And thank you for driving us home," Loris added before she scrambled out of the car, stepping to one side to let her mother close the door.

Such a bright, self-possessed little girl, Prescott thought, *but far too beautiful for her own good.* She was sure to end up like her mother—maybe worse. As she watched them climb the steps to the main entrance, hand in hand, she couldn't have said which of the two she felt sorrier for. She had to remind herself that she had yet to accomplish her mission. But all she had to do, she felt confidently, was play on Angela's love for her daughter. Once she realized that one hundred thousand dollars would ensure Loris's future, she would no longer hesitate to sign the letter of agreement.

With a self-congratulatory smile, Prescott carefully maneuvered her car back into traffic.

CHAPTER
Four

Angela closed the door and automatically flicked on the light switch. She winced as the overhead light revealed the living room in all its genteel shabbiness, mercilessly exposing the dime store knickknacks and little embroidered pillows—her every pathetic attempt to turn a furnished flat into a home. She turned the light back off.

"It's too bright—it hurts my eyes," she said in response to Loris's tiny gasp of surprise. "There's plenty of light." She motioned toward the light streaming through the sheer drapes she'd bought on sale at Gimbel's, an amber spill from the lamppost on the street corner. Additional light was reflected onto the ceiling by the giant crucifix flashing across the street in front of the mission. "You can see, baby, can't you?"

"Yes, Mommy." Going up on her toes, Loris double-locked the front door because her mother had neglected to do so.

Angela dropped her keys and purse onto a side table.

"Now, be a good girl, Loris, and get yourself ready for bed. Mommy's very tired tonight." She spoke in a dull, faraway manner, and when she crossed the living room, her go-go boots echoed heavily on the bare floor. "Call me when you're ready, and I'll come tuck you in."

"But we didn't eat dinner yet," Loris protested.

Angela had totally forgotten about dinner; it felt to her as if it were three o'clock in the morning. All she wanted was for this terrible day to end. "Please do what I ask, Loris."

"But I'm hungry!" Except for a bowl of cornflakes, and the chocolate milk and cookies, she hadn't eaten all day.

"All right." Angela's shoulders sagged as she gave in; she didn't have a drop of fight left in her. "I'll get you dinner in a few minutes."

"I'll get dinner if you're too tired, Mommy," Loris offered, thankful that she wasn't going to be sent to bed early. A sudden excitement filled her. "Can I? Can I get it?" She jumped up and down in one spot. "Please? I'll make sanguages."

Loris's mispronunciation of *sandwiches* usually made Angela smile. Tonight, it made her feel like crying. "All right, baby. Just be careful not to stain your pretty new dress."

Not that it matters anymore, Angela reminded herself as Loris skipped happily out of the room. Nothing mattered anymore. She went and sat in the faded chintz armchair in the corner. A wonderful calm came over her—the calm of a person who has nothing left to lose. Resting her forearms on the frayed arms of the chair she exhaled slowly, completely, until there wasn't a thread of air left in her lungs.

In the narrow kitchen, Loris was arranging four slices of white bread, which she'd already spread corner to corner with butter, onto her favorite tray—the one with the picture of Snoopy on it. Unwrapping a wax paper package of Genoa salami, she peeled off a long, oval slice. Her mother always gave her the first slice when she made the sandwiches, so she felt it was okay to pop it in her mouth. Except for ice cream, salami was her absolutely favorite food.

With intense concentration she began to layer salami onto two of the slices of bread, making sure they didn't stick out over the edges. She was determined to do it right and make her mother proud of her again. When the layers were nice and thick and perfectly even all around, she slapped the remaining slices of bread on top. She was absolutely forbidden to pick up anything sharper than a butter knife, so she left the sandwiches whole instead of cutting them in half, as she knew she was supposed to.

Taking a carton of milk out of the refrigerator, she carefully poured out two glasses and set them on the tray. Balancing it carefully in both hands, she then carried it into the living room. Accustomed to the bright light in the kitchen, it took several moments for her eyes to adjust to the semidarkness, but she was finally able to locate her mother.

"Look, Mommy!" Eager to show off her achievement, she hurried toward her, the tray held high. The glasses skidded to the front of the tray; only the raised edge kept them from tumbling off. Loris came to an abrupt halt as she saw her mother's face.

Angela was staring in a distant but intense way at the ceiling, where the reflection from the electrified crucifix from across the street was blinking on and off at steady intervals. The harsh white light turned her skin cadaver-pale; the shadows it created obliterated her eyes, making her face look like a skull.

"Look, Mommy," Loris shouted, holding the tray out to her like an offering. "Look!"

But Angela was beyond hearing her. The pulsing sensation in her head had intensified to where nothing could penetrate it, catching her up in that rhythm all its own, speaking to her in words only she could hear or understand. Then, something was tugging at her. She tried to shake it off, but she couldn't move. An undecipherable yet strangely familiar sound broke up the perfect rhythm, draining the words of their magic.

She became aware of increasing pressure on her chest as Loris's tiny fists pounded her. The air being forced into her lungs was a kind of violation. Her head snapped back, breaking her connection with the saving light, jerking her mouth open, and she was helpless to stop a rush of air from entering her. She recognized the sound now. It was only two syllables—*mom-my*—repeated over and over again like an incantation.

"Mom-my . . . Mom-my . . . Mom-my!"

She blinked several times, like a person suddenly thrust out of total darkness into a blinding light. It took several long moments before she realized that the squirming, demanding bundle of flesh sprawling across her lap was her daughter. A sudden nausea welled up inside her, like morning sickness. Her body recoiled from the child.

There was a soundless click in her head. She had the sensation that her body was moving steadily away from the child's until they were on opposite cliffs, overlooking a wide abyss. A long, thin wire was strung between the cliffs and, suddenly, she was hanging from the center of it, suspended over the void. With a sudden flash of lucidity, she knew that with a tremendous effort, she could once again make it back to reality.

That was Angela's last rational thought. She let go of the wire, letting herself free fall into the void.

Ellen Blake took a final toke, sucking the smoke deep into her lungs, then exhaled harshly. After what she'd been through tonight, not even pot could help her mellow out. Dropping the dead roach into the ashtray resting beside her on the window seat, she peered out the first-floor window again.

A steady rain had been falling for the past hour and Fourteenth Street, which would normally have been crowded with crosstown traffic, since it was only 10:00 P.M., was almost empty. Oil slicks from countless vehicles turned the asphalt into a glistening black mirror that reflected the flashing light of the crucifix across the way.

The sidewalks were deserted, so when Ellen spotted the

woman getting out of a Dodge Charger, parked a couple of
brownstones away, she sat up. That had to be her. The
stranger's resolute walk matched the voice she'd spoken to
on the phone half an hour ago. She was wearing a maxi-
length trench coat with a matching khaki hat, but she wasn't
carrying an umbrella. She held her head up high—something
people rarely do when walking in the rain.

When the woman passed directly under her window, Ellen
Blake craned her neck to see over the urban jungle of
oregano and marijuana plants growing out of her window
box. Just as the woman turned to go up the steps, she called
out, "You Miss Prescott?"

The woman tilted her face up to her. "Yes."

"Thank Christ!" She waved her impatiently up the stairs.
"Be right there!" She had the street door open before
Prescott had reached the front stoop. "Man, am I glad to
see you! I think she's—"

"We'd better get in out of the rain," Prescott suggested
with her typical presence of mind, just in case there were
nosy neighbors lurking behind their windows.

"Oh, sure." With a vague nod she backed into the
entrance hall, stepping to one side to let Prescott by. "I'm
Ellen Blake . . . the one who called you?"

"*You're* the landlady?" Prescott was unable to conceal
her surprise.

The young woman was barely out of her teens and,
judging from her dress, manner, and pungent aroma of pot
swirling around her, she was a hippie. Her pale blond hair
was a frizzy halo around her head. She was very pretty, in
that arrested adolescent way of a typical flower child; her
big blue eyes were dreamy, unfocused.

"This building belongs to my father, the slumlord," she
explained with a bored shrug that made her girlish, unconfined
breasts jiggle under her tie-dyed T-shirt. A coke spoon
dangled on a chain around her neck, next to a sunflower
pendant bearing the legend: WAR IS NOT HEALTHY FOR CHILDREN
OR OTHER LIVING THINGS. "He, like, let me have the place
when I dropped out. It's a great—"

"What's happened, Miss Blake?" Prescott cut in impatiently. "You said on the phone it was an emergency."

"Call me Ellen. Everybody . . . hey, wow," she exclaimed, her mind having taken a 180-degree turn. "That's right. Wait till you see her. What a bummer!"

"Where is she?"

"She's in 2A. One flight up." Ellen's collection of silver-and-turquoise bracelets jangled as she indicated the staircase at the end of the narrow corridor. "Man, I've seen some bad trips," she rattled on while leading the way, "but nothing like this."

"What exactly has happened, Ellen?"

"It started raining about an hour ago," she said dramatically, emphasizing every other word with the life-and-death intensity of a teenager. "And, like, whenever it rains, I always check to see if the windows on all the landings are closed, you know? So when I got to the second floor, I heard the little girl screaming. You could hear her right through the closed door, and—"

"Did anyone else hear her?" Prescott kept her tone deliberately casual as they climbed the stairs. "Or try to help in any way?"

"In this place?" Ellen giggled. "Who would notice? Someone's always freaking out. But, like, Angela, she's not into any kind of dope, you know. I mean, she's real nice, but she's just not with it. I figure someone must have slipped her some acid. Man, when I saw her, I could see why the poor kid was screaming her head off!"

Silence hung over the dingy, narrow hallway now as they stepped onto the second-floor landing, broken only by the sound of raindrops tapping on the window.

"What did you do then?" Prescott prompted.

"Well, like, I didn't know what to do, at first. I sure as hell wasn't about to call in the pigs."

"You did the right thing, Ellen," Prescott assured her. "Who needs the police snooping around?"

A smile mingling relief and gratitude lit up the hippie's face. "That's what I figured. Here's 2A." She pointed to a paint-peeling door just off the landing. "So, when Loris gave me your card—she said you'd know how to help—I called you right away."

"Don't worry, Ellen, I'll take care of everything." She knocked resolutely on the door.

Loris answered the door, a Raggedy Ann doll clutched tightly to her side. The child was calm now, having obviously cried herself out, but her eyes were wide with fear. She held on to the doll as though her life depended on it.

Prescott pushed her glasses firmly up against the bridge of her nose. "I'm here to help your mother, Loris. Where is she?"

"I don't know," she murmured in a lost little voice as she glanced over her shoulder to a spot on the other side of the room. "She went away again . . . but this time, she didn't come back."

"What do you mean?" Prescott brushed past the child. She hadn't taken more than a couple of steps into the living room, however, when she came to a stunned halt. "Good . . . Lord!"

Angela was still sitting in the corner armchair, her body as rigid and incapable of movement as a piece of furniture. She was in a state of total catatonic withdrawal, and seemed not to breathe at all. Her face was like a death mask, livid from lack of oxygen. She stared, unblinking, at the reflection of the crucifix flashing on the ceiling, her eyes completely veiled.

"I tried real hard, but she won't come back." Fresh tears welled up in Loris's eyes, and she hugged the doll to her with both arms. "It's all my fault." Her chin began to tremble, and tears spilled down her face. "It's all because of me that Daddy won't—"

"That's nonsense," Prescott cut her off sharply. With a snap of her head, she indicated to Ellen to shut the door. She waited until Ellen had before she spoke to the child again, her tone softer, more reassuring. "Your mother is sick, Loris. You mustn't blame yourself. Do you want to help me make her better again?"

Loris nodded, sniffling.

"First, you've got to stop crying." Taking a linen hand-kerchief from her trench coat pocket, Prescott helped Loris blow her nose. "Now, I want you to promise me that you'll do everything I say." Loris finished wiping her nose with the back of her hand and nodded again. "Where's the telephone?"

"In Mommy's bedroom."

"It's right through that door." Ellen took a step forward, as if she meant to show her the way.

"I can find it," Prescott was quick to assure her; she didn't want any witnesses. "I'd appreciate it, Ellen, if you'd take care of Loris. I'll be right back." Without giving her a chance to reply, she turned and headed toward the bedroom. She quickly weighed each and every option she could imagine. Protecting Carter was her primary concern.

Having Angela carted off to Bellevue would have been easy enough, she knew, but it would involve the police, and then there would be questions. Better to put Angela in a private clinic, where such things were handled with discretion.

Prescott just happened to know of such a clinic. Only last month she'd arranged for one of Carter's underage sluts to have an abortion there. She set her wide shoulder bag down on the bed, unzipped it, and removed her address book. She flipped through it to the Ms, found the number, and dialed it.

The Martindale Clinic on Park Avenue in the upper eighties catered to those special few whose problems and peccadilloes, if ever known, would make front-page head-lines. For a stiff price, the rich and famous could go there to discreetly dry out, get detoxified, have illegal abortions or a quiet nervous breakdown. As usual, the clinic's service was as impeccable as the Plaza's. She had only to mention the Kingsley name, give a brief description of the "problem," and a private room in the psychiatric ward was reserved instantly. An unmarked ambulance was immediately dis-patched to the scene.

As she replaced the receiver, Prescott noticed her busi-

ness card, lying on the night table next to the phone. The
hippie landlady had obviously left it there. She slipped it
into her coat pocket. Her eyes narrowed behind her thick
lenses as they scanned the nondescript bedroom.

Carter smiled boyishly from a framed photo atop the
opposite night table. The photo was set in such a way that it
was the first thing Angela was likely to see in the morning
and the last thing at night. Unzipping the largest compartment in her pocketbook, Prescott stuffed the picture inside,
frame and all. She found several snapshots of Carter in the
night table drawer, and a packet of love letters tied with a
satin ribbon; the pages were practically transparent from
having been handled so much. She stuffed the lot into her
bag as well.

She'd have to search the entire apartment before she left
and carefully remove everything that might connect Carter
to Angela. First, she'd have to get Loris and Ellen out of the
way. When she went back to the living room, she found
them both sitting on the sofa, facing away from the terrible
vision in the corner. Ellen was gently rocking the child in
her arms, crooning a lullaby. Exhausted, Loris was fighting
to keep her eyes open.

"Everything's been taken care of." Prescott gave Ellen a
meaningful look and the child a reassuring smile. "Now, in
a little while, Loris, the doctor will come to take care of
your mother. We're going to be leaving here, so you must
go—"

"Go . . . where?" Loris grabbed Ellen. "Not without
Mommy, too!"

"Why, no," said Prescott soothingly. "But if you want to
go with your mother, you'll have to get your hat and coat. I
don't know where they are. You must show me." She
smiled, but the child continued to stare at her warily. She
never had been any good with children.

The hippie came to her aid. "Like, where does Mommy
keep your hat and coat, honey?"

"In my closet."

"Okay, let's go get them."

Loris allowed Ellen to help her to her feet, but before she'd take another step, she demanded of Prescott, "Is Mommy coming, too?"

"Yes, of course," Prescott lied smoothly.

Loris made a face. "All right, then." Still clutching her doll, she led the way. "This is my room," she informed them with a proprietary air when she threw the door open. She had to stand on her toes to reach the light switch. "And that's my closet." She was too small to reach any of the hangers her clothes were neatly lined up on, or the top shelf, with its row of tiny bonnets.

Prescott quickly found her hat and coat, and draped them over the child's rocking chair, all but concealing its current occupant—a teddy bear with only one ear. "We won't be leaving for a while yet, Loris, so why don't you lie down and take a nap? It's way past your bedtime, and I can see how sleepy you are. Don't worry," she hastened to add before the little girl could protest, "we'll wake you up as soon as the doctor gets here and your mother is ready to leave."

"Promise?"

"I promise."

Her mother had never broken a promise to her, so Loris assumed all grown-ups kept their promises, and obeyed Miss Prescott without another word. Her head had barely touched the pillow when she slipped into a deep sleep.

"Poor little kid," Ellen said with a sigh when Prescott had closed the door behind them. "Like, what's going to happen to her now? And what about Angela?"

"I've made arrangements to have Angela taken to a private hospital, where she'll get the very best of care. That way, Ellen, we won't have to involve the police and we can keep this unfortunate incident out of the newspapers."

"Oh, man, I sure appreciate that." With two of her tenants running a mimeograph machine for S.D.S., she didn't need police around. Vaguely, she wondered why the press would be interested in someone like Angela.

"By the way, have you told anyone else about this?"

"There *is* nobody else. She doesn't have any family that I know of . . . no friends, either. There's the kid's father, but I don't know where to get in touch with him."

"Have you ever met him?"

"Well, like, I've seen him coming in a few times, but it was always at night, and . . ." She paused, not wanting to give away the fact that she made a habit of watching everyone's coming and goings from her window. "He hasn't been around for . . . it's got to be two years. I figured he split. Do *you* know where he is?"

"He died two years ago, Ellen." Prescott kept her tone properly hushed. "Killed in Vietnam."

"Hey, what a bummer!" She shook her head, causing her frizzy halo to wobble woefully. "But she was always saying how he was coming back to her!"

"I know." Prescott let out a suitably rueful sigh. "She's always refused to accept his death. She still speaks of him as if he were alive."

"So does Loris. Like, only yesterday she told me she was going to visit her father."

Prescott swung her purse strap casually over one shoulder. "Did she say who her father was, or where they were going to see him?"

Ellen needed a moment to think it over. "No. I just asked why she was all dressed up, and she said her mommy was taking her to see daddy."

"I'm afraid that was just another one of Angela's delusions."

Ellen blinked several times, trying to see past the fuzziness in her head. "But I saw a big limo come to get them, like, with a chauffeur, the whole works."

"A pearl-gray Rolls-Royce?"

"Yeah. A real capitalist buggy."

Prescott smiled knowingly. "I sent the limousine, Ellen. They spent the day with me at my summer place. I thought a change of scene might help Angela—she sounded so depressed the last time I spoke to her on the phone. But somehow, she managed to convince herself that *he'd* called her, not I. I tried to tell her that it was time she faced the truth, that she was harming the child by making her believe her father was still alive.'' She sighed ruefully again. ''She became very upset. I can't help feeling our talk may have triggered all this.''

''Hey, don't lay a guilt trip on yourself. She's been on a downer for ages.''

''I can't thank you enough for your kindness and understanding, Ellen.'' Unzipping the outside compartment of her pocketbook, Prescott removed a regular white envelope. Before driving to Angela's, she'd taken a thousand dollars from the petty cash fund Carter allotted her for emergencies, in case a bribe would be needed. She thumbed out five one-hundred-dollar bills, an amount she was certain would be sufficient to ensure the hippie's gratitude without arousing her suspicions. ''Please accept this as a small token of my appreciation.''

''No way!'' Ellen looked down at the money with contempt verging on revulsion.

Prescott couldn't help wondering what this new generation was coming to, but she didn't insist. ''That's very generous of you. I wonder if I may ask one last favor?''

''Just name it.''

''The ambulance should be here any minute. Would you go downstairs and wait for it so you can show them the way?''

''Sure thing.''

''Meanwhile, I'll pack a bag for Angela and one for the child.''

''Oh, the poor little kid,'' Ellen murmured sincerely. ''What's going to happen to her now?''

Miss Prescott smiled reassuringly. ''I'll take care of Loris. I know her father would want me to.''

CHAPTER
Five

The vaulted ceiling and soaring Gothic arches over the doors and windows of the vestibule of the Convent of the Immaculate Conception made Loris feel overwhelmed. Heavy brown drapes covered all the windows, shutting out the dazzling September sunlight. Every now and then a black-robed and -veiled figure floated past the main doorway soundlessly. Loris had never known so total a silence as the one surrounding her.

She couldn't have said how long she'd been waiting on the wooden bench, where they'd deposited her and her suitcase, for time itself seemed stilled within those massive stone walls. She only knew that whatever was going to happen to her now was being decided behind that closed door just across the hall, and there was nothing she could do about it.

She missed her mother terribly.

The shock of waking up and finding her gone that morning had worn off, but not the guilt of having slept while they took her away. Miss Prescott had told her that her mother was sick and had had to go to the hospital, and Loris knew she was to blame for that, too. Tears welled in her eyes, but she blinked them back. Miss Prescott said if she cried or misbehaved, then Mommy would never get better, and she'd never see her again.

The door across the way opened, revealing Prescott, who motioned to Loris to join her. She obeyed instantly.

"This is Mother Superior, Loris," she said when she'd ushered her into the office. "She's graciously consented to let you stay here until your mother is well."

Mother Superior was a handsome woman, if a bit forbidding in her severe black robes and stiff white wimple. With her every breath the silver crucifix resting on her chest rose, catching the light, making the figure of Christ appear to be breathing also.

"Thank you," Loris told her politely, "but I don't want to—"

"You will speak only when you are spoken to, Castaldi." Mother Superior's tone was firm, but not harsh. It was the tone of a person accustomed to exercising authority, fully aware of the respect due one in her position. She studied Loris thoroughly from behind her large oak desk.

Unlike the vestibule, her office was sparsely furnished, as stark as an army barracks. In fact, Mother Superior often thought of the convent she presided over as a spiritual fortress, with herself as commander in chief, waging a never-ending battle against the Devil and his cohorts; one last stand in this godless age of mini-skirts and rock 'n' roll.

Loris shifted uncomfortably from one foot to the other under the nun's clear, ice-blue gaze. She instinctively knew when someone didn't like her, and clearly, Mother Superior disapproved of her.

She was also seriously displeased by the child's frivolous appearance, and said so. She was even more appalled to learn, after she'd questioned her, that Loris was totally ignorant of Catholic doctrine. Her mother had merely taught her to believe in a loving God who would always answer her prayers. Loris knew nothing of the martyrs and saints, the Devil and temptation, or the fiery torments of hell. Nevertheless, she decided, a soul in such dire need of salvation was an irresistible challenge, an unshirkable responsibility. And the convent would benefit greatly from Miss Prescott's five-thousand-dollar donation.

It was Miss Prescott she turned her attention to now. "She will have to be baptized immediately." Her tone brooked no argument.

"Whatever you think best," Prescott agreed.

Mother Superior picked up a silver bell and rang it, her pinkie extended elegantly. She'd barely replaced the bell on her desk when the office door opened and a nun stepped resolutely inside. "This is Sister Teresa. She is in charge of the first- and second-graders."

Sister Teresa couldn't have been more than five feet tall, and seemed almost as wide, yet she bustled about with surprising energy and agility. Her pasty face protruded like a still-rising lump of dough from a wimple that seemed barely able to contain it. The tight, starched bands cut deep into her plump flesh, which could have accounted for her perpetual frown and the grim set of her mouth. She had dark, beady eyes, bushy eyebrows, and the beginnings of a moustache.

If Mother Superior was the commander in chief of their spiritual fortress, then Sister Teresa was the drill sergeant of the soul. It was her job to strip raw recruits of their individuality and impart their first lessons in conformity to the convent's strict rules and regulations. From her expression, it was clear she felt she had her job cut out for her. "Come with me," she ordered brusquely.

A sudden terror gripped Loris, and she latched on to Miss Prescott's skirt. "Please don't leave me here," she pleaded, holding on for dear life. "Please, take me back to Mommy. Please!"

"Loris, you promised to be good, remember? Do you know what it would do to your mother, sick as she is, if I tell her how you're behaving?"

"I'll be good!" Letting go of Prescott's skirt, Loris made a clumsy attempt at smoothing out the wrinkles she'd made in it. "Please, don't tell Mommy! I'll be good—honest I will!" To prove it, she hurried to join Sister Teresa, whose frown had deepened even further at her outrageous behavior.

"One word of caution, Castaldi," Mother Superior said, drawing herself up in her chair. "You are welcome here, as are all souls, no matter how lacking in divine grace. But *you* will have to work and pray harder than all the other girls in order to achieve a state of grace."

Loris stared at her blankly; she didn't know what Mother Superior was talking about.

She explained. "Since you were born to a union unsanctified by the holy sacrament of matrimony, the Devil has already put his mark on you."

Feeling a sense of shame she could barely comprehend, Loris followed Sister Teresa out the door.

The dark hairs of Sister Teresa's moustache bristled as she clucked disapprovingly. "Shameful!"

Seeking to find the source of her shame, Loris glanced at herself in the solitary mirror hanging over the wall-length row of sinks. She was seated on a stool in the communal baths, blinded by the glare from the spotless white tile walls and floor. Stalls, just large enough to hold a bathtub, lined the other three walls; a white cotton drape hid each one from view when in use.

Still clucking disapprovingly, Sister Teresa reached into a cabinet under one of the sinks and removed a towel, a small bowl, and a pair of long scissors. She dropped the towel around Loris's shoulders, then slapped the bowl on her head. "Don't move."

Loris was too startled to speak, let alone move, and since the bowl covered her eyes, she couldn't even see. She felt the nun grab one of her long curls and pull it taut, heard the terrible cutting sound as the scissors sliced through her hair. Within minutes, all her curls lay on the tile floor, and the bowl was removed. Knowing how upset her mother would be when she saw her butchered hair, she burst into tears.

"Stop crying this instant, Castaldi!" Using the flat side of the scissors, the nun gave her a sharp rap on the knuckles. Loris cried out, as much in shock as in pain. Fear froze her tears.

Sister Teresa lectured Loris on the sin of vanity while she quickly replaced the bowl and scissors in the cabinet, removed several items necessary for a bath, and marched her over to one of the stalls. She was outraged when the child began undressing as unashamedly as a pagan savage. "Didn't your mother teach you that you must never remove your clothes before another living soul?"

Sniffling, Loris shook her head.

"Then we shall teach you the proper Christian way to undress." She thrust a coarse white linen shift at Loris. "Slip this over your head; keep your arms inside." Loris did as she was told; she didn't dare do otherwise, though she couldn't see the sense of it. "Now, you may remove your garments from under the shift with no loss of modesty."

Following these orders was like peeling off her clothes under a narrow tent, but Loris managed it. Sister nodded approvingly as she readied the bath water. "Get into the tub and scrub yourself good and—no!" she cried, appalled, as Loris started to take off the shift before getting into the bathtub. "You keep that on! Don't you know it's a mortal sin to look upon your own nakedness?"

Loris stared uncomprehendingly at the nun. The concept of sin was totally foreign to her. "But, how can I wash with clothes on?"

"The same way you undressed." She waited until Loris sank down into the almost scalding water before handing her a washcloth wrapped around a bar of brown lye soap. "And use the washcloth. Never touch your body with your bare hands or you'll endanger your immortal soul."

Washing under the clinging wet shift was even more difficult than undressing under it, and Sister Teresa kept peeking through the drape to make sure Loris wasn't touching certain parts of her body. Loris wondered what kind of crazy place she had fallen into.

Wearing the regulation uniform—a dark green jumper over a long-sleeved tan blouse—Loris joined the rest of the school that evening at dinner. She was placed at the first of four long, narrow tables, which ran the length of the large refectory. Students were seated in ascending order, from the first to the eighth grade. The nuns responsible for each class were seated at a separate table, running the width of the room, that rested on a platform to give them an unobstructed view. Throughout the meal, they kept calling out to those in their charge whose conduct or table manners needed correcting.

Talking at the table, Loris quickly learned, was forbidden, and the mere scraping of a fork against a plate was an infraction. Intimidated by her strange new surroundings, she had trouble getting her food down. She found enjoying a meal difficult since everywhere she looked there were images of pain and suffering.

A huge crucifix dominated the wall behind the nuns' dining table. The writhing body of Christ was held suspended in torment by the gruesomely realistic nails driven through his hands and feet. On the opposite wall was a painting of Jesus stripped and tied to a post. Long red welts from the whip that was about to fall again covered his frail chest and back; bright red drops of blood trickled down his face from the crown of thorns embedded deep in his forehead.

Directly facing Loris was a portrait that disturbed and mystified her even more. She recognized the solitary lady with the white robe and pale blue cloak as the Madonna, because her mother had a picture of her, too. But in her picture the Madonna was embracing the baby Jesus and looked happy, while in this one, there was a terrible sadness in her eyes. And her heart, which lay exposed on her chest, was pierced clear through with seven long knives.

"Castaldi!"

Loris froze as her name rang out, unbearably loud in the

collective silence. One hundred and thirty-seven pairs of
eyes turned to look at her, making her cringe with
embarrassment.

"You must stop dawdling. Eat at the same pace as the
other girls." Sister Teresa had actually paused in the middle
of a third helping of mashed potatoes to admonish her
charge. "Each course must be finished in unison, or your
plate will be removed before you're through eating. Is that
understood?"

Loris nodded, then, before she could stop herself, blurted
out, "Why are all those knives stuck in the Madonna's
heart?"

"Swords," the nun corrected. "That is the Madonna of
the Seven Sorrows. Every time you're bad, or you don't do
as you're told—like not eating your dinner on time—you
plunge a sword into the Blessed Mother's heart."

Feeling those sad, hurt eyes watching every bite she took,
Loris forced herself to finish her meal. A bell clanged
loudly, bringing the girls to their feet in unison. Forming a
single line, they filed out of the refectory and marched in
silence to their respective study hall, to do their homework
and enjoy an hour of recreation before bedtime.

Unable to break through her innate shyness, Loris sat by
herself in a corner, longing for someone to invite her to join
in one of the games. When a group of second-graders,
who'd just been whispering and giggling in a circle, came
over to her, she was flooded with joy.

For a long moment they regarded her silently, warily, as if
she were an alien from another planet. "Why is she sitting
by herself like that?" Debbie, a pug-nosed blonde, asked the
tall, big-boned girl they were all clustered around.

Mary Elizabeth Keegan dominated the group with her
aggressive personality, as well as her height. Her hair was as
orange as a carrot, and so were her stumpy lashes, which
made the whites of her watery blue eyes seem bloodshot.
Her plain features were set in a pious cast whenever Sister
Teresa was around. But Sister Teresa wasn't around now,

and Mary Elizabeth's mouth—the smallest one Loris had ever seen—was twisted in a sneer.

"Because Miss Stuck-up thinks she's too good to play with us." She pulled the picture book Loris had been looking at out of her hands. "Just because she's a glamour puss, she thinks she's better than the rest of us. Don't you, huh?"

Loris was too hurt and confused to defend herself against the older girl's jibes and the mean-spirited giggling of the rest of her gang. She couldn't understand what she'd done to make them hate her. Was it possible, she wondered miserably, that they could all see the mark of the Devil on her?

Sitting alone in another corner of the room, Patricia Schwartz watched. A chubby second-grader with auburn hair, a mass of freckles, and eyes the color of melted chocolate that were far older than her years, she knew from experience what the new girl was going through.

She was half-Jewish, and her parents were divorced. That meant she was the school pariah. Her first year in the convent had been a living hell, yet she'd steadfastly refused to suck up to the other girls, or to try to ingratiate herself with the nuns. Only by retreating into the magical world of books had she managed to survive. There was something about the new girl—she looked so lost, so utterly defenseless— that made Patricia want to stick up for her. She stifled the impulse.

Loris was literally saved by the bell, though Mary Elizabeth promised her that she wasn't through with her yet. Quickly retrieving their school books, the girls marched upstairs to their dormitory. Sister Teresa shepherded Loris through the ritual of getting ready for bed, then the lights-out bell rang and the dormitory was plunged into darkness.

For the first time in her life, Loris knew what it meant to be utterly alone in a cold, unfeeling universe. Burying her face in her pillow, she finally gave in to the tears she'd been holding back ever since she had set foot in this terrible, scary place. She missed her mother so much she thought she would die.

Loris was jolted awake at six o'clock the following morning by the loud clanging of the first bell, and the sudden glare of fluorescent lights. It was still dark out, and freezing cold. She was the last one out of bed, and therefore, last in line to wash her face and brush her teeth. She had trouble keeping up with the rest of the students as they dressed under their nightgowns. While she was still struggling into her blouse and jumper, the other girls were standing at attention at the foot of their respective beds. Sister Teresa had already started inspection.

Any bed that hadn't been made according to regulations was stripped, earning the offender a demerit, which was duly noted in Sister Teresa's black ledger, where she kept a daily accounting of every girl's transgressions. Loris's sheets and covers were among those that ended up on the floor.

"Since this is your first day, Castaldi, we won't give you a demerit." Sister waved Mary Elizabeth, her prize bed-maker and pet pupil, over to them. "Mary Elizabeth will demonstrate the proper way to make a bed. Watch her carefully," she cautioned, "because, starting tomorrow, if you don't make your bed properly, or if you're not dressed and ready by the second bell again, you won't be permitted to eat breakfast."

Sister Teresa blew a single, shrill blast on the whistle hanging around her neck. The students formed a line and began marching out the door. The black hairs of her moustache twitched as she paused to inspect the bed Patricia Schwartz had just finished remaking. She ripped off the covers and dumped them on the floor. "No breakfast again today."

Mary Elizabeth waited until the nun was out the door before turning on Loris. "I'll probably miss my breakfast too because of you. I knew you were going to be trouble."

"I'm sorry," Loris stammered.

"Don't apologize to her," Patricia called over the beds separating them before she could stop herself. "Serves her right for being Miss Perfect and always sucking up to Sister Teresa."

"Oh, yeah?" Mary Elizabeth gave the bottom sheet a vicious tug. "You'll be lucky if they don't expel you."

The redhead with the chocolate-brown eyes laughed. "From your mouth to God's ear."

"I don't know how they could have let a dirty J-e-w in here in the first place," Mary Elizabeth tossed back contemptuously.

The other girl went pale, making the riot of freckles on her face stand out in sharp relief. Loris didn't know what Mary Elizabeth meant by "a dirty J-e-w," but she could tell that Patricia Schwartz had been called that many times before. As if to deny the hurt, Patricia pulled herself up proudly. Without another word, or a single glance in their direction, she set to remaking her bed.

Had the Devil left his mark on Patricia Schwartz, too? Loris wondered.

Carter Kingsley was in an uncharacteristically bad mood. Accustomed to having his needs—his every whim—instantly gratified, he could not tolerate frustration. Ever since Prescott's unannounced disappearance three days ago he had felt out of sorts. Not only had Prescott kept him in the dark about her progress with Angela, but the office was in a state of total chaos without her.

Carter discovered that, without his realizing it, Prescott had made herself indispensable to him. Even his father's executive secretary, whose help he'd enlisted, didn't know where anything was. In his Manhattan penthouse office with the Balthus on the wall and the Boisseau rug on the floor, Carter Kingsley was going through the files like a seventy-five-dollar-a-week clerk.

He was infinitely relieved when the woman he'd just been cursing under his breath entered his office.

"What on earth are you doing?" Prescott demanded. Her tone made it clear she didn't approve of him disturbing *her* files.

Carter let some of his frustration out in a sigh. "What does it look like I'm doing? I'm trying to find the file on the Thor-Tech merger."

She smiled wryly and closed the door behind her with a sharp click. "Try looking under *T* for Thor-Tech."

"I have been looking under *T* for—"

"In the active file. That's the inactive file." She started toward him, waving him aside with an imperious hand. "Let me do it."

The superior manner she adopted toward him whenever they were alone always irritated him, but never more than now. He wanted to shatter her cool, untouchable facade, and he knew the only way to do it would be to grab her and kiss her hard. Carter knew Prescott had fallen in love with him the day she started working with him, but she never admitted as much to herself. She devoted her life to furthering his career, and that suited him. But he hated to think he needed her, and right now he'd have given anything to see her down on her knees before him, sucking his cock, begging him to fuck her superior brains out.

He was aware of the office rumors that declared Prescott was butch. She had never given any real evidence, but people assumed as much because she refused to wear makeup, always sported the same severe, unfeminine hair style, and had a penchant for man-tailored suits. Carter didn't believe she was a lesbian. He was convinced that poor Prescott was totally asexual—a virgin most likely, and destined to remain one.

With a cool, self-assured smile, she handed him a manila folder. "The Thor-Tech merger file."

He'd been secretly hoping she'd be unable to find it, and practically tore the folder out of her hand. "Where the hell have you been for the past three days? And why didn't you call me Sunday night, as you promised? I waited up until half past one."

"Sorry to have inconvenienced you, Carter," she drawled. "I was busy cleaning up the mess you'd made."

"For three days?"

"It was an even bigger mess than usual."

Turning, Carter went back to his desk; Prescott followed at her own pace. He set the folder aside and looked up at her. "I assumed you eventually got Angela to sign the letter of agreement?"

"I'm afraid Angela won't be signing anything for a while." She took her time settling into one of the suede armchairs in front of his desk. "If ever. She's had a complete mental breakdown."

"Good God," Carter gasped. "When did that happen?"

In her typically efficient manner, Prescott gave him a quick rundown of the events of Sunday night.

Carter was silent for several moments. He was genuinely sorry about Angela. He'd never wanted anything bad to happen to her; she'd given him a great deal of pleasure. At the same time, he shuddered to think what might have happened to *him* if Prescott hadn't had her usual presence of mind. His earlier resentment toward her vanished, and he gave her a suitably grateful smile. "It was smart thinking to put Angela in the Martindale Clinic. Were there any questions?"

"Nothing I couldn't handle. That nosy landlady claims to have gotten a glimpse of you, but she's a spaced-out hippie, so we don't have to worry about her. She doesn't even know your name." Her mouth twisted wryly. "It seems Angela went out of her way to protect your reputation."

"She's like that," Carter admitted, pale-gray eyes darkening with regret. "She's the only woman I've ever known who gave without asking anything in return."

Prescott stiffened resentfully, jealously. What other woman had ever done as much for him as *she* had? She could go to jail for half the things she'd done for him. And when had *she* ever asked for anything in return?

"I did find some personal mementos, however," she told him, maintaining the cool facade that was her only defense.

"Photographs, love letters, that sort of thing." She smiled sardonically. "Do you want them as a keepsake?"

"Good God, no. Burn them."

"Consider it done." She had already stashed them in her safe deposit box. She would decide later, what to do with them. "I've gotten rid of everything else that could connect you to Angela."

"What about the child?"

"I've put her in a boarding school. The Convent of the Immaculate Conception in—"

"I don't want to know where she is."

"It has an excellent reputation," she went on. "Very traditional. The nuns were reluctant to admit her, at first, because of her questionable background. I'm afraid we had to make a five-thousand-dollar contribution. And the yearly tuition is nine hundred and fifty dollars."

Carter frowned, feeling strangely irritable again. He couldn't understand why she was bothering him with petty details like money.

She misread his reaction. "Of course, we could have put her in a state orphanage, but . . ."

His frown deepened; he wished she'd stop saying *we*.

"I felt we owed the child a decent education."

He nodded in agreement. "Just as long as she can't be traced back to me."

"I've made sure that, as far as everyone is concerned, her father was a nameless grunt who died a glorious but tragic death in Vietnam two years ago."

"Any payments and all the necessary documents will have to be in your name."

She shrugged. "It's already been arranged."

For an instant, Carter felt intense dislike for the woman. If he were a man given to examining his emotions, he might have realized that his anger was a distorted projection of his own guilt. Carter could not tolerate guilt; it was an even rarer experience for him than frustration. He had to remind himself that Prescott had saved his ass once again. He rewarded her with one of his most devastating smiles. "You did good, Pres. I don't know what I'd have done without you.''

"You know you can always count on me, Carter,'' she said, beaming under his slight praise.

"Just one more thing,'' he added. "Let me know how Angela is progressing in Martindale.''

She gave him a long look, as if she couldn't decide whether he was being facetious or just plain stupid. "Angela's stay at Martindale was only meant to be temporary. We're having her transferred to a state mental institution on Friday.''

"You can't put Angela in a place like that,'' he protested. "Nobody ever gets better in one of those snake pits. If you're not stark raving mad before you go in, you're sure to be before you...'' His words broke off as he realized Prescott's true intentions.

"I'm only thinking of you,'' she said. "There's nothing we can do for Angela anymore.''

Carter stared at Prescott with a combination of awed respect and utter loathing. Her plan was as brilliant as it was diabolical: as long as Angela didn't recover from her nervous breakdown, she posed no threat to him. If he hadn't allowed himself to be swayed by sentimental considerations, he'd have realized that before.

"You're right, of course. Let's do it your way,'' Carter agreed. But he felt that another link had been forged in that chain of deceit and betrayal that bound him, ever tighter, to Prescott.

CHAPTER
Six

Only by clinging to the belief that her mother loved her and would never abandon her did Loris manage to get through that first traumatic week in the convent. Raised in an atmosphere of total freedom, she had trouble adjusting to the nuns' rigid dogmas, and lived in constant fear of the harsh punishments they meted out for the most insignificant offenses. With each day she missed her mother more and more; every night she cried herself to sleep.

Unaware of the true nature of Angela's illness, Loris was convinced that her mother would get well in no time. After all, when she had been sick with the flu last winter, she had been back on her feet in a week.

It had been exactly one week since her mother had taken sick.

On Sundays, the study hall, where students waited to be called when parents or relatives came to visit, was abuzz with anticipation. Loris could barely sit still. She jumped expectantly to her feet every time Sister Teresa stuck her head in the doorway to summon one of the girls.

"*Your* mother's not going to visit you today," Mary Elizabeth sneered from an opposite table. "And I know why." Turning her head toward Debbie, who was sitting next to her, she whispered something in her ear. Debbie's eyes widened as they fixed on Loris. Giggling, she quickly passed the secret on to the girl next to her.

Loris refused to let them upset her. Any minute now her mother would be here to take her away from this terrible place. She jumped up at the mere sight of Sister Teresa's doughy face.

"Keegan," the nun called out, "Stevens, and Davis."

Mary Elizabeth tossed Loris a spiteful glance over her shoulder as she sauntered away.

Loris stopped bounding to her feet as the afternoon progressed. One by one, names were called and girls went skipping eagerly out the room, until she was the only one left. When the girls returned after visiting hours were over, she was staring out the window at the lengthening shadows of the trees on the lawn. The last of the cars drove down the long driveway.

"What did I tell you, Miss Glamour Puss?" Mary Elizabeth set her gleaming, gold-foil box of chocolates down on the table. "Maybe now you won't act so stuck up." Her voice was loud enough to capture everybody's attention. "What have you got to be stuck up about? I know all about you. You're a b-a-s-t-a-r-d. You don't have a father. And your mother's locked up in the loony bin!"

"Don't you say that about my mother!" Loris's chair made a terrible screeching sound as she bolted to her feet and threw herself on her tormentor, hitting and kicking her for all she was worth. Though the older girl was bigger and stronger, it took two of her classmates to drag Loris off her.

"It's true!" Mary Elizabeth spat out. "Sister Teresa told me. And sisters never lie!"

That night Loris wet her bed.

Since it was her first time, Sister Teresa informed her that her punishment would be lenient: she'd have to stand in the corner throughout breakfast and during recreation periods. Such public humiliation intensified Loris's feeling of being an outcast, as well as her fears of having been abandoned. When she wet the bed again that night, she was forced to stand in the corner during lunch and dinner as well, and during all her classes.

"So far, we've been extremely patient with you, Castaldi," Sister Teresa warned as Loris finished undressing under her nightgown. "But if you willfully wet the bed again tonight, we'll be forced to teach you a lesson you'll never forget."

"I won't wet the bed, I won't," Loris stammered as the nun brushed past her. "I promise!"

Mary Elizabeth waited until Sister Teresa was out of earshot. "Oh, yes you will, pisspot." A malicious little smile twisted her mouth and made her eyes shine. "You'll see." With a superior toss of her head, as if she knew something Loris didn't, and wasn't about to tell her, she walked away.

Mary Elizabeth and her gang lost no opportunity to further humiliate Loris, daintily holding their noses and uttering sounds of sheer disgust every time she walked by. In the study hall one evening, they made a big show of sitting at the table farthest away from the one she was at. When Susan, the shy tooth-gnasher, unthinkingly reached for the chair directly across from Loris, Mary Elizabeth called out in alarm, "Oh, don't sit *there*! Do you want to puke from the stink?"

Susan's hand froze in midair. She'd always longed to be accepted into Mary Elizabeth's clique. To be allied with Loris, even accidentally, would destroy what little chance she might have. Her hand fell to her side and she walked to another table. She was rewarded with one of Mary Elizabeth's pious smiles.

Slamming her book shut, Patricia Schwartz left the corner she'd made hers, and went over to a wooden rack that held an assortment of games. She carried one over to Loris. "You like doing jigsaw puzzles?"

Loris stared up at her blankly for a moment. "I don't know, I . . . I never did one."

"They're lots of fun." Patricia grabbed a chair, placing it so she and Loris were sitting side by side.

"Don't sit *here*," Loris warned in a fearful whisper, grateful as she was, "or they'll hate you, too!"

"With certain people, if they like you, you should feel insulted," Patsy returned, loud and clear. Under her breath she added, for Loris's benefit only, "Don't let them see they can hurt you. That's what they want."

Opening a box with a picture of Bambi on it, she spilled the colorful fragments onto the table. The sound they made was magnified by the sudden silence. None of the other girls would have dared defy Mary Elizabeth, and they were all waiting to see how she would react.

"Pee . . . uuh!" Mary Elizabeth exclaimed dramatically, holding her nose. "Now it stinks even worse than before in here!"

"Gee, I wonder why?" Patricia continued spreading jigsaw pieces out on the table. "Did you fart again?"

Mary Elizabeth's mouth twisted into a spiteful grimace. "*You're* the one who stinks. Christ killer!"

Patricia Schwartz smiled ever so sweetly. "Asshole."

"Oh! I'm going to tell Sister Teresa what you said!"

Her smile widened. "Asshole licker."

A collective gasp went up from Mary Elizabeth's gang, but there was derisive laughter from some of the other girls. "That's all you're good at," Patricia rubbed in. "Picking on those who are smaller than you, and licking Sister Teresa's ass."

More girls joined in the derisive laughter. Mary Elizabeth's face turned red with rage until it almost matched the color of her hair. She was accustomed to giving, not receiving, insults. Though she struggled to find a comeback, all she could do was sputter helplessly. Those few girls who'd remained silent, including Susan, suddenly forgot their fear and, remembering all the snubs and catty remarks they'd put up with from her, burst into laughter, too.

"See, there's nothing to it," Patsy told Loris, a friendly gleam in her eyes as she snapped one piece of the puzzle into another. "Now, you try."

Except for her mother, Loris decided that she loved Patricia Schwartz more than anybody else in the whole wide world. The two girls became best friends.

The muffled sounds emanating from the recreation room caused Sister Cecilia, the music teacher, to hesitate. Peeking through the doorway, she glimpsed a small, huddled form at one of the tables; it was the Castaldi girl. Her head was buried in her arms, and she was crying as if her very heart were breaking, while all around her, colorful Christmas decorations twinkled.

The young nun, whose dark, intense eyes seemed too large for her gaunt face, couldn't help feeling a tug of sympathy for the girl. Even those students whose parents rarely visited them on Sunday had gone home for the holidays. Loris was the only child left in the entire school. She had an impulse to place a comforting hand on that cap of unruly curls that no amount of cutting seemed able to control.

Sister Cecilia had to remind herself, yet again, that she must not become emotionally involved with any of the children. When she'd taken her vows, she'd renounced all earthly attachments; a nun was not even permitted to keep a plant. She slipped her hands inside the loose folds of her sleeves. "Come now, Castaldi," she ordered. "No more crying."

Loris straightened up with a gasp; she hadn't heard the nun approach. Like a child scared out of the hiccups, she stopped instantly. She wasn't sure whether crying was a punishable offense, but she wasn't about to take any chances.

"You must not despair," Sister Cecilia told her. "Despair is a sin against hope. You must pray to God, who is merciful and all-powerful. Only He can make your mother well."

"But I do pray to Him. I pray to Him all the time." A tear broke free of her lashes and slipped down her cheek. "But He won't listen to me."

"God always listens, but sometimes He wants more than mere words from us. You must make Him a bouquet."

Loris wiped her nose on her sleeve. "What's that?"

"A bouquet is a bunch of flowers. But your bouquet will be made up of good deeds. Here, let me show you." Sitting next to Loris, the young nun reached for a sheet of paper and one of the boxes of crayons that littered the table. "Do you know how to draw a flower?"

Loris stuck her chin up; she was proud of her drawing. "Sure." She drew a yellow circle, colored it in, then looped pink petals around it. "That's a daisy."

"Now, every time you do a good deed, or an unselfish act, or make a sacrifice, you draw a flower on a sheet of paper, until you've made a bouquet."

"How many flowers do I need for a bouquet?"

"You must fill the entire page."

Loris sighed. "I don't know if I can be that good."

Sister Cecilia had to stifle a smile. "You must try very hard, because once the bouquet is finished, and you offer it to God, He will answer your prayers and make your mother well again."

"He will? Really?"

"I promise."

"Oh, thank you!" Ecstatic with gratitude, Loris threw her arms around Sister Cecilia and hugged her tightly. She didn't realize what she'd done until she heard the nun's gasp of shock and felt the silver crucifix that was as cold as ice against her cheek. She pulled back, fearing punishment.

Sister Cecilia's undisciplined heart took another lurch. Reaching out, she smoothed a wayward curl behind Loris's ear. "And I will remember your mother in my prayers every day."

From that day on Loris strove her utmost to be obedient

and unselfish, renouncing even those few simple things that gave her pleasure, like candy. She said the rosary so often she developed a callous on her thumb. And she no longer envied those girls who were bad all week but whose parents came to see them on Sunday anyway, because she knew, as soon as her bouquet was finished, *her* mother would come to see her, too.

By the end of the month the bouquet was completed—a riot of flowers in every color in the crayon box. In bold red letters she printed underneath: TO GOD, FROM LORIS.

That Thursday, in the middle of arithmetic class, she was summoned to Mother Superior's office. "You have a visitor," Sister Teresa told her, inspecting her thoroughly before sending her downstairs. Feverish with joy at seeing her mother again, Loris ran down both flights of stairs and all the way down the hallway.

She came to a shocked halt in the open doorway. Her visitor was Miss Prescott.

"Where's Mommy?" Loris searched the office for a place big enough for her mother to hide and then jump out and surprise her, just like she used to.

"That's what I came to tell you, Loris," Miss Prescott said haltingly. "Your mother can't come to see you . . . ever. She's . . ."

"Your mother has gone to heaven, Castaldi," Mother Superior finished helpfully. "To be with God."

Loris stared blankly from one to the other. She knew exactly what the euphemisms meant; she simply refused to believe what she was being told.

"I want my mommy!" Furiously, Loris threw herself on Miss Prescott, pounding at her with her tiny fists. "You took my mommy away from me! Give me back my mommy!"

Sheer outrage brought Mother Superior to her feet. "Castaldi, stop this disgraceful behavior at once!"

"I want my mommy!"

Prescott grabbed the hysterical child by the shoulders and shook her forcefully, but she was unable to loosen her grip. "Loris, your mother is dead!"

"No," Loris screamed, over and over again. Her mother couldn't be dead. God would never allow such a thing to happen—she'd just finished her bouquet!

Only when she was standing before the plain pine box, staring with her own eyes at Angela's wasted corpse, did Loris finally accept the truth.

Never again would she pray to God for help, Loris promised herself. Never, never would she forgive Him for what He did to her mother.

PART II

CHAPTER
Seven

As she watched Miss Prescott slip behind the wheel of her BMW, Loris felt a growing sense of unease, almost dread, that spoiled the excitement she'd been feeling on this, her long-awaited graduation day.

Prescott felt a jolt of déjà vu when she checked to make sure that Loris was comfortably settled in the passenger seat. Up close, the girl's resemblance to her mother was so marked, it seemed to Prescott that Angela had come back to haunt her.

Though Loris's hair was short and the ends were as blunt as if someone had taken an axe to them, it had the same luxuriant fullness, that same blue-black sheen as her mother's. Her lips, which turned up at the corners even when she wasn't smiling, were every bit as soft and sensuous as Angela's. And there was that body, whose voluptuous curves not even her severe, navy blue linen dress could conceal.

She was a reborn Angela with long, long legs—Loris had to be at least five-feet-eight. She was an Angela with exquisitely delicate bone structure, whose beauty wasn't marred by a single flaw.

As Prescott turned the key in the ignition, she wondered why the girl's mood had changed since she'd gotten into the car. Could she be thinking of that drive to the funeral parlor twelve years ago? Or perhaps she was remembering the time she'd driven her and her mother from King's Haven back to New York. Prescott wondered just how much Loris *did* remember of that fateful Sunday.

"It seems whenever we get together," Prescott said, backing out of a space in the parking lot behind the convent, "I'm always driving you somewhere."

Loris turned her head and looked at her with Carter's pale-gray eyes, which were even more startling in contrast with her thick, black lashes. "Really?"

"Don't you remember the first time we met? I drove you and your mother home."

Loris turned her face away again. "I don't remember very much about my mother."

The day after Loris had viewed Angela's body, she had come down with a fever of 105. For three days and nights, in a delirious, barely conscious state, she called for her mother and cried uncontrollably. The doctor the sisters finally called had already made arrangements to have her transferred to a hospital when the fever broke. Afterward, Loris no longer remembered anything that had happened on the Sunday that changed her life forever. She knew her mother was dead, but she'd blocked out the visit to the funeral home. And she never cried again.

"I can remember when you drove me here to the convent," she said, as an afterthought.

"But that was the very next day."

"Was it?"

"Well, you were very young." Prescott kept her tone conversational while she turned into the exit lane. "Still, I thought you'd recall the last time you saw your mother."

"I just have a vague memory of her curling my hair. I don't know where we were going, but it must have been

someplace special because she was very excited about it.''
She shifted uncomfortably in her seat. "The rest is
just . . . feelings."

Prescott shifted smoothly into second. "Do you remember your father at all?"

"No, not at all."

"Not even his name?"

"Sure, I remember his name."

As if seized by a sudden cramp, Prescott's fingers tightened
around the steering wheel. They relaxed again when Loris
added with a wry smile, "It was Daddy."

Her smile turned rueful. "The funny thing is, sometimes
I dream about him, and I see him clearly, but when I wake
up, I can never remember his face." Impulsively, she leaned
toward the other woman. "I've never told anyone this
before, but after my mother died, I used to fantasize about
him a lot. What stories I made up about him! My own
private fairy tales." She laughed.

It occurred to Prescott that it was the first time she'd ever
seen Loris laugh. The BMW was now idling behind a line
of cars, waiting to cut into the even longer line moving
bumper-to-bumper down the driveway, allowing her to watch
the girl directly. The reserve Loris wrapped around herself
like a protective cloak suddenly dropped away. Her eyes
sparkled, and her whole face came alive. It was clear she
was happiest when lost in a fantasy world.

"My father was the king of this mythical country I'd
created all in my head," she was saying, "and he fell in
love with this beautiful peasant girl, my mother. But his evil
courtiers had my mother secretly poisoned, and they locked
me away in this convent. So my father went on a quest,
slaying dragons, besting ogres and witches, until he found
me. My favorite part was when he'd announce to the entire
convent that I was his daughter, a real princess. He'd lift me
up onto his snow-white Arabian horse, and we'd ride like
the wind to his kingdom to live happily ever after."

She laughed again, self-consciously this time, very much
a teenager who feels she's been acting juvenile. Then the

light went out of her eyes and she withdrew behind that reserved facade once more. "Of course, when I got older, I realized that it was my father, not evil courtiers, who'd hidden me away here so no one would know he had an illegitimate daughter."

"What are you saying?" Prescott protested. "Your father died in Vietnam two years before you came here."

"No, he didn't."

"You've obviously forgotten that also. You were only—"

"Please don't lie to me, Miss Prescott. The sisters may have believed that story, but I always knew it wasn't true." She leaned closer still, all eagerness. "*He* sent you to see me graduate, didn't he? And you kept tabs on me all these years just to report back to him."

Prescott adjusted the air conditioning.

"And what about the greeting cards?" Loris persisted. Every birthday and at Christmas Loris would receive a greeting card with a notation that a gift of fifty dollars had been deposited in a savings account in her name. Every time her report card showed a B or better average, a bonus of one hundred dollars was added to the account. "That was really *his* idea, wasn't it?"

"That was entirely my doing." Prescott's tone, and the look she gave her, made it impossible for Loris to doubt her.

"Oh, I'd always believed . . ." She sank back against her seat. "So, he doesn't even know you're here."

Prescott concentrated on cutting into the line of cars inching down the driveway.

"*Why* are you here, Miss Prescott?"

"I was wondering what your plans are now that you're leaving school."

Loris stared at her thoughtfully for a long moment. She had given up long ago trying to find out anything about Prescott and her father. Finally, she said, "I'm not planning on making trouble for anyone, if that's what you're worried about."

The older woman was thrown for a moment by the eighteen-year-old's perception. She was grateful that the line was beginning to move so she could pretend an interest in her driving. "What I am concerned about, Loris, is your decision not to go to college. As I wrote you, your tuition will be taken care of."

"Thanks, but no thanks. I've had enough of schools to last me a lifetime. What I need is to live. Experience is the best education there is for an actress."

Surprise made Prescott turn toward Loris. "You intend to be an actress?" She braked just in time to keep from plowing into the car ahead of her. "How on earth did you get that idea?"

"I'm crazy about the theater."

"But you've never even been to the theater!"

Loris pulled herself up proudly. "I've acted in every pageant we've done in school since I was in the first grade."

After her mother's death, Loris withdrew completely into herself; even Patsy had trouble getting through to her. In an effort to bring her out of her depression, Sister Cecilia picked Loris for the much-coveted role of the angel in the Easter pageant.

The instant Loris stepped onto the stage in her flowing white gown, a golden halo suspended on a wire over her head, gossamer wings pinned to her back, she was hooked. The colored lights transformed the drab world around her, the sound of music filled all the emptiness, and a spotlight followed her every move, warmer than the sun on her skin. The spontaneous burst of applause from the audience was all the approval, admiration, and love Loris wanted.

"I've read practically every play that was ever written," she went on excitedly. "I know all my favorite roles by heart: Antigone, Hedda Gabler, Blanche DuBois." She might have been referring to a string of her Broadway hits. Her face was animated again, glowing from within, transfigured into a girl Prescott didn't know, and suddenly she was reminded of the charisma Carter projected so effortlessly at his political rallies, where crowds were mesmerized by his presence. She wondered what his reaction would be if he found out that his illegitimate daughter, whose existence he'd never concerned himself with, was more like him than either of his other children.

"And every Saturday," Loris continued, "Patsy and I—you don't know her; she's my best friend—used to put on little plays that we wrote and acted and directed and everything. Patsy's going to be a producer."

"Is this the same Patsy whose apartment I'm dropping you off at on the West Side?"

"Yes. She graduated last year, but we write each other every week. I'll be staying at her place until I can afford one of my own."

"That reminds me." Prescott nodded toward the glove compartment. "I have something for you—a graduation present."

The envelope Loris removed from the glove compartment contained the passbook of the savings account Prescott had opened for her after Angela died; it showed a balance of thirty-four hundred dollars. A check for five thousand dollars was folded neatly inside.

"That should help you get started."

Loris shook her head. "I can't accept this." She waved the scrap of paper. "Who's money is it, anyway? Yours—or his?"

"It's *your* money," Prescott snapped. "Now, don't be a little idiot. Keep it. You're going to need it."

Loris took a closer look at the check, hoping to find a clue to her father's identity. The check was signed by Prescott, but wasn't drawn on her personal account. "What's Thor-Tech?"

She shrugged her padded shoulders. "It's a company I run. Drawing the check on my business account makes it easier for tax purposes."

"I didn't know bastards were tax-deductible," Loris quipped, well aware of the pain twisting inside her.

"Put the check away," Prescott ordered, "before you do something you'll regret."

"*He's* the one who's going to be sorry," said Loris softly, as if to herself. "Someday, when I'm a big star, he'll be sorry he didn't acknowledge me as his daughter." The BMW had finally come to the end of the driveway. As they passed through the huge iron gates, she folded the check and slipped it inside the passbook.

And I am going to be a star, Loris vowed to herself, watching in the rearview mirror as the convent receded in the distance, until it finally disappeared from view. *I'm going to be a star if it kills me.*

Loris was at first shocked to find Patsy living in a run-down tenement in one of the seedier parts of New York. But her apartment had the offbeat, bohemian charm of an artist's garret—or, at least, what Loris had always imagined an artist's garret would look like—and she was utterly captivated by it.

Pat's third floor walk-up on West Forty-eighth Street, off Ninth Avenue, consisted of a small living room with a kitchenette, a tiny bathroom, and a sleeping alcove partitioned by louvered doors. It was furnished with secondhand pieces that didn't match, and the overall effect was one of slapdash comfort. Theater posters brightened the walls, and hid most of the water stains and peeling plaster. A motley assortment of colorful throw pillows served a dual purpose: when propped up on the back and sides of the studio bed, they created the illusion of a sofa; strewn over the bare floor, as they were now, they were chairs.

Every Saturday night a group of struggling young theater people bent on starting their own repertory company met at Pat's apartment. Her living room could barely contain the thirty guests. Some were sitting three to an armchair, or thigh to thigh on the bed; the rest were lounging on the floor or leaning against walls. It all made for an intimate, friendly atmosphere, so unlike what Loris had been accustomed to in the convent. But after years of enforced silence, she felt a bit overwhelmed by the intensity of the noise surrounding her.

Traffic sounds spilled through the two narrow windows that opened onto the street—a never-ending medley of honking horns, screeching tires, disco music, and screaming police sirens. No one else in the room seemed even remotely aware of all the clamor, probably because they all spoke in such loud voices, in a rapid, staccato tempo that matched the frantic pace of the city. Cutting in while someone else was speaking had to be an accepted New York custom, Loris decided, since everyone did it and no one seemed to mind.

Sitting on the floor, but apart from the others, she wondered whether she would ever fit into this new world she wanted so desperately to be part of. The other girls present weren't much older than she was, but their sophisticated manner and appearance made them seem so. They all wore makeup and stylish hairdos, and their outfits were daringly revealing. Most of them weren't wearing bras! Loris was dressed in a high-necked, long-sleeved, shapeless navy blue dress with starched white cuffs and a Peter Pan collar. She just knew she was the only virgin there, and that everybody else knew it, too.

Loris was beginning to feel like an alien from a backward planet. The bemused smile her appearance evoked from a young man nursing a beer by himself in one corner didn't help. Defensively, she wondered what right he had to stare at her that way, since *he* didn't seem to fit in with the rest of the group either.

Like most of the men there he wore jeans, a wide leather belt embossed with a western motif, a casual shirt, and western boots. But while the other men sported designer jeans, his were just battered old Levis, and where their boots had intricate patterns or fancy snakeskin inserts, his plain brown ones were all scuffed and mottled. While the western look was merely the latest fashion fad for others, Loris knew it was like a second skin to him.

In fact, he had the stark features and hard, rangy body of a cowboy—a definite renegade quality. The sensitive, admittedly sensual cut of his mouth was, therefore, all the more surprising. Evidence of American Indian blood showed in his high cheekbones, dark, slanted brows, and straight black hair. There was an intensity about him, a moodiness behind his eyes that Loris found disturbing, and oddly intriguing.

Gazing away, Loris sipped her Coke, but she found herself wondering whether it was shyness or arrogance that kept him from joining the discussion that was taking place on the current state of the theater. From the corner of her eye she could tell that, though removed, he was listening intently to what was being said.

"Nothing original is being done anymore," Rob, a bearded playwright, concluded. "Hollywood is ripping off the classics of the thirties and forties. And Broadway—"

"Broadway's doing nothing but revivals or British imports," Pat cut in as she made her way over to Loris.

Undaunted, Rob continued, "Off-Broadway has been commercial for years. Now, Off-Off-Broadway, the last bastion of the avant-garde, is becoming tainted. Thanks to our President, that ex-second-rate Hollywood actor, grants to the performing arts have been cut to shreds."

"Tell me about it." Having finished her hostess duties, Pat sank down onto the pillow next to Loris. "My proposals have been sent back so many times I'm starting to feel like a Ford Pinto."

"It's not merely a question of money," Rob corrected. "Let's face it, we American avant-garde artists have nothing left to say. The Establishment has won. We've been totally castrated."

"Bullshit." With that single, stark comment, softened by a slight country drawl, Cal Remington finally entered the discussion. "There's plenty left to say that needs to be said. But it's easier to just sit around here and moan and groan about money problems, instead of doing something about it." He slammed his beer can down on the floor. "I don't know about you people, but I'm sick of listening to this intellectual bullshit every Saturday night."

Cal pulled himself up to his full height of six-foot-two.

"I thought the reason we've been meeting here at Pat's is to get a theater group started. Instead of just talking about it, why don't we all put our money where our mouths are." Digging into his beat-up jeans, he pulled out the twenty-dollar bill that was supposed to last him through the weekend. He knew there'd be hell to pay at home, but he slapped it down on the rickety bookcase Pat and Loris were sitting next to. "If we'd all put in twenty bucks a week, in six months or so we'd have enough money to put on our first production."

There was a moment of stunned silence and shared indecision. Then, impulsively, Loris reached into her purse, peeled twenty singles from the allowance money she'd saved up over the years, and set them on top of his twenty. As though all they'd needed was for someone to make the first move, everyone went into motion at once. Purses and wallets materialized as if by magic; Pat jumped to her feet and hurried over to the alcove where she kept her food money.

With a wry smile, Cal lowered himself onto the pillow Pat had just vacated next to Loris. "You sure you know what you're getting yourself into?"

His eyes, which at a distance had appeared to be dark, were actually blue, Loris noticed—a deep, midnight blue. "What do you mean?" she stammered, feeling flustered in a way she'd never known before.

"You've only been to one of our meetings. How do you know we're the right group for you?" Before she could explain, he added, "Or are you always this . . ." His eyes searched hers. "What is it, generous? Impulsive?"

Her chin shot up defensively. "Do you always ask people you don't know personal questions?"

So there *was* spirit behind that shy reserve of hers, Cal noted with satisfaction; he had been sure there would be. He gave what he hoped looked like a disinterested shrug. "I guess it's one of the occupational hazards of being a director. You're always trying to figure out other people's motives."

"You sound as if you expect people to have ulterior motives."

He hadn't anticipated a perceptive mind behind such an exquisite face. Something warned him not to pursue the conversation, or the undeniable attraction he felt for this girl. His personal life was screwed up enough as it was. "We all have reasons for what we say or do," he insisted, though he couldn't understand why he needed to justify himself to her. "Usually very complex, hidden reasons."

Loris found herself wondering what the reason might be for his reluctance to trust people. Or was it just women he didn't trust? "*My* reason for joining the group is pretty simple," she told him. She didn't want him to think it had anything to do with him or the impassioned speech he'd just made, because it didn't. "Pat and I have been talking about starting our own group for ages."

"You're a friend of Pat's?"

"Her best friend. We grew up together."

"Pat's real people," he stated unequivocally. "The best there is."

"I've always thought so."

As if talking about her had the power to summon her presence, Pat came rushing in from the alcove, carrying the empty coffee can she usually stashed pot in. She passed it around in lieu of the proverbial hat. While the aspiring actors dropped their contributions in, she jotted their names on a pad, making a note of those who didn't have cash on them, but had promised to bring it to the next meeting.

Cal and Loris shared an affectionate smile over Pat's organization; she was a born producer. Their smiles faded as they became aware of the growing intimacy between them, the sensual promise each glimpsed in the other. Loris took a sip of her Coke. Cal lit a cigarette.

He shot a long stream of smoke up to the ceiling. "You're an actress?" It was more a statement of fact than a question. He had a way of looking directly into a person's eyes when he spoke that she was beginning to find unnerving. "But you haven't been in New York long."

"How do you know?"

The wry look in his eyes as they scanned her unstylish dress was all the explanation that was needed. "How long *have* you been here?"

"What time is it?" she returned blithely.

Cal checked his watch. "Almost ten o'clock."

"Why, I'm practically a native. I've been her two whole hours."

He threw his head back and laughed—such a deep, ballsy laugh it startled her and made everyone turn to look at them. Loris wondered why Pat was frowning.

Leaving Rob in midsentence, Pat hurried over to them. "Twenty-two people have committed. Looks like we're finally going to get this show on the road."

Scooping their money off the bookcase, Cal dropped it into the coffee can; his gaze never left Loris. "Thanks to your friend here."

"This calls for a celebration," Pat said brightly, looking from Loris to Cal and back. "Loris, will you help me break out the wine?"

"Sure."

Cal stood up. "I've got to get going."

"Oh, aren't you staying for the party?" Loris blurted out before she could stop herself.

He took a last drag on his cigarette and squashed it out in the ashtray. "It's late. I best be headin' back."

Wherever "back" was, Loris had the feeling Cal was reluctant to return there; that moody look was in his eyes again.

"I'll call you, Pat." He bowed his head to Loris in an old-fashioned manner. "Nice meeting you."

It suddenly occurred to Loris that she didn't even know his name. With a few long-legged strides he was out the door. She turned to Pat eagerly. "Who is he?"

"That's Cal Remington. He's the artistic director."

"He seems really—"

"Stay away from him, Loris," Pat warned. "He's married. And his old lady's the type who never lets go once she sinks her nails into a man's balls.''

The disappointment she felt took Loris completely by surprise. She shrugged it off. ''I came to New York to be an actress, not to find a man.''

Pat laughed suggestively. ''What's to stop you from doing both? Just as long as you don't get hurt.''

''Hey, Pat,'' a good-looking young man called out as he came toward them. ''Where's that party you promised?''

''Coming right up. Just do me a favor, Steve. This is Loris, my best friend. She's an actress, but she doesn't know anybody here. Make her feel at home, will you?''

Steve's pale-blue eyes took a quick but thorough tour of Loris's body. ''My pleasure.''

''But, I thought you wanted me to help you serve the—'' Loris began.

''No need,'' Pat tossed lightly over her shoulder as she hurried off. ''I've got everything under control.''

''Pat's a whiz with parties,'' Steve assured her. His sandy hair fell in waves to his shoulders. She tried not to stare at the three gold studs he wore in one pierced ear, the long gold loop dangling from the other. He had no such compunction, and went on staring at her openly. ''So, you're an actress,'' he said to her bust.

''Yes,'' Loris murmured self-consciously. ''Are you an actor, too?''

''Musician. Jazz trombone.''

''Uhh, where do you play?''

''Grand Central.''

''Is that a jazz club?'' she guessed, trying not to appear as ignorant as she felt.

''No, the station.''

Even Loris was familiar with New York's famed Grand Central Station, the city's major train terminal, and the transfer point for several subway lines, but she didn't know it also contained a nightclub.

''On the lower platform,'' he explained. ''You know, the Flushing line?''

"You mean, you play... in the subway?"

"Yeah, but starting next week, I'll be playing the south-east corner of Fifty-seventh and Fifth." He sounded as though he were making his Carnegie Hall debut. "This guy I know, a tenor sax, just landed a gig on a cruise ship, so he sold me his spot for just five hundred bucks."

"You paid him five hundred dollars to play on a street corner?"

"Hey, it's one of the prime street corners in the city," Steve shot back, clearly offended. "There's a waiting list. I lucked out because we were in the same class at Juilliard."

"Oh," Loris said. She didn't know what else to say.

"I'm going to get myself a drink," Steve said.

Pat, who'd been keeping an eye on them, set down a gallon jug of inexpensive wine, picked up two of the plastic glasses she'd just filled, and carried them over to Loris. "What happened?"

"I don't know. I... I think I insulted him."

"What did you say?"

"I couldn't believe he actually paid someone five hundred dollars so he could play jazz trombone on the southeast corner of Fifty-seventh Street."

Pat laughed. Handing Loris one of the glasses, she lifted the other in a toast. "Welcome to the wonderful world of show business."

CHAPTER
Eight

Cal hesitated as he started to slip the key in the ignition. The ash from the cigarette dangling from one corner of his mouth smoldered, creating a tiny red glow in the dark interior of his car, which was parked directly across the street from Pat's. As he sat there, staring up at her living room windows, he took another long, hungry drag.

He hadn't felt this alive in years: the long dry spell between shows was finally over. Excitement pulsed through him; he was tempted to go back upstairs and join the celebration. As he scanned the figures moving in and out of the two brightly lit, framed rectangles of space, he caught sight of the new girl.

Julie Ann would be expecting him home soon, he reminded himself. Tossing the cigarette out the window, he started up the engine, then carefully maneuvered his Jeep out of the tight parking space. He never stayed to party with the others after their Saturday night meetings. Now, more than ever, he was determined to keep his end of the bargain. He couldn't afford to jeopardize what he knew was his last chance to make it as a director.

At twenty-eight, Cal was the oldest member of the group, and the one with the most theatrical experience, but he hadn't directed a play in over three years. His workshop production of Ionesco's *Victims of Duty* the previous year didn't count since he'd had to drop out after only two weeks of rehearsals. Julie Ann had been hospitalized with a stomach ailment, and there had been no one but him to look after Brian. He would not have let a stranger take care of his little boy; he hadn't forgotten what that felt like.

Cal shook his head in disbelief as he turned right onto Eighth Avenue. Three years. How the hell had they passed so quickly? Yet, paradoxically, he couldn't remember time dragging so heavy on him since he was a teenager stuck in a dusty little town in southern Utah.

His family, on both sides, had lived in the Beehive State for generations. His mother, a devout Mormon, was descended from the original pioneers who had come to Utah in covered wagons with Brigham Young. His father's ancestors had also gone West about that time, but in search of gold. They had never found it; all they had bequeathed their heirs was a restless spirit and a taste for adventure. His great-grandfather had married a full-blooded Navajo squaw.

Cal's father, a big, brawling bear of a man, had been born out of his time; being somewhat of an anachronism merely added to his charm. Few could resist him—even those who knew better—so how could an unworldly young Mormon woman remain immune? Less than a month after they had met, she eloped with him.

In between his many grand but futile schemes to strike it rich, his father had worked as a ranch hand, a rodeo cowboy, and a stunt man in B westerns. Hoping to get more work in the movies, he moved the family to Kanab, nicknamed "Little Hollywood" because so many westerns were shot in the vicinity. Soon after, when Cal was only four, his father ran off with a blond starlet. The memory of him haunted Cal's childhood.

Every time he misbehaved, his mother would accuse him of being just like his father. Afraid that he'd also end up "a godless drunkard, gambler, and fornicator," she disciplined him severely. The more she sought to curb what was merely a boy's natural high spirits, the more he resisted. He felt trapped. When he gave in to his mother's rigid moralistic notions he felt castrated; when he rebelled he felt guilty—as selfish and irresponsible as the father he'd never forgiven for abandoning him.

Unhappy at home, bored and restless as only a very bright teenager in a small town can be, he got involved in school theatricals. Soon he was reading every play he could get his hands on, and cutting classes to hang around the movie sets. He attended the College of Southern Utah, but dropped out at the end of his second year. Despite his mother's bitter objections, he accepted the job of assistant director with a theater group doing one-night stands across the country.

By the time the repertory company reached the East Coast, Cal had gained an invaluable theatrical education. He'd done everything—from building sets to designing them, from sweeping the stage to directing three-act plays. He'd run lights and sound, sometimes simultaneously, understudied all the male parts, and played leads. He'd even written a couple of one-act plays that were used as curtain raisers.

The producer of the troupe offered to double Cal's salary if he'd stay on as one of the lead actors. On stage, Cal combined the brooding sensitivity of James Dean with the sexual magnetism of the young Brando, and audiences, especially young women, adored him. Cal's reaction to such adulation was a kind of bemused embarrassment. The challenge of being a director was what really mattered to him. Though he regretted leaving the people with whom he'd spent the happiest two years of his life, Cal stayed behind when the company left to retrace its tour.

He rented himself a cold-water flat in New York's Hell's Kitchen. He drove a cab part-time, and joined an Off-Off-

Broadway experimental theater group. His very first production received rave reviews from *The Village Voice*. He was just beginning to make a name for himself when he met Julie Ann.

The responsibilities of supporting a wife and child had since brought his career to a standstill. He now lived in Astoria, a residential neighborhood just over the Queensboro Bridge. The rent was triple that of his previous place, and he was driving a cab full-time.

But his career was back on track again, Cal assured himself as he entered his ground-floor apartment. He stopped dead under the arched entrance to the living room. For a moment, he thought he'd let himself into the wrong apartment.

When he'd left for work that morning, piles of old newspapers and magazines had littered the dirty floor, discarded clothes had been sprawled over the arms and backs of chairs, toys had been scattered about like booby traps. A month-old layer of dust had covered the tops of the new coffee table and matching end tables that were so new they still weren't paid for.

He found it hard to understand why Julie Ann "just couldn't find the time" to keep the place clean since Brian had started kindergarten. He didn't mind the mess as much as the subliminal message he realized his wife was sending him: no amount of cleaning could make her proud of this place, so she refused to bother.

But now it was clean—practically spotless.

"The place looks great, Julie Ann," Cal called out as he started toward her.

She was seated on the sofa, watching a rerun of *Dynasty*. "Well, I tried." The somewhat defeated wave of her hand took in the modest room, the new French Provincial furniture that clashed with the Early Junkyard pieces they'd inherited from the previous tenants.

"You did one helluva job." Cal came around the sofa, stopping short again when he got his first close look at his wife. She was wearing makeup and a brand new dress, and she'd had her hair done. He knew their anniversary was next month, and her birthday wasn't until December. "What's going on?" he asked warily.

"What do you mean?"

"You're all dressed up. Is this some special occasion I don't know about?"

"I just wanted to look nice for you." Hurt darkened her eyes, making him feel like a distrustful clod.

Cal smiled softly, apologetically. "You do." He didn't believe that heavy makeup or fancy hairdos added to a woman's beauty because, though they might conceal her flaws, they also masked her individuality, but he was pleased that she'd gone to the trouble for him. It proved she was trying to make things right between them again. "You look lovely, Julie Ann."

Her hand flew self-consciously to her hair, which was done in a Victorian upsweep, with loose tendrils at her temples and at the sides of her heart-shaped face. "You really think so?"

It always amazed Cal that Julie Ann didn't realize how pretty she was with her dainty, doll-like features, soft, light-brown hair, and hazel eyes. "I always have."

Her lips, which were a bit thin and had a tendency to pull down at the corners, turned up into an almost desperately grateful smile. Once again, Cal was struck by the power he had over her. It was a power he'd never sought, and would have gladly relinquished. He had to watch every word he said.

"Do you like my new dress?" she asked, jumping to her feet in her eagerness to get his approval.

The loosely fitted dress was pink—her favorite color— and made of a sheer summer fabric. A double layer of ruffles edged the hem and the scoop neckline that exposed the high slope of her delicately rounded breasts.

"I like it very much." His hand reached out to tangle in the soft folds. "Very much."

She stepped back, and the fabric slipped out of his grasp. "You don't think it makes me look too fat?"

She'd never lost the twenty pounds she'd gained when

she was carrying Brian. It showed on her five-feet-five-inch frame, but she could hardly be considered fat. "You look lovely, Julie Ann." He bent over to kiss her on the cheek.

"Carolyn helped me pick out the dress," she said. He straightened up. "You know what wonderful taste she has."

Since Julie Ann felt "uncomfortable" about inviting her best friend to their apartment, Cal had met Carolyn only once, at their wedding. But he felt he knew her intimately, since a week rarely passed when her name wasn't mentioned, usually at dinner, and always with a kind of wistful envy.

Wise Carolyn, whose successful stockbroker husband had just purchased a five-room co-op on the Upper East Side, was luckier than anyone she knew. Carolyn received real jewels on her birthday and real furs at Christmas.

It was getting to where Cal couldn't stand the mere mention of the woman's name.

"Carolyn took me along on one of her shopping sprees at Bloomie's," Julie Ann was saying. "I was shocked by the amount of money she spends on resort clothes, but she says her husband doesn't care about the cost." A wistful sigh escaped her. "They're off to the French Riviera for three weeks."

Though Cal could understand his wife's longing for the finer things in life, he wished she'd stopped rubbing his nose in the fact that he couldn't afford to give them to her. "You should have married a stockbroker," he snapped before he could stop himself. "Then *you'd* be jetting off to the Riviera."

"Cal, I didn't mean—"

He turned away from her. "I'm going to look in on Brian."

"He's sleeping!"

Ignoring her protest, he stalked out of the room and down the narrow hallway, softening his steps as he reached the open door to his son's bedroom. Brian was lying on his side, sound asleep, his newest toy clutched to his chest. Kermit the Frog, his usual sleeping partner, had been exiled to the foot of the bed.

His son's hair had darkened in the past year, and the amber glow of the night light picked out the remaining blond strands from the sandy ones. He was a sturdy, active four-year-old, full of life and mischief, but when asleep he looked small and frighteningly vulnerable. The toy he clutched possessively was a foot-long robot with hard metal edges. Leaning over, Cal carefully tried to pry open Brian's fingers.

His tiny hand closing even more possessively around the robot, Brian rolled onto his back and his eyes flew open. "Daddy!" He released the toy and thrust both arms straight up, fingers grasping at the air in his eagerness for his good night hug. When his father bent his head to kiss him, the child threw his arms around his neck and squeezed tight, hanging on for all he was worth.

Intense love surged through Cal, it was rising from some unknown, primal part of him. This love for his son had gripped him from the moment he'd first stared down at the squalling, red-faced bundle the nurse had put in his arms. He cleared his throat. "So, how you doin', kiddo?"

"Okay." His sleep-tousled head fell back and he looked up at his father's deep-blue eyes. "How *you* doin', kiddo?"

"I'm doing fine, but you have to go back to sleep."

Brian's arms slid reluctantly from around Cal's neck. "But I'm all woked up already."

"You just think you are." Cal helped the boy settle back into bed. "Now, go back to sleep. You want a drink of water first?"

Brian tried, but was unable to stifle a yawn. "No, thanks."

"You have to go to the bathroom?"

He shook his head, yawning openly this time, and grabbed the robot.

"You know, kiddo, I don't think you should sleep with Robbie the Robot."

He blinked several times in an effort to keep his eyes open. "Why not?"

Bringing his lips down to Brian's ear, as if to tell him a

secret, Cal whispered, "Because you'll hurt Kermit's feelings. He'll think you don't love him anymore."

"I still love him." To prove it, he instantly relinquished Robbie the Robot. Cal shoved it unceremoniously under the bed before handing over the other toy. "I love you, Kermie," Brian assured him. Hugging the stuffed frog, he turned onto his side while Cal quickly covered them up.

" 'Night," he whispered, dropping a kiss on his son's hair.

" 'Night, kiddo," Brian's sleepy voice called back as Cal was going out the door.

Cal smiled to himself. His son's was the only unconditional love he'd ever known. As he crossed the hall to the kitchen, he found himself wondering why love between a man and a woman had to be so complicated. There were always strings attached, power plays, penalties.

When he flipped on the light, he saw that the kitchen was as spotless as the living room. He had to give Julie Ann credit for trying. The least he could do was meet her halfway. In spite of the arguments they had been having lately, they had a lot going for them. He was sure if they both tried, they could still make their marriage work. They had to, if only for Brian's sake.

When he opened the refrigerator to get himself a beer, Cal saw the half-empty bottle of rosé—Julie Ann's favorite wine. In an attempt to apologize for snapping at her earlier, he filled a goblet for her. His step was lighter when he crossed the living room this time. He'd even managed to recapture some of his earlier enthusiasm.

"This *is* a special occasion, in a way," he told her when he offered her the glass of rosé.

Julie Ann turned her attention away from *Dynasty*, and accepted the goblet with a guarded smile. "Oh?"

He sat down on the sofa next to her. "At the meeting tonight, the group finally committed to doing a production."

She set the wine down on the coffee table and, picking up the remote control, turned off the TV, just as Alexis was about to unveil her latest dastardly plot against Blake. "Robert called."

"Again?"

"He wanted to know if you'd changed your mind about the job."

"No, I haven't."

She frowned in that way she had that mingled hurt and disapproval. "He says the least you could do is talk to him about it."

"I have talked to him about it, Julie Ann—twice. How many times can you tell somebody something?"

"Well, he can't understand how you could possibly prefer driving a cab to being a production manager."

She also had a way of putting her words into other people's mouths, instead of coming out with them directly. He fixed her with a level stare. "Your brother can't understand it—or *you* can't understand it?"

She sipped her wine, her pinkie raised delicately. "Robert does have a point. A man with your intelligence and talent shouldn't be driving a taxi—I mean, really, Cal."

"I like being my own boss, and always being on the move. I sure as hell couldn't stand being cooped up in an office all day." He forced a smile, trying to lighten the tension that was building between them again. "Besides, it's only temporary, and it's the perfect job for a student of human behavior. Every director should try—"

"But, as production manager, you *would* be the boss," she persisted. "It would be up to you to make sure everybody does his job properly and that everything's running smoothly. It's just like directing. You'd love it."

"I don't want the job, Julie Ann." His tone warned her not to pursue the subject.

"Why not?"

Cal reached into his shirt pocket for a cigarette. He lit it, and took a long, calming drag. The last thing he wanted was to get into an argument. "Look, you know what I'm like. If I take on the job, I'd have to give it everything I've got. It would mean pouring all my energy and creativity into something I don't give a damn about. There'd be nothing left over for my work as a director. It's taken me six months to find the right play and get a group together, and I'm not going to quit now."

"But, what if you give up this opportunity and then the play is a flop?"

"Thanks for the vote of confidence," Cal drawled sardonically. He took a swig of beer, then set the can back down, harder than he'd intended. "It's not going to be a flop, but if it is, I'll keep *my* end of the bargain and give up directing for a permanent job. You've got to keep *your* end of the bargain, too—you agreed to go along with me on this."

"Yes, but—"

"You agreed, Julie Ann!"

"That was before Robert's offer, Cal! Be reasonable. Do you honestly believe, with your unconventional background, that you'll get another job offer like this one?"

His mouth twisted wryly. "All you'd have to do is call your dear brother and beg him to . . ." His words broke off abruptly when he caught the startled, somewhat guilty look that flashed in her eyes before she lowered them. "Jesus Christ. You didn't?"

"No!"

He didn't believe her. It wouldn't be the first time she'd pulled something like this. "How could you do that . . . knowing how important this play is to me? And after all the promises you made?"

"But I didn't, Cal, I swear!"

She leaned toward him in a supplicating manner, her scoop neckline affording him a generous view of her breasts. Cal suddenly realized why she'd gone to the trouble of cleaning the apartment and getting herself all dolled up. A cold rage began coiling inside him.

"You've got to believe me," she implored. "I'm telling you the truth."

He took a quick, hard pull on his cigarette and exhaled harshly. "Bullshit."

"It wasn't as if I'd planned it." She leaned closer still, the side of her breast brushing his arm. "But, even if I had, what's so terrible about a wife trying to help her husband because she loves him?"

"Do me a favor—love me less and respect me more." He squashed the cigarette out in the ashtray, and the paper came apart under the angry pressure of his fingers. "Maybe then you wouldn't lie to me, or go behind my back to—"

"Robert thinks the reason you won't take the job is because you're afraid to assume the responsibility."

"Fuck Robert!" Cal finally exploded. "I've never run away from my responsibilities! *You* should know that better than anybody!" She gasped as if he'd hit her. In an emotional sense he had, Cal knew—below the belt. He reached for her hand. "What I meant was—"

"I know exactly what you meant!" Julie Ann jerked her hand away, tears flooding her eyes. "You wouldn't have married me if I hadn't gotten pregnant!"

Julie Ann had never forgotten the first time she had seen Cal. A naive twenty-year-old, she'd just moved to New York from the Midwest and Carolyn, her roommate, had dragged her to a café theater in the East Village to see an avant-garde play he was in that was a big underground hit. She had been surprised when he had asked her out. From the moment she and Cal started seeing each other, she felt as if she were on an emotional roller coaster ride. One moment she was transported to the dizzying heights of happiness because the most devastatingly attractive man she'd ever known—a man who could have had practically any woman he wanted—had chosen *her*. For the first time in her life she felt special. But the next moment, she was hurtling headlong into the depths of despair. How would she ever be able to hold him? How long would it be before he got bored with her and threw her over for one of the women who swarmed around him?

Whenever she brought up the subject of marriage, he insisted they wait until he was an established director, making enough money to support her and the family he claimed he wanted. But Julie Ann knew that could take years, and in the meantime, his work continued to bring him in daily contact with young women who were far more attractive and sexually experienced than she was.

She knew she had to do something, or she would lose him. Getting pregnant had seemed a simple solution, at first. She never felt any guilt about making tiny holes in her diaphragm with a safety pin because she knew she would make Cal a wonderful wife. *She* had been willing to share the cold-water flat he lived in, but how could anyone expect a newborn baby to? Recently she had begun to regret what she had done, but she knew there was no turning back now.

Tears streamed down Julie Ann's face. "And now, you're sorry you married me. You've never forgiven me for getting pregnant. You think I did it on purpose, just to trap you and force you to give up directing."

"Did I ever say that?"

"You don't have to say it. I can see it in your eyes every time you look at me."

Cal *had* been having such thoughts lately. He didn't know it showed, but he couldn't deny it.

"And if it wasn't for me," she went on tearfully, "you'd be free to run around the way you used to . . . wild parties, a different girl every night."

He shook his head. They'd been married almost five years, and she still didn't know the kind of man he was. It was true—there had been plenty of girls during his first two years in New York. Casual sex and designer drugs were all part of the downtown scene, but he'd quickly tired of both. The reason he'd fallen in love with Julie Ann was because she was different from all the others. He had told her as much many times before. Now he was getting tired of always having to defend himself when he hadn't done anything wrong.

She began to sob. "You blame me for everything."

"Don't, honey." Guilt, pity, love, and resentment twisted through him. These tightly interwoven emotions formed the pattern of their relationship. "Please, don't." He gathered

her up in his arms. She clung to him as if she were
drowning and he were the only one who could save her.

Cal sighed regretfully. "I love you. I just wish we . . ."
Sliding his hands through her hair, he tilted her face up to
his. Her eyes were puffy from crying, the delicate skin
around them all splotchy and streaked with mascara. He felt
a tenderness for her at that moment that he hadn't let
himself feel for some time. He kissed her, softly at first,
soothingly, and then deeply.

She drew in a long, shuddering breath when he finally
lifted his mouth from hers. "If you really loved me, you'd
accept Robert's offer," she said.

Cal froze. He extricated himself from her embrace with
cool deliberation. He was seething inside, but he had the
ability, which he'd learned as a child, in sheer self-defense,
to perform an emotional vanishing act almost at will. He
gave his wife a smile, punctuated with an indifferent shrug.
"Then, I guess I don't really love you."

She burst into tears again—tears that had no effect on him
now. "That's because you're too selfish and self-centered to
be able to love anyone!" Jumping up from the sofa, she ran
sobbing into the bedroom, leaving the connecting door
open.

He waited for the creaking sound the springs would make
when she threw herself onto the bed. It was a sound he was
only too familiar with. And he knew what was expected of
him next—he'd been well rehearsed. He was supposed to
follow her into the bedroom, feeling guilty and somewhat
confused. She would be lying on the bed, sobbing convulsively.
He would sit on the edge of the bed next to her. First, he'd
apologize for upsetting her. Then, he'd take her in his arms
and kiss her to assure her that he loved her. To prove his
love, he would give in and give her what she wanted—a
VCR, a new color TV set, whatever. She would still be
feeling too deeply hurt to respond at first, but soon she
would give in to his increasingly passionate kisses and they
would make love.

Feeling as if he were trapped in a rerun of a late night

soap opera, Cal walked to the bedroom. From the doorway, he watched Julie Ann acting out her part of the scene. Then, he closed the bedroom door so her sobs wouldn't interfere with his work on the script. He made notes until 2:00 A.M. By then he could no longer keep his eyes open, but he was still reluctant to go into the bedroom. He slept on the couch.

CHAPTER
Nine

"Well, that's the best I can do with what I've got," Pat said with a self-mocking smile as she set the lipstick brush down on a japaned tray overflowing with makeup brushes of all shapes and sizes.

"You look fabulous," Loris exclaimed.

They were in Pat's sleeping alcove. Pat was seated at a triangular vanity table wedged into one corner; Loris was on a dilapidated wicker chair beside it. A low, plain wooden dresser Pat had picked up at a Salvation Army thrift shop stood in the other corner, doubling as a night table, since the queen-size bed took up the rest of the "room."

For the past half hour Loris had been watching, fascinated, while Pat applied makeup like an expert. She still hadn't gotten over the transformation her friend had undergone since leaving the convent. Pat had always been overweight and, as Sister Teresa's log of demerits could testify, downright careless about her appearance. In the past year, she'd gone from a size fourteen to a size ten, and had learned to dress with a fashionable and highly individual flair.

Ever since Loris had known her, Pat had been desperately unhappy about her strong nose and jaw; she let her hair hang in her face, as if to conceal them. Now, she wore her auburn hair in a sleek, chin-length page boy, parted in the middle, that emphasized her nose and jaw dramatically, almost defiantly. Her wide, generous mouth gleamed provocatively with coppery gold lipstick. Smoky gold lined her eyelids, setting off her best feature.

"I can't get over how wonderful you look, Pat."

"Considering what I have to work with," she said with a self-deprecating smile. "But I guess that's why God created plastic surgeons. We can't all be natural beauties like you."

In typical fashion, Loris shrugged off the compliment. "As an actress, I'd give anything to have your strong, dramatic features."

"As a woman, I'd give anything to have your boobs."

Loris laughed. "I'd exchange them in a minute for your outrageous personality."

"When a girl's mammary glands fail to develop adequately," Pat returned, "she damn well better develop some personality. I mean, just look at them." She waved a disgusted hand at the mirror. "I had bigger pimples than that when I was a teenager."

"Will you stop it? There's nothing wrong with your breasts."

"Nothing that major surgery couldn't fix. I really think I should get silicone implants. I just know it would change my life." With the tips of her fingers Pat latched onto the front of her robe, at the precise level of her nipples, pulling the fabric out. "That looks better already," she said with a smile that quickly deflated when she took in the rest of her profile in the mirror. "And I'll get my nose fixed, too, while I'm at it."

"You're not serious?"

"The hell I'm not. You've heard the expression 'beauty is

only skin deep?' Well, I've yet to meet a man with x-ray eyes.'' She released the fabric, going from a 40DD to a 32B in one fluttering instant. ''I'm afraid the dear boys are only interested in one thing.''

''You mean . . . sex?''

''They'll settle for sex, but what they really want in a woman is big boobs.''

Loris laughed again. ''You really are outrageous.''

Pat turned away from the mirror to look directly at Loris. ''I realize that, having lived most of your life in a convent stuck in a time warp somewhere in the Middle Ages, you're a total innocent,'' she said. ''But even you must have noticed the way most of the guys at the party last night were staring at you. Did you also happen to notice what they were staring at?''

''Well . . . yes.'' Admitting it made Loris feel almost as uncomfortable, and bewildered, as the experience had. ''Some of them.''

''Some of them? Even the gays couldn't take their eyes off you! You're everything they wish they—''

''The gays?'' Loris interjected. ''Who are they?''

Pat thought it best not to elaborate. It would be like trying to explain computer technology to a tribe of aborigines newly discovered in a rain forest in Brazil. ''Loris, all you had to do last night was crook your little finger and any of the . . .'' She decided to leave out ''straight'' and forgot about ''bisexual'' altogether. ''Any man in the room would have jumped at the chance to go to bed with you.''

''But, I didn't say or do anything to—''

''You don't have to,'' Pat cut in, ''because you're gorgeous and you're stacked. That's my point. Just look at what you did to Cal Remington.''

Loris felt a strange sensation in the pit of her stomach at the mere mention of his name. ''What did I do to him?''

''Perfect example.'' She shifted in her seat so she was facing Loris. ''Now, here's a man who's been coming to the meetings for months, who sits in a corner all by himself and barely says a word to anyone. There are girls all over the place just eating him up with their eyes, but he doesn't do anything about it. And suddenly, last night, he gets into this heavy conversation with you."

"But, all he did was talk, and he never once looked at my. . . my body."

"Knowing Cal, I can believe that," Pat allowed. "But the signals he was sending you—conscious or otherwise— were so strong I felt them halfway across the room."

As sexually naive as she was, Loris knew on a purely instinctive level that Pat was right. She searched her friend's face intently. "You're attracted to him, aren't you?"

"Who the hell wouldn't be?" Pat admitted with characteristic bluntness. "But I don't stand a snowball's chance in hell with him."

"Well, of course not—he's married."

Pat suppressed an ironic smile. She was about to tell Loris that in New York married men screwed around as much as single men did, but then decided against it. She'd find out soon enough. "Even if he wasn't married. You think a hunk like Cal would look at me twice?"

"Why not? He thinks you're terrific. He told me so."

She pulled back in surprise. "Me?" Then, recovering, she gave what she hoped looked like a blasé shrug. "What did he say?"

"He says you're real people—the best there is."

"That's me, all right," she tossed off sarcastically. "Man's best two-legged friend. Whenever a guy needs a shoulder to cry on, a handout, or a home-cooked meal with a no-strings-attached lay thrown into the bargain, I'm the girl."

Loris stared at her friend in shock. How could someone change so drastically in one year? "You never catered to anybody, Pat. You were always so independent."

Pat checked the bright red gloss on her long, beautifully manicured fingernails. "You can get pretty lonely being independent. I know most men claim they prefer independent women, but don't you believe it."

"And you always prided yourself on being a feminist.

Don't you remember all the talks we had—how you were always in trouble with the nuns because of your ideas?''

"Women's Lib is passé, Loris. Not only aren't we making any new advances, we're actually going back—to the fifties." She jumped to her feet. "Here, look at this." Stepping over to the bed, she ruffled the cotton batiste dress she'd laid out earlier. It had a billowing skirt and sleeves; a profusion of delicate white buds dotted the pale-green fabric like wild flowers in a spring meadow. "Feminine styles are back with a vengeance. So are high heels." She indicated her strappy white sandals before pulling open her robe. "And sexy lingerie." The ecru teddy she wore plunged to her waist and was cut high on her hips, making her long legs appear even longer.

"I don't know a woman," Pat went on, slipping out of the robe, tossing it aside, "and I'm talking about career women like me, who doesn't wear makeup, have a stylish hairdo, and wear the very latest fashion in clothes. It doesn't matter how well a woman does her job, she still has to look good doing it." She quickly slipped into the dress. "In another five years, if we keep going in this direction, a woman will have to be a virgin when she marries."

She laughed as she zipped up her dress—one of the great, bawdy laughs Loris had always admired. "At least I won't have to worry about that." She spun around to look at herself in the mirror and sobered suddenly, her eyes taking on an uncharacteristically defeated look. "I don't know what went wrong. But I do know, from personal experience, that men feel threatened by women who try to compete with them. After a woman fights the system at work for eight hours a day, she sure as hell doesn't have any energy left to fight for her rights at home." She adjusted an earring, lifting one shoulder fatalistically. "So she gives in to her man, and conforms to what's expected of her."

"But you were the one who never conformed, Pat," Loris reminded her, sitting up in her chair. "You were the only one in school who ever had the guts to stand up to the nuns."

Actually, Pat was as scrappy as ever when it came to her work. She had a job as assistant producer at a small production house specializing in TV commercials; there wasn't a single woman producer. She was determined to be the first, and, eventually, one of the top theatrical producers in the country.

But when it came to men, Pat was like a different person. She seemed to have a knack for attracting struggling artists. In the past year she'd had affairs with a blocked writer and an actor with a bruised ego. She mothered them, nurtured their talent, built up their confidence, practically supported them. Once they were on their feet again, they both dumped her for a mindless little twit with a pretty face.

"Remember that time you refused to apologize to Sister Teresa," Loris was saying, "and she made you kneel on your hands out in the hall?"

Pat nodded stiffly. She remembered that night down to the smallest detail.

"No matter how hard the sisters tried, they could never break your spirit."

"They didn't succeed in breaking your spirit, either, Loris," Pat reminded her as she finished adjusting her other earring.

"Only because I shut them all out. You fought back." Her eyes glowed with admiration as she looked up at her friend. "I'd give anything to have your guts. I always wished I could be like you."

"Like me?" It had never occurred to Pat that Loris might envy *her*.

"And I'm so glad we're going to be together again. I missed you so much this past year." Jumping to her feet, Loris gave Pat a quick, impulsive hug. "If I had a sister, I couldn't love her more than I love you."

For once, Pat was at a loss for a wisecrack, her customary defense against emotion. "You've got more guts than you know, Loris," she told her simply, meaning it. *They'll eat her up alive in this city,* she thought. For a moment, she was afraid for her friend.

"So, what's our first stop on the free guided tour?"

"The first thing we've got to do is get you out of those nuns' clothes. Even *I* don't have the guts to be seen in public with you looking like that." She picked her purse up from atop the dresser. "Come on. I'm taking you shopping."

"But, it's Sunday. Aren't the stores closed?"

"This is the Big Apple, Sleeping Beauty. You can buy just about anything you want, any day of the year. The trick is knowing the right places."

It didn't take long for Loris to realize that Pat knew all the right places, like a terrific little boutique in the East Village that stocked designers' samples at half the original price. There was a huge warehouse in TriBeCa, packed to the rafters with sportswear and designer jeans at a fraction of the cost.

Pat also just happened to know this absolutely fabulous hairdresser, Mario, who worked in a posh salon on East Sixty-first Street, where it cost $50 for a cut and blow-dry. But, since he had his heart set on becoming a theatrical hair stylist, he performed the same service for actress friends for $25, on his days off.

Mario let out a shriek of horror when he saw Loris's hair. "Who did this to you?" He'd have felt the same sense of outrage if someone had painted a moustache on the Mona Lisa. "What did the fucking butcher do, put a bowl on your head and cut around it?"

Pat and Loris exchanged a look, then burst out laughing simultaneously, causing Mario's frown of disapproval to deepen. "I'm glad you ladies find this so amusing," he sniffed, "because even *I* can't do anything with *that*."

"With your creative genius?" Pat purred. "Of course you can."

And, of course, Pat was right. When Mario had finished layering Loris's hair, a mass of sexy little curls framed her face—saucy tendrils spilling onto her forehead and down her nape. Then Pat marched her over to this absolutely

incredible makeup center she'd found that catered exclusively
to models and actors. A mind-boggling assortment of theatrical makeup lined all four walls from ceiling to floor and
overflowed the glass counters. Loris was given a free makeup consultation and the usual twenty percent discount reserved for professionals.

With Pat's help, Loris found a rent-controlled apartment
for only $356 a month on Forty-sixth Street between Tenth
and Eleventh Avenues. The railroad flat had a bathtub in
the kitchen, a bathroom the size of a closet, stained
wooden floors, and plaster-peeling walls; to Loris it was
the Waldorf-Astoria. She spent an entire week in a joyous
frenzy of painting walls, scrubbing and waxing floors,
papering cabinets.

She found her furniture at the Yin and Yang Emporium, a
combination shlock shop and Oriental bazaar that special-
ized in inexpensive rattan. Matchstick bamboo window
shades hid the slummy view and diffused the sunlight, while
a curtain of wooden beads concealed the dilapidated kitchen.

Loris loved New York. Unlike most newcomers, she
didn't feel dwarfed by its massive, towering buildings.
What she saw, when she gaped up at them in awe, was the
impossible made possible, dreams made tangible, the sheer
stubborn longing of the human spirit to transcend itself. The
very things most people hated about Manhattan—the noise,
the crowds, the frantic pace—she found exhilarating. But
what fascinated her the most about the city were the startling contrasts she encountered during her first eager explo-
rations. Tucked unexpectedly between a pair of giant corpo-
rate glass-and-steel towers she found a "mini-park" of
potted trees, dotted with benches where office workers could
eat their lunch and catch an hour's glimpse of sky, a sliver
of sunshine. An exclusive neighborhood would dead-end,
within blocks, into a virtual slum; without turning an expensively coiffed hair, mink-draped matrons swept by bag
ladies sleeping on newspapers over subway gratings.

She lived in Hell's Kitchen and worked as a cocktail
waitress at an East Side disco. All the money she made,

after paying her living expenses, went for classes. She took an acting class three days a week; a dance class, alternating between modern and ballet, every day; voice lessons to build up her range, since her voice tended to be breathy.

Loris's first five months in New York were hectic, but exciting. She threw herself into the whirl of city life as if she'd never known any other. There was only one area of her new life that she was having trouble adapting to: sex. The transition from taking baths in a shift because it was a sin to look at her own naked body to watching soft-core porno movies on Pat's cable TV channel was a perplexing one, to say the least.

"Is that what it's like?" she asked Pat when she saw sex parts pumping away like machinery for the first time.

"It feels better than it looks," Pat assured her.

"But it's so . . . so unromantic."

"If you're looking for romance, Sleeping Beauty, you're living in the wrong time and place."

Loris *was* looking for romance. She'd dreamed about love for so long she refused to just jump into bed with any of the young men Pat was always fixing her up with. She longed for a love affair, not a series of one-night stands.

"And what was wrong with *this* one?" Pat demanded the morning after another one of Loris's dates had ended in the usual wrestling match, with the young man calling her a cockteaser before slamming his way out the door.

"The same thing that's wrong with all of them. I don't even know the man, but as soon as we're alone for five minutes, he has one hand down the front of my blouse and the other one up my skirt."

Pat fixed Loris with one of her knowing looks. "It's Cal, isn't it? You're so hung up on him, you can't see anybody else."

Caught off-guard, Loris was unable to answer.

"You know, Loris, I don't have to look at the calendar to know when it's Saturday anymore. All I have to do is look at your face."

"Well, at least Cal talks to me as if I had a brain in my

head . . . when he talks to me. He's not the least bit interested in going to bed with me."

Pat smiled. "I wouldn't bet my life on that if I were you," she said.

CHAPTER
Ten

One hand skimming the banister, the other clutching her script, Loris rounded the second-floor landing, barely aware of her feet touching ground. The excitement inside her created a momentum all its own, and sent her hurtling down the last flight of stairs. She stopped short when she reached the tiny vestibule; her heart skidded to a stop also at the sight of Cal through the etched-glass panel of the front door.

He was standing out on the stoop, in that unusually still way he had, the square of metal awning sheltering him from a light drizzle. The glare from the naked light bulb over the doorway intensified the sharp line of his profile. Lost in thought, he stared down at the dark, rain-slicked street, taking slow drags on a cigarette.

What could he be thinking about so intensely, she wondered. And what on earth was he still doing here? He'd left Pat's at least fifteen minutes ago. Judging by the impatient glance he shot at his watch, she assumed he was waiting for someone. His long pull on the cigarette told her he was trying to decide whether or not to leave.

Suddenly, he turned his head and squinted through the glass toward the staircase. And then he saw her. The strangest look came into his eyes. Before she could decipher it, he turned his face away.

He held the door open for her, stepping politely to one side to let her out. When he looked directly at her again it was with a wry grin. "Fancy meeting you here."

"Well, I certainly never expected to see you," she returned in kind. Her heart was beating erratically, and it wasn't from running downstairs. "Do you come here often?"

The grin vanished. "Not often enough."

Loris was thrown by Cal's sudden change in mood, his grim tone. If he felt that way, then why was he always the first to leave the theater group meetings? She wanted to ask, but didn't. She already knew the answer.

"I thought you'd gone," she said, attempting to fill the awkward pause between them.

His eyes met hers. "Did you?"

"I mean, we all thought you'd gone," she rattled on. "Are you, uh, waiting for someone?"

Cal took a final drag on his cigarette, then flicked it into the street. "Just for the rain to let up," he told her. He sure as hell couldn't tell her he'd been waiting for her. He hadn't even admitted it to himself until he had seen her.

When he had first come downstairs, he'd had every intention of going straight home. He'd just announced the opening night of their premiere production at the meeting, and his choices for the cast and crew. It had taken him five long, frustrating months to pull together all the disparate elements needed to put on a play, but the excitement he felt now at the prospect of starting rehearsals on Monday—that sense of being totally alive—made it all worthwhile.

He wanted to hang on to those feelings just a little while longer. He only wished there was someone he could share them with. He told himself he'd smoke one cigarette before starting home. By the end of his second cigarette, he realized he didn't want to go home.

Party noises filtered down to him from Pat's third-story windows and, for a moment, Cal was tempted to go back upstairs. But he didn't want to be with a crowd of people, either. He didn't know what the hell he wanted. When he had seen Loris, he had realized what he'd been waiting for.

He had to remind himself that he had no right to hope for anything where she was concerned. She was here, now. That was enough.

"The rain seems to be letting up," Loris said, slipping her script into her tote bag.

Just as she slung the straps of the tote bag over her shoulder to leave, a burst of laughter erupted over the loud rock music blaring from Pat's windows, catching their attention.

"Sounds like one helluva party," Cal said.

"They've got good reason to celebrate tonight."

He gave her one of his long, searching looks. "How come *you're* not celebrating with the others?"

Loris lowered her eyes, afraid Cal might read the answer in them: when he'd left, he'd taken the party with him, as far as she was concerned. But there was one thing not even *he* could take away from her—her love of acting.

"Well, I never expected to get the lead in the play," she admitted. "I was so happy about getting the part of Michelle, I . . . this probably sounds silly, but I just didn't feel like being with a lot of people."

"It's not silly at all. I know exactly what you mean. We all have something we feel so deeply about that we hesitate to share it with others, for fear of being misunderstood . . . even ridiculed."

That wasn't what she'd meant at all. Was he speaking from personal experience?

"We're lucky if we find one person we can share those feelings with," he said, staring at the script he held tucked under his left arm.

His tone suggested to Loris that he had yet to find such a

person. "Anyway, I just couldn't wait to get home to start working on the play," she went on quickly. "It's such a great part, and—" She paused to listen to an ominous rumble in the distance as another strong gust of wind went up. "Was that thunder?"

"It wasn't the subway," Cal drawled. Throwing his head back, he squinted up at the huge clouds tearing themselves to shreds as they raced across the midnight sky. "The storm sure is moving fast."

She laughed. "What storm? It's stopped drizzling."

"*That* storm." He pointed toward the New Jersey shoreline, its lights glittering like earthbound stars across the Hudson River, the dark clouds sweeping in their direction. "Come on." Unzipping his leather aviator jacket, he tucked his script safely inside. "We better get going before it breaks."

Loris stiffened at his choice of pronoun; he made it sound as if they were together. "Well, see you Monday at rehearsals," she said, darting down the steps to the sidewalk.

"Hey, hold up," Cal called after her as he struggled to get his zipper closed over the bulky manuscript. "My car's parked on Tenth. I'll give you a lift."

"Don't bother," she called back over her shoulder. "I live only a few blocks from here."

"It's no bother." He took the stairs two at a time, and in a few long-legged strides was beside her, matching his steps to hers. "You shouldn't be walking around here at night alone. Besides, you'll get soaked." He eyed the threatening storm clouds again. "Looks like all hell's going to break loose any minute."

"That's okay," she tossed off lightly. "I love walking in the—"

"Christ, I told you!" Cal roared as the sky opened up on cue. "Come on!"

Grabbing her arm, he pulled her along with him and they ran down Forty-eighth Street, the rain coming in sheets, from every angle. Lightning cut a jagged slice out of the dark sky, lighting up the facades of the tenements, freezing their image for an instant, like a stage effect. Then, the world around them plunged back into darkness.

"That's it there," Cal shouted over the thunder. "The Jeep on the corner." With his keys already in hand, he opened the passenger door and practically shoved her inside. While he ran around to the driver's side, Loris reached across the front seat to release the lock button. Cal jumped in, slammed the door, and sank back against the seat. They both sat there gaping out at the rain for a moment, then turned to look at each other, soaking wet, gasping for breath. They burst out laughing simultaneously.

Loris pushed her wet bangs out of her eyes. "I don't believe that."

"Always trust a country boy about the weather," Cal told her with a crooked grin.

He certainly looked pleased with himself, she noted, as if the storm were a bit of stage business that had come off exactly as he'd directed. His straight black hair gleamed, sleek and wet, emphasizing his high cheekbones and slanted brows, the stark line of his jaw, making his mouth appear even softer, more sensual.

His smile faded when he caught her staring at him. Their eyes locked. A look passed between them that was as electric as the lightning streaking across the sky.

Loris began a frantic search for tissues in her tote bag. Sitting up, Cal tugged a handkerchief out of the back pocket of his jeans and offered it to her. She murmured a thank you. While she used the large, white linen square to dry her face and neck, Cal removed the script from inside his jacket, checking it carefully before he tossed it onto the back seat.

She thanked him again when she returned the handkerchief. He ran it quickly over his face, aware of the perfume that clung to it. She suddenly noticed that her sweater was stuck to her like a second skin. Her self-conscious attempt to detach the clinging wet fabric merely called his attention to her breasts.

"You must be cold," he muttered, shrugging out of his leather jacket. "Here. Put this on."

"No, I'm all—"

"Put it on." He slid it brusquely around her shoulders. The quilted nylon lining was warm with his body heat.

Cal concentrated on lighting a cigarette, giving it the attention he usually reserved for lighting an entire stage. While he smoked it, waiting for the engine to warm up, he busied himself adjusting the heat, lights, and wipers.

The sound the windshield wipers made seemed unnaturally loud in the strained silence that hung between them as he carefully negotiated the flooded streets to her door. Loris tried to think of something to say, but was afraid her voice would give her away again; she had mumbled her own address like a fool.

She'd never lied to herself about finding Cal physically attractive, but now she was beginning to wonder whether Pat was right, after all. Maybe she was more than just attracted to Cal. From the neck up she'd ceased to function logically; from the neck down, her body was working overtime. If he could reduce her to this absurd state just by driving her home, what would happen when they started rehearsals and she saw him three nights a week?

When he pulled alongside a fire hydrant, the only space available close to her door, she quietly asked, "Cal, why did you pick me for the lead in the play?"

He shrugged as if the answer was obvious. "Because you're perfect for the part."

"I'd have thought Lenore would make a perfect Michelle. I know everyone else in the group thinks so."

"I happen to be the director," he reminded her dryly, engaging the clutch. "I know better."

"She gave a very good reading."

"Yeah. So?" He sank back against the seat. "What are you getting at, Loris?"

She swallowed hard. "I can't do the part, Cal."

"What?"

"I'm sorry, you'll have to get someone else to—"

"Hold it," he cried, throwing his hands up. "Just a few minutes ago you told me how happy you were about it. What happened to make you change your mind?"

"I'd love to play Michelle," she admitted. Then lied: "I just don't think I can handle it."

"I'd never have given you the part if I hadn't thought you could handle it." He leaned toward her. "And I'll be there to work with you every step of the way."

That's what she was afraid of. "You need someone with more experience," she insisted, slipping out of his leather jacket. "Like Lenore. She's a very good actress. She'll be a terrific Michelle."

"No, dammit! I've been living with this play for over six months, and every time I think of it I see you!"

Loris was amazed by Cal's startling admission and the emotional intensity of his outburst. Cal was even more amazed. He hadn't realized how much a part of his fantasies Loris had become; in his mind, she and the part were inseparable.

Turning away from her, he shut off the windshield wipers with a hard snap. Then he sat staring out at the torrent of rain, which was all that was visible through the glass that seemed to ripple and melt under the water's assault. "Loris, please don't do this," he said finally, his voice barely audible. "You don't know what this play means to me."

"Cal, I'm sure it would be better for everyone if I dropped out."

"No!" He turned toward her again, his expression intense. "You can't drop out. I won't let you."

The decision was hers, not his, Loris wanted to tell him, but couldn't.

"Look, I know how you feel," he went on. "It's your first big part and you're afraid of failure. Who wouldn't be? You think I'm not afraid? I'm putting my balls on the line with this play, Loris. If I fail, I'll never direct again."

"What do you mean? Why not?"

Cal combed his fingers through his wet hair with short, jerky motions. "I'd rather not go into that. The point is, I'm

not going to fail. Neither will you. I've got every beat of
this play worked out, and I've been getting some really wild
ideas. I can't wait to get into rehearsals to try them out." He
sat up, his face coming alive. "You know the fantasy
sequences? I'm thinking of using lighting the way a film
director uses shots to build a story visually, with a series of
images. Then, whenever..." He paused suddenly, self-
consciously. "Does this make any sense to you?"

"You mean, like a montage?"

"Yes, exactly. And we'll use strobe lights to break reality
up into pieces whenever we segue into fantasy. I see the set
all sharp, slanted angles..."

Loris watched, fascinated, as Cal designed the set in the
air for her with long, lean hands. She had the feeling it was
the first time he'd ever spoken to anyone about the play
because the words were pouring out of him as if they'd been
pent up inside too long. She found herself being drawn—
seduced would have been a better word—by his creative
vision. And then she knew she had to be a part of it, no
matter what happened.

"Flats slanted, doorways, windows," he was saying,
"maybe even the furniture—I'm not sure yet—but all the
lines barely converging to create the illusion that it could all
come crashing down."

The light from the lamppost, fragmented by the rain, cast
flickering patterns on his face as he spoke. The rain was so
thick it obliterated the contours of buildings, drummed out
the sound of traffic, washed away all sense of time.

Cal realized he was talking too much, but he couldn't
have stopped if he wanted to. She was listening to him so
intently that she was barely breathing. Through her sweater
he was able to make out the unmistakable outline of taut
nipples. He told himself it had to be a reaction to the wet
fabric clinging to them, but her lips were parted, her eyes
wide with excitement and gleaming. Before he realized
what he was doing he moved toward her—causing a shrieking
sound that startled them both back to reality.

"What was that?" Loris gasped.

Cal pulled back. From under his thigh he extricated a brown paper bag that emitted another squawk of protest. "It's Donnie the Duck." He'd completely forgotten about the rubber duck he'd bought Brian to replace the one with the broken squeaker. He cursed himself silently: he'd forgotten a damn sight more than the toy. What the hell was the matter with him? Wasn't his marriage in enough trouble as it was?

Yet, part of him wished to hell he had kissed her as he'd intended, wondered how she would have reacted, what she would taste and feel like. Reaching into the paper bag, he took out the bright yellow duck and held it up in front of her. "My son won't take a bath without Donnie the Duck."

"Your son?" Loris repeated, surprised. Pat had never mentioned to her that Cal had a son.

"Yeah, I have a little one at home," he admitted, his voice filled with a tenderness that touched her.

"It's late. You should be getting home." She grabbed her tote bag with one hand, pushed down on the door handle with the other. Mumbling a quick good night, she jumped out of the car and ran through the pouring rain to her door.

When Cal arrived home, Julie Ann was waiting up for him. Her frantic questioning hardly fazed him. All he could think of was Loris and the way the street light had illuminated her face. He had more ideas for directing *High Point*, and all he wanted to do was share them with her. Julie Ann's ravings faded into the background.

CHAPTER
Eleven

Loris didn't need to check her watch to find out how late it was. She could feel 3:00 A.M. in the small of her back, as she sat cross-legged on the nail-studded, sawdust-covered floor, surrounded by two-by-fours, rolls of canvas, empty paint cans, and assorted tools and brushes. The other actors in the company had left as soon as rehearsals were over . . . she had stayed to help out.

While waiting for Greg to bring her a new can of paint, she polished off the dinner leftovers—cold chicken and warm beer—and watched the stage at the far end of the auditorium where Cal and the tech crew were putting the finishing touches on the main set.

Once-elegant white columns rose on a slant from their foundations, seemingly about to topple. Faded family portraits in peeling gilt frames hung, slightly askew, from invisible wires. Hidden among asymmetrical, precariously strung beams, spots with blue gels cast a ghostly glow over the decaying Southern mansion.

Seeing Cal's vision finally realized, Loris felt the same thrill she'd experienced that night in the car when he'd designed the set in the air for her. Suddenly, she felt sure things would go smoothly from now on. Murphy's Law had prevailed these past four months: everything that could possibly go wrong, had. The production had been plagued with bad luck from the start.

The very week they were scheduled to start rehearsals, Cal's wife had fallen off a kitchen stool while trying to reach a can of Campbell's soup, crushing a vertebra in her neck. Rehearsals had been postponed for two weeks. They were finally beginning to make some headway when Brad, her leading man, landed a part in a soap, so they had to start all over again. Thanks to the Christmas holidays and a flu epidemic, they lost still more time.

The March 15 opening was now only two weeks away. They were working seven nights a week, and until three or four in the morning on weekends. Everyone was exhausted, on the verge of losing their bread-and-butter jobs. There was constant tension in the air, an almost palpable anxiety. Loris had never been so happy.

"Looks like you finally flipped out," a voice broke into her reverie.

She glanced up to see Pat striding toward her. "Who? Me?"

"Yes, you. You're just sitting there smiling, all by yourself." She came to a halt in front of her, a can of paint dangling from one hand. "Loris, what's going on?"

"What do you mean?"

"You know Greg, the new tech guy?" Flopping down on the floor beside Loris, Pat set the paint can down. "He told me to give you this."

"None of my scenes were being rehearsed tonight," she explained between nibbles on a greasy chicken wing, "so I thought I'd help out painting flats."

"The man said, 'Would you give this to Cal's wife?'"

"What?" Dropping the chicken bone into the cardboard

bucket, she wiped her hands on her paint-streaked jeans. "Where on earth did he get that idea?"

"You never miss a rehearsal—even when you're not on call. If you're not painting flats, you're building platforms. You even keep the director's book! And the—"

"Hey, Loris," Cal shouted over to her from atop a ladder on stage. "Where are the number-two nails?"

"I've got them right here," she called back, ignoring the pointed look her friend was giving her.

Pat waited until Artie, the stage manager, had retrieved the box of nails and was out of hearing distance. "And, the two of you leave together every night. You get into his car and drive off with him. Why shouldn't Greg think you're Cal's wife?"

"Well, where the hell *is* she?" Loris cried defensively. "She hasn't been to a single rehearsal. Doesn't she care about his work? She must know how much trouble he's having finding people to help out. If I were his wife, I'd be here every night working alongside him."

"You're doing that anyway," Pat reminded her flatly. "Jesus, Loris, you're not falling in love with him, are you?"

"I'm just trying to do everything I can to make the play a success. What's wrong with that?" Picking up a screwdriver, she pried off the lid of the paint can. "I love doing all this, Pat. I've never been so happy."

"I know." She sounded worried. "So's Cal. He's like a different person. Are you two getting it on after rehearsals?"

"No, of course not. He just drives me home."

"And that's all?"

"Well, we sit in the car and talk for a while."

"You just . . . talk?"

"Yes! About how the rehearsal went, or new ideas he's trying to work out." Using a thin wooden stick, she stirred the paint with quick, jerky motions. "I mean, why can't a man and a woman just enjoy being together, without sex always coming into it? We both love the theater. We just happen to have this . . . rapport. Is that so terrible?" The

stick snapped in two, splattering them both with paint.
"Now look what I've done!"

Pat laughed. "That's okay. We're already messy."

"No, it's not okay!" Loris cried angrily. Tears suddenly
flooded her eyes. "It's not okay at all."

Pat stared incredulously. "Jesus, Loris, you *are* in love
with him."

"Oh, Pat, what am I going to do? I've never been so
miserable in all my life."

For once, her friend didn't have an answer.

The audience's growing irritation, expressed by much cough-
ing and throat-clearing, and the squeaking of metal folding
chairs, could be heard backstage, behind the frayed velvet
curtain.

"What are we going to do?" Artie whispered to Pat, who
was peering through the peephole in the curtain.

"There's nothing we can do," she snapped. She'd just seen
David Fine, a critic from *The Village Voice*—the only paper
that routinely covered avant-garde showcase productions—
jump out of his front-row seat and stomp up the aisle.
Muttering a curse under her breath, she turned away from
the curtain to find that most of the cast and crew had
gathered around her.

"Why do we have to wait for Cal?" Lenore demanded,
center stage as usual. "He's not in the play. Why don't we
just start without him?"

Knowing how fragile actors' egos were on opening night,
Pat willed herself to remain calm. "Because Cal's got the
light box."

"But, it's forty-five minutes past curtain time and he's
still not here," she returned with an imperious toss of her
head. "We'll just have to go on without a light box. What is
it, anyway?"

Pat counted to ten. She could have explained that the
school auditorium's antiquated system couldn't handle the

intricate lighting Cal had devised for the show, and that he had built his own light box, but she didn't trust herself.

Lenore turned to Ross, the actor who played her husband and Loris's lover in the play. "What's a light box?"

"What I don't understand," Ross said, upstaging Lenore, not for the first time, "is why Cal had to take the thing home with him every night."

Pat gritted her teeth.

"Because it took him over a month to build," Loris answered as she rushed in from the wings. "It's irreplaceable. He couldn't chance someone ripping it off."

"Did you reach him at home?" Pat asked.

"No. There's still no answer."

"Then, he's got to be on his way."

"That's just great," Lenore huffed, "but listen to that audience we've got to play to now."

"They're so hostile we'll never win them over," Ross seconded, and the rest of the cast murmured agreement.

"Pat, don't you think you should make another speech to the audience to—" Artie began.

"I want this stage cleared," Pat cut the stage manager off, her patience at an end. "I want actors in their dressing rooms working on their preparations, and tech crew at their stations going over their cues. Now!"

Artie snapped to attention. "Okay, everybody. Let's clear the stage."

There was plenty of grumbling but everyone complied, except Loris. She stood there beside one of the slanted columns, unable to move, barely able to voice her worst fear. "Pat, shouldn't we call the hospitals? Maybe Cal's been in an accident." If there were any doubts left in her mind about how much she loved him, the anguish she felt at that moment banished them.

"Don't worry," Pat reassured her. "Cal's okay."

"But you know how dependable he is. He's always the first one to get here. Something must have happened."

Pat laughed harshly. "Something's happened, all right.

His damn wife probably fell off another stool. Anything to wreck his opening night.''

Loris took a step toward her. "Why would she do that?"

"Because that's what she always does! This time, when he was about to go into rehearsals, she fell and hurt her neck. Last time, she had to go to the hospital with some mysterious stomach ailment.''

"You think she's deliberately trying to ruin his directing career?''

"I don't know that it's a conscious thing on her part," Pat allowed, "but the result's the same.''

"But, why does Cal—"

Loris never finished her question because Cal slammed through the side door connecting the auditorium to the backstage area.

"Christ, I'm sorry," he said, lugging the light box up the steps, onto the stage. "My goddamn car keys disappeared.'' His voice was shaking with barely suppressed rage. "It took me over two hours to find them.''

Pat exchanged a meaningful glance with Loris. "Will you tell the cast we'll be ready to go in five minutes?'' she asked her while Cal went hurrying over to the tech booth to connect the light box. "I'll tell the audience.''

The rows of faces confronting Pat when she'd finished her speech looked anything but forgiving. The only smiling face in the auditorium belonged to Julie Ann Remington.

The frayed velvet folds had barely closed on the fifth curtain call when Loris, enthusiastic applause still exploding in her ears, ran off-stage to find Cal, who was waiting eagerly for her in the wings. Caught up in the excitement of the moment, she threw herself heedlessly into his arms.

"Christ, you were wonderful!'' Lifting her by the waist, Cal whirled her around until they were both laughing breathlessly. Their laughter broke off when, her body sliding down his, he set her back on her feet. For one blinding instant everything they felt for each other was revealed in their eyes. Then they were surrounded by the rest of the company, everybody talking simultaneously, hugging and kissing. It was like New Year's Eve and the Fourth of July rolled into one.

"Okay, everybody," Pat shouted over the joyful pandemonium. "The sooner you get out of costume, the sooner we can get the party going. We've got to be out of here by midnight." As she took off for the auditorium to oversee the caterer, who was providing the buffet in exchange for free advertising in the program, the actors started for their dressing rooms.

Cal grabbed Loris's arm, holding her back. "Can I talk to you a minute?"

Without waiting for her answer, he maneuvered her around the prop table, over the tangle of light cables and extension cords, to the passageway behind the flats that the actors moved, unseen, from one side of the stage to the other. Loris couldn't imagine what Cal wanted to say to her, but she wished they could celebrate by themselves. He had made this production special for her and a success for them both.

"I just wanted to thank you," he said. "For everything." He didn't need to go into detail. Everything they'd shared during the past four months, and what it had meant to him, was visible on his face.

"I loved every minute of it, Cal," Loris blurted out. "I'm sorry it's over."

"But, it's not over," he insisted, his tone intense. "It's just the beginning."

"What do you mean?"

"Is Cal still backstage?" They both started, then turned in the direction of Pat's voice. "Have you seen Cal, Greg?"

"He was here just a minute ago," Greg called back from the tech booth, busy unplugging the sound equipment.

Cal let out a sigh of irritation, but stepped out from behind the flats. Loris followed him. "Yeah, Pat, what is it?"

"Your wife is looking for you," she told him.

"I'm not through here yet." Cal's face and tone were expressionless. "I have to take care of the light box first."

"I still have to change," Loris reminded herself out loud.

Pat waited until Loris had disappeared through the door leading to the dressing rooms before turning to Cal. "Don't you think we should stash the light box in the prop room from now on?"

"Are you kidding? Half the kids in this school are on drugs. They'll rip off anything to get money."

"The way things are going, it seems to me it'll be safer here than at your house."

Cal took a moment to think it over. "Yeah, you're right."

"I'll tell your wife you'll be right out. We wouldn't want to keep her waiting," Pat said sarcastically before walking away.

While Cal and Greg were locking up the sound and lighting equipment, Loris changed into a sweater and a pair of jeans. The opening night jitters she'd experienced earlier were nothing compared to what she felt in anticipation of meeting Cal's wife.

Julie Ann Remington wasn't at all what Loris had expected, from Pat's description of her. No wife could have been more enthusiastic about her husband's work. For the past ten minutes she'd been raving about the sets and costumes, graciously complimenting Ross, Lenore, and Loris, in turn, on their performances.

"And I'm so proud of Cal," she told them. "The play was really terrific—though, I must confess, I didn't understand half of it." She laughed, a bit too gaily, when she realized from their looks that she'd paid him a left-handed compliment. She was quick to amend it: "Cal is so brilliant, I don't know what he ever saw in me."

Loris couldn't help wondering why Julie Ann kept referring to her husband in the third person, since he was standing right next to her. Perhaps it was because Cal's attitude seemed to imply he wasn't the person she was referring to. The more his wife went on in that relentlessly cheerful manner, the more withdrawn he became.

His silence only served to spur Julie Ann on. "I just wish I could have been more help to him, but since my accident . . ." Her hand fluttered to the detachable, foam-rubber neck brace she was wearing, which held her head immobile, and contrasted oddly with her frilly pink dress and elaborate hairdo. All her fingernails were bitten off.

"How did it happen?" Ross asked, still glowing in the warmth of her fulsome praise of his acting.

Lenore stifled a groan. She would have invited her mother to the opening if she'd wanted to stand around listening to a professional martyr.

Remembering Pat's interpretation of the accident, Loris listened intently to Julie Ann's explanation.

"It was so silly, really—though, of course, I could have been killed." She laughed gaily again. "I shouldn't have climbed onto that wobbly stool to reach the kitchen cabinet, but I was rushing to get Cal's dinner ready in time. Had I known he was going to be late because he was involved in a preproduction meeting . . ." Having fixed the blame for her accident, her words trailed off. She gave the impression she wasn't the sort of person to rub things in. She even gave her husband a forgiving smile.

He was too busy lighting a cigarette to notice.

Though Cal appeared calm, Loris could sense the effort it cost him. The tension of the suppressed rage that emanated from him was almost palpable. Ross and Lenore, sensing it also, exchanged uncomfortable looks. They clearly did not want to be trapped in Cal's domestic conflict. Only Julie Ann seemed totally oblivious of her husband's feelings.

"It's been four months since your accident," Loris told her. She was simply unable to stop herself. "And you still have to wear a neck brace?"

"Oh, I don't wear it all the time," Julie Ann admitted. "Only when my crushed vertebra acts up."

Her choice of words, Loris thought, couldn't have been more revealing.

Julie Ann flinched, indicating that she was in pain even as she breathed. Her brave little smile was meant to show that she sought to overcome her ordeal. She placed a loving hand on her husband's arm. "Nothing could make me miss Cal's opening night."

Cal jerked his arm away. He'd had all he could take of her performance as wife of the year. Without a word of explanation, he stalked over to the improvised bar, which had been set up next to the buffet. Most of the cast and crew were assembled there, waiting to get a slice of the five-foot-long hero sandwich.

"I could use some food," Ross told Lenore brightly. "How about you?"

Lenore's expression was flooded with relief. "I'd love some." They hurried off, leaving Loris alone with Cal's wife.

Though she'd have liked nothing better than to take off also, Loris found she couldn't. She suspected Julie Ann of exaggerating, perhaps even inventing, her physical disability, but the pain that flashed in her eyes when Cal left her standing there was only too real.

"Cal is so moody." Julie Ann's long, drawn-out sigh made it clear how much she had to endure. "But, I'm sure I don't have to tell *you* that. I understand you've been working very closely with him all these months, so you should know how difficult he can be."

Loris didn't know anything of the kind, but she kept her opinion to herself. She was far more interested in hearing his wife's opinion of him.

"He's at his absolute worst when he's in rehearsal. Oh, I don't want you to think I'm putting him down," she was quick to add. "Usually, Cal is a wonderful husband and father. We have a terrific relationship. The theater just seems to bring out something . . . negative in his personality. That's why I'm so relieved he's not going to direct anymore."

Loris paused as she was about to take a sip of white wine. "He's not? Why?"

"He's had this really terrific job offer," Julie Ann confided. "It involves a great deal of responsibility. He wouldn't have time for anything else."

"But Cal has a great talent," Loris protested, with more emotion than she'd intended. "He has what it takes to be one of the top directors in the theater. He can't quit!"

Julie Ann made a dismissing motion with her hand. "Directing was never more than a hobby with him, anyway."

Loris stared at the woman uncomprehendingly as she recalled the hours Cal had spoken to her about his hopes and dreams. It was as if they were talking about a different man.

"Some married men play around with other women," Julie Ann explained smugly. "Cal plays at directing."

What little sympathy she'd felt toward Julie Ann dissolved as Loris realized that Pat had been right about her from the start. But didn't Cal realize that?

During their exchange, Cal was busy putting away a stiff drink of V.O. by himself. The evening, for which he'd had such hopes, had been destroyed. The fact that his wife hadn't succeeded in ruining the performance was small comfort; it hadn't been for lack of trying. The drink wasn't helping him maintain control over the anger seething dangerously inside him, he tried to recapture, at least in his thoughts, the exhilarating joy he'd known earlier.

He recalled the audience's enthusiastic applause, the five curtain calls, and finally, the moment when Loris had flung herself into his arms. He reexperienced the sound of her laughter, the arousing feel of her body sliding down his, the look of love in her startled eyes.

He poured himself a double.

An empty glass was suddenly thrust in front of him from behind. "I need a drink, too."

Cal turned and was surprised to see Pat. She'd gone out of her way to avoid him since they'd last spoken backstage. "V.O. okay?"

She shrugged. "V.O. Rubbing alcohol. Whatever."

Cal could tell she'd already had quite a few drinks, and that she was still angry with him. He didn't blame her. He poured out an inch of rye, adding ice cubes in spite of her protests.

"And what are *you* doing all by your lonesome?" she asked. "I'd have thought you'd have more company than you needed." She looked over her shoulder at Loris and Julie Ann. "Now, there's an odd couple if ever I saw one. What could they possibly have in common, I wonder?"

Letting her sarcastic taunts slide, Cal took a sip of V.O.

Pat polished off her drink in one gulp. "Did your wife enjoy the show?"

"Look, I don't blame you for being pissed off at me, Pat, but there was nothing I could do. The important thing is that the show was a success, in spite of . . . everything."

Reaching past him, she grabbed the bottle and poured herself a real drink. "Too bad David Fine didn't get to see what a success we were."

"You mean, he didn't show?"

"Oh, *he* showed, all right. *You* were the one who didn't. At least, not until he'd already left in disgust."

A raw curse tore out of Cal, catching the attention of several snackers at the buffet. "We've got to get him to come back."

"It took me a month of almost daily phone calls to get him to agree to cover us. He's so overbooked he had to cancel a personal engagement to be here, and then we ended up looking like a bunch of amateurs who can't even start the show on time! We needed that review, Cal!"

"You don't have to tell me!"

She told him anyway. "With a good write up from the *Voice*, I could have gotten the critics from the *News* and the *Post*—maybe even the *Times*. Now, how the hell am I supposed to find backers willing to put up the money for an Off-Broadway production with a play as commercially risky as this one? We needed that goddamn review!"

Cal's hand tightened around his glass with such force that Pat was sure it would shatter. She'd been so caught up in venting her own anger and frustration that she hadn't realized how upset he was. She put her hand over his, trying to calm him and let him know she was still his friend. "I know it's none of my business, but you've got an enemy in your house."

She expressed the very thought that was beginning to form in his own mind. He set the glass down slowly. He was about to say something, then didn't. Pat had the feeling he was afraid that if he uttered a single word, he would lose all control.

CHAPTER
Twelve

Julie Ann simply couldn't understand why her husband refused to speak to her throughout the drive home, in spite of her concerned prodding. "I'm not getting out of the car until you tell me what's bothering you, Cal," she said when he'd parked on the corner, a few spaces up from their apartment house. "Is it because of something I said or did inadvertently?"

He laughed, a deep, bitter laugh. "Inadvertently? You deliberately hid the car keys to stop me from going to my opening."

Her eyes widened, all injured innocence. But Cal wasn't going to argue with her. He knew that would be futile. The rage he'd been suppressing all evening surged through him, so intense it scared the hell out of him. "Get out of the car," he warned her, "or I swear to Christ I won't be responsible for what happens."

He didn't have to tell her twice. Julie Ann got out, slammed the car door, and headed toward their apartment entrance. Flooring the accelerator, he pulled away from the curb, tires screeching. Sobbing uncontrollably, Julie Ann watched the Jeep zoom out of sight from the stoop. She was sorry now she hadn't thrown the car keys down the sewer instead.

Cal had no particular destination in mind; he only knew that he needed to release his anger, to attain freedom in motion. What he found, as he sped down Northern Boulevard, was the approach to the Fifty-ninth Street Bridge. Only then did he admit to himself that Loris's apartment was his destination, and had been all along. He never once paused to think about what he was doing, or about the possible consequences.

Like Northern Boulevard, almost all the traffic on the bridge at that late hour was on the Manhattan to Queens side. As he whipped over the wide slash of darkness that was the East River, the lights of the soaring skyline rushed to meet him. It was a different city at night: it gleamed. a different kind of excitement took it over: sexual, mysterious, a bit dangerous.

By the time Cal got across town it was past the midnight deadline, so he didn't bother to stop by the auditorium. Knowing Pat, he was sure she'd moved the party to her place. But purely instinctive feeling compelled him to drive to Loris's apartment instead.

Forty-sixth Street was deserted. Loris's second-story windows were dark, the bamboo shades drawn, yet Cal felt her presence so strongly that his pulse quickened. On closer inspection, it seemed to him that a faint light was filtering through the narrow slats. He pulled the Jeep into the first available parking space.

The dim light Cal had been able to make out came from the small lamp on the table next to Loris's bed. Since the cast party had lost all meaning for her when Cal had left abruptly with his wife, she didn't see any point in going on to Pat's with the others.

Though Loris was surprised to see Cal, she didn't need to ask why he was there. "You shouldn't be here, Cal," was all she said as she let him in.

"I'll leave if you really want me to," he replied, closing the door behind him.

The next instant, they were in each other's arms. They came together with such force that it was more like a collision than an embrace; their teeth grated together when they kissed. They clung fiercely to one another as if they might be separated at any moment, kissing over and over again.

Frightened by the intensity of their desire for one another, Loris started to pull away, but Cal wouldn't let go of her. He could have taken her on the spot, right up against the door but he was reluctant to rush things between them.

He lifted his mouth from hers. "I didn't mean to be so rough . . . but I'm so damn hungry for you."

"I know," she breathed, meaning she felt the same way. She was giddy with love for him, barely able to stand on her own when he suddenly released her and pulled off his bomber jacket. He didn't bother to hang it on the bentwood coatrack next to the door, but let it fall to the floor. With the same impatience, he stripped off her robe and tossed it on top of his jacket.

He gathered her up in his arms, and the heat from his body enveloped her. His mouth took hers softly this time, with long, languorous kisses that sent waves of warm pleasure through her. She felt a rush of love for him so intense that tears burned behind her eyes. When he felt her melt against him, soft and vulnerable, it became impossible for him to restrain himself any longer.

In his eagerness, he practically tore off her nightgown, but then he was brought to a stunned halt at the sight of her exquisite body. Her skin seemed to absorb all the light from the Japanese rice paper lamp beside the bed, reflecting it with a warm, creamy glow.

"You're so beautiful," he told her, his voice awed, his gaze sliding over her like a caress.

For the first time in her life Loris felt beautiful. She
expected to be overcome by shame and a sense of sin as she
stood there stark naked before Cal, but all she felt was a
longing to have him as fully revealed to her. Just as she was
about to reach for the buttons on his shirt, he went down on
his knees before her and buried his face between her
breasts.

"Even more beautiful than I imagined," he murmured,
his breath hot on her skin, moving his hands down her back
in long sensuous strokes that lingered over the curves of her
hips and derrière. She was astonished at the pleasure he
found in touching her and at the desire he ignited in her.
When he brushed his face and then his mouth back and forth
over her breasts, she had to grab onto his shoulders to
steady herself.

His teeth caught the budding tip of her breast, making her
gasp. With barely controlled hunger he sucked her nipple
into the moist heat of his mouth. Her whole body contracted
against him when she felt the fierce pull of his lips and teeth
on her. He groaned when he felt her nipple swell with
excitement against his tongue, but he never stopped swirling
warm, wet caresses over her. She clung to him, not wanting
him to stop.

"You taste so good you make we want to eat you up
alive," he said when he finally dragged his mouth away.
His hands continued stroking her slowly, softly. Before he
could once again lower his mouth to her breast, she pushed
away from him, staggering back several steps.

Cal froze. "What's wrong?"

"I want to feel you, too," Loris explained, a shaky
motion of her hand indicating he was still dressed.

"Do you?" he asked wryly, but there was a funny catch
in his voice. He smiled crookedly. "I think it can be
arranged." He was on his feet before she could blink.

He unbuttoned his shirt and shrugged it off. Loris's finger
pulled the hem of his undershirt up. With the same long,
sensuous strokes he'd used on her, she caressed his sides,
his back and shoulders, finally letting Cal pull the white

T-shirt over his head. He tossed it onto the floor with the rest of their clothes. Loris traced the lean, strong lines of his chest, exploring the differences between his body and hers.

Her palms had become extremely sensitive, and she was amazed at the erotic sensations touching him aroused in her. She loved the sleek feel of his muscles, the way they clenched at her touch, the contrast between their hardness and the softness of his skin.

It was Cal's turn to pull away. He wanted to feel her hands all over him, to feel *her* all over him. He unbuckled his belt, unzipped his fly, and got his jeans down past his knees before he remembered his boots. Laughing breathlessly, he hobbled over to the bed, sinking onto the edge of the mattress. While he pulled off his right boot and sock, she tugged off the left ones. Getting to his feet again, he quickly slipped out of his jeans and shorts.

Loris's mouth went dry and she inhaled deeply at the sight of Cal's lean hips, tight buttocks, and the bold thrust of his sex. She'd never seen an erection before: it seemed strange and a bit scary, but beautiful.

Fascinated, she reached out and touched his rigid flesh. She ran her fingers over the glistening tip. "It's so warm . . . so unbelievably soft." A sharp intake of breath was Cal's only answer. Slowly, she explored him with both hands, a sense of wonder and excitement building inside her, making her featherly caresses turn insistent.

He pulled her down onto the bed with him. Skin sliding on skin, he molded their bodies together until they were touching at every point. "Do you feel me now?"

"Yes," she gasped, clinging to him with every part of her.

"Good." He brought his mouth close to hers—so close they had to share the same breath. "Because I want you to feel me. All of me." His hips pressed hers deep into the mattress. "Just like I want to feel all of you." He slipped between her thighs, his mouth swallowing up the moan that escaped her.

With agonizingly slow strokes, he began sliding up against

her, melting her. Heat flowed under her skin, streaming from somewhere deep inside her with a molten rush. She opened to him completely: her mouth, her body, her unknown self. Her eager abandonment nearly drove him over the edge and his movement quickened; he filled her mouth with deep, hard thrusts of his tongue. He couldn't get enough of her. And he wanted more.

Responding to her readiness, he entered her. He was surprised when Loris cried out, her body stiffening in pain. Unable to stop himself, he thrust deeper inside her, and then he was stopped by a barrier. He realized in amazement that she was a virgin, yet her response to his lovemaking had been without hesitation, sensual and uninhibited. He was even more astonished that she would give herself to him so easily her first time, asking nothing in return.

Loris cried out again when he withdrew from her, but this time from a sense of loss. "Why did you stop? Am I doing it all wrong?"

"Christ, no! I was hurting you."

"A little," she admitted, "but it was wonderful, too." Her face glowed as if lit from within, blinding him. Her lips, still wet from his and a bit swollen, remained invitingly open. He was aware of the violent tremors coursing through her body, of the aftershocks from his too-sudden invasion, but she still offered him all of herself.

Cal was taken by a surge of love for her then, an infinite tenderness that went as deep as his blood. "Why didn't you tell me?"

"Would it have mattered?"

"Yes, I . . . no. No!" He knew now that nothing could have kept him from her any longer, just as he'd always known that, once started, theirs would not be a casual fling. It was one of the reasons he'd tried so hard to stay away from her all these months. "But, if I'd known, I'd have gone more slowly with you."

"Oh, don't change anything," she said with a radiant smile. "I never dreamt it could be so beautiful."

She arched into him, entwining her fingers in his hair and

bringing his mouth back to hers in swift, tender kisses. He let his tongue trail all the way down her body.

Softly, soothingly, he brushed his face over the silken curve of her stomach, his mouth leaving warm, wet traces on her skin when he moved farther down. He nuzzled her dark, damp curls, then parted her thighs and wrapped her legs around his shoulders. He opened her up with his tongue.

Loris gasped, shocked that he would want to kiss her there, the most shameful part of her body. She started to pull away from him.

"No!" He slid both hands under her. Cupping her bottom, he raised her to his lips and his mouth worshipped her.

Liquid fire flickered through her, flared intensely as his caresses quickened, deepened, until she was twisting wildly beneath him, tongues of flame licking at her, darting inside her, burning her up alive. Everything seemed to explode in and around her at the same time. She quivered, incandescent, and melted over him. She didn't know her body was capable of experiencing any more pleasure until she felt the velvety tip of him easing inside her, his deliberately slow movements drawing out the excitement that was building in her again, almost unendurably. It took all the willpower Cal possessed to move slowly. He was dying to completely bury himself inside her. But when he broke through the obstacle to their full union, he couldn't stop.

Loris arched her hips and pushed against Cal with all her strength. She felt a sharp, tearing sensation, but she didn't hesitate. His arms tightened around her, his body seeking to absorb the impact of their coming together. He had to force himself to remain perfectly still for a moment: she felt like liquid fire shuddering helplessly around him, and he knew if he moved inside her, just once, he would lose all control.

Loris loved him so much she could barely breathe. She couldn't get close enough to him. Ecstatically, she wrapped her arms and legs around him, drawing him deeper into her heat and softness. The tremor that shook him reverberated inside her. When he took her mouth in a fierce kiss, she tasted herself on his tongue.

The world dissolved around her. She didn't know who began the tantalizingly slow movements this time because they moved as one. They were quickly caught up in the driving rhythm set by the pounding of their blood. With each deepening thrust she could feel herself slipping further away from herself, coming apart bit by bit, opening herself to him until he was so deep inside her he touched her very womb. Her body fused with his; there was no longer any point where she ended and he began. They were one, body and soul, consumed in the same burning, convulsive explosion.

They held each other for a long time—much longer than was needed for their hearts to resume beating normally. The emotional intensity of their lovemaking had left them both deeply shaken and dazed.

Then, piece by piece, the world took shape around them: traffic noises rattled the windowpanes; the amber glow from the lamp illuminated the cracks in the ceiling; someone in another apartment played an old Gershwin record. Like the plaintive strains of the love song, reality returned.

It was time for Cal to go home to his wife.

CHAPTER
Thirteen

"You're sure you don't want to spend the holidays with me and mine in scintillating New Rochelle?" Pat asked.

Seated beneath the benevolent glare of W.C. Fields, Loris shook her head.

They were having dinner at Joe Allen's, a popular hangout for theater people. The bare wood floor, low ceiling, plain wooden chairs, and red-and-white-checkered tablecloths contributed to its bistro ambiance; antique lighting fixtures gave off a relaxing amber glow. One long, brick wall was covered with theatrical posters and photos of legendary Broadway stars. A row of brick arches, through which the bar was visible, formed a wall, where they were seated. Because of the season, pots of white poinsettia dangled festively from the center of each arch.

Loris was sure W.C. Fields would not have approved. She'd never believed his dying on Christmas Day was a coincidence; he must have dreaded the holiday as much as she did.

"My family—both sides of them—will be delighted to have you," Pat persisted. "And you'd get to celebrate Chanukah, as well as Christmas."

"Thanks, Pat, but I'd just be in the way."

"You wouldn't be in the way any more than I am." Both of Pat's parents had remarried within their religion; each now had a child with their new spouse. "In my father's house I'm half shiksa, in my mother's, I'm half Jew. It would be nice to have a fellow alien on my side."

"If they make you feel that way, why do you go back every year?" Loris asked. "Why do you put up with it?"

"Who the hell knows?" Pat stirred the jalapēno pepper in her Cajun martini. "Probably for the same reason you put up with being alone while Cal celebrates the holidays with his wife: I'm used to this shit."

Loris didn't need to be reminded of what was in store for her, nor did she want to talk about it. Turning her head, she looked through the arch at the bar, which was jammed with revelers getting a three-day head start on Christmas. Two men stranded on the fringe, both in their thirties and reasonably attractive, were staring at her. She could tell at a glance that they weren't regular patrons. The ultraconservative cut of their hair and suits marked them as businessmen; the way they were ogling her made it clear they were on the prowl.

Having learned from experience that if she looked directly at a man for more than a second it was taken as an invitation to approach her, she quickly lowered her eyes. But they were already approaching her table. Pat instantly knew what was happening as soon as she saw the change in Loris's expression.

"Hi, I'm Bob," the tall, sandy-haired man said, leaning casually against the other side of the arch directly across from Loris. "I'd like to buy—"

"Ve vant to be alone," Pat said, mimicking Garbo.

"Hey, that's a great imitation," Bob said. "That's what's-her-names, right?"

"Right," said Pat. "Goodbye."

"And my name's Dick," the shorter, dark one with the boyish features told Loris boozily. "Easiest name in the work to remember." He winked suggestively. "Just think of a dick." Both men laughed uproariously, almost spilling their drinks.

Loris had let her hair grow long since coming to New York; she tucked a shoulder-length strand behind one ear.

"That *is* easy to remember," Pat agreed. "Dick. Rhymes with prick."

Dick frowned, perplexed. He wasn't sure if the flat-chested one was joking or being insulting, and the one with the great tits was ignoring him altogether. Bob clapped him on the back. "She's sure got your number. You better watch out for that one. She's smart." He took a quick gulp of his Scotch. "Hey, listen, how about you gals having a couple of drinks with us to celebrate the holidays."

"Some other time," said Pat.

"But this is our last night in New York," Bob insisted. "We're flying back to Denver tomorrow morning."

"And we always make it a rule," Dick informed Loris, "never to take any traveler's checks back with us. Between the two of us, we've got almost a thousand bucks left."

Bob flashed Loris a patently seductive smile. "We could have us a great time on that kind of money."

"Look, if you creeps don't—" Pat began before Dick cut her off contemptuously.

"We're not talking to you. We're talking to her." He turned back to Loris, leaning toward her through the opening in the arch. "Come on, what do you say?"

Loris finally looked at the two men directly, her face a mask.

"Come on, huh?" Dick urged, sweat beading his upper lip. He was already imagining the taste of her tits. "What do you say?"

"Fuck off," said Pat. "Or I'll call the manager."

Dick pulled himself up indignantly. "Nobody's got any Christmas spirit anymore," he complained as Bob dragged him back to the bar.

Pat laughed harshly. ''We already have plenty of jerks in New York. You wouldn't think they'd have to import them from Denver.''

''It's me,'' Loris said. She'd been coming to that conclusion more and more lately. ''There's something about me that makes men . . .'' Her words trailed off, and when she picked up her drink, her hand was trembling.

''Loris, you can't blame yourself for the creeps in this world.''

''Then, why does this always happen to me?''

''With that face and body, how can you expect men not to come on to you?''

''It's the *way* they come on to me, Pat. You heard that guy just now. He practically offered me money. That's not the first time that's happened. Strangers come up to me on the street all the time. You wouldn't believe the things they say to me.'' A hopeless sigh escaped her. ''I don't know, maybe they're right. Maybe they see something in me I'm not aware of. Why else would they treat me like a two-bit whore?''

''Because you let them. I keep telling you, Loris, you've got to stand up for yourself. Don't be so passive—it only encourages them.''

''I just get so confused and upset,'' Loris explained miserably. ''When they look at me or talk to me like that, it makes me feel like I *am* a whore.''

''You've got a long way to go before you qualify for that title.'' Pat signaled their waiter for another round of drinks. ''One lover doesn't quite do it.''

Loris stared into her empty goblet. ''Even with Cal lately, I . . . I can't help wondering if all he really wants from me is sex.''

''That's exactly what I've been talking about. This affair's been going on for almost ten months. Don't you think it's time you pressured him into getting a divorce?''

''I can't do that.'' She pulled herself up proudly. ''It's up to Cal to make that decision.''

''Why should he? He's got it made. He's got his family,

and he's got you. He's like two different people, Loris. At home he's a family man with typical middle-class values; with you he's an uninhibited lover and avant-garde artist. One of these days, he's going to have to decide who he really is."

"That's something only he can work out for himself."

"I don't think he can. He's incapable of committing himself totally—either to you or to his work."

"That's not fair. No one's worked harder than Cal these past few months, trying to get the group going again."

As Pat had predicted on that disastrous opening night in March, without a rave review from *The Village Voice*, she was unable to find angels to back an Off-Broadway production of *High Point*. During the following months she'd managed to beg and borrow enough money to rent a basement on the Lower East Side that had previously been a gypsy tea room. The whole company had pitched in to build a stage in the round, which Cal had designed, along with the intricate lighting system. The Lower Depths, as Pat had named the café theater, would be ready to open soon after the holidays.

"I was talking about an emotional commitment," Pat said. "He's using you, Loris, and you're letting him."

"No, he . . ." She paused as their waiter set their fresh drinks before them, then hurried off to take care of another party. "Cal's not like that. He loves me."

"His love, and a token, will get you in the subway," Pat stated bluntly. "If Cal really loved you, he'd get a divorce."

"It's not as easy for him as you think, Pat," Loris returned in her lover's defense. "You don't know how much Cal suffered as a boy because his father walked out on him. How can I ask him to inflict the same pain on his own son?"

"How long can you go on this way?"

"I don't know," Loris admitted "The happier I am with him, the more miserable I am when he's not there. Sometimes I feel, as I'm lying in bed after we make love, that if I have to watch him put on his clothes to go home to his wife one more time, I'll scream."

"You should scream. Maybe he wouldn't go home then. You've got to fight for what you want in this world, Loris. Force Cal to choose between you and his wife."

"Oh, no," she gasped, making Pat realize that it wasn't pride keeping Loris from confronting her lover, but fear. She'd never recovered from her father's rejection, and if Cal rejected her also, it would be a devastating blow to her already shaky ego.

"Maybe you should go away for a while," Pat suggested. "It would give you time to think things through, and make Cal realize what his life would be like without you. Artie's decided to accept that directing gig with the regional theater in Pittsburgh, you know."

"Yes, he told me. He asked me to join the company."

"It's only for three months."

"Three months without seeing Cal? I don't know how I'm going to get through this week without him!"

"Why? Is he going away for the holiday?"

"No, his mother's visiting, and he took the week off from work, so he won't be able to find an excuse to . . . see me." Her hands clenched into fists, long nails digging into her palms. "Oh, I get so mad at myself sometimes. I swore to myself that no one would ever make me feel like . . . like an unwanted bastard who has to be hidden away so they can all pretend I don't exist."

"Come spend the holidays with me," Pat insisted. "You shouldn't be by yourself in the mood you're in."

Loris shook her head adamantly. "I don't belong there, either. And I can't be with other people when I'm like this." She took a long gulp of her drink. "Besides, I can use the time alone to think things through, like you said. I can't go on like this anymore. I've got to do something about it."

Having had no one she could turn to for comfort after her mother died, Loris never sought the company of others when she was unhappy. She kept to herself that endless holiday week, as if unhappiness was something to be ashamed of, her own fault. Nor did she attend Pat's New Year's Eve party, as she'd promised. Everyone else would have a date—someone to share the traditional midnight kiss with—and Loris didn't need to be reminded of her single status.

It occurred to her that she hadn't received a Christmas card from Miss Prescott this year. Loris had written her when she'd first moved in, telling her about her new apartment and the theater group she'd joined. Her letter had gone unanswered. The last frail link between herself and her father, she knew now, had been severed for good.

Escaping into her own fantasy world had been Loris's only defense against feeling unwanted as a child. Since coming to New York she'd discovered the ready-made fantasy world of movies—especially old ones. Buying a VCR had been the one luxury she'd allowed herself, and she'd already taped well over a hundred films.

Tonight, she decided, it would take nothing less than an epic to lift her out of the depression that was rapidly enveloping her. She needed to lose herself in another time and place, lush sets and costumes, a wonderful love story.

The film Loris finally selected was *Dr. Zhivago*. She soon realized it was not the smartest possible choice. At first, as she sat propped up against the pillows, sipping the New York State champagne she'd bought herself, she got caught up in the sweep of historical events, the stunning power and beauty of the images. But as the tragic love affair between Lara and Zhivago unfolded, mirroring the hopelessness of her relationship with Cal, the pain she'd sought to escape overwhelmed her. She couldn't bear to watch the ending.

She switched off the movie; images of Cal celebrating New Year's Eve with his wife flooded her mind. Instead of blurring them, the champagne made them sharper still. The sound of noisemakers and tin horns, boisterous shouting and laughter, spilled out of neighboring apartments into the hallways. Firecrackers exploded outside her windows, marking the passing of the old year, and celebrating the promise of the new one.

Tears streaming down her face, Loris made a single New Year's resolution: to break off her affair with Cal.

She began January 1, 1981 nursing her first hangover. With a special actor's script on her lap, a notebook by her side, she began studying her part. She was scheduled to do Maggie's first-act monologue from *Cat on a Hot Tin Roof* in class at the end of the week, and she still didn't have her lines down.

She was having trouble concentrating. Her thoughts kept drifting back to Cal. Instead of learning her lines, she found herself rehearsing what she would say to him when they met the following evening. As if she were breaking a scene down into beats, she began writing out the reasons they couldn't go on seeing each other.

She was so involved in her task, she wasn't sure at first if she actually heard the key turn in the lock or if it was merely her imagination. Pen poised in midair, she glanced up from her notebook as the door flew open and Cal came in. He was breathless, having taken the stairs at a run. His hair was wind-blown, his skin glowing from being out in the cold, and when he looked over at her, excitement sparkled in his eyes.

Loris had the feeling that she'd been shut away in a dark room and someone had suddenly thrown open the shuttered windows, letting in the dazzling sunlight. She cursed herself silently, and him, as well. But that didn't alter her feelings. "What are you doing here?"

"I had to see you." His voice was deep, intense.

"But, I thought you said tomorrow."

"I couldn't wait till then. I've been trying all week to find a way to come and see you. This is the first chance I've had to get away." He pulled off his coat and tossed it onto one of the clothes pegs. He was wearing a fisherman's sweater that clung comfortably to the sleek muscles of his shoulders and chest; well-worn jeans sheathed his long legs.

"I just saw my mother off at LaGuardia," he explained, crossing over to her. "I'm supposed to be on my way home, so I can't stay more than fifteen or twenty minutes."

She stared at him, unable to conceal her surprise. It was close to an hour's drive, each way, from Queens to the West Side of Manhattan, when there wasn't any traffic.

He smiled crookedly. "I know it's kinda crazy, but I had to see you—even if it's only for a few minutes."

"Hardly seems worth the trouble," Loris told her notebook, keeping her eyes fixed on the list she'd just made—all the reasons she shouldn't go on seeing him.

Loris let Cal kiss her, even enjoyed the feel of his lips on hers, so soft and warm, but a part of her was watching him as if she were studying the performance of an actor whose technique she particularly admired. Sensing her detachment, he slid his arms around her back, pulling her hard against him. His kiss became intense, his mouth moving on hers with that hunger she always found so arousing.

She pushed away from him. "Cal, I—"

"Christ, but I'm dying for you." Sinking both hands in her hair, he drew her face back to him. "After all this time, I still can't get enough of you. You're so delicious." With long, slow strokes he slid his tongue from one corner of her lips to the other. "I can taste you in my sleep, you know that? All of you."

Loris fought to deny the impact her lover's words had on her, but the sensual memories they evoked were reflected deep in her eyes, and he saw them. He moved to kiss her again. "No, don't, Cal." She resented the power he had over her, the ease with which he used that power. "It's not fair."

"Yeah, you're right," he drawled, releasing her. "I better not start something I can't finish."

"That shouldn't be a problem for *you*. What you started with me you can finish with your wife."

Cal pulled back in surprise. "Is that what you think of me . . . of us?"

"Your twenty minutes are up."

"Let *me* worry about the time, okay? Just answer my question, Loris. Is that what you really think?"

"Yes. And I . . . I don't want to see you anymore, Cal."

He went very still, his face darkening as he stared at her.

Then, without a word, he got up and stalked over to the clothes tree. Her heart gave a terrible jolt, and she suddenly wished she could have taken back her words. Instead of throwing on his coat and storming out, as she'd expected, he reached into a side pocket and took out a pack of cigarettes and a lighter. Keeping his back to her, he lit up and took a couple of deep drags.

"Tell me something," he said finally, smoke trailing his words as he walked back to her. "If that's what I've got waiting for me at home, then what the hell am I doing here?" He tossed the cigarette pack and lighter on the table next to the ashtray she kept there just for him. "If I had with her what I have with you, why would I have gotten involved with you in the first place?"

"You obviously still have *something* with her."

"Yes. I have a son. That's the one thing—the only thing—she's ever given me I'll always be grateful to her for. And I'm not about to apologize for that, either. But the way I feel about you . . . I never felt that way with her. I swear to Christ, Loris, I've never loved any woman the way I love you. I never knew I could."

It was not an easy admission for Cal. Seeing the doubts lingering in her eyes left him feeling all the more vulnerable. "You don't believe that."

"I don't know what to believe anymore, you've got me so confused," Loris cried

"You're the best thing that's ever happened to me, Loris. If I thought I'd screwed this up, the way I've screwed up everything else, I . . . I don't know what I'd do." He rubbed his forehead, trying to relieve the pressure building behind his eyes. "I've known for a long time now that I've got to make a decision. I've thought about it a lot. But no matter what I do, I'm going to slam someone I love."

In the silence that followed Cal's halting words, Loris sought to extricate herself from the effect they'd had on her. "I have to go away," she said, voicing her growing realization aloud. "As long as I see you, or even speak to you, I'll never be able to break this off."

"Loris, I—"

"I've been offered a job with a regional company in Pittsburgh. I'm going to take it. It's the only way."

"Oh, Christ, don't do that. Please don't do that."

She was too stunned by the anguish in his voice, the tears flooding his eyes, to reply.

Grabbing her by the shoulders, he pulled her close. "I want us to live together . . . as much as you do. Just give me a little time. I'll find a way." A tear slid down his cheek, got caught in the corner of his mouth. She tasted it when he kissed her. "I promise," he said.

CHAPTER
Fourteen

Loris turned off the oven. Cal was late, and she didn't want the Rock Cornish game hens she was roasting for dinner to dry out. The wild rice she'd cooked on top of the stove was ready; the salad was crisping in the refrigerator. As she walked through the slightly lopsided arch that separated the kitchen from the living room, she wondered what problems he was having, and whether they would interfere with his seeing her again tonight.

Loris heard the key turn in the lock. Cal barely had the chance to close the door behind him when she threw herself into his arms. "I wasn't sure I was going to see you."

He pulled away. "It's drizzling out. I'm all wet."

"I don't care."

"You'll ruin your lovely outfit. Here." He placed the brown paper bag he was carrying between them. "I stopped off for a bottle of V.O."

"I still have some." She always kept a bottle of his

favorite liquor on hand. The bag was heavier than she'd expected. She peeked inside. "More goodies?"

"I got you a couple of bottles of wine."

"Thanks." While Cal pulled out of his bomber jacket and hung it on the coat rack, Loris stepped through the lopsided arch into the kitchen. "It hasn't started snowing yet?"

"It's supposed to snow again?"

She laughed. "Didn't you hear the weather reports? There's a storm warning. They're expecting ten to twelve inches."

"Christ, that's all I need."

His grim tone brought her up short in front of the bathtub and she looked over at him, searchingly. She'd been so glad to see him, she hadn't noticed that his face was drawn, without color. "What's wrong, Cal?"

He let out a heavy sigh. "You better put down the bottles."

Loris set the bag down on the removable metal top that covered the bathtub and served as a kitchen counter. "What is it? What's happened?"

"She's found out about us."

"Oh, my God. But how—"

"That's not all." His voice cracked and he ran his fingers roughly through his damp hair. "I sure could use a drink. Would you mind getting me one?"

"No . . . of course not."

"Thanks." He turned abruptly and walked into the living room, his shoulder sagging uncharacteristically.

Loris's mind was a jumble of questions. Her hands were unsteady as she prepared his usual drink—a generous shot of V.O. on the rocks with a splash of water. She made one for herself, though she rarely drank hard liquor. She had a feeling she was going to need it.

The sound of the rain tapping insistently on the windows filled the silent apartment, adding to her uneasiness for some strange reason, as Loris carried the drinks over to Cal. She'd expected to find him on the studio bed, sitting up against the pillows, long legs stretched out comfortably. He was sitting stiffly in the corner armchair instead, staring into space, eyes blank.

She was gripped by a sudden, paralyzing anxiety.

The feeling was only too familiar to her, but she'd never experienced it while awake before. Since childhood she'd been haunted by a recurring nightmare that was so real she often wondered whether she was reliving a forgotten trauma. Every time she dragged herself back to consciousness, heart pounding, dripping with sweat, the terrifying images dissolved before she could make any connections. She was sure it was the same dream because she was always left with an agonizing sense of loss, and the sensation—which enveloped her now as she watched Cal, so completely withdrawn from her—that she was invisible. She didn't exist.

"Cal," she called sharply, shattering the daze he was in. "Your drink." He murmured a distracted thanks when she handed him the glass.

Clutching her own glass, Loris sat on the corner of the bed directly opposite the rattan armchair. The sound of the rain was beginning to grate on her nerves. She took a quick gulp of whiskey. It burned a path through her constricted throat. She was unable to ask the question that reverberated in her mind: what was going to happen to them now that Julie Ann knew?

"It's Julie Ann. She . . ." Cal needed to take a good stiff gulp before he was able to continue. "She smashed herself up in the car."

Loris gasped, but no sound came out. "She's not . . ."

"No, but she could have been. She's hurt, though, and . . . and it's all my fault." Tears stung his eyes and he pressed thumb and index finger against his eyelids, trying to physically hold back the tears. "It's all my fault."

Wanting to comfort him, Loris rushed to his side. He pulled away from her. "No, it's okay," he insisted, his hand an open fist in front of his face, like a boxer making a last effort to defend himself. "I'm okay."

"Cal, please," she begged, unable to understand why he

felt he needed to hide his feelings from her. He never had before. "Please, let me—"

"No," With the open palm of his hand he pushed blindly at the air, waving her back. "I'm okay. Really."

Loris backed up to the edge of the mattress, then sank down onto the bed. She sipped her drink while she waited for Cal to finish lighting a cigarette. She let him take several deep, calming drags on it before asking, "Why is it your fault?"

He exhaled harshly. "Because I should have known better. I've been expecting something to happen for the past three weeks—ever since we went into rehearsals with the new play."

"So have I," Loris admitted.

"But, I sure wasn't ready for this," he went on, as if he was speaking to himself. "How dumb can you get? It's not as if it's the first time she's pulled this on me. When she told me, I . . ." His words broke off, and he knocked back the rest of his drink.

"I don't understand. You mean . . . about us?" She leaned toward him. "What did she tell you?"

"I need another drink." He hauled himself to his feet. "She really laid down the law this time," he explained on his way to the kitchen. "We were up half the night Sunday arguing." Without breaking stride he grabbed the bottle of V.O. off the metal bathtub top and brought it back to the living room with him. "I tried to make her understand that I can't be what she wants me to be. I can't give her what she needs, either. I've stopped trying to. But she actually believes things can be the way they were between us that first year, right after Brian was born." A look came into his eyes, and when he spoke again his tone was soft, rueful. "That was the happiest year of our marriage." He took a final drag on his cigarette before putting it out, then made himself another drink. "It's all up to me, of course. All I have to do is give up directing. And you."

It was a long moment before Loris could speak. "How did she find out about us?"

"She claims she called me at the theater one Friday night, several months ago. Whoever answered—it was probably Greg—told her the meeting had been over a couple of hours already. She insisted she had to get in touch with me . . . an emergency involving my son. So he gave her *your* phone number." He made an attempt at a laugh, but it came out a cough. "I guess everybody knows about us."

"But, she never called here, Cal."

"And there was no emergency."

"I don't understand any of this. If she's known about us for months, why did she wait until now to say something?"

"Julie Ann's not very good at confronting things directly. In fact, I probably could have denied everything and gotten away with it. I know now that's what she really wanted to hear, but I couldn't do it. I admitted that I love you . . . that we love each other. I told her I couldn't give you up."

Relief flooded Loris when she heard that, but then she thought of how his wife must have felt, and she was ashamed of her happiness. She knew how devastated *she* would be if Cal told her he loved another woman.

"She said she'd never give me a divorce, and unless I stopped seeing you, she would leave me and take Brian with her. She swore she'd fix it so I'd never see him again."

"She can't do that!"

"The hell she can't! And she would, too, if it ever came down to that, but she *knows* I'd never give up my son." His mouth twisted bitterly. "She knows me very well. Anyway, I . . . I just went crazy after that. I mean, I really tore into her. I said things I should never have said, but I felt so trapped—like I was being buried alive. Finally, I couldn't take it anymore. I had to get out of there. Somehow, I knew if I didn't leave then, I never would, so I threw some things in a suitcase and walked out."

His eyes met hers, and held them intensely. "I was coming here to you," he told her, as if it was important to him that she know that.

"What happened then?"

"I'd just started up the car when Julie Ann came tearing

out of the house, tugging Brian behind her. She was
hysterical. She'd dragged the boy out of bed, and she was
screaming at him to tell Daddy to come back home. I got
out of the car to take Brian back inside—it was freezing out,
and he was in his pajamas. There was still snow on the
ground, for Christ's sake! As I was picking him up she ran
past me and jumped behind the wheel of the car. The streets
were still icy and, with the hysterical state she was in, she
lost control of the car and plowed into a tree." He drew in a
long, desperately needed breath, then let it out in shreds.
"She's got a broken arm and a big gash over one eye. The
doctor thinks she might . . . that there might be other
repercussions."

All the guilt that had been festering inside Loris for so
long surged through her: *she* was the one who was to blame.
None of this would have happened if Cal hadn't met her.
"How long will she be in the hospital?"

"They just kept her overnight."

She pulled back, surprised. "Overnight? Then, it can't be
that—"

"The doctor says she's going to have to stay in bed for a
month, maybe more. She's going to need looking after,
so . . ." He sank down into the armchair with a defeated
sigh.

"So, that's why you can't leave her now," Loris concluded for him.

Cal nodded, looking away. "I wish I could. I can't. My
boy saw the whole thing! The crash . . . the blood pouring
down her face. He was crying and screaming through all of
it. I couldn't get him to stop. I kept telling him Mommy's
going to be all right, but . . ." He shook his head angrily.
"Jesus Christ, what a mess!"

He didn't pull away from her when she rushed to his side
this time. She wrapped her arms around him and held him
tight, trying to absorb his pain, share his guilt. His arms
locked around her and he buried his face between her
breasts.

Somehow, they ended up in bed.

He made love to her almost violently, with a kind of desperation that frightened her, as if he meant to leave his mark on her and make it impossible for her to ever forget him. She knew then that he was going to leave her. She tried to tell him with her body what she knew he didn't want to hear in words: how much she loved him, how good it was with them, how happy they could be together. With her hands and her mouth and her tongue, she begged him to stay.

Afterward, he dressed quickly, his back to her. "I can't see you anymore—you know that, don't you?" he said as he zipped up his bomber jacket. "I've got to straighten out the mess I've made."

Loris didn't answer; it was all she could do to nod. She felt as if she were breaking up inside.

"I really do love you," Cal added ruefully, just before he let himself out. He slid the key she'd given him under the door after he'd locked it behind him.

"What is this, the black hole of Calcutta?" Pat exclaimed when Loris reluctantly let her into her apartment. The shades were drawn against the brilliant sunshine; the flickering reflection from the TV blaring away in one corner of the living room provided scant illumination.

"The light hurts my eyes," Loris said on her way back to bed.

"But, it's a gorgeous day out. New York is a summer festival, just like the ads say." With her typical no-nonsense manner, Pat headed straight for the windows. Over Loris's objections, she pulled both shades up as far as they would go. "See? The sun is shining. The sky is bright blue. And all the window boxes are in bloom."

"I think I'll throw up," said Loris.

Pat frowned. Sarcasm was a new addition to her friend's repertoire, and she was shocked by the change in Loris's appearance since she'd seen her last. She wished she could have been more help to her these past months.

From the beginning of April to the end of May, Pat had

been in Canada, working as assistant producer on a documentary for PBS. She called Loris every Sunday, and was progressively disturbed by the way she sounded. It was almost three months since Cal had broken off their affair; instead of lessening with time, Loris's depression had deepened. Concerned, Pat had gotten in touch with her when she had gotten back to New York on Monday; for the past five days, Loris had found excuses for not seeing her.

Patricia H. Schwartz was not one to be put off, however—especially when she believed a friend of hers needed help. So, on that lovely first Saturday in June, she showed up on Loris's doorstep uninvited, determined to drag her, kicking and screaming if necessary, back to the world of the living.

"Jesus, Loris, you look horrible," she told her with characteristic bluntness. She had to raise her voice to be heard over the TV. "You're so thin and pale you could play Camille without makeup."

Lying propped up against a mound of pillows, Loris gave an unconcerned shrug and continued to stare blankly at the movie playing on her VCR.

"Do you have to play that thing so loud? You can't hear yourself think."

"That's the idea."

"Well, it's not a very bright one." Bending over, Pat grabbed the remote control unit from the bed and flicked off the TV.

"Don't, Pat," Loris said, holding out her hand. "Give it back to me." She couldn't bear the silence these days. She even slept with the TV on—when she slept.

Pat set the remote control out of Loris's reach. "I thought we'd go down to the Village, browse through the antique shops, take in the outdoor art show, then grab a pizza at Emilio's." She let out a heartfelt groan. "I haven't had a pizza in two months. And you sure as hell look like you could use one."

The thought of food was enough to make Loris nauseated. "I'm not hungry."

"The courtyard at Emilio's should be open now," Pat

went on, as if Loris hadn't spoken, "so we can eat outdoors under the trees and fire escapes, and chew the fat along with the pizza, the way we used to. Okay?"

Loris shook her head listlessly. "I can't."

"Why not? You've got something better planned?" Pat pointed an accusing finger at the telephone resting on the covers, right up against Loris's thigh. "Like spending every night and all your days off waiting for the phone to ring? He's not going to call you, Loris. You've got to stop expecting him to."

"Yes, he will," she said softly, her eyes shadowed, enormous in her pale face. "He's only staying with her until she gets back on her feet."

"Is that what he told you?"

Loris tugged a long strand of hair behind one ear. "Shouldn't they have removed the cast on her arm by now?"

"He's not coming back, Loris!"

"Yes, he is. He is. You'll see," she replied soothingly, as if Pat were the one who needed reassuring. "He was all set to leave her. I told you. that's why she had the accident. He was coming to live with me." A smile flickered across her face, lit up her eyes. "He really loves me. He told me so that . . . that night."

The light went out of her eyes again.

Pat felt a surge of anger so intense that she wished Cal were there, so she could give him a good, swift kick in the balls. She realized she couldn't hide the truth from Loris any longer. She had to destroy the illusions she was clinging to. She sat down on the edge of the bed next to her. "I saw Cal the other night. He stopped by The Lower Depths to—"

"Did he ask about me?"

The longing in her voice, suffusing her face, was so intense that Pat was almost tempted to lie. "No, he didn't. And the only reason he came by was to resign as artistic director—permanently."

"Oh, no," Loris cried. "If he stops directing now, it'll be twice as hard for him to get started again."

"Look, the man made his choice," Pat reminded her.

"And you can just forget about him ever directing again. He's accepted that job his wife's been bugging him about."

"He hates that job. He swore he'd never take it."

"He had no choice. His wife's going to have a baby."

Loris's lips parted, but no sound came out.

"He didn't tell you *that*, did he? Julie Ann was already two months' pregnant when he broke off with you. He may be in love with you, as he claims, but he's obviously been sleeping with her all along. And if he didn't leave her before, he sure as hell isn't going to leave her now." A regretful sigh escaped her. "I'm sorry I had to tell you all this, but—"

"No, you're not," Loris cut her off coldly. "You always said he was playing me for a fool, and you were right. You just couldn't wait to rub it in, could you?"

"Jesus, Loris, I'm only trying to help you," Pat protested. "I couldn't let you go on deluding yourself about Cal. No matter how painful the truth is, at least you know where you stand now. You can forget about him and get on with your life."

"Considering *your* track record with men, *you* should be the last one to give advice to the lovelorn," Loris said, turning on Pat with all the hurt and anger that were in her. "If you're so damn smart, why do you keep playing mother to a succession of losers? Everybody knows they only stay with you because they can live off you while they pursue their dubious artistic talents. And they always end up dumping you for a more convenient meal ticket, or a prettier face."

Pat was barely out the door when Loris regretted her unfair words, but she didn't call her back. Then, everything caved in on her. She hadn't cried with such deep, racking sobs since her mother died. She cried for a long time, and when she was through, she swore to herself that she would never cry over someone again. Nor would she ever love anyone again, which amounted to the same thing.

* * *

Loris had the strangest sensation when she woke up the following morning. She felt as though she'd been sick for a long time, but was better now—as though she'd almost died, but hadn't. She knew she would never be the same again.

Pat had been right, of course: she could no longer go on deluding herself about Cal. The truth was even more painful than her friend had predicted, and she did know exactly where she stood now. Alone. Unloved. She'd lived without love most of her life, she told herself, and she'd survived. She would survive this, too.

The change she'd undergone overnight made her see everything differently. When Loris looked around her apartment, she saw through her pathetic attempts to disguise what, in reality, was a dilapidated, cockroach-infested tenement flat. She remembered how happy she'd been when she had first moved in, how she'd fixed the place up. She couldn't believe she'd been naive enough to believe it was beautiful.

While she dressed, she thought about her job as a cocktail waitress; she hated it more than she'd ever admitted to herself. Most of the money she earned went for classes, or to help Pat keep the group afloat. And she had nothing to show for all the money and time and backbreaking work she'd put into their avant-garde productions. For all practical purposes, she was no further along in her career at that moment than she had been when she had come to New York two years ago.

Recalling the vow she'd made to herself on her graduation day, Loris wondered how she could have strayed so far from her original goal.

"I'm through making sacrifices for my so-called art," she informed Pat when Pat phoned that evening to find out how Loris was feeling. "I've decided to drop out of the group. I've had it with being an idealistic loser. I want to be a success. I'm *going* to be a success. And that means getting involved in the commercial theater."

There was a long pause at Pat's end. She'd been about to

advise Loris not to throw away everything she'd worked so hard for these past two years, but she stopped herself. She was only too aware of the real reason Loris was dropping out of the group, and she couldn't blame her.

"If that's what you really want, then you should go for it," Pat said at last. But she was concerned that Loris, in her desperate attempt to forget Cal, would break off with everyone who might remind her of him—including her. "There'll always be a place for you in the company, you know that. And we can still be friends."

"Of course."

"Let's get together this weekend, okay?"

"I'll call you," Loris said.

But she didn't. That same week she had her telephone number changed; her new one was unlisted.

Part III

CHAPTER
Fifteen

Seven months had passed since Loris had dropped out of the group. She had taken a new job as a barmaid at the Pussy Willow and made more money in three nights than she used to in a week. With the extra time she took new classes and attempted to find an agent.

She'd never felt more alone. Though she didn't allow herself to think of Cal consciously, he continued to invade her dreams. She missed Pat and her other friends in the group more than she would have believed possible; they were the closest she'd ever come to having a family. Several times during the past months she'd been seriously tempted to call Pat, then changed her mind. The Lower Depths, she'd learned from the trade papers, was beginning to find a receptive audience. Artie had become the artistic director of the company, and the *Voice* had given his production of the play Cal had originally planned to direct a good write-up. Subsequent productions had gotten even better reviews. In its article on up-and-coming experimental theater groups

this past Sunday, the *Times* had actually singled out The
Lower Depths; Patricia Schwartz had been compared to the
legendary Ellen Stewart of Café La Mama.

Loris couldn't have been more delighted by Pat's well-
deserved recognition. Recalling her own arrogant boast the
last time she'd spoken to her, however, made it all the more
difficult for her to call Pat now.

Like most aspiring actors, Loris found herself caught in a
dilemma: without an agent, she couldn't get professional
work; unless she was working professionally, she couldn't
get an agent. Several she'd approached had expressed an
interest in representing her—if she went to bed with them.
She'd lost out on the lead in an Off-Broadway show and a
running part on a soap because she'd refused to sleep with
the casting director. She was determined to succeed, but on
her own terms.

*Absolutely No Interviews Without Appointment. Slip Pix
And Résumé Through Slot In Door. Do Not Ring Bell. Do
Not Phone Office. If Interested, Will Call You.*

Loris didn't know why she even bothered to read the sign.
She knew it by heart. It hung on practically every agent's
door in New York City. She unzipped her portfolio automatically and took out a photo, making sure a résumé was
stapled to its back. Lifting the metal tab in the center of the
door, she obediently slipped the photo through the slot.

It's like mailing myself to nowhere, she thought as she
watched her glossy face disappear. Anger welled up inside
her. She was suddenly fed up with always playing by other
people's rules. Defiantly, she rang the doorbell, enjoying the
piercing sound that shattered the silence of the long, empty
hallway, with its double row of locked doors, forbidding
signs.

The door was jerked opened a two-inch crack. An eye
peered out at her. "Yeah?"

She quickly checked the brass name plate over the sign: *T.
Storpio Representation*. "Uhh, Mr. Storpio?"

"Yeah."

"I'm sorry to bother you, but I just dropped off my picture and résumé, and—"

"So?"

"So, I was wondering if I might make an appointment with you . . . for an interview?"

The eye looked at her severely. "Didn't you see the sign?" He sounded annoyed at having been interrupted, and impatient to get back to business. "What's the matter, you can't read?"

"Yes, but—"

"Look, the sign makes it very clear how we operate around here." Opening the door the rest of the way, he looked her up and down, quickly figuring out her age, weight, height, measurements. "Actresses!" he spat out, bending over to retrieve her photo, which he'd been standing on. "Signs don't mean a fucking thing to you people, do they?"

"Yes, usually," she told the top of his head, "but . . ."

While she was trying to think of something to say in her defense, his head moved up her legs, past her hips and waist, hovered around her bust, and ended up just under her chin when he'd straightened up completely. "Six-thirty."

"Excuse me?"

"Come back at six-thirty. I'm all booked up till then." Stepping impatiently back into the shadows, he slammed the door in her face.

Loris stood there for a moment, not quite sure how to react. She decided that Mr. Storpio's rude manner was preferable to the phony charm of those agents who were only interested in going to bed with her. He obviously meant business. She would return at six-thirty, as he'd requested.

She saw no reason to alter the schedule of rounds she'd planned for that day. She tried several other agents who had offices in the same building, but was unable to get past either their door or their receptionist, then went on to an open call for a Broadway show.

Loris showed her paid-up Equity card at the door, signed in on the yellow legal pad, and was waved inside. It was like stepping into a recurring dream. She'd seen what open calls were like before, yet somehow, never this clearly.

Though the call was for 1:30 and it was only 12:45, over a hundred hopefuls were already crammed into the sweltering studio. It was over ninety degrees outside, with the humidity typical of August in New York. There was no air conditioning, nor were there any chairs. The large, completely bare, rectangular room reminded her of an animal pen at a slaughterhouse. No wonder actors referred to these open auditions as cattle calls.

By 1:30 the studio was as packed as the subway at rush hour. A line had started outside the door, and stretched halfway down the hall. Everyone hushed as the assistant director called the first name on the list. Loris checked her watch each time a name was called: the interviews averaged five minutes.

By 2:30, the interviews averaged two minutes. Actors were being passed through like parts on an assembly line. When they left, they were quickly replaced by the new arrivals. By 3:00 there was a double line in the hallway, and the assistant director appeared totally frazzled.

"Can I please have the attention of all you Anitas?" he called out, referring to the name of the female lead in the play.

Loris strained to hear him, along with the other forty or so "exotic" types present.

"If you're over five-feet-five, there's no point in your staying, girls." He had to wave the legal pad to quiet the chorus of protests that went up. "Our star is very sensitive about his height—or rather, lack of it."

"Why didn't you tell us that before?" a brunette who was almost as tall as Loris demanded.

"Because nobody told *me* before, honey. I'm only the assistant director around here."

"That stinks!" another brunette said.

He shrugged. "That's show business."

Without another word of protest, all the taller women filed out of the studio, except for a couple of five-foot-sixers who'd assumed a slouching position. Loris decided she'd had it with making rounds for one day; she spent the rest of the afternoon in an air-conditioned movie. Then she went to her interview with Tony Storpio.

CHAPTER
Sixteen

From behind a desk piled high with scripts and theatrical photos, Tony Storpio was issuing a nonstop, staccato stream of demands into the telephone when he buzzed Loris into his office. Without even pausing to catch his breath, he jabbed an index finger at the black leatherette chair in front of the desk, indicating where he wanted her to sit. Then he proceeded to ignore her. She used the opportunity to study him.

He appeared to be in his mid-forties and was expensively dressed, his curly black hair sleekly groomed. But there was something of the street punk about him; his well-exercised body exuded a uniquely urban menace. Time had coarsened his pretty-boy features, and there was a bitter arrogance to the tilt of his jaw. His voice had a Hoboken, New Jersey accent, making everything he said sound like an insult.

He gave the impression of being intensely driven and fiercely competitive, yet she had to admire the verbal somersaults he was performing. She couldn't help wondering whether he was putting on this show for her benefit, or if it was just his style.

Pausing to let the person at the other end finally have a say, Tony Storpio downed what was left of his drink, then thrust the empty glass at Loris. "Jack Daniels on the rocks with a splash of water," he ordered. "Make yourself whatever you want. It's all there." He gestured toward the compact bar, which was part of a wall unit, facing a black leatherette couch.

"Sure I'm listening, Leonard," he assured his caller, "but you're not telling me anything I wanna hear."

Though her back was to him while she poured the bourbon, then a vodka and tonic for herself, Loris sensed him watching her every movement. He looked away when she brought him the drink and resumed her seat.

With a final, abrupt, "You're gonna have to do better than that, Leonard," he slammed down the receiver. "*Stronz!*" Leaning back in his swivel chair, he took a long, hard pull on his drink. Over the rim of the glass he looked at her, finally acknowledging her presence. His dark eyes, hooded, sardonic, moved slowly down her body. "So, what can I do for you?"

"I'm looking for an agent."

"Isn't everybody?" He set the glass down on the desk, using an actor's photo as a coaster. "But, I'm not an agent. I'm a personal representative."

"I see," said Loris, as if she actually knew the difference. He wasn't fooled, and sounded annoyed at having to explain: "I only handle my own clients. I don't just field job offers—I oversee every aspect of my clients' careers."

"In that case," Loris quipped, refusing to be intimidated by his rudeness, "I'm looking for a personal representative."

His eyes narrowed, and he studied her face as thoroughly as he had her body. "Let's see your book."

Loris quickly unzipped her portfolio and handed it to him across the desk. She sipped her vodka and tonic while he flipped through the plastic-encased photographs with a look of sheer boredom.

He took a moment to study her last, best picture, then slammed the book shut. "You need new pix. One or two of these ain't bad, but they don't sell you."

"Actually, I've been saving money to get new ones made and—"

"You don't *pay* for pix," he cut her off scornfully. "There are plenty of photographers around who'll take test shots of you for nothing. *You* pose for them for free and *they* give you half a dozen of the best shots for your book." He thrust the portfolio back at her. "You're not gonna get anywhere with these. You gotta have full-length shots in bikinis. Show off what you got." His eyes moved over her body again. "Ever done any modeling?"

Loris shook her head. "I'm not thin enough."

"I'm not talking fashion. They use boys for that," he said to her bust. "I'm talking pinups—figure modeling."

"No. But I'm not interested in modeling. I'm an actress."

"No shit?" He took a quick swig of bourbon. "Got a résumé?"

"I gave you one this morning with my eight-by-ten," she reminded him.

"Right." He shuffled things around on his desk; her eight-by-ten was under a stack of unopened mail. In less than a minute he ran through it. "This is it? No TV or movie credits?"

"All of my work has been in the theater," Loris returned proudly. "I'm a member of Equity."

He laughed contemptuously. "You gotta be in the business since the year one to get on Broadway these days." He dropped her pix and résumé on top of a stack of them. "Got any film clips, or a tape? Of a bit part, even? Anything?"

"Uhh, not really."

"Not really." A snort of disgust propelled him out of his chair and around the desk. "Not really! Christ!" His hand shot out unexpectedly. Loris sat back in her chair; for a second, she actually believed he was going to strike her. He took the glass out of her hand, instead. She hadn't realized it was empty.

"Vodka and tonic, right?" He didn't bother to wait for her answer. Pausing only to retrieve his own glass, he hurried over to the bar. "You broads are too much," he muttered over his shoulder while he quickly made the drinks. "You push your way in here with the wrong pictures, no real credits to speak of, and you expect to get a top agent to represent you."

"I may not know about the commercial end of it," she admitted defensively, "but I know I can act."

"Act?" He laughed sarcastically, making her realize that she sounded like a character in a bad movie. "The unemployment lines in this city are full of people who can act better than you."

"How do you know? You've never seen me—"

"Hey, look, I'm not interested in actors," he sneered. Picking up the drinks, he started toward her. "I deal with professionals here, not actors. And I know an amateur when I see one." He practically shoved the drink in her hand before continuing over to his chair. "It's my business. So, don't tell me, okay?"

"Then, why the hell did you ask to see my book?" Loris demanded, fed up with being treated like a nonentity. "Why did you make an appointment to see me in the first place?"

Tony Storpio smiled. "I got a thing for big boobs."

Slamming her untouched drink down on the desk, Loris grabbed her purse and portfolio and got to her feet.

"Come on, don't be so sensitive. You can't be sensitive if you're gonna stay in this business," he muttered bitterly. "Look, you came here 'cause you thought I could help you, right? Well, I can. So maybe I didn't tell you what you wanted to hear, but I told it to you straight. That's more than you're gonna get from most people in this fucking business."

Loris hesitated as she was about to step away from the

desk. If nothing else, she was forced to admit that he had been brutally honest.

He waved her back into her chair. "Go on, sit down. You might learn something." He knocked back some more bourbon while he waited until she was seated again. "Lesson number one: you could be the best fucking actress in the world, but it's not gonna get you one day's work. I don't sell actors. I sell image. You're a great-looking broad, but this town's full of great-looking broads. You got *one* thing that sets you apart from the rest." He pointed an index finger at her breasts and wiggled it from one to the other. "Those. *That's* what you gotta go with. Because that's what you got that's saleable. You married?"

"Uhh . . . no."

"Involved?"

"No."

"What do you do for money?"

"I work nights . . . as a barmaid."

He snorted derisively. "Terrific."

"The money's better than waitressing, and it leaves my afternoons free for classes, to make rounds, and—"

"How long has this been goin' on?"

Loris swallowed hard. "Almost three years."

Shaking his head, he picked up her résumé and sent it sailing across the desk to her. "Not much to show for almost three years, is it?"

She stiffened defensively. "It won't always be this way."

"You wanna bet?"

The humiliation of the cattle call was still raw in her mind, making it impossible for Loris to answer. She reached for her drink and took a long gulp.

"I might consider working with you," Tony Storpio was saying. "I got some ideas on how you should present yourself for the kinda parts I'm sure I can get you."

Since his attitude toward her was as rude as ever, she wasn't sure she'd heard him correctly.

"But we gotta change your image," he was quick to add. "You willing to go along with that?"

"If that's what it takes to get acting jobs," Loris replied unhesitatingly. "Yes, of course."

A cynical little smile flickered across Tony Storpio's face. He'd anticipated her answer, had counted on her hunger to succeed. "Then, it's a deal—on one condition." His eyes met hers with a level stare. "I tell you what you gotta do to make it in this business, and you do it. Understood?"

She held his gave unflinchingly. "Understood."

"Okay." Suddenly galvanized into action, he began a frantic search through the mounds of papers on his desk. "Now, there's somebody I want you to see. Ever heard of Alex Kagan?"

"The photographer? Who hasn't?"

"Nobody in the business has got a better eye for flesh than Kagan. He's launched most of the top models of the past twenty years. You listen to me, and I guarantee you, he'll take the test shots of you himself. You'll have the classiest book in the city. And that's just the beginning." Having found the address book he'd been searching for, he used it to wave her over to the phone. "Here, you dial it, so you can see for yourself I'm on the level—the number marked private."

Loris's hand was shaking when she punched in the numbers; she held her breath as she counted the rings. A man answered. The breath rushed out of her. "Mr. Kagan?"

"Speaking." His voice was soft, refined. "Who is this?"

Tony Storpio grabbed the receiver out of her hand. "Hey, Alex? Tony. Good, good. How you doin'? Great. Hey, listen, I got a girl here, looks real promising. I think you should see her—the sooner the better. This Thursday . . . eight o'clock . . . your place? That's great. See ya then."

He hung up the receiver, then waved his telephone hand in the manner of a magician who'd just performed his best trick. "That's all it takes when you got the right connections."

Emotion constricted Loris's throat: her luck was finally changing!

Wheeling his chair away from the desk, Tony Storpio swiveled around so he was facing her. A sardonic smile played on his lips. "Now, let's see what little favor you can do for me." He unzipped his fly, and took out his penis.

Loris stood still, as if she was nailed to the floor.

"What's the matter? You never seen a cock before?" Reaching out his hand, he grabbed her wrist to tug her to her knees. "Come on, show me how talented you are."

"No!" Loris managed to stay upright, but when she sought to free her arm, he tightened his grip.

"What do you mean, no?" He sounded hurt, insulted. He twisted her wrist. "Less than five minutes ago you agreed to do anything I told you."

"As an actress, not . . . this!"

"This," he referred to his penis, which had begun to twitch, "is part of the deal. I do something for you, you do something for me. Fair's fair."

"If you don't let go of me," Loris warned, "I'm going to kick you right in the shin." She'd had several close calls with agents in the past year, including a near rape, and she wondered now just how far Tony Storpio would go. He made a disgusted sound and tossed her arm back at her. "Hey, you don't want me to represent you? That's okay with me." With a disinterested shrug, he proceeded to stuff his penis back into his pants. "I already got more clients than I can handle."

"But I *do* want you to represent me." She hadn't expected him to back off so easily; she took it as a sign he could be reasoned with. "But it has to be strictly a business arrangement. If I get work, and you seem to think I can, you'd get ten percent of—"

"Fifteen percent."

"Fifteen percent of everything I make. I'm not asking for any special favors, just the chance to work at—"

"You're not asking for any special favors?" Sheer outrage brought him to his feet. "I'm supposed to break my balls to get you started, fix you up and introduce you to all the right people, and for what? So when I make a name for

you, you can tell me to go jerk off while you sign up with
ICM or William Morris?'' Grabbing his empty glass, he
stormed over to the bar. "Fucking actresses are all alike!
Selfish bitches every one of you!''

Once again, Loris was too stunned to react. She couldn't
understand why *he* was the one who was outraged.

"Hey, look, this is the deal,'' he said after he'd carried
his drink to the leatherette couch. "You turn me on, okay? I
see nothing but cold, flat-chested bitches all day. When I see
what looks like a real woman, I like that. I can help you,
and I never saw a broad who needed more help, but I wanna
get something out of it, too. Understood?''

"I'm an actress,'' Loris returned stubbornly, refusing to
let him strip her of the only identity she'd ever had. "If I
wanted to do this sort of thing, I'd be a call girl and make
hundreds of dollars a day, without all this aggravation
and—''

"Save it for the stage, honey,'' he cut her off sarcastically. "Yes or no.''

Without another word, Loris collected her things and
headed for the exit.

"Go on, you dumb broad,'' he called after her. "Go be a
barmaid for another three years!''

Loris hesitated at the threshold, her fingers gripping the
doorknob so tightly they went numb. She stared at the blank
wall of the hallway, but what she saw was everything that
was waiting for her out there: the bar, her crummy apartment, an endless series of cattle calls. She stepped back into
the office, shutting the door behind her.

Tony Storpio smiled, and unzipped his pants.

"It's the face.''

"The face?''

The magnifying glass moved slowly, almost caressingly,
over Loris's face and body while the two men studied the
Polaroid shots tacked onto the solid cork wall, which divid-
ed the loft evenly between the photography studio and the

living quarters. Then they turned to study Loris in the flesh—literally, since she was wearing the skimpiest of string bikinis—only to be drawn back to the snapshots, like doctors grimly examining an x-ray for the undeniable evidence of a malignant growth.

"Definitely the face," Alex Kagan stated unequivocally. He was a tall, slender man in his early sixties with silvery hair, piercing blue eyes, and a haughty manner. Except for the stripes on his shirt, and a silk pocket handkerchief in a matching shade of royal blue, he was dressed entirely in white; a white rosebud was pinned to his lapel.

"There's your problem, Tony," he concluded. "The face doesn't match the body. We're not getting a consistent image."

"You lost me, Alex."

"Observe." Setting the magnifying glass down next to a light box, he lifted his hand to one of Loris's photos. With a manicured thumb, he blocked out her face. "Notice how voluptuous the body is? But the face is like one of those street waifs with the enormous, wistful eyes in a Keane painting." He used the palm of his hand to cover her body. "I think it's that mass of long black hair. It makes her look far too serious."

Tony Storpio shrugged one shoulder. "So, we'll change her hair. Let's make her a redhead."

A frown disturbed Kagan's patrician features. "She hasn't got a redhead personality." He turned and walked to the edge of the paper background, where Loris sat perched on a high stool under the lights. Halting beside a reflecting screen, he stared at her intently for a while; it seemed like forever to Loris. From time to time, he shook his head as though he were trying on, and then rejecting, different versions of her in his mind.

Finally, he nodded his approval. "Now, I've got it. From the moment I saw her I had a nagging feeling that something wasn't quite right. I see what it is now. She's not a brunette. She's a blonde."

"A blonde?" Tony sounded as doubtful as Loris felt.

"Just look at her," Kagan insisted. "Is that the skin tone of a brunette? Can't you see how translucent it is, the way it reflects the light?" He might have been referring to an abstract painting. "Even with those . . . that voluptuous figure, there's something ethereal about her."

"Ethereal?" Tony scoffed. "With those tits and that ass?"

"Just once, Tony, could you try to see beyond tits and ass?" Kagan told him icily, wiping the smirk off his face. "I don't think you fully appreciate what you've got here. Handled properly, this girl could go very far. We're talking star quality."

Loris's heart skipped a beat. Though she wished he'd stop referring to her in the third person, she felt deeply gratified that a man of Kagan's reputation thought she had what it took to make it.

"It's true she simply exudes sex," he went on, "but she doesn't even know she's doing it. There's a kind of innocence about her. It's a very intriguing combination." He smiled. "She'd be devastating as a blonde."

Tony still didn't look convinced.

Kagan was too immersed in his vision to take notice. Nor did he need to look at Loris any longer, since he was inventing her in his head. "A champagne blonde. Nothing brassy or cheap. That Hollywood Blond Bombshell look has been done to death. What we want is a sex symbol for the eighties: savvy, independent, sensual but understated." He turned to Tony. "What's her name again?"

"Loris Castaldi."

"We'll certainly have to do something about *that,*" he muttered, stepping onto the paper background. "Loris, I don't mean to embarrass you, dear, but . . ." An elegant sweep of his hand indicated her bust. "Is that all you?"

"It's all her all right," Tony was quick to answer for her. "I can vouch for that personally."

Loris cringed.

"But does it hold up . . . without a bra?"

"You're gonna have to see this to believe it, Alex," Tony

assured him with a dirty, possessive smirk. "Hey, Loris, take off the bra."

Loris merely stared at him; she couldn't believe she'd heard him correctly.

"The bra, Loris—take it off!"

"Never mind, Tony. If the girl's too embarrassed—"

"What embarrassed? This is work—she knows that. We're all professionals here." In a few impatient strides he was standing in front of her, his back to Kagan. "So, what's the problem?"

"You didn't tell me I'd have to—"

"I'm telling you now." He spoke in a highly charged whisper, his fists clenched at his sides. "We have an agreement, remember? I set this whole thing up for you. What are you trying to do, make me look like a *stronz*? Take off that bra."

"Tony, please don't make me do this."

"You wanna make it big in this business or don't you? 'Cause unless you want it so bad you're willing to make any sacrifice, let's just forget about it right now." Grabbing her arm, he pulled her off the stool. "Put your clothes on—go on. Go back to being a fucking barmaid. Once a loser, always a loser."

Loris fumbled blindly with the back hook on her bra, but her fingers were shaking so much she couldn't undo it. Pushing her hands out of the way, Tony unhooked the bra with one yank and pulled it off. Waving it above his head, a pink polka-dot trophy, he carried it over to Alex Kagan. "Aren't they something?"

Transfixed, Kagan was unable to answer. He felt that jolt to his solar plexus which only perfection of form, the play of light on flawless flesh, could induce in him.

Tony knew that he'd hooked him. "So, what do you think, Alex?"

"I see what you mean, Tony," he managed in his best objective-critic voice. "They're full, yet firm and high. Simply exquisite skin tone." A tiny thrill shot up his spine. "With the lush, creamy glow of a Rubens."

"Is that a fantastic pair of knockers, or what?"

In her next life, Loris thought, she would be rich and flat-chested, but she'd settle for flat-chested.

Clearing his throat, Kagan turned to Tony Storpio. "Do you think you could get her to . . ."

"Take off her panties?" he finished for him, careful to hide the flush of triumph that was beginning to make him tingle. It was just a matter of reeling him in now, the superior, condescending prick. One look at that dimpled ass of hers and he'd be begging to take the pix for her portfolio— in exchange for her posing for those arty nudes he was so hung up on, naturally.

Tony gave Kagan a truly magnanimous smile. "Anything for you, Alex, you know that. Right, Loris?"

Loris stiffened. Tony was still smiling, but his eyes were hard as they locked with hers, arrogantly self-assured. He knew she'd gone too far to back out now.

They both knew it.

Alex Kagan says I've got star quality, Loris told herself as she slid the bikini bottom past her hips, her hands like ice. Nothing else matters. The pink polka-dot triangle slithered down her legs. She almost tripped stepping out of it.

"Come on, turn around," Tony ordered impatiently.

Loris did exactly as she was told: she turned around; she stood in profile; she faced front again; she walked slowly from one end of the paper background to the other. And through it all she kept repeating two words to herself—star quality. She made those two words her personal mantra. She clung to them. She wrapped them around her nakedness and they shielded her.

When she became a star, she'd make Tony Storpio pay for doing this to her. She'd make everyone who'd ever used, rejected, or humiliated her pay.

Loris submitted willingly to her transformation. Once again, she wiped the slate of her life clean—her years of struggle in New York, her aborted love affair with Cal, no

longer existed. She was reborn. Loris Castaldi was dead.
Long live Lara Layton.

Lara Layton—as the stunned reactions she got everywhere she went already proved—was someone other people
wouldn't ignore or push aside as they had Loris Castaldi. As
Lara Layton she'd finally be somebody—somebody other
people would respect and admire.

CHAPTER
Seventeen

"Where's that lousy bitch? I'll break her fucking face I get my hands on her!" Tony Storpio kicked the bedroom door open, sending it banging against the wall; the sound ricocheted inside Lara's throbbing brain. She flinched when he turned the overhead light on.

"Two o'clock in the afternoon and you're still in bed? Why aren't you at the hairdresser's?" he demanded. "And where the hell do you get off telling Dan Gordon you can't see him tonight?"

Rolling onto her stomach, she buried her aching head in the pillow; it barely muffled the sound of his voice.

"So, that's why I couldn't get through." Halting beside the night table, he picked up the receiver she'd taken off the hook. "And me, like a *stronz,* calling you every five minutes for the past hour." His knuckles whitened from the effort to contain his rage. "You gonna answer me or what? And look at me when I talk to you!"

Lara turned slowly onto her side. "Will you stop shouting? I've got a splitting headache."

"Don't give me that shit." He slammed the receiver down on the cradle, making her wince, then backed away from it as if it were a weapon he might be tempted to use. "You got bombed again." He jerked his thumb at the incriminating evidence: the bottle of Courvoisier on the night table. "You got a hangover, right? And you knew how important it was you should look great today!"

Lara fell back against the pillows. "I can't take any more of this. It's making me sick."

"Save the pitiful routine 'cause it's not gonna work. Get out of bed. Come on, get dressed." When she didn't move, he tore the covers off her and threw them across the room. "Get out of this bed, or I'll forget you gotta look good and I'll break your face for you!"

Lara sat up defiantly. "I don't care! I'm not—"

"You think I'm kidding? I'm not kidding!" He punched the Tiffany-style lamp off the night table with one sure, murderous blow. It smashed against the corner wall and shattered to bits.

Lara stiffened with fear but still refused to budge. "You can scream all you want, Tony," she told him, working at keeping her voice steady, "and you can break everything in sight, but nothing you say or do is going to make me go to bed with Dan Gordon." She had to cross her arms under the lacy, Empire bodice of her nightgown to hide the fact that her hands were shaking. "And unless you start treating me with respect, I'll—"

"Hey, what are you talking about?" Tony protested. "I always treat you with respect."

She would have laughed if it didn't hurt so much. "You told that pig, Dan Gordon, he could spend the night here, without even asking me about it, and you call that treating me with respect? That's treating me like a hooker!" Her voice rose in spite of her efforts to remain calm. "Even hookers take their johns to a hotel! This is my home!"

"Since when? I pay the bills around here," he reminded

her contemptuously. "Every stick of furniture in this place belongs to me." A wave of his hand took in the black lacquer Oriental bedroom set, the red satin drapes, and matching wall-to-wall carpet. "I rent this apartment for my West Coast clients, in case they wanna use it when they're in town. You knew what the setup was when I let you move in here, so you could get out of that rat trap you were living in when I met you." He laughed once, scornfully. "So, you hang a few prints on the walls and you buy some plants, a dumb lamp . . ." He gestured toward the stained-glass shards glinting in the corner. "And suddenly, this is your home."

"What am I supposed to be around here? One of the perks for your clients? A free piece of ass to go with the complimentary food and drinks?"

"Hey, I never said that." He sounded truly offended, like a man who'd been grossly misunderstood. "Did I ever bring anybody up here before? I even lost out on a couple of deals 'cause I wouldn't." He slid her a look that managed to be both smug and self-effacing. "I never told you about that, did I? I wouldn't have done it for nobody else but you."

"And I didn't think you cared."

"Come on, you know how I feel about you," Tony muttered, her sarcasm going over his head. Heaving a sigh, he sank down onto the edge of the bed next to her. "But this time, it's different. This thing with Dan Gordon is just too big. You gotta . . . be nice to him."

"Oh, no, I don't." Her body tensed, automatically anticipating his violent reaction.

Instead, Tony sighed again and shook his head ruefully. "Why do I always have to argue with you? Every time I ask you to do something, you give me an argument. I had to yell till I was blue in the face to get you to pose for those arty nudes for Kagan, and look what happened. Because of those pix, you landed this screen test. This could be your big break."

Kagan's nude studies of Lara had won a major photography award and had been featured in several top photography magazines. Tony had sent the tear sheets to Guy H. Griffin, the publisher of *Pleasure* magazine. *Pleasure* was second only to *Playboy* in the men's magazine field. To celebrate its twentieth anniversary, Griffin was sponsoring a contest: the Ultimate Pleasure Mate hunt.

Besides being featured on the cover and centerfold of the anniversary issue, the winner of the contest would also star in Pleasure Productions' first feature film. The talent search, which had been going on for almost a year, was the biggest and most publicized since that for *Gone with the Wind*. Thousands of young women, aspiring as well as professional models and actresses, had submitted nude photos; several hundred had been tested. Lara's screen test was scheduled for the following afternoon. "When are you going to realize," Tony concluded, "that everything I do is meant to help you?"

Lara was tempted to tell him not to help her so much, but decided against it. Smashing the lamp had obviously defused his anger, and she was grateful that he was willing to talk reasonably. "I don't want to argue with you, Tony," she said appeasingly, "but—"

"So, don't," he cut her off. "What's the point?" He threw his hands up. "We got no choice."

"What do you mean, we? I'm the one who has to go to bed with him, not you!"

"Come on, he's an old man—sixty if he's a day. What can he do? I bet he can barely get it up."

"I had to keep my legs crossed all through dinner last night. Your old man kept trying to grab my crotch under the table. If he just does half the things he told me he'd like to do to me—"

"I don't want to hear about it, okay?" he yelled. "We got no choice! That's all there is to it!"

"Then why don't *you* go to bed with him?" She turned on him with all the anger and self-disgust that had been festering inside her for the past year. "Maybe if you knew what it feels like to have someone you can't stand pawing at you, pounding away at you as if you were a piece of meat, forcing you to service him until you're ready to choke . . . then maybe you'd know how I ... why I ..." She burst into tears, surprising herself as much as she did him.

"Hey, come on, what are you doin'? This isn't like you."

"I can't take anymore ... I just can't." She drew her knees up to her chest and wrapped her arms around them tightly, then rested her face on her arms, sobbing.

"Holy shit," Tony mumbled, completely at a loss as to what to do with her. "Maybe you should lie down again." Placing his hands awkwardly on her shoulders, he pushed her back against the pillows. "That's it. You'll be yourself in a minute." Jumping up from the bed, he went to retrieve the covers he'd tossed across the room and brought them back to her. "I don't fucking believe this," he muttered while making a clumsy attempt at tucking her in. "Why are you doin' this to yourself?"

Lara reached blindly for some Kleenex. Only with the greatest effort of will was she able to bring her emotions under control; he was the last person on earth she wanted to appear vulnerable to.

"See what happens when you drink too much and you get hung over?" he said, shifting the real problem to one he could deal with. "You want some aspirin?"

She finished blowing her nose and shook her head. "I already took some. It didn't help." Using both hands, she swept away all traces of her tears. "Besides, aspirin can't cure what's making me sick."

He chose to ignore her last remark. "I know just what you need: the hair of the dog that bit you. Best thing for a hangover." Picking up the bottle of Courvoisier, he poured a generous amount of the amber liquid into the snifter resting beside it. "This'll fix you right up." Without looking at her directly, he handed her the glass, then took off for the bathroom.

As she raised the snifter to her lips the aroma of brandy, which had always appealed to her, made Lara's stomach turn over. She managed several careful sips. The usually smooth liquor burned her throat but sent a welcome rush of warmth through her.

"I could use a drink myself," Tony explained when he reappeared, clutching a glass from the bathroom. He quickly poured himself a double, made a face after he'd downed half of it. "What the hell are you drinking here?" He checked the label. "Brandy?"

"It's the only thing that helps me sleep." She nodded in the direction of the living room. "There's plenty of Jack Daniels in the bar."

"Nah, it's okay." He took another big gulp of his drink, then gave her a guarded look. "You all right now?"

"I'll be just fine as soon as you call Dan Gordon to tell him that I can't see him."

"Hey, you're not gonna start in on that again, are you?"

"Jesus God, Tony, I thought you finally understood how I feel about—"

"What about how I feel?" he cut in savagely. "You think it's gonna be easy for me knowing you're shacking up with him? I don't want that either, but that's the way this fucking business works. Everybody's out for themselves." He stabbed a finger at her for emphasis. "You put out for Gordon and he'll see to it you get as many takes as you need to look good when he's shooting your screen test, and he'll back you for the part with Griffin. You don't put out for him— and some other broad will, you can count on it—your screen test will get lost in the shuffle."

"My God," Lara murmured, "it never ends.

"Tell me about it." He knocked back the rest of his brandy. "Twenty years I've been in this business and I'm still kissing ass. You think I like it? You think I'm proud of the fact that most of the deals I make it's 'cause I fix those pricks up with broads? You know what that makes me, huh?"

A pimp, Lara was tempted to reply, but she knew better than to add fuel to the fire.

"Yeah, I'm doin' just great." He set his empty glass down hard on the night table. "Sure, I got a solid stable of actors, but I gotta bust my balls to sell every one of 'em. Twenty years and I still don't have a star! Not one star to make all those lousy producers I've been sucking up to all these years come crawling to me—make them kiss my ass for a change!''

Lara's head was beginning to pound again as a result of his yelling, but when Tony was caught up in one of his bitter tirades there was no stopping him. If she attempted to, he'd merely take his rage out on her. She had some more brandy.

"And you know how many *stronz* I gave their first real chance to, huh?" he went on. "Then, when they finally made it, they told me to go jerk off while they signed with William Morris or one of the other big agencies." He dropped abruptly onto the edge of the bed, his body straining toward her. "And now you're gonna pull the same shit on me—after all I done for you?"

"But, I'm not—"

"You land this part—and with Gordon's help, there's no way you can miss—you're gonna be a star! With *Pleasure* magazine's circulation running into the millions, Griffin's got a presold audience. The publicity alone will make you famous! Then, we can tell them all to go fuck themselves! That's what you always wanted, isn't it?"

"Tony, please stop screaming."

"You gotta do this for me, Lara! You owe me!"

He gave her a long, hard look, then cancelled it with a smile that managed to be even more ominous. "I don't know why I'm wasting my breath on you." With an easy shrug, he got to his feet. "You gotta put out for Dan Gordon. You got no choice."

"The hell I haven't!"

"Oh, yeah?" He laughed contemptuously. "I'll tell you the only choice you got, babe—a choice between the IRT and the BMT. 'Cause if you don't do this for me, I'll throw you right out on your ass. You can sleep in the subway tonight."

Lara looked up at him incredulously. "Jesus, Tony, I don't believe this . . . not even from you."

"And then what are you gonna do, huh? Go back to being a barmaid and living in a slum?" He paused to enjoy the stricken look on her face; he always knew which buttons to push to release her deepest fears. "Even a dump like the one you were in when I met you costs money, you know. You gotta have at least two months' rent, a month's security, a deposit for the utilities." He smiled again. "You got that kind of bread?"

"You know I haven't. No matter how much money I make, I always end up owing you more."

"Hey, I'm supposed to pay for all your goddamn lessons, too? And your fancy clothes, and the beauty parlor you practically live in, and all the rest of it? You know how much money I advanced you already?"

"I should know—you throw it back in my face often enough!" She was filled with shame and humiliation—a child dependent on the grudging charity of others once again, helpless and despised. Her hand was shaking when she poured herself another brandy, making her spill several drops.

"Here, give me a drink, too," Tony ordered, sliding his glass over to her. "You might as well start practicing."

"Get it yourself, you fucking son of a bitch!" She slammed the bottle down so hard she was surprised it didn't shatter. "And I hope you choke on it!" Throwing off the covers, she jumped out of bed.

Tony grabbed Lara's arm as she pushed past him, holding her back. "Where do you think you're goin'?"

"You just told me to get out."

"Quit playacting. You know I'm not gonna throw you out, any more than you're really gonna leave." He tightened his hold on her. "Christ, even if I was willing to let you go, where you gonna go?"

A wave of nausea swept over Lara, rendering her incapable of movement. It seemed to her that the room was shrinking around her, that the ceiling and the walls were closing in on her.

"You got someplace to go?" he added contemptuously. "You got somebody to go back to?"

She went limp under his hands. "Oh, you . . . bastard."

And then, she went completely to pieces. Only twice in her life—when her mother had died and when Cal had left her—had she felt so utterly alone and devastated.

"Hey, come on, don't do that," Tony was pleading roughly. "You know you got me. I'm the only one in this whole stinking world who gives a damn about you." Placing an arm around her shoulders, he eased her down onto the edge of the bed. "I need you as much as you need me, okay? 'Cause we both want the same thing, and we've both been eating shit off everybody all our lives to get it." He wrapped his other arm around her, holding her with uncharacteristic tenderness. "The only difference is, I don't kid myself. I know I'm gonna go on taking it till I get what I want. And so will you, babe." Slowly, gently, he began to rock her. "So will you."

CHAPTER
Eighteen

While the uniformed guard in the black Lucite enclosure verified their appointment, Lara and Tony signed the guest book, as requested. It was three hours past the close of business, so the usually bustling lobby of the Pleasure Enterprises building was practically deserted.

The guard hung up the phone and gave Lara a knowing smile. "You're to go right up. Mr. Griffin is expecting you. Use that elevator, please."

He pointed to a pair of brushed stainless steel doors in a side wall. Unlike the double row of equally gleaming elevators running the length of the back wall, there were no lighted numbers above it to indicate which floors it serviced in the fifty-story, smoke-glass-and-steel tower on East Fifty-seventh Street. Inside, the private elevator displayed only three floor buttons: *L* for lobby, *PE* for the executive suite on the Forty-ninth floor, and *GHG*—the one Tony had just pressed—to Guy H. Griffin's penthouse pied-à-terre.

As the elevator glided upward without a sound, Tony

checked Lara out for the tenth time in as many minutes, and frowned for the tenth time. "You should have worn the red outfit, like I said. Why the fuck don't you ever listen to me?"

"I told you, Tony, it's so tight and low-cut I look like a hooker in that dress."

"The kind of competition you're up against, you got to show off what you got, not hide it."

Lara didn't bother to defend her choice of clothes; she'd already won that battle. She realized that Tony was just letting off steam because he was so anxious about her interview. It amazed her that she was so calm.

"White, she wears," he muttered bitterly. "You wear white to your first communion, not to an interview with a man like Griffin. You think the other girls wore white?"

"No, I'm sure they all wore something red, tight, and low-cut, or the equivalent. At least I'll be different."

"Griffin doesn't want different." Pulling a handkerchief out of the breast pocket of his sharkskin suit, he wiped his sweaty palms. "He wants the same, only better."

"I look fine, Tony. Stop worrying."

"This could be the most important interview of your life. *You* should be worrying, not me."

"Then, let me worry about it."

The elevator came to a stop, depositing them in a vast, two-story-high atrium. Eucalyptus trees were embedded in the marble floor, perfuming the air, and lush greenery spilled over the hanging balcony. A waterfall cascaded down a travertine wall, flowing into a huge circular swimming pool ringed with exotic plants. Amid the stark, gray towers beyond the walls of glass, the atrium glowed like a tropical oasis in the sky.

"Do you believe this fucking place?" Sweat beaded Storpio's upper lip. He could taste the money and power such surroundings glorified. "But, where do we go now?"

As if in answer to his question, huge, solid-bronze doors at the end of an adjoining corridor parted slowly, unaided by human hands. Lara was reminded of *The Wizard of Oz*. "Down the yellow brick road," she said, pointing.

Tony dabbed at the sweat on his upper lip as they started down the hall. "Now, listen, you got a good chance to land this part, so don't fuck it up. It's down to you and one other girl, and Gordon's been pushing for you like he promised."

Lara's face darkened as she recalled the demeaning sexual demands Dan Gordon had forced on her when she had gone to bed with him.

"Griffin's gotta make a decision tonight. You just make sure he picks you."

"What do you mean by that?"

"You're a woman. I gotta tell you what to do to make a big impression on a man?"

Lara halted just before they reached the doorway. "Is something going on here you haven't told me about?"

Wiping his hands a final time, Tony stuffed the handkerchief back in his pocket. "Just don't fade into the woodwork, like you usually do. That's all I'm saying." Taking her elbow, he pulled her along with him. The huge bronze doors with the bas-relief of a griffin at the center slid closed behind them after they crossed the threshold.

Griffin's duplex took up two entire floors of the building, occupying the space of over a dozen conventional apartments. The living room alone was the equivalent of five flats. Its walls were of glass from ceiling to floor, affording breathtaking views in every direction, creating the illusion that they were suspended in space with all of glittering Manhattan sprawled at their feet.

Pale, tawny tones predominated in sensuous fabrics; the sleek, ultramodern decor sustained the feeling of limitless space. The ingenious use of levels separated the various areas, added a sense of drama. Several steps above the living area, past the sunken marble bar, was a media center as dazzling as a space shuttle's cockpit with its intricate network of lights, controls, and TV monitors.

The inside of the private elevator was displayed on one of the screens; the hallway on another. The entrance to the penthouse was on the one Griffin was now watching. The man, he noted, was gaping in awe at the surroundings—the usual reaction—but the girl seemed unimpressed by such luxury. He wondered what it would take to impress her.

Guy H. Griffin was not only a self-made man, he was a self-created one, as well. Born in a small town in Indiana in 1937, a long-awaited son after the birth of three daughters, he'd always felt that he was destined for greater things. Many children entertain the notion that they were born of bluer blood and switched in the cradle—Guy believed this for a fact. He reasoned there was no other explanation for the vast difference between himself and his drab, strict Baptist family.

On the surface he was everything a well-brought-up sixteen-year-old was expected to be in 1953; inside, he was a seething mass of barely perceived longings. He might well have followed in his insurance broker father's plodding footsteps if only, that summer, he hadn't borrowed his older cousin Wilbur's copy of a new magazine called *Playboy*.

Suddenly, everything made sense. His destiny became manifest: he was born to be a swinger, like Frank and Dean and, especially, Hef. In homage to his idol, Hugh Hefner, Guy Griffin insisted that, henceforth, everyone call him Grif, and he bought himself a camera.

Grif soon discovered that, while looking at photos of Playmates was arousing, getting the girl next door or one of his classmates to take off her clothes and pose for him—no mean feat in 1953—was even more exciting. It gave him a sense of mastery he'd never known. The photo sessions usually ended with Grif and the model drinking champagne and making out to the accompaniment of the Sinatra records he also provided.

Throughout college Grif continued to perfect both the art of photography and the art of seduction. Soon after graduating, he made his long-dreamed-of escape to Los Angeles, the city of real, live angels. Fallen angels were his favorite kind. He quickly acquired a reputation for being one of the best pinup photographers in the business. With his lopsided

grin and undeniably boyish charm, he had a knack for
getting young women to trust him and expose the parts of
their bodies. It was illegal at the time, but that didn't stop
Grif.

In 1964, as the sexual revolution was about to burst on
the scene—along with mini-skirts, the no-bra look, and the
Beatles—*Playboy* began to seem like pretty tame stuff to
Grif. With his boundless confidence and enthusiasm, he had
no trouble raising money to start a new kind of skin
magazine, which he named *Pleasure*.

"Hef is then," he told his investors, wealthy swinger
friends he'd made since coming to L.A., "Grif is now." His
intention was to knock *Playboy* on its airbrushed ass by
featuring nude layouts that were far more realistic and
sexually explicit. *Pleasure* created a sensation with its
premiere issue. The rest was history.

Before the year was out, *Pleasure* had become a serious
challenge to *Playboy*'s dominance of the skin rags. Grif
cleared his first million before he was thirty. As the magazine's logo, he selected a fluffy white kitten. "I'll take a
pussy over a bunny any day," he quipped at the time. The
merchandising department of Pleasure Enterprises, Ltd.,
sold an average of two hundred and twenty million dollars a
year worth of satin sheets, accessories, and boudoir fashions
with the pussycat logo.

At forty-five his hair was steel-gray, but except for a few
crinkles at the corners of his pale-blue eyes, his face was
unlined. Not conventionally handsome—a sharp nose and
triangular bone structure, combined with a sly expression,
made him look like a fox—he nonetheless managed to give
the impression of being immensely attractive. Just under six
feet, he had the slender build and muscle tone of a man
twenty years younger, though he'd never been known to
exercise—unless sex could be considered exercise. And he
still retained a boyish enthusiasm and boundless confidence.
He had the aura of a man who truly believed there was
nothing he couldn't do and no one he couldn't win once he
set his mind to it.

But there was the proverbial fly in Griffin's ointment: in spite of his accomplishments, most people merely considered him a second-string Hugh Hefner. He became obsessed with the idea of becoming a star maker—the one goal his former idol had consistently failed at. To that end, he had conceived the Ultimate Pleasure Mate hunt.

After almost a year of choosing, appraising, and sampling most of the finalists, he was beginning to despair that he would ever find the girl who most perfectly represented the Pleasure Mate ideal. The contest had officially ended a month ago. The winner's name was scheduled to be announced at a press conference at the end of the week, and he still hadn't made his choice.

He'd needed only one glance at the tear sheets of Kagan's exquisite nude studies of Lara to know that he'd finally found what he'd been looking for: the dream girl of all time. He had quickly dispatched his producer, Dan Gordon, to New York to make a screen test of her over the weekend. Impatient to see the results, Grif had flown to New York himself Sunday night. Lara's screen test confirmed what his instinct had already told him. First thing Monday morning, he got in touch with Tony Storpio.

With a feeling of anticipation he hadn't experienced in years, Grif now rose out of the high-backed chair, finally making himself visible to his guests.

He'd barely cleared the steps to the living area level when Tony Storpio came hurrying toward him. "Hey, I gotta tell you, this is some place you got here."

Grif managed a polite reply but his attention, his whole being, was focused on the girl who'd remained by the doorway. His pale eyes swept over the Grecian-style dress she was wearing. The soft folds of the cowl neckline permitted only a tantalizing glimpse of cleavage; the fluid white column of silk crepe merely suggested the lush curves of breasts and hips. She lingered by the door, making no attempt to come to him. Nor did she smile invitingly or give off any of the attention-getting signals he was accustomed to receiving from eager young women.

If the mountain won't go to Mohammed . . . he thought wryly, leaving the agent gushing over the spectacular view. Never taking his eyes off her, he crossed the wide expanse separating them, every step bringing him closer to the realization, once again, that instinctively he'd been right about her. That unique quality he'd first glimpsed in the photos hadn't been a result of Kagan's artistry. The photographer had merely brought out what was already there.

There was an innocence about her that was sadly lacking in most girls these days. Innocence, he'd found, was the greatest turn-on of all. And an air of mystery. But the most extraordinary thing about her, he recalled from viewing her screen test, was her ability to remain mysterious while she was naked. Women, in his experience, gave up all their secrets along with their clothes. He had the feeling she'd never allow any man to possess her entirely. Which, of course, made him want to possess her all the more.

He halted beside her. "I've been looking forward to meeting you, Lara. You're even more beautiful in person. I didn't think that was possible."

She looked as if that was exactly the sort of thing she expected him to say to young women who posed in the nude. It usually was, but in her case, he'd really meant it. "I've just been viewing your screen test. I was very impressed."

Lara's stomach constricted nervously; she wasn't as calm as she pretended. Halfway across the room, every muscle in Tony's body tensed. The same thought crossed both their minds: Did that mean she had the part? They waited for Griffin to elaborate.

He smiled. "You must think me a very poor host. Why are we standing here, when I should be offering you a drink before dinner?" Proffering his arm gallantly, he escorted her to the circular Art Deco bar.

Tony almost tripped in his eagerness to follow them down the carpeted steps. "I knew she'd test great. She's fantastic, isn't she?"

"She certainly is," Grif agreed, seating Lara on the

semicircular banquette; a curved bar of marble and brass completed the circle. "I thought we'd have champagne— unless you'd prefer a cocktail, Lara."

Trying to appear relaxed, she sat back and crossed her legs. The banquette was upholstered in the finest glove leather, and had the smooth, supple texture of flesh. "Champagne's fine."

"And what'll you have, Tony?"

"Champagne, sure." He laughed expansively and sat next to Lara—close enough to let the other man know who owned her, but not so close as to discourage his interest. He knew Griffin was dying to possess her. "I don't usually drink the stuff, but if this is a celebration," he added pointedly, trying to get him back on the subject.

Guy H. Griffin was not so easily led. He was accustomed to doing the talking. He busied himself with opening and pouring the Dom Perignon, then raised his flute in a toast. "To *Ecstasy*."

Lara smiled. "The film or the experience?"

Grif returned her smile. "Why not both?" He touched his glass to hers, the crystal ringing, then sat down on the other side of her.

"Speaking of the movie," Tony said between sips. "I really need to know your shooting schedule, Grif. There might be a problem with conflicting dates. Lara's been offered the lead in another movie, you know."

"Really?" Griffin didn't sound convinced. Lara knew he was aware that Tony was lying.

"Personally, I prefer she did your movie," Tony was quick to assure him. "Because I'm sure it'll be a much classier production. But I need to hear your offer before I make a decision on which way to go."

Grif twirled the stem of his glass between slender, mani-cured fingers. "This meeting was meant to be purely social, Tony. I'd rather not discuss business tonight, if you don't mind."

"Sure, Grif, whatever you say." Tony's tone was fawning. Inwardly, he cursed the wily son of a bitch.

"Unless *you* have a question," Grif amended, turning to Lara.

"I'd just like to know what the film is about." She leaned toward him. "And the character you're considering me for—what's she like?"

She was serious about her acting, Grif realized, and that pleased him. "It's a remake of *Ecstasy*, the silent film classic based on *Lady Chatterley's Lover*."

"I've always loved that book," Lara admitted. "No one's ever done a film version that could compare to it."

"Until now," he corrected with a confident smile. As Grif went on to explain how he visualized the movie, Lara was relieved to find out it wasn't going to be just another sexploitation flick, as she'd feared. "There will be nude love scenes, of course, but—"

"She can handle that," Tony cut in boastfully.

"—they will be done with taste and style," Grif continued as if Tony hadn't spoken. "What we're dealing with primarily is a love story—one of the greatest, most sensual love stories ever written. For the past twenty years we've had nothing but buddy movies, violence, or high-tech sci-fi. I believe the public is ready—not ready, but starving—for the kind of glamour and romance that were once synonymous with Hollywood. And I'm going to give it to them. *Ecstasy* will be—"

This time Grif interrupted himself. The Swiss couple who looked after the penthouse while he was in L.A., and all of his needs when he was staying in New York, were setting caviar, with its accompaniments, on the dining table. Lara had never seen gold caviar. Relegated, at one time, for the exclusive use of the Shah of Iran and his family, small quantities of gold caviar were now being smuggled out of Iran at a prohibitive cost.

"Dinner's ready," Grif announced, standing, "I hope it meets with your approval. I'm afraid I gave Clara and Hans very short notice."

After a five-course meal, which included cold medallions of lobster in champagne, braised duckling in a flamed

brandy, truffle and wild mushroom sauce, Lara couldn't help
wondering what kind of dinner the couple prepared with
advance notice. It was certainly the most sumptuous meal
she had ever enjoyed. A different wine was served with each
course. She only wished Tony would shut up and stop trying
to sell her so hard.

Griffin was aware of Lara's embarrassment, and his
dislike for Tony Storpio increased with every course. He
was barely able to restrain himself as he watched the
uncouth bastard knock down his cognac—a Hennessy Paradis
costing $150 a bottle—in one greedy gulp.

Setting down the empty snifter, Tony jumped to his feet.
"I hate to eat and run, but one of my clients is opening
tonight and I promised to catch the third act."

Lara stared at him blankly; this was the first she had
heard about the play. Thanking Griffin for his hospitality,
she picked up her purse and got up to leave with Tony.

"No, you stay," he ordered, waving her back in her
chair. "I'm sure you two still have lots to talk about."

She stood there, frozen, as she suddenly realized why
Tony was deliberately leaving her alone with Griffin. Grif
had been set up like this before, so it came as no surprise to
him.

"Talk to you tomorrow, Grif," Tony tossed over his
shoulder as he hurried toward the exit. He figured Lara
wouldn't dare give him any shit in front of Griffin, but he
wasn't about to take any chances.

Reaching into the pocket of his jacket, Grif took out a
remote control unit, which he used to open the brass doors,
then close them again once Tony had left. While he replaced
the unit he studied Lara intently. As an actress she might
have been able to fake the stricken look in her eyes, but not
the high spot of color on her cheeks. "You didn't know
anything about this, did you?"

"No, *I* didn't," she returned accusingly.

"I assure you, neither did I. I'm not going to pretend I
don't want to make love to you, Lara, because I do—very
much. But this isn't my style. I've never made sex a

condition in my professional dealings with women." He
smiled disarmingly. "I've never had to."

With his money and power, and easy charm, she might
have believed that, if she was capable of believing men
anymore.

Cradling his snifter in both hands, Grif slowly swirled the
amber liquid within. "Sit down and finish your cognac,
Lara. There are several things I'd like to talk to you about
now that he's gone. Then I'll have my chauffeur drive you
home. Unless you think I'm planning to ravish you right
here on the table."

She smiled in spite of herself and the tension between
them was broken. "This is just the sort of thing Tony would
pull," she admitted, resuming her seat. "He knows you're
still undecided between me and another girl, and he figured
I'd help you make up your mind in bed."

Grif paused as he was about to take a sip of cognac.
"What other girl? I've never seriously considered anyone
else for this role. The moment I saw Kagan's photos, I
knew you were the one, but I had to make sure. That's why
I had Dan make a screen test and why I flew to New York
especially to meet you."

Lara shook her head as if to deny the awful realization
spreading through her: Dan Gordon had lied just to get her
into bed. Was there no end to the betrayals?

Ignorant of the facts, Griffin misread Lara's reaction.
"You still don't believe me. The part is yours." From the
inside pocket of his jacket he took out an envelope containing
two copies of the contract he'd had drawn up. He handed
one across the table to her. "See for yourself."

"But, why didn't you say so before?" she demanded
after quickly scanning the contract. "Instead of toying with
us all evening."

"I don't like your friend Tony Storpio," he said bluntly.
"How did you ever get involved with someone like him?"

"He believed in me when no else did."

"Well, *I* believe in you now. You don't need him anymore. You're going to be a big star, Lara. He's a cheap

pimp and he makes you look lousy. Get rid of him.'' Grif took Lara's surprise at the glimpse of steel behind his suave facade for reluctance. ''Are you in love with him?''

''God, no, I hate him.''

Guy H. Griffin smiled approvingly. ''That should make it easier.''

Tony was waiting for her when Lara got home a couple of hours later. ''Did you get the part?'' he demanded before she barely had a chance to close the door.

She regarded him coldly. ''How dare you set me up like a two-bit hooker?''

''What do you mean, set you up? I was trying to help,'' he protested, ''and if I told you what I'd planned, you'd have given me an argument. But you'd still have gone through with it, like you did with Dan Gordon, because you got no choice. So, what was the point? I didn't want you getting all upset and crying, like the last time.''

Lara's mouth twisted sarcastically. ''You're the soul of consideration.''

''Hey, I'm on your side, remember? I only want what's best for you.''

''Like putting me in bed with Griffin?''

''Come on, you think I like that? I've been going out of my fucking mind here thinking about you being with him.'' He frowned and ran a hand through his hair. ''I don't want to talk about this anymore, okay? Or else *I'll* get upset. Let's just forget it ever happened.''

She didn't bother telling him that nothing had happened, since that was also beside the point.

''So, did he promise you the part, or what?''

Snapping open her purse, Lara pulled out her copy of the contract and thrust it into his hands.

''Holy shit, you got a contract?'' he cried, jubilant. ''You're fantastic. I knew you'd come through.''

''Did you?''

Tony was too busy skimming through the contract to

answer. Lara was glad he was making it so easy for her. She spun on her heel and stalked into the bedroom. Pulling a canvas suitcase off the top shelf of the closet, she began to pack. She was only taking her jeans and some summer tops and the few dresses she'd bought herself. She would leave behind the gaudy outfits Tony had purchased. Griffin intended to buy her a whole new wardrobe to go with her new image.

He'd talked to her for over an hour about it. She couldn't understand why she simply couldn't be taken for what she was. First Storpio and Kagan, and now Griffin reinforced the importance of an image to her. Lara decided she would shine through any image they created for her. She agreed to the changes Grif had suggested. Once she was a star, Lara assured herself as she tossed some underwear into the bag, once *she* had the power, she'd be exactly what she wanted to be. Until then, she would do whatever it took to make it to the top.

Lara straightened up as she heard the raw curse that Tony screamed from the other room. Then she heard something being knocked over, smashing to pieces.

He rushed into the bedroom, yelling. "What are you, fucking crazy? You go and sign a contract before I okay it? Do you know what you signed here?" He waved the crumbled pages in her face. "This is an exclusive, seven-year contract. The man owns you, body and soul!"

"I'd have signed anything to get away from you."

"What are you talking? You're not getting away—" Tony finally noticed the suitcase lying open on the bed. "What the fuck is this?"

"I'm leaving you, Tony. You're never going to do this to me again." Pulling the contract out of his hand, she brandished it like a banner celebrating her new-won freedom. "Not you—not anyone—ever again!" She dropped the contract and her purse into the canvas bag and quickly zipped it up. "Griffin's car is waiting for me downstairs. He's flying back to L.A. in his private jet tonight. I'm going with him."

He stared at her for a long moment. "If you think you're

going to dump me now," he said finally in that slow, flat tone he used when he was on the verge of exploding, "you better think again."

Lara began to shake inside. She knew from experience how violent Tony could be when he was crossed, but she didn't back down. "You'll get your fifteen percent commission on whatever I earn on the film. I owe you that much." She lifted the suitcase off the bed. "But you don't represent me anymore, and I never want to see or hear from you again."

He stepped directly in front of her, raising his clenched fists over his head. Her mouth went dry. Instead of the blow she'd anticipated, tears filled his eyes.

"Don't *you* do this to me," he pleaded, shaking his fists in the air. "Not when you know how I feel about you. Not now when I'm so close to making it happen after all these years. Don't *you* fuck me over, too, like all the others." His fists fell impotently to his sides.

"It's *you*, Tony," Lara cried, no longer able to contain the anger and contempt she felt toward him. "You're not an agent, you're a glorified pimp. You exploit people and treat them like animals. That's why they all end up leaving you the first chance they get. You're a bum!" Pushing past him, she stormed out.

"You haven't heard the last of Tony Storpio," he yelled from the doorway as she was crossing the living room to the exit. "I'm gonna sue you. I'm gonna sue Griffin, that shark in sheep's clothing. Just wait, you'll find out what he's really like, and then you'll be sorry you ever left me. But don't come crawling back because I won't take you. You hear me?"

The sound of the front door slamming was her only answer. "Fucking actresses!" She'd left her slippers beside the bed; he kicked them halfway across the room. "Selfish bitches—every one of 'em," he screamed. Through the open closet door he saw the clothes he'd bought her; she hadn't taken a single one. He yanked the dresses off the hangers and ripped them to pieces. Then he went through the dresser drawers and shredded every piece of lingerie. With one sweep of his arm he cleared the vanity table of all her lotions and perfumes.

When there was nothing left in the room to smash, or to remind him of her, Tony Storpio sat down at the foot of the bed, alone.

CHAPTER
Nineteen

With the mincing steps of a geisha, Lara paced before the antique white-and-gilt telephone. The skirt of her gown was extremely tight, restricting her movements, making it impossible for her to sit down even if the state of her nerves would have permitted it. Although she was waiting for Griffin's call, she jumped when the phone rang.

"It's almost time," he reminded her.

"Grif, do you have a Valium? I need a tranquilizer or I'll never be able to go through with it!"

There was a pause at his end of the line, then he said, "I've got something better. I'll be right up."

Lara sighed with relief as she replaced the receiver. She knew she could count on Griffin. She'd come to depend on him more and more since coming to Los Angeles with him. He'd taken charge of her life from that very first evening three months ago.

"I don't like the idea of you living alone, unprotected,"

he told her on their flight in his luxurious, custom-designed jet. "I've made arrangements for you to stay at the Chateau."

Lara meant what she had told Tony earlier: no one was going to treat her like a hooker again. She wanted Grif to know that, too. "I have no intention of being another notch on the gun, Grif, if that's what you have in mind."

"That's not what I had in mind at all," he replied cryptically, and left it at that.

"Thanks, anyway, but I'd rather get a place of my own."

"It would be just like your own. You'd have your own private suite with your very own key," he assured her. "No strings attached." He flashed a self-mocking smile. "The drug parties and wild orgies I'm sure you've read about in the tabloids are held on a purely voluntary basis. You don't have to attend unless you want to."

She laughed. She liked the fact that he could make fun of himself, and she assumed he was joking.

"Why not try it for a week?" Grif suggested. "If it's not to your liking, we'll make other arrangements."

Lara agreed. It was difficult not to agree with Grif, she quickly learned. Unlike Tony, he made no demands or threats. He merely suggested, offered advice, and patiently instructed. True to his word, he respected her privacy and made no sexual advances. Instead, he courted her. It had been a long time since Griffin had had to pursue a woman, and the novelty of the chase added a dimension of excitement to his growing obsession with Lara. He overwhelmed her with solicitude. If he was overprotective of her at times, she decided she preferred such attention over neglect.

He personally supervised every detail of the perfecting of her beauty, as he graciously put it—from the color of her hair down to the shade of nail polish on her pedicured toes. He drove everyone involved crazy. Dissatisfied with the way things were going during the Ultimate Pleasure Mate photo session, he actually grabbed the camera out of the hands of the photographer. "I'll take over now, Leo."

Leo Koenig, as volatile as he was talented, bristled. "In case you've forgotten, Grif, I've worked with girls who don't know their ass from their tits before, and I've always gotten great results."

"In case you haven't noticed, Leo, none of the girls you're accustomed to working with is in the same class as Miss Layton. Perhaps that's why you don't know how to handle her."

Lara knew the fault was hers, not Koenig's, who stomped out of the studio. She kept freezing up. The nude studies Kagan had done of her were meant to glorify the female body, while the kind of pinup poses Koenig had insisted on made her feel dirty and exploited.

"Don't try to act sexy," Grif told her, countermanding Koeing's previous instruction. "You're sexy just the way you are." He put soft music on the stereo and plied her with champagne. "Forget about the camera. Think of the lens as the eyes of the man you love. Imagine him watching you, wanting you."

Lara imagined Cal's eyes watching her; she felt Cal's hands caressing her body with sensuous strokes and Cal's mouth kissing her. The assistants no longer needed to rub ice on her nipples to make them erect.

The twentieth anniversary issue of *Pleasure*, featuring Lara as the Ultimate Pleasure Mate, sold out the same day it hit the stands. The first week her Pleasure Mate video was released, it made *Billboard*'s top ten list. As Tony Storpio had predicted, Lara became a celebrity before she'd set foot in front of a motion picture camera.

Ecstasy was scheduled to begin shooting on Monday. Tonight, Griffin was throwing an extravagant, well-publicized party in Lara's honor. Outside her sitting room window the vast grounds and formal gardens were floodlit, illuminating the Porsches and Mercedes and custom-built Rolls-Royces approaching the white-pebble driveway. At the main entrance to the Chateau, which was guarded on either side by a pair of large marble griffins, uniformed attendants waited to park the arriving cars as they relinquished the rich and famous, the powerful, and the merely beautiful. Everything seemed unreal to her, except for the sense of panic threatening to overwhelm her.

"What's wrong, Lara?" Grif asked from the doorway. Party sounds drifted up the stairs.

The knot in her stomach tightened another notch. "Do you know who just pulled up in the driveway? Jack Nicholson. Jack Nicholson, for God's sake! One of my favorite actors."

Griffin smiled, and locked the door as a precautionary measure.

"Some of the biggest stars in Hollywood are here," she rattled on, "and some of the most important people in the whole country."

"In the whole world," Grif corrected. "And they all came here to see you, Lara."

"No, that's just it!" She hobbled over to him. "They came here to see the Ultimate Pleasure Mate. They're all expecting to meet this wild, uninhibited creature they saw running around bare-assed in the video. She has nothing to do with me!"

As though to verify that fact, she looked at herself in the mirrored wall, which also reflected the white-and-gilt rococo decor, a fitting backdrop to her gaudy image.

Her hair was platinum blonde, and with the addition of a fall, it cascaded halfway down her bare back. A double fringe of false lashes gave her eyes a sultry cast; tinted contacts changed them from pale gray to Technicolor blue. Flecks of eighteen-carat gold gleamed on her eyelids and in the special face powder that added a glowing radiance to her skin. She wore no undergarments beneath her skintight lamé gown; her body appeared to have been dipped in molten gold.

"This isn't me," she wailed.

"It's what you were meant to be. You've never looked more exquisite." Griffin beamed proudly at his creation, already relishing the sensation she would cause when they made their entrance down the baronial staircase, as they'd rehearsed. His eyes shone. "You'll devastate them."

"I'll never be able to carry it off, Grif."

"Yes, you will." He added confidentially: "With a little help from your friends." From the inside pocket of his dinner jacket he removed a glass vial filled with a powdery white substance. He carried it over to the marble-topped console table that was used as a bar.

Lara followed as quickly as her gown would permit. Carefully, Grif poured the contents of the vial onto the mirrored tray. She drew in a shocked breath. "Cocaine?"

"Pharmaceutical quality." He took a small alligator case, not unlike a portable manicure set, out of his other pocket. "Not even rock stars can get blow this good. It's almost one hundred percent pure." Gold implements gleamed when he unzipped the case. He slid out a straw and a single-edge razor blade, leaving the roach clip untouched.

Lara shook her head as she stared at the lines he was chopping out of the snowy mound with the gold razor blade. "I'm not into drugs, Grif."

He slanted her an indulgent smile. "Sure you are. Alcohol's a drug. So are tranquilizers. And they're physically addictive. Coke isn't."

"That's what I've heard," she admitted, "but all I need is a Valium."

"Valium's going to bring you down. What you need is something to help you rise above it all." He set the razor blade aside. "You've got to shine tonight, lady."

Lara's stomach gave another twist as she recalled the celebrities who were waiting for her to make her grand entrance. "I just don't want to start on drugs."

"The choice is yours, Lara." Grif's tone was patient, understanding. "You can go down there in this state, or you can be in total control of the situation." He used the straw to point to the four white lines he'd assembled. "I'm going to do a couple of lines, too. Do you think I'd take or give you something that would mess us up, tonight of all nights?"

"No," she allowed. "Of course not."

"A couple of lines of coke and all your fears and insecurities will vanish. You'll be as dazzling as I know you can be." He offered her the gold straw. "Trust me." She did.

Lara dazzled. She sparkled. She captivated everyone in sight. She was so witty and clever she amazed even herself. She was Cinderella at a ball where midnight never struck and Prince Charming never left her side.

Grif introduced her to all the really important people, taking such evident pride in her that it was impossible to mind the way he kept his arm about her, clutching her possessively to his side. Having been disavowed all her life by her father and forced to hide her true relationship with Cal whenever they were in public, Lara found she enjoyed being shown off by Griffin.

Despite the hundreds of women Griffin had bedded, and an endless parade of "favorite ladies," he'd never found the one woman who could match his idealized image of himself. Perhaps that was why he'd had to invent her. In Lara, he felt, he'd finally found the perfect consort.

"You were sensational," he told her when he managed to get her alone.

It surprised her to find how much his approval meant to her. "I couldn't have done it without you, Grif."

"I'd like to believe that's true," he admitted with a disarming grin, "but you even surpassed my fantasies. You eclipsed every woman present. There isn't a man here tonight who doesn't want you." His eyes gleamed with a kind of excitement she'd never seen in them before. "I've shared you with everyone else long enough. This is our night." His eyes met hers meaningfully. "Let's finish celebrating it together. What do you say?"

"I thought you'd never ask," Lara said.

" 'Come into my parlor, said the spider to the fly.' " With a playful leer, Griffin waved Lara inside. The effects of the cocaine had worn off, but the excitement they both felt about her triumph at the party lingered.

This was Lara's first visit to Grif's private apartment. She'd heard about it, of course. Only a very select few had actually seen it, however, so Lara was fully aware of the honor being accorded her. She glanced around with wry amusement. "Some parlor, said the fly to the spider."

In contrast to the rococo decor of all the other rooms of the Chateau, Grif's apartment was ultramodern. The living room, from the vicuna carpeting to the chamois-covered walls, was done entirely in chocolate brown. The long, low-slung sectional was upholstered in the identical soft, buttery chamois, and it overflowed with fur throw pillows. The only vivid colors in the room were provided by the assortment of nudes that hung on the walls—part of Grif's celebrated collection of erotic art. Prominently displayed over the marble fireplace, like an exotic flower whose translucent pink petals seemed to quiver, was a sculpture of female genitalia.

Lara followed Grif from one extraordinary room to another. There was something of the unreality of science fiction about his apartment, she thought. It was a world within a world that was so isolated and self-contained that it could have been spinning somewhere in space, or anchored twenty thousand leagues under the sea.

She was struck, as she had been on other occasions, by the contradiction in his personality. Though he was obviously trying to impress her with his money and power, there was an ingenuousness about him as he showed off each priceless object, demonstrated every state-of-the-art gadget. He was like a child eager to share his favorite toys.

"These were designed by Miró," said Grif of the bronze doors gliding open at their approach. "And this..." A self-mocking grin played on his lips. "... is the notorious bedroom."

His bedroom could more appropriately be described as one big bed, since it was composed of a wall-to-wall mattress a foot thick, surrounded by a raised mahogany deck. The sable bedspread covering it could have kept a dozen zaftig Siberian women warm through the bitterest winter. Built into one side of the deck was a fully stocked bar; a refrigerator filled with assorted delicacies that dispensed soda, spring water, and diamond-shaped ice cubes; a hidden safe wherein pot, hashish, and cocaine were stashed; and a popcorn machine. "I can't really enjoy a movie without popcorn," Grif explained. The other side of the deck contained a complete rack stereo system and two VCRs. A huge projection-TV screen stood at the foot of the bed.

"This is Max," said Griffin when they were sitting up against the fur-covered headboard, referring to the space-age computer panel at his side. "He can be very useful." He pressed several buttons. The tracks of spotlights running across the ceiling changed to low-voltage museum lighting, tinted peach and pink; the mellow sounds of vintage Sinatra floated out of concealed speakers; and seascapes appeared on the white matte screens that covered the windows.

All the windows were sealed, Lara suddenly realized. It was impossible to tell whether it was day or night, what the season or weather was. Light, climate, and view, as Grif was quick to demonstrate, were determined by his whim with the mere touch of a button. At the moment it was winter and snow was falling softly on a quaint New England town. With a flick of a switch it was springtime in the Rockies. He controlled night and day; rain or shine; sunrise, sunset.

"This place is like a Disneyland for adults," Lara said. "I've heard you don't leave this room for days."

"Why should I, when I have everything I could possibly desire right here?" Grif brought his face down to hers. "Now I even have you. I may never leave this room again." He kissed her lightly, expertly, taking his time exploring her mouth. Then he looked deep into her eyes. "I want the first time with you to be special, Lara—unforgettable. That's why I waited this long." He brushed her lips with his.

"Let's do some more coke. I want to make love to you all night."

Though at first she was somewhat startled by his suggestion, Lara didn't hesitate to snort a couple of lines with him this time. She found Griffin fascinating, even attractive, but she wasn't in love with him. With the help of cocaine, as she'd already learned, she would be transformed into that scintillating fantasy creature he seemed to believe she was, and it would also help her make love to Grif.

When he'd set the gold straw aside, Grif licked the tip of his finger and plunged it into the snowy mound. "Open your mouth," he ordered. He rubbed cocaine all over her gums; it melted on contact. The coke she'd snorted hit her with an icy numbness at the back of her throat and a rush of pure energy. Then her gums, her whole mouth, went numb as if she'd been shot full of Novocaine. The air was suddenly so light and easy to breathe that she felt it go all the way down to her toes. Her senses had never been more acute.

When he began making love to her, every sensation was magnified. Emotionally, she felt oddly detached. Nothing existed beyond her own sexual hunger, an infinite greed. The drug had the same effect on him. He dabbed some cocaine on her nipples and sucked them until she wanted to scream, then he rubbed even more of the snowy powder between her thighs. His tongue licked her clean. What little control she still possessed dissolved, as well. She could feel herself reaching climax, but he pulled away from her abruptly, leaving her stranded on the edge of orgasm.

"I don't want you to make it yet," he explained. "I want to keep bringing you to the edge until you're half out of your mind."

Lara laughed breathlessly. "I *was* half out of my mind."

"Until you're completely out of your mind, then." He reached for some more coke and rubbed it on his penis to prolong his erection and delay his own orgasm. Positioning her body to allow him the deepest penetration and the greatest degree of control, he entered her with one thrust, only to withdraw almost entirely before plunging all the way in her once again. Her body shuddered from the impact.

Over and over again he did this, his withdrawals becoming increasingly slower, more maddening, his thrusts ever deeper and more powerful. Though he tried to, he was unable to stop her this time as the uncontrollable spasms took her. She felt as if she were splintering into a million pieces of glass.

As she lay beside him, drenched in perspiration, her heart pounding wildly, Grif stretched out his hand and pushed a button on the computer panel. There was a whirring sound, which Lara instantly recognized as the sound of a video cassette being rewound. Another button flashed an instant replay of what had just occurred onto the large TV screen at the foot of the bed.

"You don't mind, do you?" asked Grif solicitously when he saw the shocked look on Lara's face. "Don't worry, I'll erase it afterwards. I just couldn't resist seeing the two of us together."

Taking her stunned silence for approval, he settled back with the eager anticipation of a kid at a Saturday matinee. "Just look at you. God, you're gorgeous." He hit the pause button, freezing her naked image. It hung suspended for a moment, like one of his centerfolds.

"Mmm, remember that?" Reaching for her, he pulled her onto her side so he could snuggle up against her back while he watched the performance. "I really had you going there, didn't I?" She felt him between her legs, growing harder. "You were really out of your head there, weren't you?" He slipped easily inside her, never taking his eyes off the screen. "Just look at you. You're fantastic." He moved slowly at first, trying to prolong the sensation, but he soon became caught up in the rhythm of her excitement as she lost control. He made it at the same time she did in the film.

CHAPTER
Twenty

For ten days in May every year a kind of madness swept through a small luxury resort town on the French Riviera. Many of the local inhabitants literally took to the hills during the Cannes International Film Festival as nearly 30,000 movie people—including producers, directors, publicists, major stars, and eager starlets, along with a horde of media hounds and fans—invaded Cannes.

It was movie madness that compelled the visitors to disregard a sea and sky of cobalt blue, miles of fine, sandy beaches, and the almost tropical brilliance of the sunlight to lock themselves up in the dark. Screenings of over four hundred movies were held from six-thirty in the morning until well past midnight. A combination carnival, lofty artistic event, and hucksters' convention, the film festival at Cannes was like no other.

Films of the highest artistic merit competed for the prestigious "Palme d'Or" while movies like _Assault of the Killer Bimbos_ and _Space Sluts in the Slammer_ were being peddled at the independent Film Mart. Movie deals were the main order of business. Films were the main subject of conversation, their relative merits debated in a variety of languages. An international brigade of prostitutes worked the bars.

All of the major hotels had been booked solid months in advance, and a room the size of a broom closet in an out-of-the-way pension cost $250 or more a night. A drink at even the least fashionable bars was priced at $12.50. A full course meal for two at any of the four-star restaurants practically cost enough to feed several starving families, yet no one seemed particularly dismayed. The ostentatious display of wealth was, after all, one of the primary attractions of the festival.

Women wore diamonds at breakfast, and full-length sable coats, despite the balmy climate. To keep cool they simply wore as little clothing as possible underneath their furs. The limousines inching bumper-to-bumper along the Boulevard de la Croisette were almost as long as some of the yachts moored in the harbor. Cannes was the boating capital of the Côte d'Azur—no where else did the yachts gleam so sleekly or entertain such a dazzling assortment of the rich and famous. Lara and Griffin received so many invitations to exclusive parties that they attended as many as three or four a night.

Ecstasy, which was being shown out of competition, was the most talked about and sought after property at the Film Mart. Lara was mobbed everywhere she went. Between galas and functions she was barricaded in her suite at the Carlton. Each excursion outside was planned like a major military campaign, complete with armed bodyguards. Because of a terrorist scare, most of the Hollywood superstars who had been scheduled to attend had cancelled and the media was therefore desperate for news. Bored with the usual starlets dropping their bikini tops at the sight of a camera, reporters eagerly pursued Lara.

Paparazzi stalked her every move, ignoring established European stars in their frantic efforts to get more pictures of her. Her face and body were on display at every newspaper kiosk. She made the covers of *Paris-Match*, *Epoca*, and *Stern* in the same week. In the States all the major newspapers detailed her triumph; both *Time* and *Newsweek* featured photos of her in their articles on the festival. LUSCIOUS LARA STUFFS HER WILD BIKINI WITH THE CANNES FILM FESTIVAL headlined *People* magazine's cover story.

Never had an unknown American actress made such an impact at Cannes. Lara was amazed to find herself being touted as the Brigitte Bardot of the eighties and as the long-awaited successor to Marilyn Monroe. Blinded by adulation, she ignored the fact that Bardot had become so disillusioned with humanity that she now dedicated herself to animal rights, and Monroe, burnt out at the age of thirty-six, had committed suicide.

All Lara thought or cared about was that her lifelong dream of being a success had finally come true, and that Griffin had made it possible. Success was the ultimate trip, they both found—an even greater high than the one they got from snorting cocaine daily. Success was a far more seductive and powerful addiction, and it bound them closer together. On a wild impulse, which at the time seemed like a perfectly logical conclusion to the wonderful madness of the past ten days, they got married.

The ceremony was performed in Vallauris, a quaint little town perched high above Golfe Juan, in the same town hall where Rita Hayworth and Aly Khan were married. Lara had wanted a private ceremony, but Griffin's publicity man "accidentally" leaked the news to the media. Over a thousand people descended upon the town, which was famed for its ceramics, and a near riot ensued. Her wedding made the front page of every major newspaper, and it was the lead story on television news broadcasts all over the world.

Lara wondered what Cal's reaction would be when he heard about it.

* * *

Cal loosened the knot in his tie, which felt like a noose around his neck, and unbuttoned his collar as he entered his study. The triangular-shaped room was so small he had only to stretch out a hand to turn on the desk lamp. Built into the stairwell in the foyer of his home, it was originally intended as a storage area, but he'd been able to fit a chair and a single-drawer desk up against one slanting wall, a recliner into the corner. It was the one room in the house he considered completely his, the only place where he could go to be alone with his thoughts.

Sitting behind the desk, he took a bottle of V.O. out of the drawer and poured himself a double, neat. Eyes closed, he leaned back in the swivel chair, the drink in one hand, a lighted cigarette in the other. It was silent in the house. His wife and son were tucked safely in their beds for the night. No sounds disturbed the quiet of the suburban street outside his split-level home in Valley Stream on Long Island. Tears slipped from beneath his closed eyelids. He didn't brush them away. Nor did he attempt to stop the flow of memories. Loris filled his consciousness.

After his wife's car accident, Cal had tried to shut her out of his mind as completely as he'd shut her out of his life. He dedicated himself to taking care of Julie Ann. Consumed by guilt, he buried the resentments he felt toward her. Julie Ann tried to forgive him for his affair with Loris.

Together, throughout her pregnancy, they sought to recapture the closeness they'd shared when she was carrying Brian. If either of them sensed the futility beneath their pretense of conjugal happiness, they managed to ignore it. All their hopes of saving their marriage were wrapped up in the baby. Julie Ann was so sure it would be a girl, she insisted on having the alcove she'd turned into a nursery painted pink; a bureau filled with tiny pink outfits awaited the new arrival.

The baby girl was stillborn.

Despite her obstetrician's assurances to the contrary, Julie Ann was convinced that her car accident seven months earlier had been the cause of her child's death. "*You* killed her," she screamed at Cal. "You and your whore killed my

baby!'' She went into a prolonged depression, sleeping ten
to twelve hours a day. When awake she gorged herself on
junk food and binged on ice cream. She gained over forty
pounds. Oddly enough, her face and limbs remained slender; all the weight was concentrated in her stomach. She
looked nine months' pregnant.

The mere sight of her kept Cal's guilt and remorse alive.
Swallowing what was left of his pride, he accepted his
brother-in-law's offer of a loan for the down payment on the
house she'd always wanted; a bank loan helped pay for new
furniture. It would be years, he realized, before he was out
of debt. He buried forever his dreams of being a director.

Julie Ann's depression lifted. She threw herself into the
job of decorating the house with an enthusiasm he hadn't
seen in her in ages. There was a victorious air about her
now that she'd finally won the battle to turn Cal into a
model suburban husband. He didn't fight her any longer. He
gave her everything she wanted—except himself.

In her presence he was always withdrawn, silent. The
only time she ever saw him smile was when he was with
Brian. The love and tenderness he lavished on his son
merely added to her sense of being shut out. She reverted to
her clinging, possessive manner with him. He began working late at the office.

On weekends, after he put Brian to bed, Cal would spend
entire evenings alone in his study, reading the latest theater
news or sketching sets for plays he would never direct. For
hours on end he'd sit, lost in thought about the way his life
had turned out. He thought about what might have been.

He began writing his feelings down as a way of releasing
emotions he knew were getting dangerously close to exploding. He needed to express those feelings in order to make
some sense out of them. The artist in him refused to die and
he filled page after page of the journal he started, seeking to
understand the reasons for the choices he'd made. And no
matter which path he took through the tortuous maze of his
own mind, in the end, he always came back to Loris.

He wrote about her, pouring out his love for her, which

neither time nor guilt nor all his will had been able to
diminish. Even if he'd still wanted to forget her, the notori-
ety she'd achieved as Lara Layton would have made it
impossible. Her image beckoned to him from newsstands,
TV screens, and movie billboards. At the office, her nude
centerfold tormented him from a wall in the mail room. On
his way home that evening, he'd seen the headlines an-
nouncing her marriage to Guy H. Griffin.

Cal lit another cigarette on the end of the one he'd just
finished smoking, then poured himself another drink, tears
sliding silently down his face. Caught up in his memories of
Loris, he was unaware at first that his wife was standing in
the doorway watching him.

In all the years they'd lived together, Julie Ann had never
seen her husband cry. "You're thinking about her, aren't
you?" she said, furious. "You've never stopped thinking
about her!"

He looked up at her. For once he made no attempt to hide
his real feelings from her. "I told you I couldn't give her
up. Did you think I just meant physically?"

"You're still in love with her," she screamed. "You've
never stopped loving her! Don't deny it!"

"I wasn't going to deny it," said Cal.

He knew it was absurd, hopeless. He didn't care. He
could not give up his love for Loris. It was no use reminding
himself that his passion almost destroyed his family. Given
the choice, and with full knowledge that their love affair
would end in pain for everyone, he would have done it all
over again.

If their trip to Cannes had seemed like a dream at times,
reality quickly set in upon their return to the Chateau. To
Lara's amazement, Grif insisted they maintain separate
apartments, though he did arrange for her to move to a
luxurious suite—the one usually reserved for his "favorite
lady." Flushed with success, he threw himself into preproduction work on *Ecstasy II*, supervising everything,

down to the smallest detail. She sometimes didn't see him for days.

"But I'm doing all this for you," he reminded her when she requested they spend more time together. "I want everything to be perfect for you."

She could not argue with that.

On those evenings when Griffin summoned her to his apartment, for a candlelight dinner and cocaine-flavored sex, he couldn't have been more charming or attentive, but she always felt as if they were on a date. And there was still a bevy of Pleasure Mates in residence, lounging about the pool, disporting themselves in the Jacuzzis.

"They're here to entertain my guests," he insisted. "It's expected of me. I have an image to maintain."

"It's like living in Grand Central Station," Lara complained. He frowned, seriously displeased.

Lara soon learned that her husband couldn't tolerate the slightest complaint or emotional demand, any more than he could bear to see her without makeup or with her hair in curlers. When she had her period, he shunned her as if she were diseased.

"I guess I'm too much of a romantic," he explained. "You're the only woman who's ever lived up to my fantasies, and I don't want anything to spoil that."

He didn't seem to realize that he was forcing her to play the role of Lara Layton, sex goddess, in both real life and reel. She was getting the two confused. And she was feeling the strain along with a growing resentment.

Like most sequels, *Ecstasy II* was a disappointing ripoff, Lara thought. Griffin was sure the movie would make even more money than *Ecstasy*, and an even bigger star of Lara. Time would prove him correct. A month before the New York premiere they took up residence in the penthouse on East Fifty-seventh Street so Grif could personally supervise the advertising and publicity campaign.

Because of her years of struggle in the Big Apple, Lara

got deep satisfaction from seeing her posters all over Manhattan. That morning she watched the three-story-high billboard displaying her image being raised on the corner of Third Avenue and Fifty-ninth Street, just one block away from the approach to the Queensboro Bridge.

She wondered how Cal would feel as he drove by the billboard.

No print interviews or television talk show appearances had been scheduled for that afternoon, and Lara was lounging in bed reading *Time* magazine. Politics held no interest for her, but as she slipped through that particular section to get to the movie and theater reviews, a photograph caught her eye. There was no mistaking the woman; she'd barely changed in the five years since Lara had last seen her. And she certainly had come up in the world. Jane Prescott, as the caption stated, had become campaign manager for a Senator Kingsley. The distinguished-looking senator from New York, Lara went on to read, had just announced his entry into the 1988 presidential race.

Still coasting on the high she'd gotten from seeing the billboard, Lara decided to call Miss Prescott. Information quickly located the number for the senator's campaign headquarters, and she dialed it.

"Prescott here."

The voice was exactly as Lara recalled: cool, controlled, which was more than she could say about the sound of her own voice when she said, "Miss Prescott, this is . . . Loris Castaldi. Do you remember me?"

There was the slightest pause; that was all the time Prescott needed to recover from the shock. "Loris Castaldi?" she repeated emphatically for Carter's benefit. He glanced up from the computer printout of the latest polls. His eyes met hers across the desk, filling with alarm. "Why, of course, I remember you, Lor—I suppose I should call you Lara now. I've been following your career with great interest."

Lara was pleased to hear that Miss Prescott was aware of her success. She was sure it would make things easier.

"Has my father been following my career with great interest, also?"

"Your father is dead, Loris, as I've told you before." She tilted the receiver so Carter, who was now bending over her, could hear his daughter's voice.

"I'm not a child any longer, Miss Prescott. Please don't treat me like one. We both know he's alive. I want to get in touch with him."

"I'm sorry, but I can't help you."

"Doesn't it occur to you that he might want to see me now?" She tried to keep the pleading note out of her voice, but was unable to. "I want nothing from him, except to see him. Please tell me where I can reach him."

Carter shook his head adamantly.

"I haven't the faintest idea," said Prescott. "It's been a long time since I worked for him, you know."

"Well, then, tell me his name, and I'll—"

"I can't do that, either."

Her authoritarian tone infuriated Lara, made her feel like a five-year-old. "Who the hell do you think you're dealing with—that helpless little girl you shut away so everybody could pretend she didn't exist? I'm not a nobody anymore. I'm Lara Layton! And I have a right to know who my father is. If you won't tell me his identity, I'll hire a private detective to—"

"Do you think that's wise?" Prescott cut her off again. "According to the interviews you've given, your mother and father were killed in an automobile accident when you were five. Do you really want the truth to come out? The whole world would know then that Lara Layton is a bastard whose mother died hopelessly insane."

Lara drew in a sharp, audible breath.

Prescott continued. "I'm sorry I had to be so blunt, but you would have the truth. And the truth is, your father has never wanted to have anything to do with you. Your very existence has always been an embarrassment to him. Never more than now, I would imagine, since you've become a notorious sexpot."

Without another word, Lara hung up.

Prescott replaced her receiver. "I don't think Miss Lara Layton will be hiring a private detective."

Carter didn't look convinced. "What if she does?"

The intercom on Prescott's desk buzzed before she could reply. She pressed the appropriate button. "Yes?"

"Everyone's assembled in the conference room, Miss Prescott," her secretary informed her.

"We'll be right there, Molly." She got to her feet. "If she should be foolish enough to hire a detective, I'd be the first to know. I'm the only lead she's got."

"Are you positive she doesn't remember anything about that day at King's Haven?"

"I questioned her about it the last time I saw her. It was obviously such a traumatic experience that she blocked out the entire incident. You heard her yourself, Carter. She doesn't remember you."

"What if she starts remembering? Once the campaign gets underway, my picture will be—"

"Stop worrying. She doesn't want anything from you. She's a fool, just like her mother. All she wants is your love." She picked up the computer sheets. Carter was running a close second to George Bush. "I took care of Angela, didn't I? I'll take care of her daughter, too, if it ever comes down to that." She handed him the printout. "We're going to be late for the meeting."

CHAPTER
Twenty-one

Prescott's contemptuous words had cut deep, filling Lara with shame and humiliation. In spite of her success, the slightest rejection could still make her feel utterly worthless. The elaborate structure of her present life had been constructed on the shaky foundations of her loveless childhood. Those foundations, she feared, might crumble at any time, bringing everything she'd achieved crashing down around her. She cursed herself. Out of her eagerness to meet her father, she'd acted prematurely. She should have waited until she'd proven herself as an actress. More than anything—more than ever—she wanted him to be proud of her. She desperately needed a drink.

When she descended the carpeted steps to the sunken bar, she found Griffin and Bernie Kaplan, the publicist, in the middle of a brainstorming session.

Kaplan was an old pro who'd cut his publicity teeth working for MGM in the late forties. Now in his mid-sixties, he was as trim and dapper as ever, with a full head

of white hair of which he was inordinately proud, a dashing
moustache, and an unquenchable twinkle in his eyes for the
ladies. Lara was usually delighted to see him. He had an
endless supply of anecdotes about the outrageous publicity
stunts that were popular during Hollywood's golden era.

"Lara! Such a wonderful surprise," he said with an
appreciative glance at her mauve silk lounging pajamas.

"Bernie and I are still working on a publicity gimmick to
tie in with the New York premiere," said Griffin.

Roughly translated, Lara knew, that meant he was busy
and she was in his way. He never allowed her to sit in on the
meetings involving her films, claiming it would prove too
great a strain for her. What she'd once interpreted as a
desire to protect her, she was beginning to realize was a
need to control her. "Don't let *me* interrupt you." She
walked over to the bar.

"Interrupt," Bernie said, eyes atwinkle. "Interrupt all
you want. Inspiration, that's what I'm missing. With you
here, I'm sure to come up with a brilliant idea."

"I hope you're not going to have me jump naked into the
fountain in front of the Plaza, Bernie."

Bernie actually gave her sardonic jibe serious consideration before shaking his head. "It's been done."

"Since you've decided to join us, these are the layouts
for the print campaign." Grif proudly indicated the black-
and-white newspaper and the four-color magazine ads propped
up against the leather banquette. "What do you think?"

Lara slammed a snifter down on top of the marble bar.
"Because of pictures like that, people refuse to take me
seriously as an actress."

"You're not an actress, my pet," Grif reminded her with
an indulgent smile. "You're a star."

Ignoring him, Lara reached for a bottle of Courvoisier. "I
know you're not going to believe this, Bernie, but I've
actually acted on the stage."

Bernie looked as if he didn't. "On the legitimate stage?"

"That's right." Lara poured herself a brandy. When she
caught Grif's disapproving frown, she made it a double. "I

once belonged to a repertory company here in New York. Maybe you've heard of it—The Lower Depths?''

Bernie nodded. "It's one of those avant-garde groups, am I right? They don't make much money, but they're big with the arty crowd.''

"I starred in their first production.''

"No kidding?'' Bernie looked at her with new eyes, which suddenly lit up as if an idea had struck him. "This could be it.'' He jumped to his feet. "Hollywood sex symbol comes back to her roots in the legitimate theater. It's a new twist, all right. We could have like a . . . a big reunion.''

Lara stared at the publicist over the rim of her glass. "A reunion?''

"We'd have to get the original company together, naturally, but . . .'' Bernie paced; it helped him to think. "But we'd also invite other arty types, like, uhh, Joe Papp, say, and Mike Nichols. You know the media coverage we'd get?'' He halted in front of Griffin. "And if you could, God willing, get Woody Allen to show up . . .'' The mere thought rendered him speechless.

Lara laughed—as if that caliber of artist would show up for Griffin, the soft-core porno king. Griffin wasn't laughing. That was precisely the sort of recognition that had always eluded him—the very reason he'd gone into film production in the first place.

"I'm sure the group would go along with it,'' Bernie was saying. "They couldn't afford that kind of publicity in a million years. You'd have to foot the bill for the shindig, but . . . maybe you could make, like, a contribution. It's tax-deductible, and it would be great P.R.'' Bernie had a tendency to think in headlines; his hand swept one before their eyes: "PLEASURE PRODUCTIONS SUBSIDIZES THE ARTS.''

Grif nodded in agreement. The idea was also beginning to appeal to Lara—on a personal level as well as a professional one. "The reunion would have to include all the original members of the group, wouldn't it, Bernie?''

"Sure. That's what gives it human interest. They're the

ones who knew you when you were a struggling actress. Just imagining how they'll feel to see you now—a star."

Lara smiled with satisfaction as she imagined how Cal would feel. "I like your idea very much."

"I like it, too," said Grif. "Let's do it."

Bernie beamed. "I'll get started on it right away. First, I've got to find out if they'll go for it."

"Let *me* call," Lara insisted. "As a personal gesture." Picking up her brandy, she started toward the stairs. "I'm sure I still have the number in my address book. It's in my bedroom. I'll be right back."

Lara didn't need to check her address book for the phone number of The Lower Depths; she knew it by heart. She wanted to keep the conversation private. She wasn't sure Pat would speak to her, and she didn't know how she'd react to another rejection. She punched in the number and took a long gulp of brandy. She barely had time to swallow: Pat answered the phone on the first ring. "Hi, Pat. This is—"

"Loris!" Pat exclaimed. "I don't believe this. We were just talking about you."

Lara's mouth went dry. "We?"

"Artie and me. About that gigantic billboard of you on the corner of Fifty-ninth and Third. You're stopping traffic. But what else is new?" She laughed that great bawdy laugh of hers and Lara felt her throat tighten with emotion.

"You certainly don't sound like *you've* changed. Pat. How have you been?"

"You know me. Still hanging tough. How are you?"

"Oh, everything's great . . . just great."

"I would think so. We heard you were in New York to do publicity for your new movie."

"That's one of the reasons I'm calling." Quickly, Lara filled Pat in on Bernie's reunion idea. "Are you interested?"

"I'm game," she said without hesitation. "We sure as hell could use the free publicity."

"That's great. I'll have Bernie call you. But let's get together, just the two of us. Are you free for lunch tomorrow?"

"If I'm not, I'll make sure I am. One o'clock? Pizza at

Emilio's like the good ole days?'' When there was no answer, she repeated, "One o'clock okay with you?''

"I've missed you very much, Pat," Lara admitted haltingly. "I've wanted to call you so many times. But after the terrible things I said to you, I was sure you were still angry at me.''

"I think I was more hurt than angry, Loris. I've missed you, too. I'm very glad you called.''

"See you tomorrow, then.''

"Just one thing,'' Pat added before Lara could hang up. "You said you wanted me to get *all* the original members of the company together. Does that include Cal?''

"I don't see how we can exclude him,'' Lara said, managing to keep her tone neutral. "There wouldn't have been a company if it wasn't for Cal.'' She was tempted to ask Pat if she'd heard from him recently, but she didn't.

With her usual perception, Pat answered Lara's unspoken question. "I haven't seen Cal since he dropped out of the group. The last I heard, he'd moved to Valley Stream. I shouldn't have any trouble tracking him down.'' There was a pause. "You're sure you want me to?''

"Oh, yes,'' Lara said with more emotion than she'd intended. "I'm sure.''

Woody Allen declined the invitation to the gala reunion. If he hadn't, he'd have been surprised to find himself among some of the most respected names in the theater and the New York-based movie community. There was also a collection of power brokers and politicians, a glittering array of the Nouvelle Riche. The party was lavish in an understated, elegant manner. It was definitely not a typical Guy H. Griffin affair. There wasn't a single Pleasure Mate in sight.

In his droll, inimitable fashion, Mayor Koch delivered a speech about New York's contribution to the arts, and was rewarded with a round of applause. Photographers rushed forward to snap pictures of him with Lara and Grif.

"Ed, how about a shot of just you and Lara?" one of them called out.

Hizzoner obliged by putting an arm around Lara's bare shoulders. He grinned mischievously. "How am I doing?" Recognizing the mayor's trademark question, everyone laughed. Flashbulbs exploded. TV news cameras turned.

Griffin stepped forward. "Thank you, ladies and gentlemen, but that's enough photos for this evening. It's party time."

Lester Lanin, the famed society bandleader, took the cue, gave the upbeat, and the lilting strains of *Night and Day* poured forth invitingly from the area of the penthouse living room, where a dance floor covered the carpeting. Champagne corks popped. Liveried waiters snapped to attention behind the buffet table, which was almost a city block long, and overflowed with a smorgasbord that would have given Henry the Eighth pause.

While Grif exchanged pleasantries with the mayor, Lara excused herself to look for Pat. She found her mingling with a circle that included playwrights David Mamet and Lanford Wilson. "Cal still hasn't arrived," she told her when she'd drawn her aside. "You're sure he said he was coming?"

"Yes. He sounded surprised that he'd been invited at first, which is understandable under the circumstances, but he agreed." Pat took a sip of her vodka martini as she recalled his exact words over the phone. " 'I wouldn't miss it for anything,' he said."

"He's over an hour late." Lara shifted impatiently from one foot to the other. "Maybe he changed his mind."

Pat secretly hoped he had. "Or maybe his wife hid the car keys again."

Lara laughed, though Pat hadn't meant it as a joke. "Déjà vu—my least favorite experience." She tossed her head, sending her platinum hair swirling. "The reunion is a great success, isn't it?" It was more a statement than a question. Lara's eyes were sparkling as she scanned the glamorous assemblage.

In fact, her eyes were unnaturally bright, Pat noted. And there was a recklessness to Lara's movements as she downed the rest of her champagne, exchanged the empty crystal flute glass for a brimming one from the silver tray one of the liveried waiters was carrying, and waved to Hal Prince, whose eye she'd caught, though she'd never met him before that evening. Remembering how shy Lara used to be, Pat assumed fame had given her the confidence she'd once lacked, yet she sensed a desperation behind her gaiety.

She's still in love with him, Pat thought grimly, *and she doesn't even know it.*

"I hope you don't mind my interrupting," a polite voice inquired. They turned to find a dark-haired man, his neatly styled beard just starting to go gray, his eyes deep-set and piercing.

Lara recognized him instantly. "Not at all. I'm so glad to get the chance to tell you how much I admire your work. I never miss any of your films."

Phony compliments always made Martin Stacy squirm. The genuine article, paradoxically, made him smile self-consciously, as the famous director now showed. "Could we talk business for a moment, Miss Layton?"

Lara had already learned that most movie deals were conducted at parties. "Yes, but only if you call me Lara." Pat took the cue to get herself another drink.

"As you may have heard, I'm casting my new movie. Bobby De Niro's set for the male lead. I think you'd be right for the female lead. Would you be interested?"

"Interested? I'd work with you if you were going to film the telephone directory!"

Stacy smiled again. Lara's refreshing lack of artifice, so at odds with her blond bombshell appearance, was what had impressed him about her performance in *Ecstasy*—that, a certain wistful quality, and a touching vulnerability. "Then, you wouldn't mind doing a screen test?"

"Stars aren't usually required to test," Griffin chided lightly, having suddenly materialized at Lara's side. "You should know that, Marty."

"If I had any doubts about your talent," Stacy told Lara directly, "I wouldn't be considering you for the role, but it's not a glamorous part. It's only fair to both of us to make sure it's right for you."

"I'm willing to test," Lara admitted openly, ignoring the look her husband slanted her.

"I'll air-express your agent a copy of the script."

"I don't have an agent."

The director stared. It was unheard of for a professional actress not to have an agent.

"My wife's under exclusive contract to me," Grif explained. "She doesn't need an agent. I select all her scripts and make sure her interests are protected."

He's going to protect her right out of a promising career if she's not careful, Stacy thought. It certainly wouldn't be a Hollywood first. Nevertheless, before taking his leave, he agreed to send the script directly to Griffin and to "take a meeting" with him in Hollywood in two weeks. He hoped his intuition was wrong.

Lara's eyes gleamed with genuine excitement; the cocaine she'd sniffed earlier was rapidly wearing off. "Grif, I'd sell my soul for that part." It would mean a chance to break away from her sex symbol image and do some serious acting. It never occurred to her that her soul was no longer hers for the selling. Its current owner smiled reassuringly. "If it's that important to you, Lara, I'll do everything in my power to see that you get it," Grif said. "But it's got to be on my terms, not his."

"What do you mean?"

"We'll talk about that later. We're neglecting our guests." Taking her arm, he led her to a nearby group that included Mike Nichols, Sidney Lumet, and Meryl Streep, the actress she most idolized.

Normally, Lara would have needed to make another trip to the snowman in order to cope with such an illustrious trio, but her encounter with Martin Stacy had given her confidence a boost. She soon found herself discussing the technical differences between stage and film acting with Meryl Streep who, to Lara's amazement, treated her as an equal. All that was lacking to make her triumph complete was Cal's presence.

And, then, she saw him.

Her heart shuddered to a stop, and her mind put the rest of the world on hold. He was standing by the great brass doors. Not bothering to make her excuses, she started toward him. She didn't catch the look of annoyance that flickered across her husband's face. Without noticing, she brushed past Donald and Ivana Trump. Several people attempted to gain her attention as she passed, but she didn't hear them. She moved slowly across the vast space separating the two of them; she'd waited too long for this moment to rush it. She knew she had never looked better. She'd spent hours making sure of that.

Cal waited for her, his blood pounding. Desire went through him like a shot of adrenalin at the first sight of her. But what he felt was more than mere sexual longing. He hungered for the smile that used to light her face whenever she saw him. He yearned to see her eyes soft with love for him. There would be no love in her eyes for him now, he knew. And he was having trouble reconciling the Loris he remembered with the drop-dead glamorous, supremely confident woman approaching him.

She was sheathed in a strapless black satin gown, and black satin gloves encased the length of her arms, making her bare shoulders, the exposed slopes of her breasts, gleam all the whiter. Diamonds and emeralds glittered at her ears and throat; a string of diamond bracelets dazzled at her wrists.

So many things had conspired to keep them apart, but at that moment, it seemed to Cal, she'd never been more unattainable. Smiling coolly, she halted beside him.

"Hi, Cal," Lara said breezily, the perfect hostess. She was shaking inside. "I'm glad you could make it."

His mouth twisted wryly. "Did you think I could stay away?"

She took a sip of champagne, letting the implications of his question slide. Without seeming to, she looked for

changes in his appearance since she'd seen him last—changes
for the worse. Those little lines at the corner of his eyes
hadn't been there before, nor the two deep lines bracketing
his mouth. But, if anything, they served to enhance the
stark, dramatic quality of his face. His black hair showed a
premature sprinkling of white at the temples, but it was as
unruly as ever. His deep blue eyes were as intense as she
remembered. And he still had the most beautiful mouth
she'd ever seen.

"Though, I must admit I was surprised as hell that you
invited me," he was saying.

Lara shrugged her perfumed shoulders and gave him the
same excuse she'd given Pat. "How could I not invite you?
You're the one who started the company. You've more right
than anyone to attend the reunion."

"I couldn't care less about the reunion," he said, not
needing to justify his actions, as she had. "I just wanted to
see you again, Loris. I was hoping your invitation meant
you've forgiven me for having hurt you."

Lara was completely thrown. She'd forgotten how direct
he could be.

"I often wonder how you are, if you're happy."

She laughed ever so gaily. "How could I not be happy? I
have everything I could possibly want." Diamonds flashed
as she waved her bejeweled arm, indicating her luxurious
penthouse.

Cal took a moment to finally look around. To his eyes the
admittedly stunning decor was devoid of life, a mere deco-
rator's statement. Nowhere could he find a touch of Loris.
Not a single trace of her warmth or spirit was evident amid
that brazen display of wealth and power. "Very impressive."

His sardonic tone made it clear just how unimpressed he
was. That irked her. Living well was supposed to be the
best revenge. "You have to admit this is a damn sight better
than living on West Forty-sixth Street."

"It had its moments." When his eyes met hers and she
saw the memories reflected within, she felt the past coming
alive between them.

She was swept by a sense of loss, and then anger. "And that's all there were—moments."

He dropped his eyes.

"I have a full life now," she added defensively, as if he were giving her an argument about it. "Success, money—everything I could possibly want." Realizing that she was repeating herself, she took a gulp of champagne. Dom Perignon. Sixty-five dollars a bottle. "Including a husband who adores me."

"That's not so hard to do," he muttered.

"By the way, where's *your* adoring spouse?" Lara glanced around her. No one else was standing anywhere near the entrance. Grif, she saw, was in the raised media center, probably showing off his state-of-the-art electronic equipment. The party was now in full swing. Pat's red hair flashed under the strobe lights, setting her apart from the other disco dancers. The music blared.

Lara had been oblivious to everything around her since she started speaking with Cal. Damn him that he could still do that to her, she cursed silently.

Putting on her hostess smile, she turned back to her former lover. "I don't see your adoring wife anywhere. Didn't you bring her?"

"No." He offered no explanation.

Having Julie Ann witness the tangible proof of her success had been part of the scenario Lara had been acting out in her head for weeks. Nothing was going according to her plan. She was suddenly furious. The next words she heard herself utter came tumbling out all by themselves. "You mean, she actually allowed you to go alone to a party being given by your ex-mistress? Or didn't you bother to tell her you were coming here? That's the way you used to do it, wasn't it?"

"Christ," said Cal.

What the hell am I doing, Lara thought. She had planned to play it cool, to be so far above him he could never hope to reach her. How could everything have unraveled so quickly? "So, tell me, Cal," she rattled on sarcastically, "how have *you* been? Has your life turned out the way you wanted it to? Are you happy?"

Cal's eyes darkened, in response to her question, Lara first assumed. Then she realized he was reacting to someone or something behind her. Glancing over her shoulder, she saw her husband approaching.

"I wondered where you were, Lara," Grif called out lightly, not wanting her to know he'd been observing her— them. "What on earth are you doing way over here?"

"Just talking old times, darling," she said.

Griffin managed to conceal his bemusement. She never called him darling, not even in private. Her face was flushed. In contrast, the tall, strikingly good-looking stranger was unnaturally pale.

"This is Cal Remington, darling," she told him when he halted beside her. Taking his arm, she clung to him in a wifely manner. Another first. The attractive stranger looked away. "Cal's The Lower Depths' original artistic director."

And her former lover, Grif had already surmised. He had been watching them on the TV monitor, and he'd felt the heat that passed between them when they looked at each other.

Grif gave Cal his most charming smile. "Sorry to intrude. I'm sure you two must have a great deal to talk about." His arm went around his wife's back, his hand coming to rest on her bare shoulder. It was a casual gesture—that of a man supremely confident of his possessions.

It irritated the hell out of Cal.

"You two can finish catching up on old times later. We're about to screen a preview of *Ecstasy II*."

"When did you decide that?" Lara asked.

"I thought I'd give everyone a treat," Grif told Cal. "Personally, I never get tired of watching it. Lara's never looked more exquisite." His hand slid over the curve of her shoulder in a way that was evocative of far more intimate caresses.

Cal's hand went for his cigarettes.

Grif was accustomed to other men desiring his wife. The

look of envy they regarded him with had always been a source of great satisfaction to him, but this was different. What he saw reflected in Cal Remington's eyes when they looked at him was not envy but jealousy, dark and corrosive. He was still in love with Lara. Knowing he couldn't have her was eating him up inside.

Grif could feel himself getting hard. "Why don't you two go on ahead to the screening room, while I make a general announcement, darling?"

Cal finished rippling open the silver foil from a fresh pack of cigarettes. "I can't stay."

Lara stiffened, but said nothing.

"You just got here. The fun is just beginning." The disappointment in Grif's voice was genuine. He'd been looking forward to seeing her ex-lover squirm in his seat while he watched Lara's naked image. He'd planned to hold her hand throughout the movie. "I'll leave you to get Cal to change his mind, darling. Who can deny you anything?"

He dropped a kiss on her shoulder. A perverse little smile curved his lips when he caught the look Cal shot him.

Lara was too busy watching her husband to notice Cal's reaction. *What game is he playing now*, she wondered irritably as he sauntered off.

Cal lit the cigarette he just tore out of the pack.

"Do you really have to leave?" Lara said. How many times in the past had she asked him *that* question?

He took a long drag on his cigarette. The last thing he needed was to watch her rolling around naked in another man's arms. He exhaled harshly. "Yes."

Lara's laugh was just as harsh. "You wife keeps you on a very short leash these days, I see."

"We all have our problems," Cal snapped. "Tell me something—doesn't it bother your husband to parade you naked in front of the whole world?"

It was a question Lara had asked herself often enough, but she wasn't about to admit that to him. Her chin went up defensively. "No, why should it?"

"It would bother me a lot knowing that other men were

jerking off on my wife.'' She gasped, her eyes widening with pain. He didn't care. He wanted her to hurt, as much as he was hurting. ''Don't you mind being treated like the choicest piece in his collection of erotic art?''

''I'm used to men treating me like a choice piece,'' she returned bitterly. ''And that includes you.''

''I never treated you like a—''

''A piece of ass on the side—that's all I ever meant to you. But I loved you, you bastard.'' Tears burned behind her eyes. She refused to shed them. She'd shed all the tears over him she was ever going to. ''So, I wouldn't feel so superior to Grif if I were you, Cal. You're two of a kind.'' She left him standing there.

But it was precious little satisfaction to her.

CHAPTER
Twenty-two

The man owns you, body and soul.

Tony Storpio's words came back to haunt Lara. She'd never realized the Faustian pact she'd made when she had signed that exclusive seven-year contract with Griffin, or to what extent he controlled her career, until he destroyed her chance to do the Stacy film.

"I did it for you," he said.

She shook her head angrily. "You insisted on being made executive producer because you always have to control everybody and everything."

"I was trying to protect you, Lara."

"Protect me from what? The first decent part I've ever had? Working with a co-star like Robert De Niro?"

"From making a fool of yourself. That great Hollywood cliché: the sex symbol who wants to be taken seriously as an actress. The critics would have a field day with that one."

"Martin Stacy loved my screen test."

"A ten-minutes screen test does not a two-hour movie

make.'' He seemed truly saddened to have to expose her to such obvious truths. "I'm not trying to put you down, Lara. I think you're sensational—at what you do. But we're talking heavyweight competition now. You're way out of your class."

"Why did you push so hard for me to get the part if you felt that way?"

"Because I knew how much you wanted it. And with me as executive producer, you'd have a fighting chance. I'd see to it that your best takes were used. If De Niro looked too strong, I could cut him down to size in the editing. But if you were to go it alone, without me, an actor like De Niro would wipe you right off the screen."

"I'm willing to take that chance. Jesus, Grif, don't I have the right to decide what movies I make?"

He smiled. "No." He didn't bother to elaborate, since she was only too familiar with the terms of her contract: she couldn't do so much as a walk-on, on stage, screen, or television, without his consent.

"It's my career!"

"You're my creation!"

She laughed right in his face. "You sound like a mad scientist in a grade B movie."

The look he shot her sobered her instantly; she'd never seen such rage in his eyes. Yet, when he finally spoke, his voice was controlled. "Why do you think I've never cast a male star in any of your movies—just good-looking studs? It was so you'd never have to play opposite anyone better than you. Lighting, makeup, wardrobe, every camera angle, every word you spoke, were chosen just as carefully, and for the same reason: to make you look good. To emphasize all your strong points, and hide your weaknesses as an actress. That's why you're a star."

Lara was too shaken to reply. It didn't take much to undermine her confidence in herself, as he well knew.

"*Dominique* is going into production as originally sched-uled," Grif went on coldly. "Your first costume fitting is at ten o'clock tomorrow morning. Be there. And don't ever question my judgment again.''

He turned away from her for a long moment; when he turned back, he was his usual charming self. From the inside pocket of his smoking jacket he removed a black velvet jewelry box. "I meant to give you this at dinner tonight, to make up for your little disappointment." He lifted an opera-length strand of pearls out of the velvet box and slipped it over her head. "Exquisite," he said. "I knew only Ceylonese pearls could compete with the translucence of your skin. Do you like them?"

Lara's hand felt the spherical perfection of each pearl. They had to be at least twenty-five millimeters, worth close to a hundred thousand dollars.

The smile Grif gave her was appealingly boyish. "Am I forgiven?"

Her fingers closed around the lustrous strand. With one yank she tore it from her neck, sending pearls flying in all directions.

They did not speak to one another, except through intermediaries, for the next two months.

Lara had attended the costume fitting and she started the film on schedule. She had no choice. *Dominique*, a costume epic set during the French Revolution, was little more than a series of sex scenes strung together by the flimsiest of plots. She hated it. She used to rely on her memories of Cal whenever she had to do a sex scene. All she was able to summon up now was the contempt she'd seen in his eyes at the reunion.

Cocaine gave her the sexual glow she needed in order to fake a passion she hadn't felt on or off the screen in years. She was doing so much coke it deserved a screen credit. But she had to be careful. If she did too much she got strung out, and then she crashed into the most paralyzing depression.

She was terrified of ending up like her mother, of being unable to function in the real world. But she could not stop snorting cocaine and gulping down shots of brandy. The

only way she could endure the endless filming of what had
become ludicrous in her mind, was to get high.

"Is she here yet?" The assistant director's voice bellowed.
Lara heard him before he entered her dressing room. An-
nouncing his presence gave him the sense of authority his
short stature and slight build sadly denied him.

Duval ignored him and continued brushing out the sleep
tangles in Lara's hair.

"Thank Christ!" he exclaimed upon seeing Lara, his
voice grating on her raw nerves. He always sounded as
though he were shouting through an imaginary megaphone.
He crossed the boiserie-paneled room, feeling more awkward than usual among the delicately carved and gilded
Louis Quinze furnishings. "How is she? Is she okay?"

An angelic smile lit up the hairdresser's face, making his
cherubic features appear even more so. "She needs a
touch-up."

The AD's Steven Spielberg-type beard jutted out aggres-
sively. "A touch-up? Now?! Madden's been set up to shoot
for over an hour, and Grif is calling down every five
minutes to find out if we've started yet."

Duval calmly tucked the brush under one arm and grabbed
a couple of fistfuls of Lara's hair, separating them to expose
an inch of black roots. "She needs a touch-up."

"Shit!"

Lara cringed behind her dark glasses, but continued to
play the invisible woman, which was exactly how their
references to her in the third person always made her feel.
She tried to concentrate on the script lying open on her lap.
She was having trouble memorizing her lines—all four of
them.

"*You* tell Madden, okay, Duval? He's already pissed off
because she's late again, and—" A mechanical squawk cut
in. Grif's voice cried out from the depths of the AD's
designer jeans: "Joel?" Wrestling the walkie-talkie out of

his back pocket, Joel quickly extended the antenna and snapped to attention. "Yes, sir?"

"Is she there yet?"

One would have thought to hear them that Lara had to travel miles to reach the set when, in fact, *Dominique* was being shot almost entirely at the Chateau, though the walk from her bedroom to her dressing room had seemed like miles to her that morning. In spite of the sleeping pills she'd washed down with brandy, she hadn't fallen asleep until dawn again.

"She just got here. I was about to call you."

"How does she look? Is she all right?"

"She" felt like hell, as though she were wearing her body inside out. Her nerves were where her skin should be, and everything kept scraping against them. The light hurt her eyes, and loud noises felt like blows to the head.

"She's okay," Joel shouted into the walkie-talkie, "but Hair says she needs a touch-up."

The walkie-talkie shouted back, "A touch-up—now? He picked one hell of a time to schedule a touch-up."

Duval adjusted his six-feet-one to the AD's five-feet-five, his voice to the instrument. "I've had a touch-up scheduled every morning for over a week, but she's been too—"

"Tell Hair he's got to work around it," Grif's disembodied voice ordered. "I'm counting on him and Makeup to get her together and on the set in record time. Call me when we're ready to shoot." He clicked off.

But not soon enough for Lara. She hated the sound of that thing. It made her feel like there was a war going on and she was the main hostage. Her head was beginning to throb.

"Where the hell is Makeup?" Squinting through his George Lucas-style glasses, the AD scanned the dressing room. "Don't tell me Jason's not here now?"

Smiling pleasantly, Duval began teasing Lara's hair. "He just went for a cup of coffee."

"Great!" Joel exploded. "That's fucking great!"

Lara felt as if the top of her head was about to come off. "Joel, will you please stop—"

"Doesn't anybody realize we're making a movie?"

"Joel, *please*. I'm trying to memorize my—" Lara started to say.

"Here's our little star," Jason purred, making his customary grand entrance. "We couldn't get her out of bed again today, hmm?"

"Come on, Jason, you're holding up production," the AD said. Jason swept by him, ignoring him as usual. "How long will it take you to get her ready?"

"How long?" Pinkie extended, Jason lifted the styrofoam container to his chiseled lips. He rolled the answer around in his mouth along with the coffee, taking his time to savor both. "As long as it takes, dear boy."

"Come on, Jason, not today, huh? What the hell am I supposed to tell Madden?"

A perverse gleam lit up Jason's eyes; his features were as sharp as his tongue. "A great *auteur* such as yourself should be able to come up with something original."

"Jee-zus! Why am I wasting valuable time with you people? I'm needed on the set." Walkie-talkie clutched in one hand, the AD went storming out of the room, like a commando on a suicide mission.

"Bloody little twit." Jason detached a small ivory pillbox from the gold chain around his neck. "Film Institute graduate, wouldn't you know, with an Orson Welles complex." With long, fastidious fingers he picked through a multicolored collection of uppers and downers, settled on a dexy. He popped the upper, washing it down with coffee, then held out the pillbox. "Happiness, anyone?"

Duval smiled his angelic smile while he went on teasing Lara's hair. "I just had a 'lude." Which explained the smile.

"No, thanks," Lara said. Not that she couldn't have used a 'lude in the strung-out state she was in. What she really needed was a pill that would make the rape scene they were shooting today disappear. She'd have swallowed an entire bottle of pills to make the movie disappear.

"You sure? You bloody well look like you need something."

Lara was seriously tempted. She fingered the antique poison ring she wore all the time now, drawing some comfort from it. Its concealed center could hold a full gram of cocaine. "I've got something stashed for later."

"You don't look like you're going to make it to later, luv." Snapping the box shut, Jason hooked it back on the chain as he turned to Duval. "I assume we'll have to work on our little star at the same time again today." He took his position between Lara and the vanity table, where the gilt-framed mirror reflected the collection of many-hued jars and bottles, the wide assortment of brushes and sponges that were lined up as precisely as surgical instruments on the tray. He waved an imperious hand at her face. "Let's have a look at it, shall we?"

Reluctantly, Lara removed her sunglasses.

"Good Lord," he gasped, seeing the dark circles under her eyes. Her lids were swollen, and her usually translucent skin was a sickly yellow. "Just what am I supposed to do with that? I'm a makeup artist, not a bloody magician."

Duval gave Lara an encouraging wink in the mirror before lifting the platinum fall off its stand. "A real artist would consider it a challenge, Jason."

Jason smiled acidly. "Fuck you, dear boy."

"Anytime."

While Duval anchored the fall to Lara's head, which was now one solid, throbbing ache, Jason started applying make-up, working in double-time—dexy time. With the deft movements of professionals, they handled her face and hair as if they were objects apart from her. Everything seemed strangely detached to Lara, out of focus.

Before applying the final touch of lipstick, Jason stepped back to view his artwork. He frowned. "We can probably get away with it in long shot—perhaps even in a two-shot. But I'm not too sure about close-ups."

"Who the hell is going to look at my face, anyway?" Lara snapped, her patience finally at an end. "They're all going to be looking at my naked tits and ass." She flinched as her own voice reverberated in her brain. Her headache had escalated into a full-fledge migraine.

"A close-up—that's the moment of truth, that is," Jason returned, snap for snap. "That's where it all shows: that pill too many, that drink too many, that little extra toot." With a sable brush he added another layer of rouge. "We might have been able to overindulge when we were eighteen or twenty. But not at your age, luv. From here on in it's wrinkle city, and unless—"

"That's enough!" Lara put both hands up in front of her face to ward off the brush. "I've had enough!" She jumped up, sending her script flying and Jason crashing into the vanity table. The can of hair spray sailed clear out of Duval's hand.

"I think she's finally flipped out," Jason said as Lara pushed past him.

"You're on a real bitch trip today, you know that, Jason?" Duval tossed off as he went after her.

"Me?" Jason's eyes widened. "What did I do?"

Duval caught up with Lara, just as she was about to shut the bathroom door behind her. "Lara, don't." He grabbed the doorknob, stopping her. "The state you're in, you shouldn't be doing any shit. You're in no condition to work today. Let me call the nurse in. She'll take one look at you and sign you out."

"No, don't! Grif said if I'm too sick to work one more time, he'll have me put in one of those . . . clinics."

"Maybe that's what you need, Lara."

She shook her head wildly. "God, no! It's the same as being locked up in the nut house." *Just like my mother. I'd rather die.* "I'll be all right, really." She forced a smile. "I just need a few minutes by myself to . . . to calm down." He released the doorknob. "Thanks, Duval." She gave him a quick kiss on the cheek. She was genuinely grateful for his concern; nevertheless, she slammed the door on it. And locked it.

She headed straight for the cabinet where she kept her toilet articles. She took out her alligator case and a milk-glass bottle labeled ASTRINGENT LOTION. Pulling out the stopper, she spilled what she judged to be four lines worth of cocaine onto the mirrored shelf above the scalloped sink. She used her monogrammed gold razor blade to shape two lines out of the mound of sparkling crystals, her hand shaking. The lines made up in thickness what they lacked in evenness.

When she sniffed the powder's crystalline dazzle into her nostrils, she felt a burning, stinging sensation, followed, within minutes, by a soothing numbness. Then that exhilarating heart-pounding rush. The hit exploded behind her eyes, blowing up her migraine into a million icy pieces. Everything came sharply into focus. There was a wonderful feeling of space behind her eyes now. Endless space. She could breathe again.

Scooping up the rest of the cocaine with the tip of the razor blade, she filled her antique poison ring. A little insurance never hurt, and she no longer dreaded doing the rape scene. She'd just gotten this absolutely staggering insight into how the scene should be played.

Earlier, she'd left the ivory lace negligee that completed her costume hanging on the back of the door. Discarding her robe, she slipped the negligee over her frilly corselet, which constricted her figure into the shape of an hourglass, pushing her breasts up so high they all but spilled out of the lacy top. Long garters held up her white silk stockings, leaving the flesh of her upper thighs exposed.

Pausing only to grab a tissue for her runny nose, Lara sailed back into the dressing room. "I'm ready. Let's go."

"Where the bloody hell is she off to now?" Jason wailed, lipstick brush flailing in midair. "You're not finished, you know?"

Lara couldn't possibly sit still. "You can finish me on the set." She had to keep moving. She had to tell Madden about her absolutely staggering insight immediately. So many other brilliant ideas were flooding her mind it was difficult to keep track of them all. "Come on, Jason, you're holding up production." She blew her cooler than cool nose, dropped the soiled tissue at his feet as she swept by him. "Let's go, everybody. Magic time!" She flung herself out the door.

"Oh, this is too bloody much," Jason muttered savagely to Duval as they went stumbling down the hall after her, lugging their paraphernalia.

Lara laughed. There was no way they could keep up with her, and she wasn't about to wait for them. She couldn't afford to waste a single atom of all this energy and brilliance. The world trembled around her at the speed of light.

Madden was conferring with Ron, his cinematographer, over the storyboards detailing that morning's shoot. The key grip and his best boy were testing the dolly tracks to make sure the camera's movements would be fluid, while the head gaffer was rechecking the arc lights his crew had positioned earlier, just to have something to do while he waited. Everything came to a halt the instant Lara glided onto the set. From halfway across the rococo bed chamber, with its lushly frescoed ceiling, inlaid, multicolored marble floor, and authentic Louis Seize furnishings, Lara saw the enthusiasm drain out of the director's face.

Josh Madden, though only in his mid-twenties, had already established his reputation as a director—of TV commercials. His specialty was those lush, tropical, thirty-second fantasies that lured people to the Bahamas and the Virgin Islands. No one could touch him when it came to evoking the white expanse of deserted beaches, sun-struck water, moonlight-drenched, romantic hideaways.

Soft focus, his favorite cinematic device, seemed to extend to his persona. His pudgy features had a blurry look to them—his hair and eyes were so light as to appear washed-out, his body was shapeless. He moved and spoke as if in slow motion. This was his first feature film. The way things were going, he feared it might be his last.

"How are you feeling today, Dominique?" Madden always called his actors by their characters' names, something he had picked up from reading *Stanislavski Directs*.

"Great. I've been working on the scene," Lara confided proudly. "I have several ideas I'd like to—"

"I can't wait to hear them." The smile he gave her was as condescending as his tone. It made her stiffen resentfully. "But we're running behind schedule, so why don't we try it the way we rehearsed it, first?" He peered at her as if through the lens of a camera. "You sure you're feeling all right? You look very. . . pale."

The concerned look in his eyes as they searched her face didn't fool Lara for a second. What he was really trying to figure out was how much trouble she was going to be today. She was on to all of them. Attuned to every nuance, to levels of meaning none of them could even begin to comprehend, she was fully aware of the hostility behind the crew's phony smiles.

"This is going to be a tough scene," Madden was saying. "Physically, as well as emotionally. If you don't feel up to it, it might be better to—"

"I never felt more sure of myself," Lara interrupted for a change, projecting her voice to reach one and all. At that moment, her husband came strolling in.

The current Pleasure Mate of the Month was draped over his arm, her long, strawberry-blond hair mussed suggestively. She was in full war paint—aquamarine shadow to match her eyes, lashes several inches long—but a tiny red smudge was all that was left of her lipstick. Which raised the inevitable question in everybody's mind as to what she'd just been doing with her pouty mouth. Grif couldn't have looked more cheerful or relaxed.

Everyone stared. The silence was total and so thick, Lara thought, she could have sliced it with a gold razor blade. All eyes now turned to her, eager to witness her humiliation. She denied them the satisfaction.

Without so much as a glance in her direction, Grif escorted the busty eighteen-year-old to a silk-damask-covered love seat on the sidelines, from where they could clearly see the action, and be just as clearly seen. Miss Pleasure Mate had on an ivory lace jump suit. Lara didn't need that special clarity cocaine afforded in order to get Grif's message: *You can be replaced.* She'd show him.

Head held high, Lara walked over to her starting position beside the silk-draped canopied bed where Rod, her co-star, was waiting to rape her.

"Cut," the director called out, making Lara freeze under the key light. "How did it look in the camera, Bob?"

The cameraman nodded. "Looked good to me. She hit her mark right on the money this time."

Madden's sigh of relief was audible. "Print it."

Lara slowly released the breath she'd been holding. The first setup, a four-line-apiece exchange of dialogue between Dominique, favorite of Louis XVI, and Tonio, her ex-stableboy-turned-revolutionary, had required twenty-four takes. Once the cameras had started rolling, all her brilliant ideas had deserted her. She had trouble remembering her lines, and she kept missing her mark. Her mouth was so dry she could barely speak, and her arms and legs had that strange, draggy feeling she'd been experiencing lately. All that fabulous energy had drained clear out of her.

"Get ready for the next setup," Madden ordered.

The cameraman and the cinematographer looked at each other, then at the director, as if they were sure they hadn't heard him correctly. "Shouldn't we get a few more good takes?" Ron asked. It was the customary procedure.

"I think we'd better get the rest of the scene in the can first, just in case . . ." Madden's voice trailed off. He glanced over at Griffin, who nodded his approval from the love seat. "Next setup." He pulled himself out of his director's chair as the crew sprang into action.

"Now, here's where we go into the rape," he explained on his way to the canopied bed. "I don't want any acting. I want the real thing." He smiled, just to keep things light. "Short of actual sex. But I want you both to pull out all the stops. This is going to be the hottest thing ever put on film. Now, we don't have time for a run-through. Do you remember what we did in rehearsal, Dominique?"

"Of course." That's why she dreaded doing the scene.

He gave her the rundown anyway. "At first you fight Tonio with all you've got. Then, you start getting excited in spite of yourself. Finally, you're as hot for it as he is. Any problems with that?"

"No problem at all," she returned flippantly. "Everybody knows women secretly love being raped," she added, but her sarcasm was lost on Madden.

"That's exactly the subtext of the scene," he said, clearly surprised by her perception.

It was time for another trip to the snowman, Lara decided. She'd have to move quickly, cautiously. The director's back was to her as he returned to his place; the crew was too involved with making the necessary adjustments to take any notice of her; Grif was huddling with the Pleasure Mate. She stepped behind Rod, who was busy making sure his wall-to-wall chest muscles would show to advantage under the deep slash in his flowing peasant shirt.

She flicked open her poison ring. Using the longest of her fingernails to scoop up the crystals, she snorted instant energy into one nostril, limitless brilliance into the other. She made a second trip. She wasn't taking any chances. Already inflamed, her nasal passages felt as though she'd stuck a red hot poker up them. Her eyes teared. The pain would be gone within minutes, she assured herself, returning to her mark just as the director gave the signal.

The AD held up the clapper board. "This is a take. Roll sound."

"Rolling."

"Camera."

"Mark it."

"*Dominique*. Scene fourteen. Take one."

The sudden, overwhelming jolt to her nervous system took Lara completely by surprise, making her stagger. *Something's gone wrong*, she thought. Before she could recover Rod grabbed her, threw her roughly down on the bed, and climbed on top of her, his massive body crushing hers into the mattress. She fought to push him off her, but it was like pushing against a stone wall. Her legs felt so heavy she couldn't have moved them even if they weren't pinned under his. She could barely lift her arms.

His mouth came down on hers, hard. Parting her lips forcibly, he shoved his tongue so deep in her throat she almost gagged. Somehow she managed to grab chunks of his hair and pull his head back, but it seemed to her that she was moving in slow motion, while the rest of the world had speeded up, like a merry-go-round spinning out of control.

She never realized how hard she was pulling on his hair. Gripping her wrists, he twisted them until she was forced to let go. His hands were so huge he needed only one of them to secure both of hers. With his other hand he tore loose the silken cord holding back the drapes. Quickly, effortlessly, he tied her arms to the bedposts, stretching them high above her head. Then he sat back, straddling her hips, a slow grin spreading across his face. He was now free to do anything he wanted to her.

And there was nothing she could do to stop him. That exhilarating rush of euphoria she always got on cocaine had turned inward, against her. Her heart was beating too fast. His meaty fingers thrust apart her negligee, hooked the lacy top of her corselet. With one motion he ripped the length of it wide open. She felt completely overwhelmed by his superior strength and her own helplessness. With the wounded fury of a trapped animal, she thrashed from side to side, struggling to free herself. He grabbed her bare breasts and kneaded them as if they were unfeeling lumps of dough. When he rammed his knee between her thighs, forcing them apart, a primal panic seized her.

She no longer knew the difference between make-believe and reality.

Before the stunned, dilated pupils of Lara's eyes, Rod became Tony Storpio, who changed into Dan Gordon, who looked just like Griffin. He was all the men she'd ever been forced to submit to sexually. The silken cord finally gave way under the pressure of her frantic tugging. She went for his face with both hands, nails first.

"Cut," Madden sighed, hauling himself to his feet. "No,

Dominique, you're not supposed to fight it anymore, remember?'' He dragged himself over to the canopy bed. ''He's got it in you now, and you love it. That's what we want to see, not . . .'' His words broke off as he got his first close look at Lara. Rod had climbed off her and was sitting back on his heels at the foot of the bed, also staring incredulously. She was hyperventilating, Madden realized; he'd assumed all along it was heavy breathing.

Lara was still flat on her back, drenched in sweat, shaking uncontrollably. Adrenalin was pumping through her, readying her body for escape, but every muscle was locked. Her heart was pounding furiously, and spasms of pain radiated up her chest and neck. Wouldn't it be funny if she was having a heart attack, she thought dazedly.

''I think something's wrong,'' Rod was saying, looking like himself again. ''I could feel her shaking all over, and she's sweating cold.''

''Joel, get the nurse down here right away,'' the director called over his shoulder.

A crowd quickly formed around the bed, then parted to make way for Griffin. ''Lara, can you hear me?'' It took her a moment to realize that it was her husband's face looking down at her, not a hallucination. He sat on the bed next to her. ''You're going to be all right.'' He bent over her solicitously. ''We'll take a break until you're feeling yourself again. There's only one more setup left to shoot. You can do it one more time, can't you?''

Lara opened her mouth to answer, but a scream came out. She didn't stop screaming until somebody jabbed a hypodermic needle into her arm.

She flinched as the harsh glare of the fluorescent lights hit her, full force. *Why did I come in here?* she wondered, shielding her eyes against the bathroom's relentless brightness.

The last thing she could remember was someone jabbing a hypodermic needle into her arm—she'd always been terrified of needles. Whatever it was she'd been given must have been strong enough to knock out a bull elephant. But how long had she been out?

She was dying of thirst.

That's why she'd come in here, she finally realized. She needed a glass of water.

Still feeling groggy, but wonderfully out of it, Lara floated over to the shell-shaped marble washbasin . . .

. . . where the mirror was waiting for her to finally confront herself. And the gold razor blade gleamed invitingly.

PART IV

CHAPTER
Twenty-three

On his way back to his office, Cal stopped by his secretary's desk to pick up his messages and drop off the notes from the production meeting he'd just concluded.

"Meg, did Charlie Barnett call while—" he began.

"Oh, my God," Meg Dowd gasped, and her left hand shot up from the typewriter keys to press the audio plug deeper into her ear. Her brown eyes widened as she strained to listen to the miniature TV she kept in the top drawer next to the typing paper.

Dire happenings were transpiring on *General Hospital*, Cal surmised with an indulgent smile.

His secretary, a middle-aged widow with two grown sons, was addicted to soap operas. Since she was somehow able to listen to them while typing ninety words a minute, and keeping her right ear cocked to answer the phones, he saw no reason to discourage her habit.

"My God," she said again, looking up at him. "Lara

Layton—you know, the movie star?—she tried to kill herself. She's in a coma!"

Everything went silent around Cal; all he could do was
stare at the woman. He could see her lips move as she
repeated the rest of the news bulletin, but that was all. Then
the varied sounds of the bustling, sprawling production
room returned with a roar. ". . . rushed to the hospital," she
was saying, "but the doctors fear it may be too late to save
her."

Cal turned and went into his office. He closed the door
behind him and sank back against it. All the strength went
out of his legs; he barely managed to get to his desk, where
he collapsed into the swivel chair.

His phone rang. Meg usually answered the telephone by
the second or third ring, but she'd obviously left her post to
spread the news. The phone kept ringing and ringing. When
he couldn't stand it any longer, he tore the receiver off the
hook. "Yes?"

"Have you heard the news?" his wife asked breathlessly.

He murmured an assent.

"Isn't it awful?" she tsked. "She was only twenty-
six."

"*Was*? You mean, she's . . ."

"Dead, yes. They just announced it. I thought you said
you'd heard."

"Oh, Christ, no," he said. "No!"

"She slashed both her wrists," Julie Ann went on,
unable to keep the glee out of her voice. "She practically
bled to death before they found her. I know it's terrible, but
with the life those people lead—drugs, liquor, wild parties—
what can you expect? Thank God *you* had the good sense to
get out before—"

Cal hung upon her, slamming the receiver down so hard
the bell inside the instrument jangled, and sprang to his feet.
He was on his way out the door when the phone started
ringing again. He knew it was Julie Ann. He didn't stop.

* * *

He walked the streets for hours, without direction, oblivious of time, his surroundings, or the jostling crowds. Hunched over, hands sunk deep in his pockets, he walked swiftly, trying to outpace the memories that pursued him. His feet stopped, suddenly, and when he looked up, he saw that he was standing in front of the steps leading down to The Lower Depths.

The theater was between productions; the door was locked when he tried it. He pounded on the wooden frame, causing the stained-glass panels in the door to rattle dangerously. He let out a stream of curses that grew more intelligible and increasingly graphic the louder he yelled. A shadowy form approached.

Pat unlocked and opened the door, her irritation turning to surprise when she saw that it was Cal. She needed only one look at his face to know that he'd heard the news. Stepping back, she let him in.

While Pat was double-locking the door behind him, Cal's eyes swept over the empty theater. A work light stood center stage, its naked glare illuminating unfinished flats, a mess of two-by-fours, paint cans, and carpentry tools. The smell of paint and raw lumber mingling in the air caught in his throat.

He thought he'd been running away from the memories, when all the time, he'd been running toward them. They rushed in on him now. He saw himself standing in the wings as Lara threw herself heedlessly into his arms. Her ecstatic laughter rang in his ears, her body pressed against his, soft and warm, as he relived that blinding moment when pretense was no longer possible and everything they felt for each other was finally revealed in their eyes. That moment when he knew, for the first time, that she loved him.

"The six o'clock news is about to go on," Pat said, breaking into his reverie. "They're sure to have more information by now. The TV's in my office."

Cal followed as Pat quickly led the way. He dreaded hearing the details about Lara's suicide, yet he had to know what had driven her to such a desperate act. The news had already started when they entered Pat's cubby-hole of an

office. A close-up of a publicity still of Lara filled the TV
screen, her face radiantly alive, heartbreakingly beautiful.

"... at 1:15 Pacific Standard Time," Bill Beutel was
saying. "For an update, let's switch live to Judy Fields, our
Los Angeles correspondent."

"This is Judy Fields. I'm standing here in front of
Westside Hospital, where over a thousand Lara Layton fans
have been gathering since early afternoon to hold a vigil for
the world-famous sex goddess." The camera panned the
crowd surging against the police barricades, many of them
holding lighted candles. "According to a reliable source, the
star suffered a breakdown on the set this morning during the
filming of her latest movie."

"Why wasn't she taken to a hospital then?" Cal demanded.
The anchorman echoed his question.

"No one seems to know, Bill," Judy Fields replied. "She
was sedated by the company nurse, who claims to have left
her sleeping peacefully in her bedroom while she went for a
cup of coffee. When the nurse returned, she found that Miss
Layton had locked herself in her bathroom and wouldn't
answer her calls. When they broke the door down they
found the queen of glamour semiconscious on the blood-
soaked carpet. She'd slashed both her wrists."

"Why the hell can't they refer to her as an actress?" Cal
muttered angrily.

"They've never referred to her as an actress," Pat reminded
him bitterly.

"The star's husband, Guy H. Griffin," the correspondent
continued, "did not accompany his wife to the hospital. A
spokesperson said the world-famous publisher of *Pleasure*
magazine was unavailable for comment. Sources claim he's
in seclusion at an unnamed friend's villa in Malibu."

"Fucking son of a bitch!" Cal gave the dilapidated file
cabinet he was standing next to a vicious kick.

"Miss Layton was already unconscious when she was
rushed into emergency, having suffered a traumatic loss of
blood. The cuts on her wrists were sutured and she was
given a massive transfusion, but she remains in a coma—"

"What did she say?" gasped Cal. Pat shushed him impatiently, eager to hear the rest.

"—and the doctors, who'd despaired of saving her life earlier, now give her an almost fifty-fifty chance of survival. Like her adoring fans..." The camera panned over the crowd once again, while they raised their lighted candles aloft, as though they'd been rehearsed. "... all we can do now is wait—wait and pray for her recovery."

Cal blinked several times as the realization that Lara was still alive sank in. Joy flooded him with such intensity it was an almost physical sensation. He broke down in tears. Turning, he stumbled blindly over to the corner. Stretching out his arms, he pressed his hands against the wall for support while the anguish he'd been holding back for the past two hours poured out of him.

Pat stared, too astonished to say or do anything. It took her several minutes to recover. She'd always doubted the depth of Cal's love for Lara. No more. She went to him. "Lara is going to pull through, Cal. I'm sure she will."

"I thought she was already dead." Head bowed, the tears fell unchecked from his eyes, hitting the floor like raindrops. "She told me she was dead."

"Who told you that?"

Cal fought to pull himself together. "Julie Ann."

"Why would she tell you such a vicious lie?"

"Because she knew how it would rip me up." Pushing away from the wall, he drew in a long, deep breath and let it out slowly. "Christ, how that woman must hate me."

"Has it really taken you this long to figure that out?" On her way to her desk, Pat shut off the TV. While Cal dried his face with a handkerchief, she dialed the number of a travel agent, who also happened to be a friend. "Susan, can you get me on the first available flight to L.A.?"

Cal's head snapped around. "Book me a seat, too."

"Look, you're angry and upset right now," Pat cautioned while Susan checked flight availabilities. "Why don't you wait until you've cooled off, so you can think things through before you do something dumb?"

"I've had it with thinking things through. This time I'm going with my feelings. Book me a seat, Pat."

"Cal, you'll be making the trip for nothing. If and when Lara comes out of the coma, you're the last person on earth she'll want to see."

"I know that." Removing an American Express Gold Card from his wallet, he tossed it on the desk in front of her. "I have to be there, that's all."

Pat shook her head, then listened as Susan rattled off various departure and arrival times. "There's a nine o'clock flight from LaGuardia," she told him. "Will that give you enough time to go home and pack?"

"Take it. I'm not going home. I'll buy whatever I need in L.A."

Against her better judgment, Pat had Susan book the flight, reserve a rental car, and line up two rooms at a Holiday Inn.

White blurs moved silently around her, adjusting covers, hooking up IVs, monitoring her vital signs as she drifted in and out of a darkness as all-enveloping as a womb for almost thirty-six hours, while her fans kept a ghoulish vigil outside the hospital gates. Pain, throbbing insistently beneath the bandages on her wrists, finally brought her back to the inescapable reality of who she was and what she'd done.

They removed the IV, but the right sleeve of her hospital gown remained fastened to the covers with a large safety pin, and the wide leather strap still held her firmly down on the bed. She didn't need to be told she'd been moved to the psychiatric ward. She wondered if this was the kind of place they had put her mother in. There were bars on the windows and no door on the bathroom. When they brought her dinner, they gave her a plastic spoon to eat with, and then they took it away as soon as she was finished. She was given an injection. She didn't ask what it was for.

During the night while she slept, heavily sedated, Lara was smuggled by private ambulance into Whispering Palms,

an exclusive sanitarium that catered to a strictly Hollywood
clientele. At any given time there were enough actors,
writers, and directors in residence to put on a full-scale
production. Unlike Lara, most of the patients were voluntaries,
there to dry out or get clean. Many of them were frequent
patrons of the establishment. All of them were reported
vacationing in some remote corner of the world.

She woke to find herself in a room painted a pale shade
of blue, furnished like a private home; the decor was
California casual. She was no longer pinned or strapped
down to the bed, and there were no bars on the chintz-
draped widows, though a closer inspection would reveal a
fine, steel-mesh barrier. Soothing music was piped in during
the day. The food was nouvelle cuisine.

That night the nightmares started. She hadn't had them in
a long time, but now they returned with a vengeance,
waking her twice, sometimes three times in a single night. It
was as if her unconscious mind desperately wanted to reach
out to her, to tell her something. But all Lara could
remember was fear.

The sound of a typewriter being pounded incessantly
could be heard clear out in the hallway as Pat knocked on
the door to Room 406.

"It's open," Cal called out, still typing furiously while
she let herself in. She waited until he'd finished getting the
rest of the line down on paper before asking how it was
going.

"Good," he sighed around the cigarette dangling from
the corner of his mouth. Cigarette butts filled the ashtray on
the narrow motel writing table, crumbled pages overflowed
the wastebasket and littered the floor at his feet. "I finished
Act II last night."

His bed had not been slept in, Pat noticed. "Did you stay
up all night again to write?"

He shrugged. "I caught a couple hours' sleep." He was
unshaven, his hair in tangles, but his eyes, though blood-

shot, glowed with satisfaction. "I'm already halfway through the first scene in Act III."

Unable to sleep while waiting for Lara to come out of the coma—if she did come out of it—Cal had started writing. He needed to understand the reasons she'd been driven to take her own life. As he thought about it, a larger pattern began to emerge: Marilyn Monroe, Jean Seberg, Brigitte Bardot, Dorothy Stratton, and so many others—all of them had been beautiful, exploited, and finally destroyed, one way or another. He felt there had to be something terribly wrong with a society that punished female beauty and sexuality so harshly.

Since coming to Los Angeles almost a week ago, Cal had spent every night on the play, writing in a white heat. During the day he and Pat kept busy trying to track down Lara. While she remained in Intensive Care, the hospital refused them permission to see her. The news that she was out of danger broke only after she'd been secretly trans-ferred to the sanitarium. Griffin had left strict orders that no one was to be told of her whereabouts. He, himself, remained incommunicado.

But they refused to give up. After three days of steady badgering, the butler at the Chateau threatened to call the police, but the head nurse of the psychiatric ward at Westside Hospital finally relented and agreed to pass their message on to Lara's psychiatrist at the sanitarium.

"Have you heard from Dr. Aarons yet?" Cal asked Pat now.

"That's what I came to tell you. We've got a two o'clock appointment to see Lara."

"Christ, finally!" He quickly stubbed out his cigarette and pushed away from the table. Cal's longing to see Lara was so evident that Pat didn't have the heart to remind him that Lara might not want to see him.

As they were walking up the winding path, past lush lawns dotted with the tall, frond-swaying trees that gave Whispering Palms its name, Cal was the first to voice Pat's thought aloud. "I think I'd better wait out here until you've asked her if she wants to see me."

She agreed. Together, they climbed the steps to the veranda of the huge, Mediterranean-style mansion that had once been the home of a silent-screen star. As Pat was about to go in Cal put a hand on her arm, holding her back. "Please tell her how much I . . . I want to see her."

"I'll do what I can," Pat promised. "It also depends on what state she's in."

Although she was prepared for the worst, Pat was shocked by her first glimpse of Lara, and angry. It infuriated her that Lara had deliberately tried to destroy the beauty Pat would have sold her soul to possess. She was never one to hide her feelings. "Jesus H. Christ, what the hell have you done to yourself?"

Lara laughed softly. "I look awful, I know." She ran her hand over the dark stubble that was all that was left of her hair. It made her eyes look enormous, haunted. Her face was drawn, her skin almost as white as the bandages on her wrists. "I look like a Nazi collaborator in one of those World War II movies from the forties." Her hand dropped into her lap. "I guess, in a way, I did collaborate with the enemy, didn't I?"

"How are you feeling?" Pat asked when she'd joined Lara, who was sitting on the window seat, long legs stretched out.

"Believe it or not, I feel better than I have in years." She shifted her legs to make more room for Pat. "It's nice here. Quiet. No pressures. Nothing to do but relax."

Pat made a face. "Just like being in a country club."

"Okay, so it's tough at times," Lara admitted. "I keep having these godawful nightmares, night after night, but Dr. Aarons says that's good."

"Nightmares are good?"

"It's supposed to mean that all the subconscious emotions and conflicts I've been suppressing with drugs are very close to the surface. I remember having these nightmares back in the convent when we were kids, but I never tried to make any sense of them then." I've been running away from these feelings all my life." She drew in a long breath and let it out in ragged pieces. "I can't run anymore. I've come to the end of myself."

"Lara, why did you do it?"

"I felt trapped. I wanted to break free, and I couldn't see any other way out."

"But you've got everything: beauty, money, fame. What do you mean, trapped?"

"Trapped—like in a cage! Only the cage I was trapped in was myself. Or, at least, what I've become. I wasn't a woman anymore, Pat. I was a female impersonator. I was this *thing*: Lara Layton, sex symbol. I just couldn't go on being that anymore. I had to put a stop to it somehow."

She paused and stared at the bandages on her wrists. "I never meant to go this far, but I was strung out on coke. My brain was fried. I look back on what happened now and I can't understand how everything could have seemed so overwhelming, so . . . hopeless." A wry smile flickered across her face. "I guess there's nothing like watching your life spilling out onto a bathroom floor to put things in perspective."

Pat reached out and put her hand on Lara's. "Why didn't you call me and let me know you were in trouble? I'd have taken the first plane out here."

"There was nothing you could have done. I've been heading for this for a long time, I know that now. Anyway, I really appreciate your coming to see me, Pat."

"We've been trying to see you for almost a week."

"We?"

"Cal's here."

Lara sat up. "What do you mean, here? Here in L.A.?"

"Right here. Outside. He wants to see you, but he's afraid you don't want to see him."

She shook her head. "He's right. I don't want to see him."

"He's been frantic with worry over you, honestly. He's still in love with you."

A single, bitter laugh escaped her. "In love with a choice piece?"

"What?"

She sank back against the upholstered wall. "It's a private joke."

"Will you at least think about it?" Pat persisted. "We'll be coming out to see you again tomorrow, so if you change your mind . . ."

"I won't change my mind," Lara said with a certainty Pat had never seen in her before. "I'm having enough trouble trying to straighten out my life without having to deal with Cal. Tell him to go back home, where he belongs."

"Okay," Pat sighed. "If that's how you feel."

"Can you stay another week, Pat? I'll pay all your expenses. No, I insist," she added as Pat started to protest. "There are some important things I need done that I can't do myself while I'm in here. I'd have my secretary take care of them, but I know she'll report back to Griffin. That's the last thing I want."

"Has he been to see you?"

"Are you kidding?" She laughed caustically. "Grif has a phobia about hospitals. He can't handle sickness or death, or anything that's too real. He doesn't love me, but he won't let me go. He's like a Dr. Frankenstein—completely obsessed with this creature he's created. He's been pushing his weight around, trying to have me released so I can finish that goddamn movie of his."

"You're in no condition to work!"

"Dr. Aarons told him that on the phone. They had quite a run-in, I understand, because she can't be charmed or bought, like everybody else around him. But you don't know Grif. He'll stop at nothing to get me to finish *Dominique*, even if it means risking another breakdown." Fear darkened Lara's eyes. "I can't go back to that life, Pat. Will you help me?"

"Of course. Just tell me what you want me to do."

CHAPTER
Twenty-four

From behind the dusty-rose drapes on her bedroom window, Julie Ann watched as the Chrysler LeBaron containing her husband and son halted in front of the stop sign at the end of the block. She waited to make sure Cal executed a right turn and was out of sight before going over to the French Provincial dresser. With a growing urgency, she pulled opened the middle drawer where she kept her lingerie. She would have to move fast, she knew. Cal was just dropping Brian off for Little League practice.

Sliding her hand under a pile of full-length slips, she found the key where she'd hidden it, and dropped it into the pocket of her house coat. Quickly, she crossed the bedroom and the hallway, taking the stairs to the ground floor at a run. She couldn't wait to find out what Cal was hiding from her.

Since he had returned home two weeks ago, Cal's manner toward her had undergone a subtle, though perceptible change. She was furious with him for disappearing for a week without getting in touch with her, especially since he had called Brian at school every day. The instant he walked in the front door, she sensed he was just waiting for her to start an argument. What he was really hoping she'd do, she was sure, was throw him out of the house, once and for all.

She had no intention of letting him off the hook so easily.

From time to time Julie Ann had thought of leaving Cal. She seriously considered going on a diet and joining an exercise class, perhaps even getting a job, in the hopes of finding a man who would appreciate her and take care of all her needs. After all, she was only thirty—still young enough to make a new life for herself.

But that would leave Cal free to make a new life for himself. He would be free to find a woman who could do the one thing she herself seemed incapable of doing, no matter how hard she tried: make him happy. He didn't deserve to be happy. He hadn't finished paying for destroying her love for him.

So, Julie Ann didn't throw Cal out as he'd hoped, nor did she make a scene. She acted as if he'd just come home from working late at the office. She didn't even ask where he'd been. And in the days that followed, she was all sweetness. She just knew it would drive him up the wall.

Her behavior, however, left him unfazed.

Something, she felt instinctively, had happened to him during the week he'd been away from her. She began to watch him every chance she got. There was a new vitality to his movements—a light in his eyes that hadn't been there in years. At first, she thought he was having an affair with another woman. But he came home for dinner every evening, though he shut himself up in his study once Brian had gone to bed, rarely going to sleep himself before one or two in the morning.

"What do you do in there night after night?" she demanded, dying to know.

"Just working on a project. It wouldn't interest you," was all he'd admit to her. He made sure the door was locked when he wasn't there.

It drove her crazy!

She became obsessed with the idea of getting into his study to find out what he was up to. The way she saw it, it wasn't an invasion of privacy. A man had no right to keep secrets from his wife.

She borrowed his keys while he was sleeping late that Saturday morning, and had a copy made of the one to his study. She'd intended to tell him she had misplaced her house key and needed to make a fast run to the store to get some things for breakfast. When she returned, Cal was in the shower, so she simply replaced his key chain on the dresser. He never knew it was missing.

Julie Ann held her breath in anticipation as she unlocked the door to Cal's study and switched on the light. The first things she noticed were the sketches he'd tacked on the slanting wall. One of them appeared to be a blueprint for a revolving stage; the other three were set designs.

"The impossible dream," she muttered contemptuously. When was he going to grow up?

A closer inspection revealed that these weren't mere sketches: all were drawn to scale, painstakingly detailed. Each one must have taken him days to complete.

Why would he go to such trouble? Unless . . .

Julie Ann went through the papers on Cal's desk, which were in two stacks. The shorter pile, she saw immediately, was the last scene of a play; the thirty-odd pages, roughly typed, bore a number of scribbled changes in Cal's handwriting. In contrast, the completed pages of the manuscript in the other pile were neatly typed and spotless.

She felt for the chair behind his desk and sank slowly into it. It had never occurred to her that he might be writing a play. That explained the excitement she'd sensed in him these past weeks. She pictured him sitting here working on it, night after night, oblivious of her, hiding his happiness behind a locked door. With rage building inside her, she skimmed the completed manuscript. So, this was how he planned to escape her.

She found a pair of scissors in the drawer. Taking half a

dozen pages at a time, she cut the finished manuscript lengthwise, into long, thin strips, then into confetti-size pieces. When she was through she yanked the sketches off the wall; those she tore into bits by hand, one by one.

Then, as though they really were confetti, she scooped the bits up by the handful and tossed them high into the air. They were floating down around her when Cal came to a surprised halt in the doorway. "What the hell's . . ."

He looked around incredulously. He saw that his designs were no longer on the wall; that the completed pages of his manuscript were gone from his desk. He saw the scissors lying there, open. Bending over, he grabbed a handful of what looked like confetti all over the floor. Even as he stared at the evidence right there in the palm of his hand— the bits of white paper with black letters printed on them— he couldn't bring himself to believe what his mind had already grasped.

Until he saw the vindictive triumph in his wife's eyes.

The depth of her hatred and malice left him stunned. As the realization of what she'd done to his play began to slowly sink in, he expected to feel a surge of rage toward her. Instead, he felt . . .

He couldn't have said what. The feeling was so odd, so new. A sort of calm? A kind of peace? It was as though an invisible rope made up of twisted strands of guilt and regret and futile hopes, which had kept him bound to her, had just been severed with one clean, final blow.

He was free.

"After this," he told her, "we can no longer pretend there's anything left in this marriage worth saving. I'm leaving."

Julie Ann gasped. "But I only did this *because* I was trying to save our marriage." Tears flooded her eyes, making a strange contrast with the festive look of the confetti dotting her hair. "I did it because I love you, Cal!"

"You could probably go on playing the loving and long-suffering wife with your brother, or the neighbors, or even with Brian. But not to me anymore, Julie Ann—or to yourself.'' Turning his hand over, Cal let the shreds of his play spill to the floor. ''Because, now, we both know what a castrating bitch you really are.''

He walked out the door, and went upstairs to pack.

CHAPTER
Twenty-five

As Lara had predicted, Griffin used his influence to have her released from the sanitarium before either Lara or Dr. Aarons felt she was ready to resume her "normal" life. But the two weeks she'd been there had given her enough time, with Pat's help, to set her plans into motion. She'd only agreed to return to her apartment at the Chateau so she could tell Griffin in person what her intentions were. If she could get him to stand still long enough so she could get him to listen to her.

"Grif, we have to talk," she insisted again.

"We can talk after the party," he agreed amiably on his way to her dressing room. "Everybody's waiting to welcome you home. You can't disappoint them."

She followed him to make sure he heard her, loud and clear. "I didn't come here to party, Grif."

If he heard her, he pretended not to. "It shouldn't take you long to make yourself presentable." He opened the door to the dressing room and switched on the light.

Lara blinked. She half expected to see Jason and Duval waiting impatiently there for her, the AD barking orders into his walkie-talkie.

"I've already taken care of everything for you." A grand sweep of his hand indicated her plastic double, posing beside the vanity table. The mannequin, like the ones in dress shop windows, had movable and detachable parts. Custom-made, "she" had the exact same measurements as Lara, and a face cunningly painted in her likeness. Usually employed for preliminary costume fittings, the dummy was currently dressed as Grif had decided Lara should appear at the party.

He had indeed taken care of everything, she noted resentfully from the doorway: a platinum-blond wig, glamorously styled, with which to hide her butchered hair; an evening gown, all glittering black sequins, with a V-neckline that plunged to the waist to show off her breasts, and long, tight sleeves to hide the scars on her wrists. Everything—right down to the strapped gold sandals on the dummy's feet, the gold mesh evening bag hanging from "her" arm.

Lara couldn't resist: "Why don't you take her to the party? I'm sure nobody would know the difference."

He frowned. "Please don't make things any more difficult than you already have, Lara."

"Actually, I intend to make things as easy as possible for you, Grif." She walked over to him. "Just give me a divorce and let me buy up the rest of my contract, and you'll never be bothered by me again."

He gave her a look, his expression unreadable. "Perhaps you're right," he said then, smiling. "I should have realized a party would be too much of a strain for you your first day home. I have a better idea. Why don't you take a nice long soak in the Jacuzzi?"

"Griffin, didn't you hear what—"

"Let me prepare it for you," he insisted, the picture of marital solicitude. "I know just the way you like it." He hurried eagerly toward the bathroom. "I'll come in with you. It's been a long time since we made love in the Jacuzzi.''

One of us is crazy, Lara thought. *It's either me or him, but one of us is definitely crazy.*

From where she stood, she had a clear view through the open bathroom door of the washbasin and the mirrored cabinet above it. Everything was spotless, gleaming white. The section of the flokati carpeting that had been soaked through with her blood had been replaced; the job had been done so expertly no seam was visible.

It was as though nothing had happened.

''Which of these bath oils do you prefer?'' Griffin called out to her, referring to the assortment kept in a gold filigree cage beside the sunken marble bathtub. ''Jasmine? Sandalwood? How about musk?''

''Since you refuse to talk to me, there's no point in my staying,'' Lara called back. ''When you're ready to take me seriously, call me.'' With determined strides she left the dressing room, and was halfway across the sitting room before he caught up with her.

''I didn't think you'd feel up to a heavy discussion this evening,'' Grif explained. Taking her arm, he held her back. Eager to get this over with, Lara allowed him to lead her to a Regency-style love seat covered with Beauvais tapestry. He sat close beside her. ''I want to resolve this misunderstanding between us as much as you do.''

''But,'' she said before he got the chance to. There was always a *but*.

''But, first, we have to wrap *Dominique*.''

She'd expected him to make finishing the film a condition to their talks. ''No, I can't. I won't.'' She cut him off in mid-protest: ''And nothing you say or do will make me change my mind.''

He slumped back against the Beauvais fantasy landscape. ''You're really out to get me, aren't you?'' He sounded deeply bitter. ''What you did to me already...'' He nodded in the direction of the bathroom. ''...that wasn't bad enough. Now, just to spite me, you refuse to finish the picture.''

"Jesus God, Grif, can't you ever think beyond yourself? I can't finish the picture for my own sanity. I can't go through that again. That's what pushed me over—''

"If you're concerned about doing the rape scene,'' he broke in, sitting up again, "no problem. We're not going to reshoot it. It's fantastic. Everybody who's seen the dailies has flipped over your performance. We're—''

"Performance?''

"—talking Academy Award time!''

"To bad you didn't get to shoot my 'performance' in the bathroom. I bet that would really clinch the Oscar.''

"That's not funny.'' He appeared genuinely offended by this display of bad taste on her part.

She laughed. "You're telling me?''

He needed a moment to take a long, calming breath before he was able to continue. "Lara, we're talking four, maybe five setups. The two scenes that were left to shoot before you . . . took ill, we've already shot around you. All we need are inserts: close-ups, reaction shots. That's it.''

"You don't need me for that, Griffin. Just take some of my close-ups or reaction shots from other scenes in the film. Or from the other films we made, for that matter. Nobody will ever know the difference.''

"You *are* doing this to spite me.''

"Isn't that what you'd have done if I'd died?''

"You're really into morbid jokes today, I see.''

She fixed him with a long, hard stare. "I'm not joking. It's just coming out that way.''

Throwing his hands up in sheer disgust, Grif got to his feet. "I can't talk to you when you're in this state.''

Lara stood, also. "Maybe you'll have less trouble communicating with my lawyers. I'll have them get in touch with you.'' She took a moment to enjoy the stunned look on his face. From a zippered compartment inside her alligator bag, she then removed a small square of note paper and held it out to him.

He regarded it warily. "What's that?"

"I've rented a house—a bungalow, actually—in the Valley. This is my phone number."

"Who put you up to this?" he demanded. "That lesbian psychiatrist?"

"It was my idea, and Dr. Aarons isn't a lesbian. To you, any woman who's smarter than you are and wears sensible shoes is a lesbian, and stop changing the subject! Is it really that inconceivable to you that I could make a decision on my own?"

"She didn't use hypnosis on you, did she?" he asked, alarmed. "Posthypnotic suggestions?"

"I should have known I couldn't talk to you." Lara tossed the scrap of paper onto a gilded side table. "I'll have my lawyers contact you. You can discuss the settlement of the contract and the terms of the divorce with them."

He shook his head. "I don't believe any of this."

"My God, Grif, did you actually think we were just going to go on as if nothing happened?"

"This is much worse than I realized."

"Things have been much worse than you realized between us for a long time."

"No, I meant *you.* I thought those paranoid reactions you'd been having, like blaming me for everything, were from doing too much coke. Now I realize you're *really* . . ." He couldn't bring himself to finish.

"Are you saying I'm crazy?"

"The doctors told me how sick you were. I should have listened to them. They warned me that you weren't ready to be released from the clinic."

"You're enough to drive anybody crazy, Grif, you know that? Psychiatrists should pay you a finder's fee."

He took a step toward her. "Lara, I'm not the enemy. That's only in your head. I want to protect you—from yourself. You're the one who wanted to die."

"No, I didn't want to die," she insisted. "I just wanted to kill Lara Layton."

"Kill Lara Layton? Don't you hear how crazy you sound?

Lara Layton is the most desired woman in the world! Most women would sell their souls to be you!''

"I'm a joke—a dirty joke everybody's either laughing at or jerking off on! That's what I wanted to put an end to, not me!''

Griffin sighed at the sheer futility of trying to make sense out of her lunatic ravings.

"I can't be this fantasy creature you want me to be anymore, Grif. Don't you understand that?'' He didn't contradict her. She was relieved to see that she was finally getting through to him. "Please let me go. You won't stand to lose any money, I swear. I'll give you every cent I have. All I want from you is my freedom.''

He smiled. "No way, lady.''

That superior, confident smile of his angered Lara even more than his refusal. "Why the hell not? You don't love me. You only married me so other men would envy you because you got to fuck Lara Layton. Is that supposed to prove to the world what a great cocksman you are?''

Griffin went pale under his Malibu tan. His right hand lashed out, slapping Lara hard across the face, sending her staggering back several steps. "Now, you listen to me!'' Grabbing her by the shoulders, he slammed her up against the mirrored wall with such force that it cracked the glass. "You've already caused me irreparable damage. You've made me look lousy on the front page of every newspaper from here to Timbuktu. If you think I'm going to allow you to make me look ridiculous by walking out on me, you're even crazier than I thought.''

Lara was so completely thrown by Grif's violent outburst that she was barely aware of the stinging sensation on her cheek or of the pain where his fingers had dug into her flesh. She'd never known him to lose control of his emotions.

"Just remember one thing.'' His hands slid down her arms to grip her wrists; he practically shoved the scars in her face. "I can have you certified and put away because of the crazy stunt you pulled. Even your precious Dr. Aarons was against your leaving the hospital. You were released in my custody." He threw her arms back at her. "So you can forget about retaining lawyers and renting bungalows. You can't even leave this house without my permission."

"I don't believe you," Lara cried. "This is another one of your—"

"Just try it, and see what happens." The look in his eyes made it impossible for her to doubt him. "I didn't want to do it this way, Lara. *You* forced me to."

Stepping back, he adjusted his jacket to make sure it was hanging properly; it had gotten somewhat mussed in the course of his violent actions. "Monday morning, either you're on the set, ready to work, which proves you're mentally competent, or you'll find yourself back on the funny farm. The choice is yours." He shot the cuffs of his silk shirt. "I'd think it over carefully if I were you. It's the only choice you've got."

Lara thought of nothing else for the next two days, during which she was kept locked in her suite. Only Grif and the trio of nurses he'd hired to watch her 'round-the-clock had the key to the main door. With his usual thoroughness, he'd had the locks on all the other doors removed, as well as the telephones. She was allowed no calls or visitors. Her meals were sent up on a tray, served on paper plates with plastic spoons. And she was forced to leave the door open whenever she went to the bathroom. It was a not-too-subtle reminder of what was in store for her in the mental hospital if she didn't give in to his demands.

No matter how she analyzed her situation, Lara always came to the same inevitable conclusion. Legally, Griffin held an unbeatable hand; he had all the aces. The only way she could beat him at his own game, she finally realized, was to adopt his favorite strategy: Never fight a stronger opponent; use his own weakness against him.

She devised a plan. The next morning she sent word to him that she was ready to submit to his demands.

* * *

"That's more like it," Griffin enthused, when he was through inspecting his wife's appearance.

Lara was wearing the platinum-blond wig he'd bought her, but she'd altered it to match the style Brigitte Bardot had made famous. Her shoulder-length rhinestone earrings and white satin negligee, edged with ostrich features, were right out of a Jean Harlow movie. The bouncing breasts and exaggerated swing of the hips as she negotiated the mahogany deck were pure Marilyn Monroe.

"You've never looked more ravishing," he said, clearly pleased with what she'd intended as a parody.

Lara was also pleased by what she saw as she quickly scanned Grif's bedroom. Everything was exactly as she'd anticipated. The lights were low, a bottle of champagne was chilling in a silver cooler, moonlit seascapes shimmered on the windows, while all around them, the seductive sounds of vintage Sinatra played. She was especially gratified to see the mound of cocaine set out on a mirrored tray.

Resplendent in a pair of red silk pajamas with a griffin embroidered in gold on his breast pocket, Grif was lounging against the sable-covered headboard of his orgy-size bed. He was freshly shaved, and every hair on his steel-gray head was smoothed sleekly in place. He sent her one of his most disarming smiles. "I'm delighted to see you, Lara."

Lara was not taken in by her husband's seeming willingness to forgive and forget. Her capitulation would not be considered complete, she knew, unless she submitted to him sexually. Still smiling, he patted a place for her next to him on the bed. Kicking off her satin mules she stepped off the deck, her bare toes sinking into the sable bedspread as she swayed over to him.

While she settled beside him, Grif proceeded to open the bottle of champagne, his thumbs working the cork expertly. "This champagne is unique," he boasted, flashing her a glimpse of the label so she could see it was a Bollinger Vieille Vignes '81. "At twelve hundred dollars a bottle, I originally bought it as an investment. But I felt an occasion like this warranted a champagne as special." He popped the cork with a flourish, sending it flying up to the ceiling dramatically.

Jesus God, Lara thought, *he's got to make a big production out of everything*. She had to remind herself that that was exactly what she was counting on.

As he filled a pair of hand-blown crystal flutes, Grif slanted Lara a look. "Aren't you the least bit curious about what we're celebrating?" he prompted as though she'd forgotten to pick up her cue.

She batted her double fringe of false eyelashes at him. "Oh, of course."

"I've decided what we both need is a vacation—as soon as we wrap *Dominique*." He slid the Bollinger into the silver bucket, picked up the brimming flutes, and handed her one. "I thought we'd go back to the French Riviera. We had a fabulous time in Cannes, remember?" He gazed into her eyes soulfully as he touched glasses with her. "We'll have a second honeymoon. Wouldn't you like that?"

The tip of her tongue flicked out to wet her suggestively parted lips. "Sounds fabulous!"

"It will be, I promise," he said with a rather touching smile.

Lara remained untouched. She sipped champagne, calculating that each swallow cost about fifty bucks, and waited for him to make the next move.

"Things will be just the way they used to be between us—you'll see." Bending his head, he nuzzled her neck while his free hand slipped inside her negligee to caress her bare breast. She tensed, and felt his lips curve into a smile against her skin. He'd obviously interpreted her reaction as sexual excitement. He began to sing.

"Isn't it romantic," he whispered in her ear, following along with Frank Sinatra, though slightly off-key.

Lara snickered into her champagne glass.

That was not the response Grif had been hoping for. Straightening up, he removed the glass from her hand, setting it, along with his, on top of the deck. He managed to give the impression that his action was prompted by a sudden, overwhelming desire for her. "Let's start our honeymoon right now." He flipped open her negligee. "Let's make love all night, and all day tomorrow. I've got enough coke to last us till Monday."

Lara's eyes widened in her best imitation of a classic dumb blonde. "Grif, do you really think I should? Dr. Aarons said—"

"What does she know? A couple of lines can't hurt you. I'll make sure you don't do too much." His hand slid down her body. "Trust me."

"Okay," Lara purred, the most submissive of sex kittens. "I'll do some coke with you." She giggled. "God knows you can't make it without it."

He pulled himself up indignantly. "The reason I choose to do cocaine with sex is to give my partner as much enjoyment as possible—not because *I* need it."

"Oh, come on, you know you do. Just like you need all of this." A wave of her hand took in his bedroom, with all of its electronic gadgets and seductive trappings. "It's okay, Grif. Really. I understand."

"I don't *need* all of this," he insisted defensively. "Can I help it if I'm a romantic? I want everything to be beautiful. What's wrong with that?"

"Nothing's wrong with it, honey," she reassured him breathily. "Unless you can't function without it." Another little giggle escaped her. "It's just funny, that's all. I mean, here you are, the high priest of sex, and if it wasn't for all this artificial stimulation, you couldn't even get it up."

Griffin turned an unfashionable shade of green.

"Of course, I could be wrong," Lara was quick to add. Before he could stop her, she reached over and pressed several buttons on the computer panel, turning the lights up, "Ole Blue Eyes" off, and blanking out the seascapes. Then she lay back on the bed, looking up at him, her gaze unflinching. "You want to try it and see?"

Grif looked as if he'd rather strangle her. But there was no way he could back out. His compulsive need to prove that he was the world's greatest cocksman made it impossible for him to ignore her challenge.

He practically attacked her, but it was with more panic than passion. Without drugs or the usual voyeuristic stimulation, he was unable to maintain a full erection. He was beginning to sweat—something she'd never known him to do. He escalated his attack, pushing every known erogenous zone button on her body, a living illustration of a sex manual. Lara responded accordingly. She was about as aroused as a turnip.

"You're doing it on purpose," he accused bitterly. "Just to make me look lousy."

"No, I'm just not faking it anymore," she admitted, shriveling him up completely.

"You never faked it with me! I have the tapes to prove it!"

"So I've heard. And that you show them to guests you want to impress. Well, now *I've* got a tape!" Lara punched the REWIND button on the VCR, and then PLAY.

Griffin watched the instant replay of his impotent performance in horrified silence.

Lara laughed. "How do you think your distinguished guests will react to this video?"

His rage was catatonic; he could neither speak nor move as she popped the tape out of the VCR and jumped up onto the deck.

"You know, Grif, you think you're the world's greatest cocksman," she told him before she went sailing out the door, "when all you really are is the world's biggest prick."

An impressive array of guests was assembled in the Salon d'Honneur on the last Saturday Lara was to spend at the Chateau.

As she'd anticipated, preserving his image as one of the greatest cocksmen of all times, that self-created illusion upon which his entire empire stood, was as vital to Griffin as breathing. In exchange for the video tape of his impotent performance, he allowed her to buy up her contract and he agreed to a divorce. In fact, he couldn't wait for her to leave. The mere sight of her threatened his manhood.

His guests, as Lara noted from the doorway of the salon, were the usual glittering assortment of well-known actors, power brokers and politicians, with a more than adequate supply of Pleasure Mates to go around. Everyone was seated. Grif was snuggling up with the strawberry-blond, eighteen-year-old centerfold, who'd already been elevated to the status of "favorite lady." A low murmur indicated everyone's curiosity about the movie that was about to be screened. Grif's sex movies were legendary.

Leaving her suitcase beside the door, Lara hurried over to the audio/video studio, which was just behind the boiserie wall of the salon. Ironically, though Griffin had had every room of the Chateau searched in a frantic effort to find where Lara had hidden the compromising videotape, no one had thought to look in the most obvious place of all: among the video cassettes that lined one entire wall of the studio. "Hank, are you ready to run that copy of the video you made for me?" she asked the projectionist. "You know, my special surprise for Grif."

"All set, Miss Layton." He indicated the intricate computer panel he was seated before. "I'm already switched over to video. Just waiting for Mr. Griffin's signal."

Lara rewarded him with a dazzling smile. She made it back to the doorway of the salon just in time to hear the collective gasp that went up from the audience as the tape of Griffin's impotent performance unreeled. Picking up her suitcase, she started toward the exit.

The story was in all the Hollywood tabloids by midmorning of the following day; before nightfall, it had reached New York. Though Lara felt justified about paying Grif back in kind for flaunting tapes of their lovemaking, her action did create a backlash against her in the movie colony. Those very producers who had snickered gleefully over Griffin's fall from the pantheon of sexual athletes refused to hire her. The only film offers she received over the follow-

ing month were for raunchy sexploitation or outright porno
flicks. The industry had written her off. Overnight, she'd
become yesterday's blonde.

Lara refused to give up. She decided to go back to the
theater in New York. Pat agreed to look for a play through
which Lara could regain her reputation as a theatrical
actress. She realized the critics would be sharpening their
long knives for her. Everyone would be hoping she fell flat
on her celebrated ass. But as scared as she was, she was
determined to prove, once and for all, that she was more
than a choice piece.

CHAPTER
Twenty-six

Her screams woke her. Her heart pounding, Lara bolted upright in bed. Her body was covered in cold sweat, her face wet with tears. A child's screams reverberated in her mind. The child in the dream, Lara suddenly realized, was her. She was that little girl with the corkscrew curls and the red polka-dot dress.

For the first time, the nightmare that had haunted her all her life lingered in her consciousness. Like pieces of a jigsaw puzzle—the tray with milk and sandwiches; the motionless form in the corner armchair; the crucifix of light slanting across the ceiling, illuminating the darkness in flashes; the staring, lifeless eyes—the images made sense to Lara.

It was her mother's face that finally woke her.

Lara felt for the lamp on the bedside table and switched it on. The soft glow it gave off wasn't bright enough to dispel all the shadows in the room. Indeed, the shadows seemed alive still with the nameless fears of childhood. The frightening vision of her mother's face kept flashing in her mind. She drew her knees up and wrapped her arms around them, hugging them tightly to her chest.

Another image sprang to mind: She saw herself sitting in her mother's lap in front of a window, watching the parade of people going by under the huge, lighted crucifix. The image was now so vivid that she recalled the sign over the storefront mission: *Christ the Savior.*

Lara had assumed the cross in her dream was merely a symbol. Now she knew that it was real. And it was the only clue she had about where she lived all those years ago. Moment by moment, the events of that terrible night began to unfold in her mind.

She remembered how carefully she'd made the sandwiches, so her mother would love her again. She couldn't recall what she'd done to upset her, only the excitement she'd felt as she carried the tray in to her, and the terror when she had found her in that condition. Her screams brought the hippie who lived downstairs and was always so nice to her. The hippie's name was something like Eileen . . . or Elaine . . . or *Ellen*. Ellen had called Miss Prescott. The last thing Lara could remember was Prescott putting her to bed, with the promise to wake her when the doctor came. But when she woke up the next morning, her mother had been gone. Forever.

Fresh tears spilled down Lara's face as guilt, buried since childhood, twisted through her. If she hadn't fallen asleep, she could have stopped them from taking her mother away. She finally realized that she'd blamed herself all these years for what had happened to her mother. She had even believed that *she* had been the cause of her breakdown, and the thought had been so painful that she had completely blocked it from her memory.

But no matter how hard she tried, Lara could not recall the events that had taken place earlier that day. She had a vague memory of her mother curling her hair and getting her all dressed up. She seemed so happy. They were going someplace special. But where?

She sank back against the pillows. There were still so many unanswered questions. Which psychiatric hospital had

Miss Prescott taken her mother to? What kind of treatment had she been given? How had she died? She didn't even know where she was buried. Prescott had never volunteered any information, nor, Lara was forced to admit, had she ever asked for details concerning her mother's death.

Because she didn't want to know. For twenty years, she'd been running away from the truth.

It was time, Lara decided, to stop running. She was determined to uncover the events of the day her mother went insane. Hoping the house in which they had lived would trigger further memories, Lara set out to find the flashing crucifix.

Lara's throat tightened when she caught sight of it—a huge cross, blocks away. She'd already been to two storefront missions dedicated to Christ the Savior that morning. Neither of them had displayed the type of cross she remembered in her dreams. She was beginning to think it had been symbolic after all. But now, there it was, a flashing beacon of light suspended over the concrete sidewalk, slicing through the steady April drizzle.

She quickened her pace, continuing east on Fourteenth Street. She had to caution herself not to get her hopes up. The building she'd lived in with her mother might no longer be there. Twenty years was a long time in a city that seemed to remake itself daily. She'd just passed an entire block of tenements slated to be demolished—all the windows were marked with white paint.

Even if the building she was searching for was still standing, it was highly unlikely that Ellen would still be the landlady. Lara was hoping the real estate company that owned the building had kept a record of its employees and would be able to furnish her with Ellen's last name, and perhaps a forwarding address.

Her efforts to get in touch with the only other person who knew what had happened to her mother that night had proven futile: Jane Prescott was on the campaign trail with Senator Kingsley. According to a volunteer at his campaign headquarters, it would be weeks before they were back in New York, and Lara was fairly certain that even when Miss Prescott did return, she would not help her. It would take a full month for the Bureau of Birth and Death Records to mail Lara the copy she'd requested of her mother's death certificate. Only then would she finally learn where and how her mother had died.

Lara came to a halt in front of the mission. The five-floor walk-up directly across the street had to be the one she'd lived in as a child. The view of the cross indelibly fixed in her mind would be visible only from its windows. The exterior was still intact. The interior, however, was little more than a shell. Through the scaffolding running the width of the building, she could make out the forms of construction workers involved in its renovation.

That took care of her feeble hope that Ellen might still be the landlady, as well as her idea of questioning whoever was currently in charge of the building. A trailer was parked at the curb with BLAKE REALTY, LTD. painted in bold red letters on its side.

She made a note of the phone number before taking a taxi back to the apartment she'd been subletting for the past month on a quiet, tree-lined street in the Village. Not even bothering to remove her raincoat, she quickly dialed the number of the realty office.

"Miss Blake is out right now," the receptionist told her when Lara had explained the purpose of her call. "Can I take a message?"

Lara left her name and number. "Please tell her it's urgent," she added before hanging up. She was in the middle of preparing herself a light lunch when the phone rang. She hurried to answer it.

"Lara? Pat. I found it—the perfect play for you. It's called *Bright Lights, Dark Shadows*. It's an expressionistic drama about the rise and fall of a Hollywood sex symbol."

"That sounds like me, all right—especially the fall part," Lara replied with a self-deprecating laugh. "Who's the author? Established or a new talent?"

"Damn, there's my other phone," Pat fibbed. "Be right

back." She put Lara on hold and looked up at Cal, who was standing across the desk from her in her backstage office.

"What did she say?" he asked.

"She wants to know who the author is."

"I told you it wouldn't work."

Pat shushed him. "Listen, Lara," she said, getting back to her, "I've got a potential angel on my other line, so I've only got a second. I'm sending the play over to you by messenger. Call me as soon as you've read it. Better yet, meet me here at the theater around six, so we can talk about it."

"You mean . . . today?"

"I guarantee you, once you start reading it, you won't be able to put it down." Pat wasn't trying to hype Cal's play; her feelings about it were genuine. "I can't remember the last time I was this excited about a play."

Intrigued, Lara agreed. "See you at six."

Pat was beaming when she hung up. "She's going to read it."

"You should have told her up front that I'm the author, Pat."

"She'd have turned the part down, sight unseen."

"But, when she finds out afterward that—"

"If she reads it, she'll do it," Pat assured him, setting aside the title page with his name on it before slipping a copy of the script into a manila envelope. "It's a terrific play, Cal—a once-in-a-lifetime part."

Hands jammed into his pockets, he began to pace. With his long legs, he covered the length of Pat's cubby-hole of an office in a few strides. "Even if she liked the play, when she finds out we lied to her, she'll be furious."

Pat chuckled as she slapped the label with Lara's address onto the envelope. "She'll be pissed at first, that's for sure. But when she calms down, she'll do it."

"She's got to do it!" He kept pacing back and forth. "I wrote it for her!"

"Will you stop pacing, already? You're making me dizzy. Here." She handed him the parcel across the desk. "Put some of that manic energy to use. Drop this off with her doorman. Make sure he sees that she gets it immediately, if not sooner.''

Cal nodded, yet he stood there staring down at the envelope containing his script, suddenly unable to move at all. "I feel like I've literally got my life in my hands."

"You've got all our lives in your hands," quipped Pat. "This play has the potential of being a big commercial and artistic hit. It could make your reputation, salvage what's left of Lara's, and finally get my theater to run in the black."

"I wasn't thinking about the professional end of it," Cal murmured, slipping the package under one arm. "I've been hoping that . . ." His words trailed off, but his meaning wasn't lost on Pat. She knew how much Cal was hoping his play would bring Lara and him back together.

"It'll work itself out, Cal. Just give it time," Pat assured him. "And stay glued to the phone this evening. I'll get back to you with her answer."

"Don't worry, I will." Despite his anxiety, he managed to smile. "Thanks, Pat. See ya."

When Cal got outside, he was relieved to find that his taxi hadn't been towed out of the no-parking zone in front of The Lower Depths. Sliding behind the wheel, he flipped on the OFF DUTY sign and swung smoothly into traffic.

Cal had resumed driving a cab during the day since he had left his wife; he wrote at night. Julie Ann hadn't destroyed his earlier drafts of the play, so he'd been able to salvage some of it, but piecing it back together had been a long, painstaking struggle.

Julie Ann had made good on her threat to move back to her parents' home in Akron, taking Brian with her. Cal missed the boy deeply, but he had refused to go after them. He was through giving in to emotional blackmail. Once she realized he was now totally committed to his work, that she could no longer use his love for his son to get him to do as she wished, he was sure she'd come back to New York of her own volition. If not, he was prepared to fight for joint custody.

When Cal pulled up in front of Lara's place, he left the motor idling and sat behind the wheel for the length of a cigarette. He was seriously tempted to deliver the script to her in person. He was dying to see her again. And the thought of deceiving her, even with the best of intentions, rankled. He had to remind himself that she didn't want to see him, and that she would refuse to read the play if she knew he'd written it. Following Pat's instructions, he left the script with the doorman, but it bothered the hell out of him.

Pat spent the rest of the day on the phone, trying to line up a tech crew capable of handling the intricate sound and lighting demands of Cal's play. She'd just started making a breakdown of the characters by sex, age, and type for the casting notice that would run in *Backstage* and *Show Business*, when she heard the front door chime.

As she went to answer it, she checked her watch automatically: Lara was half an hour early. *A good omen*, she thought. Her welcoming smile turned into a frown when she saw it was Cal. "What the hell are *you* doing here?"

"I've decided I should be here when Lara arrives," he explained, walking past her resolutely.

"Are you crazy? You'll screw everything up. I need some time to talk to her first, to break it to her—"

"I won't have you lying to her on my account, Pat."

"Cal, I'm doing this as much for her as for you. Lara needs this play desperately. If I can get her to admit she wants to do the part, I might be able to argue her out of turning it down because of her stubborn pride. This part could save her career."

He hadn't considered that point. He walked to where the last row of theater seats began, and stood there with his back to her for several moments. When he turned to her once more, his face was set. "No. I won't lie to her."

"We're not lying to her," Pat protested. "We're just not telling her the whole truth. It's for her own good!"

Cal shook his head ruefully. "That's how I used to justify my half-truths when Lara and I were lovers. I can't do that to her again."

"Okay, but she'll probably refuse you."

"I'll just have to take that chance." His tone was grim, making Pat aware of how difficult a choice this was for Cal.

"You know, there was a time," she admitted to him, "when I wouldn't have believed you'd have the guts to put yourself on the line like this."

His mouth twisted wryly. "There was a time when I didn't have the guts. I was torn between so many..." He paused to squint at a point over Pat's head. Through the stained-glass panel in the door behind her, he saw a female figure come hurtling down the steps. "It's her," he breathed just before the doorbell chimed.

Pat spun around. Mentally keeping her fingers crossed, she let Lara in. "You're early."

"I tried calling you several times, but your line's been busy." Lara sounded upset, out of breath, as if she'd rushed to get there. She was clutching the script in one hand. "Pat, who wrote this play?"

With a resigned sigh Pat moved aside, allowing Lara to glimpse the tall, lanky figure standing in the shadowy recess behind the last row of seats.

Cal stepped out of the shadows. "I did."

Lara's reaction was barely audible: a tiny murmur of shock escaped her lips. Like shock waves, the full impact of seeing Cal again reverberated inside her.

"I knew it," she murmured. "I didn't see how it was possible, yet I knew it couldn't have been anyone else. No one else..." Her voice splintered.

"It was *my* bright idea not to tell you he was the author," Pat was quick to inform her, "not Cal's. I was sure you wouldn't read the play if I told you."

Lara seemed not to hear her friend. Her attention was fixed on her former lover. "Why did you write this?"

"I wrote it for you," he said simply.

"For me?" A bitter laugh escaped her. "You've exploited my most personal feelings and memories. You used the love I... once felt for you..." Her voice was breaking again, and it infuriated her. "You even used my own words! Things I said to you—and to no one else!"

Cal was completely thrown. He'd have understood her being angry at him because he'd concealed his identity, but not because of what he'd written. He'd poured all his love and longing for her into that play.

"Yes, I used your words in the love scene." Neither his tone nor his manner as he went to her held a trace of apology. "Every artist uses experiences from life in order to create. I used my own words, too, and my feelings of love for you."

His blunt admission left her without an argument. Or perhaps it was the fact that, unlike her, he'd spoken of love in the present tense.

He lowered his head to look into her eyes, and let her see deep into his. Then he spoke again, very softly. "Lara, I never meant to exploit your feelings. No matter how badly you think of me now, you can't really believe I'd do that to you."

Lara didn't, couldn't, answer.

Straightening up, Cal ran his fingers roughly through his hair, a gesture she remembered as an expression of frustration. "I was trying to show the real woman behind the sex symbol image! That's why I split the action and wrote part of it as a play and part of it as a movie. In the live sequences we see her as she really is—vulnerable, sensuous, loving—while in the film sequences, we see the dumb blond sexpot they turned her into, and how that destroyed her."

Lara had to look away. It would have been so easy to let herself become caught up in Cal's creative visions. It bothered her that he could still do that to her. Yet she realized, now, that she'd been so shaken by the memories the love scene had evoked, she'd been unable to judge the play objectively, or Cal's motives.

"My play isn't a ripoff of your life," he was saying. "It's about anybody who compromises his ideals and dreams. It's about the price we pay when we try to be what other people want us to be, instead of who we are. Christ, I'm an expert on that subject."

There was a long moment of silence, during which Cal

searched Lara's face intently. Her eyes were shadowed, and he couldn't tell what she was thinking.

Finally, she said, "I'll do the play—on one condition. Someone else has to direct."

This time, Cal was too stunned to reply.

Pat, who'd thought it best to keep to herself up to then, hurried to join them. "Lara, nobody could direct this play better than Cal, and you know it."

Lara nodded in agreement. "But, unfortunately, whenever he directs, it causes problems for him at home, which always ends up causing problems for all of us. I refuse to go through that again."

"Is that the *only* reason you don't want me to direct?" His sardonic tone made it clear that he was aware of her other motive.

"Of course," she shot back defensively. "What other reason could I have?"

His eyes met and held hers in that direct, intense way she remembered. "The last time we did a play together, we became lovers."

She held his gaze unwaveringly. She was shaking inside. "There's no chance of that happening again."

"Then there's no problem, either. You see, Julie Ann and I split up months ago. So I'm free now to commit myself totally to the play." He smiled crookedly. "Or anything else you have in mind."

At that point, what Lara had in mind was cold-blooded murder. There was no way she could back out now, she knew, without admitting that she was afraid that working with Cal would revive her love for him.

"So, when do we start rehearsals?" she asked, ever so nonchalantly.

CHAPTER
Twenty-seven

The five-story walk-up Lara had lived in with her mother was still little more than a shell. Whatever progress the renovation crew had made in the week since she'd last seen it was not evident from the outside. Her attempts to contact the owner of Blake Realty had been equally unproductive. Crossing under the scaffolding running the width of the building, she approached a worker sneaking a cigarette break. "Excuse me. Do you know Miss Blake?"

The young man took a moment to imagine the figure beneath her jump suit, but Lara was confident the floppy hat and wraparound sunglasses she wore hid her identity. "Yeah, sure. She owns this building."

"Her office told me she might be here today."

He thumbed his hard hat back at a rakish angle. "She was here earlier." He turned to the construction worker who'd just joined them, hoping to get a closer look at Lara. "Miss Blake didn't leave yet, Al, did she?"

Al rolled his eyes. "Nah, she's still here. She's on Charlie's case today."

"Is it all right if I wait for her?" Lara asked.

"Be my guest," the first one said with a cocky grin. "If you're looking for an apartment, maybe I can—"

"What in hell is going on here, Tom?" a petite woman in a smart business suit, which contrasted oddly with the hard hat she wore, demanded as she came down the stairs to the sidewalk. "No wonder we're behind schedule, with everyone standing around shooting the breeze instead of working."

Tom adjusted his hard hat. "This lady was asking about an apartment, Miss Blake. I was just telling her to see you about it."

The attractive, fortyish blonde appraised Lara with the knowing eye of a professional, making note of her designer outfit and expensive accessories. "Okay, boys, I can handle this. You can get back to work now." She waited for them to start. "If I don't watch them like a hawk, nothing gets done around here."

Taking off the metal hat, she smoothed her straight, chin-length hair and, before Lara could speak, went into her sales pitch. "These apartments are a fantastic value for the money. You won't find another co-op this close to midtown at twice the price. Let me show you the floor plans." She gestured toward the trailer parked at the curb, her collection of gold bracelets jangling. "Right this way."

Lara followed her into the trailer, which was furnished like an office, taking the seat across the narrow desk from her. "How long have you owned this building, Miss Blake?"

"It was one of my father's buildings. He started the company." She began searching through some blueprints. "When he passed away sixteen years ago, I took over the—oh, here we are." She opened the folded blueprint and spread it out on the desk. "How many rooms are you looking for?"

"Actually, Miss Blake, what I'm really looking for is information. I'm trying to locate a woman who was the landlady of this building in nineteen sixty-seven. I assume your office keeps records of its employees?"

The woman sat up stiffly. "That's the law."

"Unfortunately, I don't know her last name. Her first name was Ellen, and she was—"

"Why are you trying to locate her?"

"It's a personal matter."

Miss Blake kept her vivid blue eyes fixed on Lara. "I'm sorry, but I'd have to know why."

"I'm trying to find out what happened to my mother. You see, we lived in this building when I was a child. Ellen has certain information about her that would help me a great deal."

"What's your mother's name?"

"Angela Castaldi."

The woman's mouth dropped open. "*You're* Angela's little girl?"

"Did you know my mother?"

"*I'm* Ellen," she said, laughing. "You don't remember me?"

"I do remember you, but with a huge Afro and funky clothes and a whole lot of silver and turquoise jewelry."

"That's when I was going through my hippie phase." She laughed again, ruefully this time. "We were going to change the world. Instead, the world changed us."

Lara leaned expectantly toward her. "But you do remember my mother?"

"Oh, I'm not likely to forget Angela. I don't think I'll forget the night she flipped out as long as I live." She reached her hand across the desk. "I'm sorry, I didn't mean that to sound so unfeeling. I always liked her very much. How is she? Is she all right now?"

"She died seven months after we left here."

"What a bummer," Ellen murmured, reverting to hippie slang. "How did it happen?"

"I was never told. That's what I'm trying to find out. I was hoping you could help me."

"How can I help you? I never saw Angela again after that night."

"Do you know what caused her breakdown? Something must have happened earlier that day."

Ellen Blake made an effort to go back in time. "She was fine that morning. She dressed you all up. Your hair was in curls." The memory caused her to smile. "You looked like a little doll. She always dressed you so beautifully. I remember that."

"I know we were going somewhere special," Lara prompted. "She was very excited about it. Something must have happened to her there. Do you know where we went?"

"To visit her girlfriend—you know, the woman who came over later and took care of everything?"

"Don't you remember the first time we met? I drove you and your mother home," Lara suddenly recalled Prescott saying to her on her graduation day.

"I don't know what I'd have done without her," Ellen went on, "but her name escapes me. Anyway, she was the one who sent the Rolls-Royce to take the two of you to her country place for the day."

"But Miss Prescott was a secretary at the time. How could a secretary afford a Rolls and a country place?"

"That's what she told me. I'm sure of it. Because I remember thinking how weird it was that Angela believed she was taking you to see your father instead."

Lara's eyes widened in shock. "My father?"

"I mean, that was her problem. She refused to accept the fact that your father was killed in Vietnam."

"Who told you he was killed in Vietnam—Prescott?"

"Yes."

Lara needed several moments to fully absorb what Ellen had told her. "Where did they take my mother? To Bellevue?"

"No, that would have involved the police. Prescott had her taken to some private clinic she knew of."

"You don't happen to know the name of the clinic?"

"I didn't even ask. I was so grateful to her for taking care of everything, I wasn't about to question anything she did. With all the druggies living here then, I couldn't risk a run-in with the pigs, as we used to call them."

"But why should Prescott have been afraid of the police?"

"All I know is, she seemed pretty concerned about them.

And about having the incident get in the papers." She shrugged. "Though I can't understand why the press would be interested in someone like Angela."

"Loris, I told you, your daddy is a very important man." Her mother's words echoed in her mind as another piece of the puzzle snapped into place. "Do you know if she managed to keep the incident out of the papers?"

"I have no idea. I'm sorry, I wish I could be more help to you."

"You've helped me a great deal, Ellen," Lara assured her with a grateful smile. "You've just given me a lead."

Following the directions the Information clerk gave her, Lara took the escalator one flight up. The Mid-Manhattan branch of the New York Public Library lacked the architectural splendor of the main building, but its decor was modern and functional. The walls of the spacious, high-ceilinged reading room were painted white. Taupe carpeting absorbed the sound of her footsteps, preserving the hush that prevailed, as she walked over to the section marked PERIODICALS.

"Newspaper or magazine?" asked the short, stocky woman behind the counter automatically. In back of her, lined up in vertical rows, were open bookcases containing stacks of newspapers. Black metal file cabinets hemmed her in on both sides.

"Newspaper," Lara said.

"What year?"

"Nineteen sixty-seven."

"Anything that old would be on microfilm." She slapped a requisition slip down on the counter before Lara. "Write the date and the name of the paper. Each reel holds a week. You're allowed two weeks."

Using one of the ballpoint pens attached to the counter by a slim metal chain, Lara quickly filled in the information and returned the slip. The woman disappeared behind the metal cabinets, reemerged carrying two square, white boxes.

She handed them to Lara, along with a card that had a large number printed on it. "Machine number ten."

"Thanks."

Directly across the aisle from the Periodicals counter stood three rows of tables with microfilm viewers. Lara settled in front of the one assigned to her. As she slipped the first reel onto the prong, she wondered whether she'd find what she was searching for. Following the instructions on the base of the machine, she wound the wide ribbon of film through a metal contraption and onto the take-up reel. A few turns of the hand crank brought a blurry image up on the monitor. A twist of the center knob was needed to bring the front page of *The New York Times* into sharp focus.

For a long moment Lara stared at the date she had never forgotten: Monday, September 8, 1967. The day her childhood had been shattered. Then, page by page, column by column, she went through the newspaper, searching for a name she didn't know, a face she couldn't remember.

Her father, she was sure, was the person Prescott had sought to protect. A scandal involving the mistress and illegitimate child of "an important man" would have been newsworthy, not her mother's breakdown.

Several scandalous events had been reported that day, Lara found—including bribery, political corruption, and illicit sex in high places—but none involved an unknown young woman named Angela Castaldi. Since her mother had been taken to the hospital during the early morning hours, she reasoned, the story wouldn't have been reported until the following day. But there was no mention of the incident in Tuesday's paper, either, or any day that week.

Refusing to give up, she slipped on the second reel of microfilm, which contained the news of the following week. By the time Lara had worked her way through the Saturday edition, she was forced to concede the obvious: Prescott's cover-up had succeeded.

She went through the Sunday *Times* just to finish up the reel. According to Best & Co.'s full-page ad, the layered look was in. Macy's was having a white sale: queen-sized sheets were reduced from $4.49 to $3.99. And a studio apartment on the fashionable East Side could be rented for $155 a month. As she was cranking past the society page, a familiar name leapt out at her. She reversed the film to get another look at the headline.

CLAUDIA PIGGOT DELAFIELD
TO WED CARTER KINGSLEY, JR.

Could it possibly be the same Carter Kingsley whose campaign Prescott was managing? She read on:

> Mr. and Mrs. Lionel Piggot Delafield have announced the engagement of their daughter, Miss Claudia Piggot Delafield, to Mr. Carter Kingsley, Jr.
> The bride-to-be attended Marjorie Webster Junior College in Washington, and was presented in 1960 at the Debutante Cotillion and Christmas Ball in New York.

Lara examined the accompanying photograph. The high-society beauty no longer wore her pale hair in a shoulder-length bouffant, but there was no mistaking the patrician bones or haughty expression. It was undeniably the senator's wife.

She went on with the text:

> Mr. Kingsley graduated from the Woodrow Wilson School of Public and International Affairs at Princeton University, where he was elected to Phi Beta Kappa. For the past two years he was a junior member on the staff of the American Consulate in Saigon.
> Currently president of Thor-Tech—

Lara gasped, but never took her eyes off the screen.

——Mr. Kingsley plans on entering the political arena in the near future.

It took several moments for the full impact of her discovery to sink in. She saw the check for five thousand dollars Prescott had given her on her graduation day as clearly as if it were up there on the screen, as clearly as when she'd held the check in her own hands and had eagerly read the name of the account it was drawn on, hoping to find a clue to her father's identity. It had been a Thor-Tech check.

When she thought about it later, back in her apartment, Lara was surprised by her reaction. All her life she'd longed to know who her father was, and now that she was certain that she did know, she wanted no part of him. His marriage to another woman must have precipitated her mother's breakdown. Several questions continued to nag her. What had happened that day they had gone to see him at his country home? Where had Prescott taken her mother? How had she died?

Until she received a copy of her mother's death certificate, she'd have to put her search for the answer to those questions on hold. Rehearsals for the play were scheduled to start in another week and would severely limit her time, she knew, but she couldn't stop now. She wouldn't stop until she knew the whole truth.

On Sunday, May 3, 1987, a stakeout by a team of *Miami Herald* reporters yielded a front-page story claiming that Gary Hart, the leading Democratic presidential hopeful, had spent most of the weekend with a part-time actress named Donna Rice. Five days later, Hart was forced to withdraw his candidacy.

Prescott called an emergency strategy session with her deputy campaign manager, Fred Barker, her media consultant, Jack Benson, and her communications director, Chuck Wilson.

"The blood is in the water, gentlemen," she predicted accurately. "From now on, political journalism will be a frenzy of feeding sharks. The character issue will become the number one story of Campaign Eighty-eight."

It was immediately determined to scrap the current TV campaign, which emphasized Senator Kingsley's charismatic personality, and replace it with ads meant to position him as the perfect family man. Henceforth, his wife, Claudia, would accompany him on the campaign trail. It was Fred Barker's responsibility to make sure she was sober. Prescott took the responsibility upon herself to terminate the affair Carter was currently conducting with Cindy Smith, one of their volunteer staff members.

"I want Carter to tell me himself that he doesn't want to see me anymore," the eighteen-year-old insisted.

"He wanted to tell you himself," Prescott lied with her usual conviction, "but I wouldn't let him take such a risk. Reporters are crawling out of the woodwork these days. If you really love him, you'd—"

"I do love him." Cindy burst into tears. "I can't bear the thought of never seeing him again."

This was going to require all the patience at her disposal, Prescott realized. The ones who were in love with him were always the most difficult to get rid of, and she couldn't afford to antagonize the little slut. One never knew what someone in love was capable of doing.

She offered the pretty redhead her handkerchief. "And Carter loves you, too, Cindy." She almost choked on the words. "This separation is just for a little while—until this Gary Hart thing blows over."

Cindy brightened instantly. "Then, he does love me."

"I know what a great sacrifice this is for you." Prescott's tone held more tragedy than a Greek chorus. "But just think of what's at stake—the presidency of the United States!"

The appeal to her patriotism caused Cindy to burst into fresh tears. She capitulated.

CHAPTER
Twenty-eight

Lara wrapped her arms around Brad's neck to draw him close again. "I never dreamt it could be so beautiful." Her words reverberated in the almost deserted theater. Brad moved to kiss her.

"Okay, let's hold up right here." Cal's deep voice came out of the darkness beyond the footlights. "This isn't working."

"Give me a break, Cal," Brad called back in mock exasperation as Lara pushed away from him and slid to the edge of the bed. "You could have let me kiss her."

Sitting next to Cal in the first row, Pat gave one of her great, bawdy laughs. "Didn't you 'rehearse' enough kisses with me last night?"

Brad's handsome face split in a rakish grin. "Just trying to apply what you taught me, coach."

Checking his watch, Cal got to his feet. "It's too late to go over this again tonight." He'd sent the tech people home two hours ago. "Pat, can we schedule this scene for tomorrow?"

"We've got the big scene in Act II tomorrow, Cal."

"Can you push it back a couple of hours?" he asked on his way to the stage.

"I guess I'll have to." She made a note of it.

Cal took the steps up to the stage two at a time. "You can go, Brad. It's coming along, so don't worry about it, okay? We'll get it tomorrow." As Lara moved to get up also, Cal motioned her to stay. "I need to talk to you a moment, Lara."

She wasn't surprised: *she* was the one who was having trouble with the scene, not Brad. She couldn't feel anything when she said her lines.

"Cal, you don't need me anymore tonight, do you?" asked Pat when Brad joined her.

"No, we'll only be a few minutes. I'll lock up." He smiled crookedly. "I know you're eager to 'coach' Brad some more."

From opposite sides of the stage, Cal and Lara watched while Pat and Brad, laughing and joshing in that silly, giddy way new lovers have, quickly gathered their things. Cal tried not to be too envious of their happiness. And, though Lara was delighted that her friend had finally found someone who appreciated her, she wished Pat wouldn't leave her alone with Cal.

Pat and Brad tossed off quick, cheerful good nights. Their laughter spilled out the door with them, magnifying the silence they left behind.

Crossing upstage to Lara, Cal negotiated the silence as though it were another kind of distance between them. During the three weeks they'd been in rehearsals, Lara had gone out of her way to avoid him on a personal level; it was really getting to him. This was the first chance he'd had to be alone with her.

She was sitting in the center of the bed, long legs tucked demurely under her, the lush curves of her body softly outlined beneath a white nightgown cut as simply as a slip.

Her long, dark hair tumbled loosely around her bare shoulders. Her exquisite face was devoid of makeup, making her look exactly as she had the first time he'd made love to her.

Spots with blue gels cast a midnight glow over the "bedroom," adding to the illusion that time had slipped its moorings and they were back in her apartment on West Forty-sixth Street. Even in the dim lighting her skin glowed, her wide, pale-gray eyes were luminous. She'd never lost that aura of vulnerability that had always made her infinitely desirable to him. She was irresistible.

From clear across the stage, Lara felt the impact of Cal's gaze. It was as naked as a caress. Every step that brought him closer increased her erratic heartbeat. Heat flowed over her skin, as though someone had suddenly turned all the white-hot lights full up. Yet the lights pouring down over his hard, rangy body, she saw when he halted before her, were still a deep, midnight blue—like his eyes.

"You seem to be having a lot of trouble with the love scene," Cal stated. He had to work to keep his tone and manner toward her strictly professional. "Why do you think that is?"

"I don't know." Lara shifted self-consciously. Because of his nearness, her nightgown was no longer a costume, and the bed had ceased to be a mere stage prop. "It's a tough scene."

"The last scenes in Act III, where you're building to a breakdown, are a helluva lot tougher, yet your work is so real, so deeply felt. How do you explain that?"

"That's easy. I've been there. I know what that's like."

A wry smile played on his lips. "Are you telling *me* you don't know what it's like to be in love for the first time?"

Lara tugged on the front of her wig. "I have a vague recollection of the experience," she managed facetiously.

"I remember the experience vividly." His strictly professional tone slipped several notches. "And the one thing you never did with me was hold back. I don't just mean

sexually, I mean emotionally. That's what you're doing in
the scene: you're holding yourself back.''

"I've tried to let go. I can't!"

His eyes met hers. "What are you afraid of, Lara?"

"I'm not afraid," she insisted defensively. "I just can't
feel anything. The scene leaves me cold.''

"Really?" Cal sat on the edge of the bed, facing her. "I
think it's just the opposite. This scene is too close to
you for comfort. It brings up feelings and memories you're
afraid to deal with." He leaned toward her. "Feelings about
us.''

Lara pulled back. "If you start getting personal, Cal, I'm
leaving.''

There was a pause. A tiny muscle beat in his jaw as Cal
fought to keep his frustration under control. "Why do you
keep shutting me out like this?''

"I'm leaving!" Before she could move he grabbed her,
pulling her over to him.

"I love you," he said bluntly, almost angrily. "I know
you don't want to hear that, but there it is. I've never
stopped loving you, though it wasn't for lack of trying. And
you still love me, whether you want to or not." He hauled
her into his arms. "We tried not to love each other once,
remember? Neither one of us has ever been able to do a
damn thing about it!''

His mouth came down on hers, hard, his arms crushing
her to him as if he meant to make her part of him. His kiss
was all heat and hunger, almost bruising in its intensity. It
went right through her. She could feel her mouth begin to
warm under his; she felt him shaking with emotion. The
longing she'd fought so hard to suppress welled up inside
her—that blind, helpless longing she'd known only with
him. All the barriers she'd so carefully erected against him
began to give way; everything in her cried to open to him.
She couldn't believe he could still do this to her!

She pushed away from him almost violently. Immediately,
he sought to gather her up in his arms again. "No . . . don't!"

She was shocked by the sound of her own voice: it was like something tearing.

"All right," he said softly, soothingly. "I won't." But he took her hands in his as if he feared she would bolt. There was a long silence, broken only by the sound of their ragged breathing.

Finally, Cal said, "Lara, I can understand why you're afraid to let yourself love me again. I know I hurt you, badly. But at the time, I felt I had no other choice. I was trying to do the right thing, so I sacrificed you to save my family." His hands, warm, vibrant, tightened around hers. "But all that's changed now. We can finally be together, have a life together, just as you'd always wanted."

"No, it's too late." Lara tugged her hands out of his. "I can't forget the past as easily as you can."

"I haven't forgotten the past!" Anger, born of frustration, slipped out of his control once more. "I live with the mistakes I made every day of my life. I know I can't change what happened, or erase the pain I caused you, but you weren't the only one who suffered!"

Surprised by the very real anguish in his voice, Lara stared at Cal intently. For the first time, she saw beyond her fear and distrust of him to what living with the choice he'd made had done to him. The premature lines etching his face, the slash of gray at his temples, and especially, the darkness that always seemed to be behind his eyes now testified to the price he'd paid. She'd only been aware of the suffering his choice had caused her. Up to that moment, it had never occurred to her that he'd suffered, also.

"Lara, very few people are lucky enough to get a second chance in life. We could be happy together. But you have to let go of the past."

"All my life I've fought to break free of the past," Lara told him, her eyes despairing. "How do you do that?"

"By accepting it," Cal said. But he could see she wasn't ready for that.

* * *

Robert Stone sat in the last row of the theater, watching the rehearsal with a practiced eye. It didn't take him long to realize that Lara Layton was a damn good actress. Who would have believed it? He'd been a pretty good actor himself once, before he realized that with his ordinary looks and stature, he'd be forever condemned to minor roles. So he gave it up. Sort of. He'd been able to put his acting talent to considerable use as a detective. Now he liked to think of himself as the Marlon Brando of private eyes.

Since Lara was so deeply involved with rehearsals the past few weeks, she'd hired Stone to finish searching for the evidence that would prove Carter Kingsley was her father, and to uncover his involvement, if any, in her mother's breakdown and death. The information he'd succeeded in gathering was tucked inside the accordion folder resting on his lap. He waited until Lara was through rehearsing before approaching her.

"I thought you'd forgotten all about me," she told him when they were in her dressing room.

"Are you kidding? I've been working on your case exclusively. I've been running all over the place—upstate, to that convent you were in. Tracking down that private clinic they first took your mother to. I just spent the whole day at Creedmore." He laughed. "And, believe me, you don't want to spend the whole day in Creedmore."

It hurt Lara just to think of her mother being confined in such an institution. She forced a smile. "I didn't mean to run you ragged."

"You told me you had to have the results by this weekend."

"Senator Kingsley is going to be back in New York this weekend. Then, he's off to Iowa to—"

"No, he's not going to stay in New York," Stone cut in, taking the chair Lara offered. "He's going to be spending the weekend at his father's place in Newport. No politics— just the family. And, of course, the ubiquitous Miss Prescott." He smiled sardonically. "Quite a clever lady, that one. She's the one who should be running for president."

Lara sat upon the edge of her chair. "Is he my father?"

"The evidence sure points to it, but it's all circumstantial. You don't remember him at all?"

Lara shook her head. "No matter how hard I try, I still can't remember my father, or what happened that day we went to see him." She leaned toward him. "Did you find out what happened to my mother?"

"I found out, all right." Stone handed over the accordion file. "But you're not going to like it."

CHAPTER
Twenty-nine

The rented Lincoln Continental limo sped smoothly down the deserted two-lane highway toward King's Haven. The fluid motion, the insular comfort, that unreal silence peculiar to limousine travel, added to Lara's feeling of being suspended in time. She heard her mother's laughter.

"Oh, look, baby. Look at the beautiful horse."

Beyond the side window, their coats glistening in the sun, Thoroughbreds galloped in a wide, grassy field enclosed by a corral fence. She watched them through a mist of tears, feeling a rush of memories. If only she had the power to turn back time, she thought. Then, on that Sunday long ago, she'd have had the Rolls-Royce drive straight on ahead, instead of turning off the highway onto the country road, as the limo was doing now.

When they came to the end of the road, to the high, spike-topped wall that stretched as far as the eye could see, they were waved through the huge, wrought-iron gate by a

uniformed guard. Giant oak trees lined both sides of the
long driveway.

The Victorian mansion, gleaming white, still crowned the
man-made hilltop; the triangular beds of the formal garden
still edged its marble-columned veranda. The limo glided up
the manicured slope, past the clay tennis court adjoining the
orchard, the marble terrace enclosing the swimming pool,
and left her in front of the entrance.

She asked the chauffeur to wait, assuring him that she
wouldn't be long. Lifting the brass ring clutched in the
maws of a lion, she knocked on the door. She was admitted
by a liveried butler, whom she guessed to be in his early
fifties. His manner, which was all she could recall of the
previous butler, was every bit as supercilious.

"I'm here to see Senator Kingsley."

"Is the senator expecting you, madam?"

"No, but I'm sure he'll see me. The name is Loris
Castaldi."

His expression made it clear what he thought of people
who paid unexpected visits. Nevertheless, he said, "I shall
inquire."

"You do that," Lara returned.

While the butler was busy on the house phone, Lara
glanced around the entrance hall. On her first visit, she'd
been overwhelmed by the enormous cut-glass chandelier,
the sweeping mahogany stairway, and the sumptuous ap-
pointments. She was not overwhelmed now. She tucked the
accordion folder she was carrying firmly under one arm.

"Mr. Kingsley will see you in the library, madam." Ramrod
straight, the butler led the way down a long, carpeted hallway.

As Lara retraced the steps she'd taken as a child, it
seemed to her she could feel her mother's presence at her
side. Her left hand was hot and moist, as if someone were
clutching it tightly; her right hand was like ice. When she
stepped through the door into the library, it was like stepping into the past. Swamped by memories, she neither saw
nor heard the butler leave.

Her eyes swept over the shelves of morocco-bound first

editions lining one entire wall, the early-eighteenth-century English landscapes and hunting scenes, the collection of silver racing trophies on the marble mantelpiece. She stared into the fireplace that, as a child, she'd feared was large enough to swallow her whole. It was strange to remember how big everything had seemed to her then. It no longer seemed big at all.

The side door concealed in the wood paneling at the other end of the library opened and Carter Kingsley entered with Jane Prescott. They both froze when they saw her. Lara was wearing the long black wig she'd borrowed from Wardrobe (though she couldn't have explained the impulse that had compelled her to do so), and a mini-length shift that had come back into fashion. Carter's lips moved soundlessly, forming a single word: *Angela*.

Prescott was the first to recover. "Even for someone in your dubious profession, this surprise visit is highly melodramatic, Miss Layton. What are you doing here?"

"We all know what I'm doing here," Lara told Carter Kingsley. "I want to talk to my father."

Her resemblance to Angela had completely unnerved him. He stammered, "But, how—"

"Don't pay any attention to her, Senator," Prescott cut in to keep him from giving himself away. "Ever since I've known her, she's had this fixation about finding her long-lost father. It's obviously turned into a full-fledged delusion since her crack-up."

Lara ignored her. "It's amazing how little people or things change in twenty years. This room, for example. It's almost exactly as I remember it that day my mother and I came to see you." She began to stroll about the library, pointing things out as she spoke. "These Chesterfield couches aren't the same, though. The other ones were maroon leather, these are tan. And you switched the Oriental rugs around. The one with the maroon tones used to be under the couches, and the gold one that's there now was over here under the writing table."

She stopped beside the bureau plat, just a few steps away

from her father. "You haven't changed much, either." At
fifty-two, he'd retained that golden-boy look—the aura of a
man to whom everything had come easily. "But you had a
full moustache then, and long sideburns."

She turned to Prescott. "*You* haven't changed at all. You
still wear your hair pulled back in a bun, and those thick
glasses that hide your eyes so no one can see what you're
thinking. And you're still trying to hide the truth from me.
You had the butler take me to the kitchen for milk and
cookies to get me out of the way the last time, remember?"

"I don't know what you're talking about."

"No more lies!" Lara cried angrily. "I've been lied to all
my life. I won't stand for any more. I know he's my father.
Believe me, it's not something I'm proud of. All these years
you've been covering up for him because of what he did to
my mother."

"You must understand," Carter began, only to be cut off
by Prescott again.

"Don't indulge her paranoid delusions, Carter." From
behind her thick lenses, she fixed Lara with an icy stare.
"With your history, you should be very careful of what you
say. If you go around making unfounded accusations about
people, you could end up being put away, like your mother."

"I'm not so easy to get rid of these days, Miss Prescott.
But if I should be put in Creedmore, like my mother, I'll
make damn sure *you* don't sign the commitment papers this
time."

There was a stunned silence. The furtive look of accom-
plices who'd been found out passed between them.

Lara opened the accordion folder and took out a document. "This is a photocopy of the commitment papers you
signed." She dropped the page on the bureau plat. "Here's
a copy of the bill from the Martindale Clinic, where you
first took my mother so the police wouldn't get involved.
And these are my tuition bills from the Convent of the
Immaculate Conception." She added them to the rest. "All
these bills are made out to, and paid by, Thor-Tech."

Prescott forced a contemptuous laugh. "What does that

prove? Thor-Tech is an electronics company I ran once—I told you that.''

"What you didn't tell me was that Carter Kingsley owned the company. You worked for him even then. These bills prove that he paid to have his mistress's breakdown kept secret and his illegitimate child hidden away so no one would know she existed.''

Carter could see headlines that would make the Gary Hart scandal look like a whitewash. Angela's words echoed in his mind: "*Sooner or later, we all have to pay for our sins.*" He took a step toward Lara that was more like a stumble. "What do you intend to do with these documents? Go to the press?''

Prescott stepped in before he lost his head completely. "Let *me* take care of this, Carter.''

"You've already taken care of it!'' He turned on her furiously. "This is all your doing! I'll be damned if I'm going to be crucified by the press for your mistakes!''

"She doesn't have a shred of evi—''

"I can explain everything,'' he told Lara. "Please sit down.'' A sweep of his elegant hand indicated the fauteuil chair in front of the writing desk. He smiled gratefully, appealingly, when she complied. "Would you care for a drink?''

Lara shook her head.

"Get me a Chivas on the rocks,'' he ordered Prescott, as if she were a servant. She flushed from the humiliation, but turned and went to the bar while he took his seat behind the bureau plat. Father and daughter regarded each other for a long moment.

This is the man whose love and acceptance I've longed for all my life, Lara thought, *and all I feel for him now is contempt.*

"You're very beautiful,'' he said finally, almost proudly. "You remind me so much of Angela. I loved your mother a great deal. She's the only woman I ever really loved.'' He cleared his throat, giving the impression that it was difficult, perhaps even painful, for him to talk about it. "You see, my father was against our relationship from the start. He'd always had plans for me to go into politics and felt that, because of her background, Angela would not be a suitable wife. He did everything he could to keep me from marrying her. He even pulled strings in Washington to have me posted to Vietnam for two years, hoping to break us up. *He* arranged my marriage to Claudia.''

"If you really wanted to marry my mother, why did you agree?''

"What *I* wanted never mattered. You must understand something, my dear. A man of my position isn't free to do as he chooses.'' He let out a sigh heavy with the weight of his predicament. "My life has been mapped out for me since the day I was born. I have unshirkable responsibilities to my family and to my country.''

He was beginning to sound like one of his political speeches, Lara thought. "But not to the woman you loved or your child?''

"Certainly. That's why I invited you both here that day. I wanted to explain the situation to Angela in person. In order to ensure her future—and yours—I offered to give her a hundred thousand dollars.''

"In exchange for what?''

Carter was thrown by her perception, but quickly recovered. "I didn't set any conditions.''

Lara laughed scornfully. "I'll bet.''

"It was understood, of course, that she would give up whatever . . . claims she felt she had on me.''

"Like, expecting you to marry her. Or admitting you were the father of her child.'' Lara shook her head sadly. She could imagine how her mother must have felt when the man she loved tried to buy her off with money. "She refused your offer, didn't she?''

He nodded. "She became extremely agitated. She went into a . . . a kind of trance. But then she came out of it. She seemed perfectly all right when she left here.'' He looked up at Prescott, who was setting the drink before him. "Didn't she?''

Prescott was quick to give him the confirmation he sought. "Yes. She was fine when I drove her home."

"And then she had a breakdown," Lara concluded softly, to herself, as the last piece of the puzzle slipped into place.

"Angela had no family," her father went on, "so we thought it best to place you in boarding school." He gave her a smile that was positively heartbreaking in its appeal for her sympathy. "I realize it must be difficult for you to understand why, as much as I wanted to, I was unable to acknowledge you as my daughter."

"No, I understand your motives perfectly. If it were known—even today—that you have an illegitimate daughter, you'd be finished in politics." She paused to enjoy the sight of her father squirming in his chair. "I might have been able to find it in myself to forgive you for shutting me out of your life all those years. But I can never forgive you for what you did to my mother."

"Are you blaming me for your mother's mental instability?"

"I'm blaming you for putting her in a state institution instead of a private psychiatric hospital, where she could have been helped." Gripping the edge of the writing table, she leaned toward him. "But that's the last thing you wanted, wasn't it? As long as she was locked up, you'd never have to worry about her exposing you."

"I greatly doubt that Angela could have been helped," Prescott offered in Carter's defense. "She was catatonic. Even today, with the latest medical advances, catatonics are considered practically incurable."

"*You* should know better than anyone that she could have been cured!" Lara cried angrily, jumping to her feet. "It's true she suffered a catatonic episode, but she came out of it. In fact, her doctor was so encouraged by the progress she'd made in six months, he recommended her parole when she went to staff. It was denied because *you* refused to sign the necessary papers! You deliberately left her there to rot. You killed her—both of you. And the worst part of it is, that you have no remorse for what you've done."

Grabbing the documents she'd set out earlier, Lara stuffed

them back in the folder. "But there's a law of retribution. The evil we do in this world comes back to us. You're both going to pay for what you've done."

"But, I knew nothing about this," Carter insisted, his voice rising in panic. "I never saw Angela again after she left here. Prescott took care of everything. She assured me that Angela was getting the best medical attention money could buy. I knew absolutely nothing about this parole. She told me Angela was hopelessly insane."

Lara had only to look at the horrified expression on Prescott's normally placid face to know her father was lying. Without another word, she turned to leave.

"Stop her," Carter ordered Prescott, as Lara sailed past her, heading for the door. "Pres, do something!" he said once Lara was out the door. Prescott hadn't moved. "We can't let her go to the media! Call Baxter, have him stop her at the door!"

"You idiot." Prescott's tone, like her face now, was utterly devoid of expression. "She was bluffing, and you believed her. She hasn't got a shred of evidence against you. All she had was suspicions, which you were stupid enough to confirm."

"You saw the bills. How can you be so sure?"

"Because I don't make mistakes. I made sure nothing and no one could ever connect you to Angela. *My* name is on every document, every single check. There's nothing to—"

"Then, that'll be our story," Carter cut in, jubilant. "It was all *your* doing. And in a way, it really was, wasn't it? I don't think there was anything illegal in what you did— except for that little matter of the parole. Oh, don't worry, if there should be a problem about that, my lawyers will see you get off." He patted her on the shoulder, the way one would pat a loyal dog. "But it might be a good idea to call Ramsey right away to see where you stand. While you're at it, find out if we can hit her with a libel suit. That should take the wind out of her sails."

"And what are *you* going to do?" Prescott asked evenly. He checked his watch. "I'd better start getting dressed for dinner. You know how impossible Claudia can be if dinner is held up. We'll talk later.''

Jane Prescott watched Carter Kingsley leave the library with his typically light, confident stride before she went into her adjoining office and sat behind her desk. She removed her glasses and set them on top of the computer printouts of the latest Iowa media buys.

She was not concerned about her safety. Without hard evidence, no newspaper would dare print Lara's allegations, for fear of being sued. Before the current law had been enacted, thousands of mental patients had lingered in state hospitals because their own relatives refused to assume responsibility for them. Though some might consider her refusal to sign Angela's release a morally reprehensible act, it was not an illegal one.

But if she and Carter *had* literally killed Angela, she knew now, he would still have blithely expected her to take the fall.

For twenty-two years she had made Carter Kingsley the center of her life. She'd run his business, covered up his inadequacies, and created a political machine that had carried him to within reach of the White House. And she'd never asked anything in return—except to be needed by him.

For twenty-two years she'd loved him. She'd put up with his wife, who treated her like a glorified servant, as well as an endless succession of mindless little sluts. She'd always believed that *she* was as vital to him as he was to her—that she was the only woman he couldn't do without. To find out now that she was as expendable as all the others was a devastating blow to Prescott. She didn't intend to play the fool any longer.

She picked up her glasses and put them on. Thumbing through her Rolodex, she found the telephone number and dialed it. The phone was answered with a sniffly hello. "Cindy?"

"Oh, it's you." Disappointment was evident in the girl's voice. She'd obviously been crying. "You didn't have to check up on me, Miss Prescott. I'm leaving, just like I promised. I was about to call a cab to take me to the airport."

"Forget about the cab. You don't have to leave."

"Did Carter change his mind? Oh, I knew he would!"

"No, Carter never changes his mind. When he's through with a woman, it's for good."

"But you said he loved me! That in time—"

"I was trying to let you down easy."

The teenager gave a tiny gasp of pain and the tears started flowing again.

Prescott had to raise her voice to be heard over the sobs. "Cindy, how would you like to be on TV?"

"On TV?" Cindy repeated, brightening up considerably. "How?"

And Miss Prescott explained.

As Jane Prescott had surmised, Lara had never had any intention of going to the press. She'd merely played on her father's fear of exposure to get him to admit his involvement in her mother's breakdown. And though she did believe in a law of retribution, she certainly hadn't expected it to operate so swiftly: the story of Carter Kingsley's involvement with an eighteen-year-old hit the papers the very next day, forcing him to withdraw from the presidential race.

Morally, Lara felt he deserved his fate. She shuddered to think that a man who could treat another human being with such casual cruelty, as he had her mother, might have become President of the United States, holding the lives of millions in his power. Yet, to her own surprise, she felt no vindictive satisfaction at her father's downfall. His innocent family was also paying for his sins.

On the other hand, Miss Prescott, according to the latest reports, appeared to have vanished from the face of the earth.

The week after the Carter Kingsley scandal broke, a

package was delivered to Lara at the theater. There was no return address on the envelope, nor was there a note of explanation inside. The package contained photos of her mother and father, and a packet of faded love letters.

CHAPTER
Thirty

The curtain was scheduled to go up at seven on opening night, to allow the TV reviewers time to make their eleven o'clock news shows. The actors' call had also been moved up an hour, to five. Lara had gone out of her way to avoid publicity since coming back to New York, so she wasn't prepared for the mob scene that awaited her as her rented limo glided to a stop in front of The Lower Depths.

Police barricades had been set up on either side of the theater to hold back the crowd of fans that had been gathering since early morning, as if in eager anticipation of a major movie premiere, rather than an Off-Broadway opening. There were enough uniformed cops on duty to handle a full-scale riot. A horde of reporters and photographers was milling about restlessly; as one, now, they rushed the limo.

Cal got there first. Unnoticed, he'd stationed himself at the curb when he saw what was happening, ready to act as a buffer between Lara and the media. He had the car door open in an instant and helped her out. "Hang on to me," he ordered under his breath. "I'll get you out of here."

Wrapping his left arm protectively around her shoulders, he pulled her close to his side, using his right arm to wedge an opening through the mass of bodies surrounding them. He had to raise his voice in order to be heard over the barrage of questions the reporters started shooting at her. "Miss Layton has to get ready for a performance. You can interview her after the show."

Cal might as well have been speaking to himself. Microphones were thrust in Lara's face, halogen lights blinded her, minicams whirled.

Walking backwards, as though that was the normal means of locomotion, a reporter from the *Post* demanded, "How do you like acting on stage, Lara?"

Unlike Cal, Lara knew from experience that ignoring the press would only make them escalate their attack. She managed a smile. "I've never enjoyed acting more."

A stringer from the *Enquirer* shoved by the others, her tone as aggressive as her manner. "*We* heard you were having so many problems during rehearsals that the opening almost had to be postponed."

"That's bullshit," Cal snapped, pushing past the woman unceremoniously.

She stuck to their heels with the tenacity of a bull terrior. "Lara, how do you feel about your ex-husband's claim that, as an actress, you're just a Trilby to his Svengali?"

Lara forced a laugh. "That's the reason he's my ex-husband."

"What do you think of the rumor going around," a disembodied baritone called out, "that the bookmakers in Hollywood are giving four-to-one odds the New York critics will slaughter you tonight?"

Lara laughed again. Only Cal was aware that she was shaking as he continued to pull her along with him. "I must be improving," she tossed off lightly. "When I first went into rehearsals, the odds against me were ten-to-one."

Cal and Lara had almost reached the stairs leading to the

theater entrance when the reporter from the sleaze sheet managed to shove her way in front of them again. "What *will* you do if you bomb as a 'serious' actress, Lara?" she purred. "Go back to taking off your clothes?"

Everyone snickered. Flashbulbs popped, capturing the stricken look on Lara's face. She found it impossible to fake a response this time. It was all she could do to follow Cal down the steps with some semblance of pride.

Cal was still cursing at the woman when they were safely inside Lara's dressing room. Then, frowning with concern, he searched her face. "Are you all right?"

She nodded, but Cal could see the self-doubt widening in her eyes. He knew how fragile her new-born confidence in herself as an actress was. They really did a number on her in Hollywood, he thought resentfully, and they still won't leave her alone. He longed to take her in his arms and reassure her, but the way things were between them, he was afraid he might upset her even more.

"Don't let those bastards get to you, Lara," he told her instead. "After your performance tonight, they're all going to have to eat their words. Including 'Svengali.' "

Lara made a gesture of weary fatalism. "It doesn't matter how good a performance I give, Cal—I know that now. I can't win. They'll find some way to bring me down. What I'm really sorry about is that I'm going to drag you and Pat down with me." She turned away so he wouldn't see the tears she was blinking back.

"Lara, you've already won." Taking her by the shoulders, Cal turned her back to him. "Every time you step onto that stage it's a victory. That's what those bastards won't forgive you for. You had the guts to buck the system because you wanted to be more than a sex goddess. You know now what a fine actress you are. You've proven it in rehearsals. No one can take that away from you, ever again."

His hands moved to cup her startled face and tilt it up to his. "Christ, I wish you could see how beautiful you are in the play. I'm not talking about your face or body. There's a radiance inside you, that—in spite of everything that's happened to you—nothing, no one, has been able to destroy. You light up the whole stage.''

Cal's deeply felt words, the love burning in his eyes, left Lara speechless, but her lips parted in unconscious response, soft and vulnerable. Irresistible. Suddenly, Cal didn't give a damn about the consequences. ''Lara, I love you so much,'' he told her not caring whether she wanted to hear it or not. He had no way of knowing how very much she needed to hear those words.

He kissed her, softly, with an aching tenderness that dissolved her. She went all open to him, in that way she never had with anyone else, unfolding in layers like the petals of a flower. He gathered her up in his arms as if she were a promise he was almost afraid to believe in. Denied for too long, the rush of love that went through her shook her with its force. She clung to him with every part of her.

The sound of hurried footsteps outside in the hall finally brought the reality of opening night back to them.

''Damn!'' He'd dragged his mouth away from hers, but continued to hold her. ''You've got to start getting dressed, and I'd better get out front to make sure the tech crew's setting up.'' Swiftly, he brushed her lips with his. ''To be continued,'' he vowed before he finally let her go.

The image at the center of the rear-projection screen at the back of the stage dazzled: a platinum halo framing sky-blue eyes; glossy, suggestively parted lips; a body that seemed to have been dipped in molten gold. During the course of the play, her image as a Hollywood sex symbol would fill the wide screen more and more, until it completely dominated the stage—just as it continued to dominate Lara's life.

Despite her doubts and fears, Lara was determined to end that domination tonight. Heart pounding, head held high, she made her entrance on cue.

A buzz of excitement went up from the audience—whispered

comments on her appearance, low giggles of anticipation. *The kind of crowd that enjoys freak shows must sound like this,* she thought. Instead of defeating her, as it would have at one time, their eagerness to see her make a fool of herself for their amusement added to her determination.

Convinced that she couldn't win, that she had nothing more to lose, she gave herself up to the sheer self-satisfaction of creating. Acting, she finally realized, had always been a means to fulfill her lifelong hunger for acceptance and recognition—an insatiable craving for the audience's love. No longer. The look of love she'd seen on Cal's face earlier remained imprinted behind her eyes. His was all the love she would ever need, she knew then.

She held nothing back during the love scene, expressing her feelings for him, all her longing, as she'd never dared to do in rehearsals.

Somewhere along the periphery of her consciousness she was aware of the hush that had come over the auditorium, as if the audience was holding its collective breath, and of the almost electric charge flowing between them. When the final curtain fell there was a long moment of silence, and then the theater came apart. When the curtain lifted again the entire audience was on its feet, cheering wildly.

The standing ovation they gave Lara lasted almost ten minutes. It was a greater vindication than she'd ever dared hope for. Yet the loving pride she saw in Cal's eyes when she ran to him in the wings was worth a hundred standing ovations to her. And as she lay in his arms all night, talking and making love, feeling him so deep a part of her she didn't know where she ended and he began, Lara finally knew the fulfillment that not even the adulation of the entire world had been able to give her.

GET
LOVESTRUCK!

AND GET STRIKING ROMANCES
FROM POPULAR LIBRARY'S
BELOVED AUTHORS

Watch for these exciting

LOVESTRUCK

romances in the months to come:

March 1989

BETRAYALS by Gina Camai
LOVE'S SWEET CAPTIVE by Blaine Anderson

April 1989

BEGINNINGS by Eileen Nauman
BOUNDLESS LOVE by Jeanne Felldin

May 1989

THIS TIME FOREVER by F. Rosanne Bittner
LOVE'S MIRACLES by Sandra Lee Smith

June 1989

LOVE'S OWN CROWN by Laurie Grant
FAIR GAME by Doreen Owens Malek

July 1989

SHIELD'S LADY by Amanda Glass
BLAZE OF PASSION by Lisa Ann Verge

 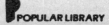